FATAL FRAUD

FATAL SERIES, BOOK 16

MARIE FORCE

Fatal Fraud
Fatal Series, Book 16
By: Marie Force

Published by HTJB, Inc.
Copyright 2020. HTJB, Inc.
Cover Design by Kristina Brinton
Print Layout: E-book Formatting Fairies
ISBN: 978-1950654864

The Fatal Series

One Night With You, *A Fatal Series Prequel Novella*
Book 1: Fatal Affair
Book 2: Fatal Justice
Book 3: Fatal Consequences
Book 3.5: Fatal Destiny, *the Wedding Novella*
Book 4: Fatal Flaw
Book 5: Fatal Deception
Book 6: Fatal Mistake
Book 7: Fatal Jeopardy
Book 8: Fatal Scandal
Book 9: Fatal Frenzy
Book 10: Fatal Identity
Book 11: Fatal Threat
Book 12: Fatal Chaos
Book 13: Fatal Invasion
Book 14: Fatal Reckoning
Book 15: Fatal Accusation
Book 16: Fatal Fraud

More new books are always in the works. For the most up-to-date list of what's available from the Fatal Series as well as series extras, go to *marieforce.com/fatal*

CHAPTER ONE

I f there was one benefit to Sam's husband, Nick, being vice president of the United States, it was the motorcade that conveyed them with admirable efficiency wherever they wanted to go. As they made their way northbound on the Baltimore-Washington Parkway, Sam appreciated that she also got to bring friends on this mission to see their colleague Sergeant Tommy Gonzales in rehab. Since the other benefits of Nick being VP were few and far between, Sam decided they needed to enjoy this one.

"This is the life." Sam's partner, Detective Freddie Cruz, had his arm around his wife, Elin, who was snuggled up to him.

"Seriously," Michael Wilkinson said. His wife, Detective Jeannie McBride, sat across from him, next to Sam, who was in her happy place—pressed up against Nick.

If they had to be trapped in the car for more than an hour, and neither of them had to drive, you bet your ass she was going to enjoy the ride. "The best part is that people get the hell out of the way of the Secret Service," Sam said.

"Why do they get all that respect when people ignore us?" Jeannie asked.

"A very good question," Sam said. "What is it about the Secret Service that gets people to do what they say?"

"It must be about the very important people they protect," Freddie said.

"We're incredibly important," Nick said, drawing a laugh from the others. He never took himself as seriously as the Secret Service and others took him.

"Can we discuss the elephant in the SUV?" Michael asked.

Sam groaned. "Do we have to?" One of the network Sunday shows had been on fire that morning, speculating on the next presidential race and the likely candidates for both parties. Naturally, Nick's name was at the top of the Democratic ticket, even if he'd given no public indication of his plans.

Sam was painfully aware that he was struggling with the decision. She prayed he wouldn't run but kept her mouth shut on the matter to give him the space he needed to decide for himself. In the meantime, she held her breath and waited while the rest of the world went wild with speculation and assumptions. "Of course he'll run," one pundit had said recently. "He'd be insane not to."

In Sam's opinion, he'd be insane if he *did* run and brought that kind of endless scrutiny down on them. The thought of that spiked her anxiety into the red zone, so she tried not to go there. They received more than enough scrutiny as the second couple.

"You may not want to talk about it, but everyone else does," Michael said.

"People need to mind their own business," Sam said.

"I hate to tell you," Freddie said, "but when you're the vice president, your business is their business."

Sam scowled at him. "That's not helpful."

Nick squeezed her shoulder in a show of silent support. They were both excruciatingly aware that they were going to have to decide sooner rather than later. Sam hoped it would be much, much, *much* later. She didn't want him to run for president, and he didn't want to run either. But sometimes it felt like nobody was listening to either of them as invisible forces propelled them toward an inevitable destiny.

"On another note," Freddie said, "did you see the thing in the *Star* this morning about the Kent woman who defrauded all her rich friends in some glorified Ponzi scheme?"

"We didn't get a chance to read the paper before we left," Sam said. "We were busy getting Scotty and the twins ready to spend the day with Tracy and Mike." Her sister and brother-in-law had a full day planned for Sam's kids and their cousins.

"Apparently, the Feds have been working on this case for almost a year, and it all came to a head this week when they charged her in federal court. Up until then, most of the friends didn't know they'd been defrauded. From what the paper said, it sounds like there were some fireworks among the privileged class as the word got out that their money is probably gone."

"So let me get this straight," Sam said. "She basically *stole* from her *friends*?"

"Yep," Freddie said, "and family. She got them to invest in some business she was supposedly starting, and then lo and behold, she walked away with the money and won't tell anyone what she did with it."

"How much are we talking?" Jeannie asked.

"About twenty million," Freddie said.

"I have so many thoughts about this," Sam said. "First of all, who just gives their money to somebody and expects they're just gonna do the right thing with it? Second of all, how did she think she was going to get away with it? Were her friends going to suddenly forget they'd given their money to her?"

"Why does anyone think they're going to get away with fraud?" Nick asked. "I'd be so afraid of getting caught that I wouldn't be able to enjoy the money."

"Me too," Sam said. "How do people sleep at night when they're stealing from their friends and family? I want you all to know I'll never steal from you."

"I'm strangely comforted to know that." Freddie ducked his head to see out the window. "We're getting close to Baltimore. Is anyone else nervous about seeing him?"

"I am a little," Jeannie said. "I want our Gonzo back, the way he was before Arnold died. Part of me wonders if that's too much to hope for."

The shocking murder of Gonzo's young partner had sent him spiraling over the last ten months, culminating in a dependence on prescription meds that'd gotten out of control before he was sent to rehab.

"It might be too much to hope for the same Gonzo," Sam said, "but right about now, I'll take any Gonzo I can get. It hasn't been the same without him."

Since he'd been in rehab, Sam had lost her father, and they'd closed her dad's long-unsolved shooting case. Sometimes she felt like she'd lived a whole lifetime since she last worked with her sergeant.

"How come Christina didn't come with us today?" Freddie asked of Gonzo's fiancée.

"She said Alex wasn't feeling great, and since we were going, she decided to stay home," Sam said.

"What do you think will happen with them?" Jeannie asked.

"I wish I knew," Sam said, sighing. "I just hope they're able to stay together, because I think that'll be critical to his recovery."

"Have you heard any more about the Feds looking into the department?" Jeannie asked.

"We had a commanders' meeting about it the other day," Sam said. "From what the chief said, the FBI will be conducting a top-to-bottom look at the department in light of several of our own being charged with violent felonies. We have a meeting with the Feds this week."

"That ought to be fun," Freddie said, frowning.

"I heard someone call it a proctology exam," Jeannie said.

"That's about right, but we've got nothing to worry about," Sam said. "This is why I'm always talking about dotting the i's and crossing the t's. Our asses are covered. The Feds can poke around all they want. They won't find jack shit to investigate in Homicide." At least they'd better not. Sam went out of her way to run an exemplary unit, and if there was corruption to be found within the department, they weren't going to find it in her pit.

When they arrived at the rehab center in downtown Baltimore, Nick's Secret Service detail went in ahead of them while they waited in the car.

"Do you have to go through this everywhere you go?" Michael asked.

"Every single time," Nick said. "And you wonder why I'm not jumping at the chance to be president?"

"I'm not exactly wondering," Michael said as the others laughed.

They waited fifteen minutes until Brant, Nick's lead agent, came to let them out of the car. Inside, they were shown to a private room that'd been arranged in advance by the Secret Service.

Gonzo joined them there a few minutes later, hugging each of them and thanking them for coming. "It's so great to see you guys."

Sam was relieved to see him looking and sounding more like his old self than he had in the dreadful months since January. The haunted look in his eyes was gone, and the bright, engaged friend she loved so much seemed to be back. "You look great."

"I feel really good."

With the Secret Service positioned outside the door, they sat on folding chairs around the table.

"I wish I could offer you drinks or something," Gonzo said.

"Don't worry about us," Sam said. "We're fine. We want to hear how you're doing."

"Much better. The extra month has made a big difference. Andy was here last week," he said, referring to Nick's attorney friend.

"How come?" Sam asked.

"We've been talking with the U.S. Attorney's Office, and I'm going to plead guilty to a misdemeanor." He'd bought pills on the street during the worst of his addiction and somehow that had been reported to the U.S. Attorney. "It's the best possible outcome and allows me to keep my job and rank."

"That's *bullshit*," Sam said, immediately incensed. "You have an *illness*. You shouldn't be charged for things you did when you were sick after your partner was murdered."

Gonzo offered a small smile. "If anyone else in the department got caught doing what I did, you wouldn't feel that way."

"Yes, I would. Drug addiction is an illness. If it can be proven that someone is sick when they're out scoring, they ought to be given a break. I've always thought we needed to spend more money on rehab and less on prosecution."

"I've heard her say that before," Freddie said.

"It's my fault you got caught in the first place," Sam said. "My feud with Ramsey led to this. He was looking for a way to hurt me by going after you." There'd been bad blood between Sam and the Special Victims sergeant for some time now. From what she'd been able to gather, he resented her rise through the ranks, among other beefs he frequently liked to air out to anyone who'd listen. Their feud had intensified when the U.S. Attorney declined to indict her after she punched him and he fell down a flight of stairs, breaking his wrist and suffering a concussion.

"This is *my* fault, Sam," Gonzo said. "I took a massive chance with my career, my reputation and my life. I knew it at the time, and I didn't care."

"That was the addiction speaking," Sam said. "The Gonzo I've worked with would've cared. It's not something you would've done if you hadn't been sick. And why were you sick? Because your partner was *murdered* right in front of you on the job."

"I know this is upsetting to you, Sam—"

"If you do this, you'll never move past sergeant," she said.

"I know, and I've made my peace with that."

"It's wrong," Jeannie said. "You're the best of us all. You could be chief someday."

"Once upon a time, I might've wanted that, but I'm learning to find comfort in what *is* rather than what used to be or what might've been."

"Before you sign anything, let me have a word with the chief," Sam said.

"I agreed to the deal. I'm due to sign the paperwork when I get out of here, and that's what's best for me, to not have this shit hanging over my head."

She wanted to scream, yell and break shit over the sheer injustice of him pleading to a criminal charge when scumbags like Ramsey were getting away with ruining the career of one of the best cops Sam had ever worked with.

"When do you get out?" Freddie asked.

"They're saying this week sometime."

"How're things with Christina?" Jeannie asked.

"Better," Gonzo said. "We talk a lot, and we're both ready to get back to normal, whatever that is after everything I've put her through."

"She loves you, man," Freddie said. "It's gonna be okay."

"I hope so. I guess we'll see. So, enough about me. What's going on with you guys? Tell me everything about the Tara Weber case. I feel so cut off in here."

They filled him in on the case they'd recently closed in which the president's mistress had been murdered, leaving Sam and Nick once again breathless with dread as they waited to see if President Nelson could hang on to his office through yet another scandal.

"You guys must've been dying," Gonzo said to Sam and Nick.

"Ah, yeah, kinda," Nick said. "I expected that being his VP would be mostly boring—and it's been that *too*."

"You couldn't have predicted his son would become a murderer, or that he'd have an affair while his wife was undergoing cancer treatment," Gonzo said. "I still can't believe that. It's so disgusting."

"That was the hardest part for me to swallow too," Sam said. "Gloria is a really nice lady, and she's stood by his side through his entire career. She deserved better than what she got from him."

"At least she left him," Jeannie said. "None of that 'stand by your man' nonsense that political wives are known for."

"This political wife has already told her man the same thing," Sam said, grinning at Nick.

"And my wife knows she has *nothing* to worry about on that front."

"The word *castration* was used," Sam said, making the guys wince.

"She's all bark and no bite," Nick said.

"Um," Freddie said, "I think there's some bite behind her bark. Just sayin'."

"That's right," Sam said with a big grin, "and don't you guys forget it."

"I miss you all so much," Gonzo said with a sigh. "I can't wait to get back to work."

"How much longer?" Freddie asked.

"A few more days in-patient, and then they want me to take a week or two at home before I come back part-time."

"We'll take whatever we can get," Sam said.

They spent another hour chatting with him before they stood to leave. Nick went to the door and gave a knock to let Brant know they were ready.

"We have to wait for him to come get us," Nick said.

"This is fascinating," Michael said. "Truly."

"Glad you think so," Nick said. "It drives me bonkers."

"But it beats the alternative." Sam took hold of her husband's hand, hoping to calm the agitation he felt whenever he was reminded of the many restrictions of being vice president.

They said their goodbyes to Gonzo and loaded up the SUV for the ride back to the District.

"He seems really good," Nick said when they were on the way out of Baltimore.

"So much better than he was," Jeannie said.

"I'm *fuming* about him pleading to anything," Sam said.

"Ah, yeah, we could tell," Freddie said. "As usual, you had no poker face."

"It's complete *bullshit*," Sam said. "I'm not about to pretend otherwise."

"Is there anything that can be done?" Nick asked.

"I'm going to talk to Malone," she said, referring to the detective captain who was her boss and mentor. "And the chief."

"Gonzo sounded pretty determined to take the plea," Freddie said tentatively.

"He's going to screw his entire career if he takes that plea," Sam said. "We can't let that happen." She caught Freddie and Jeannie exchanging concerned glances and knew what they were thinking. Tommy's recovery was fragile. This was what he wanted. And she respected that, but if there was anything she could do to save him from taking this massive hit to his career, she was going to do it.

Her phone rang with a call, and the single word on the caller ID made her groan. "Dispatch."

Which meant someone in the District had been murdered, and that was now her problem.

CHAPTER TWO

"Lieutenant Holland."

"Lieutenant, we've received a report of a body found in a garage off MacArthur Boulevard in Kent."

Sam ducked her head to see out the window to figure out where they were. Greenbelt, Maryland. "I'm about fifteen minutes outside the District. Have Patrol secure the scene until my team can get there. Don't let anyone in or out."

"Yes, ma'am."

"Let them know I'll be about an hour."

"Will do."

Sam slapped her flip phone closed and filled in the others. "Figures it had to be on the whole other side of the city."

"Murder is inconvenient that way," Nick said, "or so you tell me."

"Yes, it is. This means you're in charge of dinner, baths and bedtime."

"I can handle it."

"I know."

He put his arm around her, and Sam took the minute with him while she could, disappointed she wouldn't get to spend the evening with the kids when they got home. Since Aubrey and Alden had come into their lives, Sam had a whole new appreciation for working mothers and the challenges of trying to balance it all. It was tough, even with the tremendous help that Shelby provided, especially since the twins had joined their family. Scotty had been quite a bit older than the twins, who'd soon be six, when he joined their family and much more self-sufficient from the get-go.

The motorcade pulled onto Ninth Street and stopped in front of the double townhouse Sam and Nick called home.

"Thanks for the lift," Freddie said, kissing his wife and sending her home in his car while Jeannie said goodbye to Michael.

"Let me run in and get my stuff," Sam said. "Be right back."

Nick followed her up the ramp that had been installed for her late father so he could come visit them in his wheelchair. One of these days, they needed to see about removing the ramps at her house and his, three doors down. But not today.

A new agent was working the door and opened it for them.

"Good evening, Mr. Vice President, Mrs. Cappuano."

"Evening, Henry," Nick said.

Of course he knew the agent's name. He knew everything.

Sam grabbed her keys from the hook in the kitchen where she kept them, ran upstairs to the master bedroom to retrieve her cuffs, weapon and notebook from the bedside table drawer and returned to the kitchen to speak to Nick. "Tracy promised to have the kids home by six, and there's leftover pizza from last night if you don't feel like cooking."

"We'll figure something out."

Sam wanted to be there to help him figure it out, but duty called. "I guess I'll see you when I see you."

He put his arms around her and kissed her. "Be careful with my cop. She means everything to me."

"Take good care of my family. They mean everything to me."

"I gotcha covered, babe. Don't worry."

"I'll try to call the Littles before bedtime."

"I won't promise it in case it doesn't happen. We'll be fine."

Sam had to pull herself away from him. "Love you."

"Love you too. Be safe."

"I will."

Henry opened the door and nodded to her, probably

wondering who she thought she was, running around without her own detail.

She walked down the ramp to the sidewalk, where Freddie and Jeannie waited for her.

"All aboard," Sam said.

They got into the tricked-out black BMW retrofitted for her as a surprise from Nick. Sam joked that she could survive a nuclear explosion in that car, but it wasn't far from the truth. She used her flashers to get them across the city as quickly as possible, but Sunday-night traffic was light to begin with.

Sam took a call from Captain Malone when they were about five minutes out. "What's up?"

"Heard we caught a new one and was just checking in."

"Not sure what we've got yet. I've got Cruz and McBride with me, and we're almost there. We were on the way back from seeing Gonzo."

"Let me know what you've got when you can."

"Will do. Can we talk tomorrow about Gonzo?"

"What about him?"

"He's about to accept a deal on misdemeanor drug charges."

"I heard about that."

"And you're okay with it?" Sam had to remind herself that going ballistic with her boss wasn't the best idea.

"I'm not thrilled with it, but it'll take care of the problem and allow him to keep his job."

"Without any chance of ever being promoted again? That's complete bullshit, and you know it."

"I do know it, but I also know there're people within the department who aren't going to let this go, and he's better off to plead than have it become an even bigger deal. Especially right now when his sobriety is fragile. I talked to him. This is what he wants."

"It's freaking *infuriating* that he's having to put up with this shit because of people who're coming at *me*. This doesn't even have anything to do with him."

"He's the one who scored pain meds on the streets, Sam. Not you."

"You know as well as I do that the only reason he's having to plead this out is because of Ramsey's beef with me."

"It might've come to light without Ramsey."

"No one else is looking for shit to pin on my team." Sam wasn't sure how to process the sheer rage she felt at this drug charge putting the brakes on Gonzo's career.

"I'm sorry. I agree it's unfortunate. But it is what it is. While I have you, I wanted to remind you of the commanders' meeting at zero eight hundred tomorrow."

"I'll be there." They were meeting with Special Agent in Charge Avery Hill and others from the FBI about the upcoming investigation of the department. "This job is nothing but nonstop fun lately."

"That's what we're all about. Check in after you're done at the scene."

"Will do." Sam closed the phone and wished it wouldn't be such a hassle to get a new one, or she might be tempted to hurl it out the window.

The GPS on Freddie's phone guided them to the exact address, a palatial house surrounded by public safety vehicles and gawking neighbors. Why did the neighbors always gawk? Sam wanted to ask them why they were so curious about murder.

"Get Patrol on the neighbors. I want them nowhere near here."

As she got out of the car and made her way around the vehicles that blocked the driveway, she heard one of the gawkers say, "That's the VP's wife!"

"No pictures," she said to the man who was reaching for his cell phone. Sam was always concerned about saying or doing something that would embarrass Nick in his position as VP, but sometimes she just didn't care. She was so pissed about the situation with Gonzo that she probably shouldn't have been let out of the house. But alas, murder didn't wait for her to be in the right mood.

"What've we got?" she asked the female officer who met them at the yellow tape line. Sam noted her name tag read Phillips.

"Virginia 'Ginny' McLeod, age fifty-six, found in the garage by her husband, Kenneth, when he returned home from playing golf."

"Where is he?"

"In the kitchen with my partner. I instructed him not to touch anything and to remain seated at the kitchen table until you arrived."

"Excellent. Let me see the vic."

"Sam," Freddie said.

"I'll be right with you," she said to the officer as she stepped back to consult with her partner.

"Virginia McLeod is the woman we were talking about earlier who ripped off her friends," Freddie said.

Sam processed that information as she signaled to the officer to lead the way. With Freddie and Jeannie following, Sam thought about what she'd heard earlier about this woman. How many people would've wanted her dead after she defrauded her own family and friends? Was it ten people or hundreds?

She would find out soon enough.

They walked past a navy-blue Mercedes sedan with District plates parked in the driveway.

In the garage, they encountered a bloodbath—on the floor, walls, ceiling, and splattered on the silver sedan parked on the far side. The victim was on the floor by the door that led into the house, surrounded by a massive pool of blood. The unmistakable smell of death filled the air.

"Any sign of a murder weapon?" Sam asked the officer, who was making an effort not to look at the victim. Once was probably enough.

"Not that we could find on a quick canvass."

Whatever it was had been sharp and lethal, judging by the wounds to her face and neck. "Where's Crime Scene?"

"On the way," the officer said. "As is the medical examiner."

"Good job, Officer Phillips. Watch for them while we go in to talk to the husband."

The young officer hightailed it out of the garage, probably relieved to get away from the dead person.

"McBride, take a good look around the garage and the grounds for the weapon."

"On it," Jeannie said.

Sam and Freddie went into the house through a breezeway that connected the garage to the kitchen. A silver-haired man was sitting with another Patrol officer, this one a young man who jumped up when he saw Sam coming. She scanned his uniform and found his name tag. Jestings.

"Lieutenant, this is Kenneth McLeod. Mr. McLeod, Lieutenant Holland."

"I know who she is. Everyone knows who she is."

All righty, then, Sam thought. "Thank you, Officer Jestings. You can wait for us outside."

The officer took off, leaving Sam and Freddie alone with the charming husband.

"If your first question is did I kill her, the answer is no, even though I had good reason to. I'm sure you know all about what she did, how she fucked over our family and friends."

"When did you find that out?" Sam asked, taking a seat at the table while Freddie did the same.

"The same time everyone else did, when she was charged in federal court last week."

"Prior to that, you had no idea?"

"None."

"It must've made you pretty mad to find out that she'd defrauded people you call friends."

"Mad," he said with an ironic smile that made him look mean. "That's one word for what I was. Do you have *any idea* what she did to my life? The people she stole from, some of them are my clients."

"And what do you do?"

"I'm an attorney."

"What kind?"

"Estate."

"How many people were taken for a ride by your wife?"

"Hundreds."

Sam had been afraid of that. Nothing like a murder with

motive for days. "And you know them all?"

"Not all, but many of them."

"How much money are we talking about?"

"Twenty million, give or take."

"I'm not aware of the case against your wife beyond the basics. Fill me in on what she did and how she did it." Sam wanted to hear the story in his words.

"She's in finance, or she was. She puts together investment opportunities for her clients."

"What kinds of opportunities?"

"Everything from construction to travel to tech. You name it, she's dabbled in it. The project that got her in trouble was for a real estate business she started, to rehabilitate run-down properties. She would identify properties, get people to invest in them and then promise them returns on their investments when the properties sold."

"Except," Freddie said, "most of the properties people were investing in didn't actually exist."

"Right," McLeod said, his expression grim.

"So what'd she do with the money?" Sam asked.

"I have no idea," McLeod said. "That's one of many things Ginny will take to her grave with her. However, I've come to believe she had a gambling addiction, so that might account for some of it."

"Where were you today?"

"At the Potomac Country Club all afternoon. I played eighteen holes with three close friends, some of the only friends I have left because they didn't have enough cash to make them worth her time."

"We'll need their contact info."

"Why?" he asked, seeming astounded that they would check what he'd said.

"Because people lie to our faces all the time."

"I'm not lying! I played golf."

"Great, then you won't have any problem giving us the names and contact numbers for the people you played with."

He sagged and seemed to accept the inevitable, which was

good because not cooperating would count as wasting her time, and Sam hated when people wasted her time.

Using his cell phone to get the info, he wrote down the names and numbers of the three men. Sam handed the notebook over to Freddie to make the calls.

"When was the last time you saw your wife?"

"Before I left this morning."

"Spoke to her?"

"After her arraignment when I drove her home and asked her what the fuck she'd been thinking stealing from people, let alone people we *know*. When she couldn't give me a satisfactory response, I told her to stay the hell away from me. I was planning to immediately file for divorce and wanted her out of the house."

"Was she aware you were planning to divorce her?"

"Not yet, but I hardly think she would've been surprised in light of what I've learned about her. I didn't want to be on the hook to make restitution to her victims." As he said those words, it seemed to occur to him that he might be now that she was dead. "I didn't kill her, but I can think of hundreds of people who had reason to. One of our closest couple friends, Dan and Toni Alino, both his parents have Alzheimer's, and she got them to invest in her scheme with money she knew they'd need to care for his parents. She took money from her own cousin as well as my brother. Who does that?"

"I don't know," Sam said. "Was anyone particularly outspoken after she was charged?"

"Her phone was ringing nonstop for days. She ignored the calls. People were calling and texting me, but I didn't know what to tell them except I was as surprised as they were to find out what she'd been doing. I'm sure they don't believe I didn't know, but I really didn't. I was horrified when I heard the full extent of what she's charged with. If I'd known…" He looked at them, seeming shattered. "I would've done something to stop it. I'm an attorney, an officer of the court. There's no way I would've let this go on and not tried to stop it."

"Take me through what happened when you found her."

"I came home from the club, opened the garage door and saw

the blood all over the place, and then I realized it was her. Ginny. I... I recognized the running shoes she had on. I immediately called 911 and waited outside until the MPD arrived."

"You never touched her or went near her?"

"No. I could tell there was nothing I could do for her."

"Is her phone here?"

He nodded toward the kitchen counter. "It's there."

"Do we have your permission to take it into evidence?" Sam asked.

"Yeah, sure."

Sam pulled an evidence bag out of her coat pocket and handed it to Freddie.

"Is there somewhere else you can stay tonight? Crime Scene will be coming in to work the scene and will probably be here at least until tomorrow."

"I, um, I can go to my brother's. I think. Is it okay to text him?"

"Yeah, go ahead."

Sam stayed with him while he texted his brother.

"I can tell him what happened with Ginny?"

"Yes."

He typed the information into the phone and then waited for his brother to respond. "He said I can come over."

"We'll get Patrol to take you."

"I can't drive myself?"

"Everything here is considered evidence until Crime Scene is finished processing it. Where is your brother's home located?"

"Chevy Chase."

"Detective Cruz, will you ask Patrol to arrange transport for Mr. McLeod?"

Freddie nodded and left the kitchen.

"Are you guys going to ruin my life in the process of figuring out who killed my wife? I watch TV. I know you always think the spouse did it."

"Not always, and we'll only have to ruin your life if you lie to us."

"Everything I've told you is the truth."

"Then we shouldn't have a problem."

CHAPTER THREE

After sending Mr. McLeod off to his brother's house with Patrol, Sam stayed with the body and waited for the medical examiner while Jeannie and Freddie conducted a canvass of the neighborhood. On a search of the grounds, Jeannie hadn't found anything that might be the murder weapon, but Crime Scene would do a more thorough search of the house, yard and surrounding area.

Dr. Lindsey McNamara, the District's chief medical examiner, arrived with her team a short time later. With her long red hair up in a ponytail, Lindsey looked much younger than her thirty-seven years. "Sorry, I was out at the farm with Terry when I got the call." The family of her fiancé, Terry O'Connor, lived in Leesburg, Virginia. "I got here as fast as I could."

"No worries. We were on the way back from Baltimore when we got the call."

"How is he?"

"He seems really good."

They walked into the garage together.

"Did he say when he might get released?"

"In the next week or so and then back to work part-time at first."

"I'm glad for him and all of you that he'll be back soon."

"We are too." Since Lindsey was alone, Sam filled her in on

Gonzo's plan to plead to misdemeanor drug charges. "If you ask me, it's total bullshit."

"I agree with you." After putting on gloves, Lindsey squatted for a closer look at the bloody wound to Ginny's neck. Lindsey moved the woman's hair. "Looks like death by sharp object, but not tidy enough to be a knife. I'll know more when I get her cleaned up."

"I'm going to need a time of death as soon as possible. We've got motive up the wazoo here. Apparently, she was running a scam that bilked people out of millions."

"I read about that in the *Star* this morning! Terry and I were talking about it. How do you scam your own family and friends?"

"We were saying the same thing on the way to Baltimore. I guess we need to inform the prosecutor on the fraud case that his case just became mine." She'd get someone on her team to take care of that detail.

"Probably so." Lindsey took some photos and then signaled to one of her assistants to bring in the gurney for transport to the morgue. "I'll get on this right away and have a report to you by morning."

"Thanks, Doc."

Sam caught up with Freddie and Jeannie in the street. "Anything?"

"Of course no one has seen a thing," Freddie said, "but they'd all heard about Ginny being charged with fraud."

"Hmm, well, I guess that'd be big news around here."

"We've still got one house." He pointed to the last house in the cul-de-sac.

"Let's do it," Sam said.

They knocked on the first door, and an older man with thick white hair and glasses answered, seemingly taken aback to see three cops on his doorstep. "What can I do for you?"

"We're investigating the murder of Virginia McLeod," Sam said.

"She was *murdered*? Well, I suppose that's not surprising in light of what she did."

"Did you invest with her?" Sam asked.

"I did not. She came after all of us, though." He waved his hand to encompass the neighborhood. "I don't know of anyone who actually went in with her around here. If they did, they didn't tell anyone."

"Why weren't you interested?"

"Her proposal didn't pass my smell test."

"How so?"

"Long on big ideas, short on details."

"Did you know of anyone who might've been angry enough to kill her?"

"Based on what I read in today's paper, that's a very long list."

And Sam could hardly wait to talk to all of them. *Ugh.* "Did you see anyone around the McLeods' home today?"

"I just got home after being out for most of the day. So no, I didn't."

"Do you have one of those doorbell-cam thingies?" His front door was the only one that had an unobstructed view of the McLeods' house.

"No, I don't."

Because that would've been too easy. Sam handed him her business card. "If you think of anything relevant, give me a call."

He glanced at the information on the card. "You're the VP's wife, right?"

Sam hated when people stated the obvious. "I am."

"I hope he doesn't run for president."

She didn't want to ask. She honestly didn't. "Why's that?"

"I don't think he's got the experience required to be president."

"I'll pass that on to him."

The man gave her a curious look. "Is he going to run?"

"I'll ask him and get back to you on that." To her team, she said, "Let's go."

"It's no wonder you hate people," Jeannie said when they were across the street, far enough away that the man wouldn't be able to hear them if he was still in the doorway.

"Eh, whatever. Does he honestly think I care? That Nick would care?"

Freddie shrugged. "Who knows? People are weird."

"I tell you that every day." Sam noted that Lindsey's team had left with Ginny McLeod's body and Crime Scene was on the job. They'd pore over every inch of the place looking for evidence. Sam took a minute to confer with CSU Lieutenant Haggerty. "We're looking for a murder weapon, something sharp and lethal, but probably not a knife."

"On it."

"I'll check with you in the morning, or call me if anything pops."

Always a man of few words, Haggerty nodded and headed inside.

"What's the plan, LT?" Freddie asked.

"Let's go home and pick it up in the morning. I'll dig into the coverage of the case against her and figure out who we need to talk to. I'll drop you guys." After she'd delivered them to their homes, she headed for hers, thinking through the new case in the context of what she'd learned about her victim in the last hour. A deep dive into the coverage of Ginny's fraud case would help to frame Sam's next moves.

At a stoplight, she opened her new cherry-red flip phone and put through a quick call to Malone to update him. "Will you have someone notify the prosecutor on her fraud case as a courtesy?"

"I'll take care of that," Malone said.

She could check that item off her list. "Great, thanks. See you in the morning." Next, she called Nick.

"Is this my lovely wife?"

"No, it's the sidepiece."

"Remember—my wife can never know. She's vicious and possibly a bit feral."

"I hear she's got one hell of a steak knife too."

"Indeed. How's it going?"

"I'm on my way home. I called so you could get your sidepiece out before I get there, but somehow, it all went wrong."

His rich, lusty laugh was among her favorite things. "Thanks for the heads-up. I'll send her packing before you get home."

"Good plan. So my vic is the woman who swindled her friends."

"Seriously? Where do you even start with that?"

"With the swindled friends, I suppose. By the way, one of her neighbors thinks you shouldn't run for president because, and I quote, you don't have the required experience."

"Well then, that's it. I'm out."

Sam laughed. "I thought you'd like that."

"What I would've liked was to see your face when he said it."

"He almost got himself a throat punch, but I'm on my best behavior these days." After nearly being indicted for assaulting Ramsey, who'd totally deserved it, Sam thought first and punched second these days.

"What's your ETA?"

"About ten minutes. Is there food?"

"There is. I grilled burgers and saved one for you."

"Look at you."

"I'm capable of feeding myself and our children, even if I don't have the experience to be president."

"Almost to the checkpoint. See you in a few."

"I'll be here."

Sam ended the call, smiling as she always did after talking to him. He was so fun and funny and sexy and the full package, as far as she was concerned. "And he *has* a full package," she said, laughing at her own joke. Maybe it was weird to be cracking herself up or flirting with her husband after leaving a murder scene, but that was how she stayed sane while working an insane job.

After being waved through the checkpoint, she parked in her Secret Service-assigned spot on Ninth Street, locked her car and headed up the ramp to home, thankful she'd made it in time to see the twins before bedtime.

Henry opened the door for her. "Evening, Mrs. Cappuano."

"Evening, Henry."

She walked into the usual after-dinner chaos of the twins wrestling with Scotty and Nick standing watch over them to make sure no one got hurt.

Scotty had both of the Littles captured in his arms as they tried to get away, screaming their heads off as they laughed as hard as they screamed. "Do you surrender?"

"Never!" Aubrey said.

"That's my girl," Sam said. "Never give in."

Scotty tightened his hold on the squirming twins and shot a grin in Sam's direction. "Is there *any* concern for the older brother?"

"None," Sam said.

"Ha! Good to know."

"Two more minutes, little people, and then it's bedtime."

"If we go now, I'll read you an extra story," Scotty said.

"Let's go," Alden said.

Scotty released them, and they started to get up before diving back on top of him and taking him completely by surprise.

"We win!" Alden declared.

"Oof," Scotty said. "I'll give you that one, but no fair ganging up on me. You better start running, because I'm coming for you."

They went screaming up the stairs with Scotty in hot pursuit.

"Another night in paradise," Sam said to Nick, who put his arm around her and led her into the kitchen so she could eat.

"That's the best word I can think of to describe it," he said. "Absolute paradise."

"Nothing makes me happier than to walk in that door and see you watching over our three kids and obviously enjoying every second of it."

"I do enjoy every second of it." He poured her a glass of wine and sat with her while she ate a burger and fries while picking at a side salad.

As always, the burger and fries were far more interesting to her than the salad would ever be. "This is good. Thanks for cooking."

"No problem. It's funny you mentioned what that guy said about me running for president, because I've kind of made a decision about that over the last few weeks."

Sam glanced at him, noting his unusually serious demeanor. Usually, he was at his most relaxed when it was just the two of them. "Am I going to like this?"

"I think so. I'm not going to run."

While she wanted to stand up and cheer, she forced herself to consider him first. "Are you sure that's what you want?"

"I'm sure that I want to be here—all the time—and I can't do that if I'm on the road campaigning for months on end."

"Is it okay to say *phew*?"

"Yeah," he said, laughing. "It's okay."

"Do you want to talk about it?"

"There's not much to say other than it came down to you and the kids and how I don't want to be away from you guys for more than a year to campaign for a job I don't really want. You know how much I always wished for a family of my own. Now I have it, and the last thing in the world I want is to miss anything."

Sam reached over to put her hand on top of his. "I think you're doing the right thing and not just because I'm a selfish cow who doesn't want you anywhere but right here with me and the kids. It's also because of the scrutiny and the nastiness and the vitriol and the haters. The thought of even more of that aimed at you and us makes me queasy to think about, let alone live with."

"That's part of it too. If my insomnia is as bad as it is now, I can't fathom what it would be like with that job."

"It'd be unbearable. Have you talked to Graham yet?" Retired Senator Graham O'Connor had been a father figure and mentor to Nick since he befriended Graham's late son John as a freshman at Harvard. Graham and John had played critical roles in Nick's career, and no one wanted Nick to be president more than Graham did.

"Not yet. He's going to be bummed. I hate to disappoint him or anyone, but this feels like the best decision for our family right now. I was already leaning toward not running when the Littles came into our lives. Now I know for sure it's the right thing to be here for them."

"It might upset people, but I have to say I'm thrilled. No one wants to see you succeed more than I do, but there're so many other things you can do besides that. Remember how you said you wanted to go to law school?"

"Because that'd be no big deal with three kids underfoot."

"You could do it. Whatever you want."

"I might want to teach, actually."

"Really? You've never said that."

"It's something I think about."

"College?"

"High school."

"Get out of here. Are you serious?"

"I might be. I love the time I spend with kids when I visit schools. I think I could do some good there, get them excited about public service. That's my thought, anyway."

"You'd be amazing at it."

"You really think so?"

"Hell yes."

"We'd have to take a bit of a pay cut."

Sam shrugged. "We have what we need."

"I'd probably have to go back to school to get certified."

"You and Scotty can do your homework together."

He laughed. "I'd trade him help with algebra if he writes my papers for me."

"I bet he'd jump all over that offer."

"You really think this is a good idea?"

"I think it's a great idea. You know what it's like to meet someone like Graham, who opened your eyes to all the possibilities at a critical time in your life when you could've gone in any direction. You could do for your students what he did for you."

"That's kinda the idea."

"I truly love this, and I think you will too."

Nick's phone chimed with a text. "From Scotty. The Littles are fading fast if we want to say good night."

"Let's go."

They went upstairs to tuck in the twins, who were cuddled up to each other in the big bed they shared. There would come a time when they wouldn't want to sleep together anymore. Until then, Sam and Nick supported whatever gave them comfort in their grief after losing their parents to murder. And they drew tremendous comfort from each other.

She kissed them both, and then Nick did the same. "Have

sweet dreams," she whispered on the way out of the room. In the hallway, she said to Nick, "Could I borrow your laptop? I need to do some reading about what my vic was charged with."

"Sure. I'll run downstairs and grab it for you."

While he did that, she knocked on Scotty's door.

"Come in."

He had homework spread out on his bed. "You saved it all for the last minute again, huh?"

"Why should I ruin the rest of the weekend?"

"True." She sat on the edge of his mattress. "I did the same thing when I was in school. Always the last minute for everything. It drove everyone crazy."

"And look at you now. Two degrees and a gold shield."

"That's right, but with hindsight, I can see I made things harder on myself than they would've been if I'd chipped away a little at a time rather than trying to write an entire paper the night before it's due."

"I can sorta see that, but I can't bring myself to actually do it."

"You should try it for the next big thing. Do thirty minutes a day for two weeks before it's due, and see what you think."

"I'll take that under advisement."

"That's my line, and you're not allowed to use it."

"The last time you used that line, we were talking about the dog this family needs. What's the status of that?"

"Still under advisement."

"How long does advisement take, anyway?"

"Depends on the issue. Taking on another living, breathing thing that would be dependent on us to feed and care for it requires some time."

"You took on five-year-old twins without even five minutes of so-called advisement."

A snort from behind her let her know Nick was listening.

"Am I right?" Scotty asked him.

"When you're right, you're right."

"Whose idea was it to send him to school so he could outsmart us?" Sam asked Nick over her shoulder.

"It was most definitely not my idea," Scotty said. "I want to be homeschooled. That sounds like fun."

"Not happening," Sam said.

"But the dog is, right? See what I did there? The dog looks pretty good compared to homeschooling. And P.S., I call Dad for my homeschooler."

"That's a good call, and nice try with the outsmarting of your parents."

"Back to the dog..."

"We're thinking about it." Sam leaned in to kiss his forehead. "I swear we are."

"Think faster. I'm not getting any younger over here."

Sam tried not to laugh, but failed miserably. "You're too much, Scott Cappuano."

"You know I'm only joking, right?" He looked up at her with a vulnerable expression that tugged at her heart. Even after all the time they'd been together, did he still worry about doing or saying the wrong thing with them?

"Of course I do. And I know you really want a dog. Dad and I are thinking about it. That's the best I can do for right now."

"We've had a lot going on with Gramps dying and everything. I don't want you to think I'm being selfish."

"Buddy... Make room for your mother."

Rolling his eyes, he moved some of the papers so she could sit close enough to hug him as tightly as she could. "You don't have a selfish bone in your body, and the number one reason why you don't already have a dog is because we have to resist the urge to give you everything you want the second you ask for it. We're trying to do this parenting thing right, and not giving you everything you want is apparently how we keep you from being completely spoiled."

His snort of laughter was muffled by the tight hold she had on him. He pulled back to look at her. "Did you read that on some how-to-be-a-good-mom website?"

She play-punched him in the arm. "What if I did?"

"You're funny. I promise if you get me a dog, I won't turn into a spoiled brat."

"That's good to know, and it's not lost on us that you never ask for anything, which makes you the best kid ever."

"Could I ask you something kind of weird?"

"Anything you want. We specialize in weird around here."

Once again, Nick laughed behind her.

"What does it mean when people ask if you're going to have 'real' kids?"

CHAPTER FOUR

S am felt like she'd been sucker-punched. "Where... where did you hear that?"

"At school. Someone said they asked if you were having real kids, and I didn't know what that meant. I think it means babies, but I wasn't entirely sure."

Sam wanted to weep and wail and throat-punch the insensitive reporter who'd asked that question at a recent briefing. "What it means is that people are stupid."

"Well, I already knew that much," Scotty said with the cheeky grin she loved so much. It was very similar to Nick's.

"A reporter asked me if Dad and I were going to have kids of our own, and I went off on her, letting her know I already have three kids of my own who I love with all my heart."

"So she meant babies are real kids?"

"Who knows?"

He gave her the withering look that was her trademark. Apparently, he was borrowing from both their playbooks. "They meant babies that you would have, right?"

"Yeah, I guess."

"For what it's worth, pal," Nick said, "I lost my shit with that reporter's boss and let them know how offensive we found that question. You, Alden, Aubrey and Elijah are our family, our kids, the only kids we need, and we love you all very much. You know that." Elijah, a sophomore at Princeton, was the twins' older brother and legal guardian, but Sam and Nick had let him know he had a family in them now that his father and stepmother were gone.

"I do. Of course I do. We all know that. But, if you want to have babies too, that'd be cool."

"That's kind of a tough subject for us. Have you heard the word *infertility* before?"

"Isn't that what your speech was about that time?"

"Yeah, it was. I have trouble getting pregnant and staying pregnant." Sam really hoped she wasn't giving him more information than he needed, but it was important to her to tell him the truth—always.

"Oh, so like you can't have babies?"

"Right. I would if I could, but it just hasn't happened."

"And that's why you adopted me."

"No! We adopted you because we fell madly in love with you and needed you in our family. It had nothing to do with whether we could have babies. It was entirely about you."

"Mom is right," Nick said. "From the first time I met you, I couldn't stop thinking about you or wanting to see you again. Making you part of our family was the best thing we ever did. *You* made us a family, buddy."

"That's really nice of you to say."

"You know I mean it," Nick said. "We love you, Scotty. We have from the very beginning. Please tell me you know that."

"I do."

"People say the most insensitive things sometimes," Sam said. "Making it sound like adopted children aren't our own is the most insensitive thing anyone could say to someone who has adopted children. I wanted to stab her."

"With your rusty steak knife?"

"Yes! With the rustiest steak knife ever."

Scotty laughed. "I'll bet you were pissed."

"You have *no* idea."

"We both were," Nick said. "I went ballistic when I saw that. Her network got an irate phone call from the vice president."

"That must've made their day."

"I'm pretty sure it made their day very shitty, which is exactly what they deserved," Nick said. "There was a lot of outrage over it, not just from us. People wrote op-eds in the *Post* and the *Star* about the importance of adoption and the need to respect the sanctity of families, however they're composed."

"I think our family is pretty cool," Scotty said. "It's not just us and the twins, it's also Elijah and Shelby and Avery and Noah and the grandparents, aunts, uncles, cousins, not to mention all the friends, like Graham and Laine, who're like extra grandparents. And then there's my biological father..." Since meeting the man who'd fathered him, Scotty had maintained contact with him and saw him occasionally.

"That's right," Sam said. "Our family is the coolest. I'm going to be honest with you about something really big. Are you ready for this?"

Scotty glanced at Nick. "Is it normal to be afraid when she says something like that?"

"Completely normal. You never know what she's going to say."

"I can hear you two," Sam said, amused as always by them. "Before you joined us, my most pressing need was to have a baby. It was all I thought about. I've had a lot of disappointments in that regard." The statement glossed over years of infertility, miscarriages and heartbreak her son didn't need to know about. "But after you came to live with us, and I got to be your mom, that stuff doesn't hurt me the way it once did. I'm still sad about the fact that I can't seem to do what comes so easily to other women, but I'm not heartbroken anymore, and that's because of you." She placed her hand on his face and looked him in the eyes. "You made me a mom, and you're the realest and bestest kid I've ever known. I wouldn't want any other boy in the world to be my son but you."

His lips lifted into a small smile. "*Bestest* isn't a word."

"I say it is, and you are the very bestest."

"So are you. Thanks for telling me all that gross stuff about babies."

"It's certainly not for a lack of trying on our part."

"Stop it right now."

Sam lost it laughing at his look of complete horror, and when she hugged him again, he let her.

"Can we talk about something else?" Nick asked as he stepped into the room.

Scotty gave him a wary look. "Something bad?"

"No, buddy. I think it's actually good news. I've decided I'm not going to run for president."

"Oh. Really?"

"Yeah."

"How come?"

"Because I'd much rather be here with you, your mom and the twins than on the road campaigning for more than a year."

Scotty appeared to give that careful thought. "Are you sure? Because I read on NPR's website that you're, like, the most likely candidate to be elected if the election were tomorrow."

"You're reading NPR?" Nick asked, seeming amazed.

"I keep track of what's going on," Scotty said with a huff of indignance that made his parents laugh. "And I thought it'd be kind of cool to live in the White House."

"I think it's one of those things that sounds good on paper, but it occurred to me that if I ran and somehow managed to win—"

"You'd *so* win," Scotty said.

"Thanks for your vote, but it occurred to me that if I did win, you'd live in the White House the whole time you're in high school, and that might begin to feel a bit confining for you."

"Hmm, yeah, that might kinda suck after a while."

"That's my fear. One of them, anyway."

"And Mom would hate it."

"That too."

"That's not true!" Sam said. "I'd do it for you."

"And you'd hate it," Scotty and Nick said together before laughing at their own joke and sharing a high five.

"If you two are finished..."

"I hear what you're saying," Scotty said, "and I get why you're saying it, but I wouldn't want to be the reason you don't run."

"Me either," Sam said.

"You're not the reason, but you're both part of it. I waited all my life to have a family, and now that I do, the last thing in the world I want to do is be separated from you guys for any reason. It's enough that I have to travel as VP, but campaigning would be an eighteen-month grind of primaries and then the general election. I just don't want to do that. I don't want the job badly enough to put any of us through that, not to mention the scrutiny, the security, the attention and nonstop media coverage. Ack, just no. Being VP has been more than enough for me."

"As long as it's not because of me, then I support your decision," Scotty said.

"I appreciate that," Nick said, clearly amused by his intelligent comment. "Do me a favor and don't mention it to anyone until I can talk to Graham?"

"I won't say anything."

"Appreciate it, buddy."

"And with that," Sam said, "we're outta here. Finish your homework and go to bed."

"Did you get that line from the mother website too?"

"Nope, that one's all mine." She kissed the top of his head. "If anyone gives you shit about anything at school, let me know. I'll make sure they get arrested and sent to juvie."

"You can't do that," he said, his tone dripping with disdain.

"*They* don't know that. I could make them sweat, and I'd do it for you in a red-hot second."

He rolled his eyes, which was another trait of hers. "It might be better for all of us if I take care of the middle school nonsense while you worry about the killers."

"You're a wise young man, Scott Cappuano," Nick said. "And we love you."

"Love you too. Go away so I can finish this nightmare called homework."

"Don't stay up too late," Nick said.

"I won't."

Sam got up to leave the room, giving Nick a murderous look that she knew he'd understand. That they'd even had to have a conversation with Scotty about "real kids" made her crazy.

"You guys?"

They turned back to him.

"I'm thankful all the time that you came to Richmond that day and we met each other. I just wanted you to know that."

"That was one of the best days of my entire life," Nick said.

"Better than becoming VP?"

"A thousand, million, *bazillion* times better. See you in the morning."

Smiling, Scotty said, "Night."

Nick let Sam go ahead of him, closed Scotty's door and followed her into their bedroom, where she whirled around to face him.

"I want to kill that woman."

"Don't do that, babe. Think of the paperwork..."

"I'm going to call her and let her know what her dumbass, ignorant, what-the-ever-loving-fuck-is-wrong-with-her question led to."

He smiled at her choice of words. "That might not be a bad idea."

"It's the best idea I ever had. In fact, maybe I'll go there and have it out with her in person and really make her day."

"Uh, well..."

"Don't tell me not to protect my kid, Nick. Please don't do that."

"I'd never tell you not to do that, but you tend to shy away from the kind of publicity a confrontation like that is apt to generate."

"In this case, I don't care." She glanced up at him. "Unless it'll cause heartburn for you."

"I couldn't care less about that."

"Maybe," Sam said, giving him her best diabolical smile, "we should go together."

"A date with my beautiful wife in the middle of a workday? Sign me up."

"Only you would see it as a date."

He closed the distance between them, placed his hands on her hips and kissed her. "Any minute I get to spend with you is the best date I've ever been on."

"I'm so *mad*."

"Me too, babe."

"Let's do something about it."

"I'm with you."

"This idea makes me giddy."

"Giddy is a good look on you." He kissed her again. "What you said to Scotty about it not being for a lack of trying on our part was classic. The look on his face..."

Sam flashed a big grin. "Right? I was rather pleased with that myself."

"The poor kid," Nick said, chuckling. "He's going to need PTSD therapy by the time we're done with him."

"No, he won't. He's our masterpiece. He's going to make us so proud. I know it."

"I tend to agree. He'll make us proud despite us."

"No, *because* of us. He thinks we're so gross with the kissing and stuff, but we've shown him what to aspire to when it comes to love and marriage and happily ever after."

"That's true," Nick said. "I can't wait to see him fall madly in love so I can tease him mercilessly."

"Same."

"But until the day comes when we can mock and torture our son, I'd like to focus on my own happily ever after."

Sam put her arms around him. "Is that right?"

He kissed her neck and seemed to breathe her in. "Uh-huh."

"What did you have in mind?" She needed to spend time online, digging into the life of her latest victim and finding out more about the scheme that'd probably gotten her killed. But with her husband hot and hard and talking about happily ever after, the case would have to wait a little while longer.

"What I have in mind will require full nudity."

"Your plans usually do."

"Only the ones that involve you."

"Well, that's a relief."

His low laugh echoed through his big, muscular body. She loved to make him laugh, to make him smile, to make him happy. Whatever it took, she was there for it, even if it meant putting work on hold for a bit.

Once upon a time, before he came back into her life, the idea of putting work on hold for anything never would've occurred to her. Now, she did it regularly, because she'd learned there was nothing more important than him or their family. She gave her job everything she had for eight to ten hours a day, plus weekends, holidays, vacations... She'd learned that allowing a minute or two for herself in the midst of an investigation made it so she could continue to fight for justice for her victims.

And the minutes she allowed herself to have with Nick were the best of her entire life.

Being naked in bed with him was one of her favorite things in the world, and after the long, emotionally charged day with Gonzo and the new case, not to mention the conversation with Scotty, she felt the tension leave her body when he wrapped his arms around her and held her close to him in bed.

"This is the best thing ever."

"The absolute best thing."

For the longest time, they did nothing more than cuddle and touch and kiss, which was more than enough for her. It was so relaxing, in fact, that they both dozed off after a while, and because it was so rare for him to actually sleep, Sam had to sneak out of bed an hour later so she wouldn't disturb him.

He'd left his laptop on the dresser, and after she put on Nick's discarded T-shirt, she retrieved the computer and brought it back to bed, moving carefully, hoping he'd stay asleep.

She checked her email to see if there was anything from Lindsey, which there wasn't, but there was a message from Detective Cameron Green.

LT,

Took the liberty of a deep dive into the case against Virginia McLeod and summarized the details for you below. I also made a very LONG list of the people we need to speak with. I figure we can maybe divide and conquer tomorrow? Hope this helps.

Cam

"God bless you, Cameron Green," she whispered as she

scrolled down to read the details of the scheme Ginny had perpetrated against her family and friends.

The gist, Cameron had written, was that she got them to invest in properties, such as old warehouses and run-down apartment buildings, that would be rehabbed and sold at a profit, though many of the properties didn't even exist. She used photos of properties located in different parts of the country to build detailed prospectuses about the possibilities for each one, along with projections for profitability for each development. Working with a local Realtor, she'd shown potential investors properties similar to the ones she had in mind for rehab. And the money came pouring in, to the tune of twenty-two million dollars from four hundred and eighty high-end investors.

Ugh, Sam thought. That gave them four hundred and eighty people with motive to kill.

The scheme was uncovered, Cameron wrote, when the FBI was tipped off by one of the investors, named Brett Haverson, who'd spotted some cracks in the scheme and asked an FBI agent friend to check it out for him. That had led to a full-blown investigation by the FBI and IRS that found Ginny was collecting the money, living large, not paying taxes and not rehabbing anything.

Sam composed an email to Cam.

This is fantastic work! Thank you so much for getting a jump on it. You saved me a ton of time. Questions:
How do people think they will get away with this stuff?!?
Don't they know that eventually the investors are going to be asking for progress reports on the properties?
How do they explain their new extra lavish lifestyle to the friends and family whose money is being used to pay for it?

He wrote back a few minutes later.

I wondered the same things. If you're going to do something like this, there're smarter ways to get your friends to invest in something less tangible. And if you're an investor, don't you view the property in question BEFORE you turn over a shit ton of money?! But people who have shit tons of money in the first place probably don't do the same due diligence ahead of time that you and I would do. Which also leads to the fact that she was asking friends and family to invest, and that lends a certain credibility. Who would suspect a FRIEND or FAMILY MEMBER of blatantly stealing from them? In that way, it's kind of brilliant...

Diabolically brilliant, Sam replied. *We'll talk to Haverson to start with in the a.m. Divide up the rest of the list among the team. And thanks again for getting a jump on this. You earned multiple gold stars!*

Ha-ha, how do I cash in on these gold stars you speak of? Also, we need to talk about the OTHER THING in the a.m. I might have something for you.

I'm intrigued. Gold stars to be redeemed as the LT sees fit. The system is somewhat arbitrary and undefined. Have a good night and thanks again.

The "other thing" was a side investigation into Sergeant Ramsey they were conducting completely off the books. They believed he reported Gonzo for buying drugs on the street and was looking for any way to discredit Sam and her squad.

She'd asked Freddie, Jeannie and Cameron to do some digging into Ramsey, leaving no paper trail that could come back to bite them. She couldn't wait to hear what Cam had uncovered.

She read through the reports Cam had forwarded to her from the FBI investigation into Ginny's scheme and how it had unraveled, as well as the IRS audit of how she'd spent the money. The home she'd been murdered in was relatively new, as were the luxury cars she, her husband and children drove. They'd been on trips to Europe, a safari in Africa and a cruise in the South Pacific, but all that represented only a small fraction of the missing money.

The Feds believed the rest had been stashed offshore, but they'd been unsuccessful in locating the accounts.

Sam tried to imagine living large right under the noses of the people she'd stolen from. It was so brazen as to be unreal. Ginny was either the smartest criminal in the history of criminals or the stupidest. Sam couldn't decide which. This would be one of those cases where she'd have to really work to remain empathetic toward her victim. Often, those she sought justice for were innocent people who were either in the wrong place at the wrong time or caught up in something bigger than they realized until it was too late.

Sam would never go so far as to say that someone deserved to be murdered, but after what Ginny had done to the family and friends who'd invested in her scheme, it wasn't surprising that someone had exacted the ultimate revenge.

That motive would drive the investigation, and Sam was looking forward to digging into the case in the morning. Because regardless of Ginny's despicable crimes, she would still get Sam's best effort—and that of her team—to bring a killer to justice.

CHAPTER FIVE

"Did you actually sleep all night?" Sam asked Nick after her alarm went off, waking both of them.

"I did. Can I sign up for snuggle therapy again tonight?"

"Tonight and every night."

"I'm in."

They got the kids up and dressed and ate breakfast together while they waited for the lead agent on Nick's detail, John Brantley Jr., to report to work.

The young, handsome, intense agent knocked on the kitchen door before he stepped into the room. "You wanted to see me, Mr. Vice President?"

"Morning, Brant. The lieutenant and I would like to pay a visit to News Channel 6 around lunchtime today if we can make that happen."

Sam loved watching Nick in vice president mode, even as she thanked her lucky stars that she'd never have to see him in president mode. Dear God, the very thought of him as president made her weak in the knees.

"Uh, pardon the inquiry, sir, but neither of you is exactly known for courting press attention."

Nick smiled at the comment the agent never would've made when he first started working with them. He'd become increasingly more comfortable with expressing his opinions to them, which was fine with her. Knowing the super competent agent was protecting her husband went a long way toward keeping Sam sane.

"Right you are, Brant," Nick said. "But we have a very large bone to pick with one of the reporters there, and we'd like to pop in for a face-to-face discussion."

"Right. Pop in."

The logistics involved in coordinating that "pop in" would take over Brant's day.

"Can we make that happen?"

"Yes, sir."

"And of course the element of surprise is highly desired..."

"Of course. I'll get back to you with an approximate time."

"Excellent. Thank you, Brant."

The agent nodded and left the room.

"He hates our guts, doesn't he?" Sam asked.

Nick laughed. "I don't think it's gotten to that point quite yet."

"He's going to write one hell of a tell-all after you're out of office."

"No, he won't." Nick crooked his finger to bring her close enough to whisper in her ear. "And now we have a nooner to look forward to."

Sam laughed at the way he waggled his brows suggestively.

"I heard that," Scotty grumbled. "I don't even know what that is, but I'm pretty sure it's gross."

"Go brush your teeth," Sam said, laughing at his grumpiness.

Scotty scowled at her and took off to finish getting ready.

"Love you," Sam called after him. "Have a good day!" Next, she kissed the twins, made sure their lunches were ready to go and left them with Nick for face washing and teeth brushing.

"See you at noon," Nick said when he kissed her goodbye. "Take good care of my cop this morning. I love her forever."

"She loves you too."

As she drove to work, she thought about how the twins' mother had volunteered at their school, overseen craft projects and planned elaborate birthday parties. Sam felt inadequate compared to her, but showered them with all the love she had to make up for the things she lacked. She could only hope it was enough.

Their sixth birthday was coming up next week, the weekend after Thanksgiving, and they would have a party while Elijah was home from Princeton. Sam had relegated the details to their personal assistant, Shelby Faircloth Hill, the ultimate party planner, who would pull it off without breaking a sweat, whereas Sam would've been lost on where to even start.

Thank God for Shelby.

She arrived at HQ and drove around the building to the entrance by the morgue, her first stop being a check-in with Lindsey. "Give me something, give me anything."

Lindsey looked up from where she was typing on a computer. As usual, she had her long red hair in a ponytail and a tall coffee sitting on her desk. "I got something. Come see?"

"Do I gotta?" Sam hated the morgue and everything that went on there.

"Yep."

Sam hoped her breakfast would stay where she'd put it and not come rushing up at the sight of something that could never be unseen. "Here I come." This was one of those times when deep breathing didn't help, unless the smell of formaldehyde settled your stomach. It only made Sam's feel worse, so no deep breathing.

Lindsey led her to the table where Ginny was laid out, a sheet covering her that Lindsey peeled back to reveal the nasty injury to her neck that had killed her. "See this?" she asked after she snapped on gloves and pointed to the edges of the wound.

"What about it?"

"I believe you're looking for a yard implement or something with pointed, sharp edges that would've created this pattern."

Now that she pointed to it, Sam saw the pattern.

"Like a garden cultivator or what's sometimes called a Garden Weasel."

"A what? So not a gardener here."

"It's a handheld tool that's used to clear weeds and such. Has three very sharp rotating tines that churn up the dirt."

"Rotating tines? Ouch."

"I know."

"But that would indicate that whoever killed her maybe didn't go there with a plan. They likely grabbed the yard tool in the garage and attacked her."

"That's what I'm thinking too."

"This is good stuff, Doc. You've given me a thread to pull."

"And we all know how much you love your threads."

"Indeed."

"The tox screen came back negative for drugs or alcohol in her system. No sign of sexual assault, and I saw no other obvious injuries besides the one to her neck that killed her and the cuts on her face. If I had to speculate, your perp grabbed the first available object and took her out."

"That sounds like a plausible theory—and he or she got lucky with the first strike."

"It would seem so."

Sam stepped out of the freezing-cold room to call CSU Lieutenant Haggerty.

She got his voice mail, which irritated her. "It's Holland. Call me when you can. I've got something." After slapping her phone closed, she turned to speak to Lindsey, who'd followed her out into the hall. "I'll tell you something Terry is going to hear today that also affects you as Terry's fiancée, but it's top secret otherwise."

"What's that?"

"Nick isn't going to run."

Lindsey's eyes went wide. "Wow, that's huge."

"I know, and frankly, I'm relieved."

"I'm sure. Did Nick say why?"

"You know how he was raised, right? Teenage parents and a grandmother who didn't really want him around?"

"I've heard that."

"He doesn't want to be president. Plus, he's waited all his life for what we have now, and he doesn't want to spend months on end away from us on the campaign trail."

"That's so sweet."

"I think so too, and I'm thrilled he won't be gone all the time. I almost lost my shit when he was in Europe for a week, and when he went to Iran. Ugh..."

"I feel you. It's tough for me when Terry travels with him, so this is good news for me too, even if I loved the idea of Nick being president. He would've been really great."

"I agree, but we're looking forward to getting our lives back after he leaves office. As much as we love Brant and the other agents, their presence is a tad intrusive at times."

"I bet it's way more than a tad intrusive. I'd hate being watched all the time like that."

"Nick says he understands now what it's like to be a goldfish in a bowl with everyone looking at him."

"That's a great way to put it."

"It's the truth. Well, I need to hit it. I've got a noon date with my husband to pay a visit to the reporter who asked if we're going to have kids of our own."

Lindsey's mouth fell open. "You're *going* there?"

"Yep."

"What brought this on?"

"Our son asking us what it means to be a 'real' kid."

"No."

"He heard it at school and didn't know what it meant."

"Sam..."

"I know. It's infuriating, and we thought it might be fun to tell the reporter who asked the question what she started."

"I'd give anything to be there to see you two walk into her office."

"You can come if you'd like."

Lindsey laughed. "Thanks, but I'll wait to hear about it from you."

"I'm actually looking forward to it."

"God help that woman. She has no idea what's about to hit her."

"Nick and I can take whatever shit they fling our way, but don't come for our kids, you know?"

"Absolutely. You're doing the right thing and teaching her a lesson she'll never forget."

"Let's hope so. Have a good day, Doc."

"You too. Let me know how the visit to the TV station goes."

"Will do." On the way to the pit, she took a call from Haggerty. "Hey, so the ME has determined our cause of death was most likely a Garden Weasel or a similar implement that would've caused a ragged wound."

"Got it. We're back on the scene today finishing up. I'll let you know if we find anything that fits the bill."

"Thanks very much. Was there anything else useful?"

"Not yet. We took a ton of prints and collected lots of other evidence. It's all with the lab. Today, we're working on getting the prints of anyone who had regular access to the house so we can rule out family members."

"Perfect. Keep me posted."

"Will do."

When the line went dead, she smacked the phone closed and jammed it into her back pocket. In the pit, she signaled Cameron Green to come into the office.

Squared away as always in a starched light blue dress shirt and matching tie, Green came in carrying a file folder. "Can you ask Cruz and McBride to join us?" he asked.

Sam picked up the phone and buzzed Freddie's extension.

"Yes, ma'am?"

"Come into the office, and bring McBride with you."

"Yes, ma'am."

She put down the extension and waited for them to come in.

Freddie closed the door behind them. "What's up?"

"I've got something on Ramsey," Green said.

Sam's backbone tingled the way it did when something was about to break on a case. "Do tell."

"He's having an affair." Green put a series of photos on the desk.

Sam, Freddie and Jeannie leaned in for a closer look.

"The woman's name is Amy Turnblat. She's thirty-five and works as an executive chef at La Belle Vie in Potomac. I tailed him over a week, and he spent three nights with her and four at home in Columbia Heights." Cam put more pictures on the desk, all of them taken from Facebook. "He's been married to Marlene Ramsey for thirty years, and they have four adult children."

"Holy bombshell," Sam said, her mind racing with thoughts of how they could use this info to force Ramsey to back the hell off.

"I'm incredibly impressed, Cameron," Jeannie said.

"It was actually kind of fun," Cam said, smiling. "Nothing like catching a scumbag being a scumbag."

"How do we use this to get him off our backs?" Freddie asked.

"I was just trying to figure that out myself."

"If I may suggest something?" Cam said.

Sam waved her hand to give him the floor.

"Send the photos in an interoffice envelope with a note that says something like, 'When you dig for shit on your colleagues, they do the same.' Nothing more, nothing less. Just that."

"I love that," Jeannie said.

"Let's do it. Type the note on plain white paper and wear gloves so there's no evidence to trace this back to us."

"I'll take care of it," Cam said.

"Are we all in agreement?" Sam asked.

Freddie hesitated. "I worry about making it worse somehow."

"How can it get any worse than him basically ruining Gonzo's career?" Sam asked him.

"I don't know, and I'm not sure I want to find out."

"If we don't do something to put him on notice that what goes around comes around, he'll continue to make our lives a living hell in every way he possibly can," Sam said. "We have to do something."

"I don't disagree with that. I'm just worried about what his next move might look like."

"If he makes another move, we send the pictures to his wife," Sam said. "He'll understand that without us having to spell it out." To Cameron, she said, "Do it. Just like you said."

"Will do." He handed her another stack of pages. "I split up the McLeod investors list by locals and out-of-towners, figuring we'll start local."

"He's showing us all up," Jeannie said when she leaned in for a closer look at the lists.

"He certainly is," Sam said. "Pass them out, and let's get to it."

"You've got the FBI meeting at eight," Freddie reminded her.

"Shit, fuck, damn, hell. Why do I have to go to that stupid meeting?"

"Um, because the chief asked you to?"

"Whatever." Despite her hatred of meetings that got in the way of real work, Sam actually welcomed the FBI probe into the department. The recent spate of lawlessness within their ranks and the accompanying press coverage had led to the inquiry. At least with Avery Hill overseeing the investigation, they would get a fair shake, but attending that meeting was the last thing Sam wanted to do when she had a fresh homicide to investigate.

"Hopefully, it won't take long," Freddie said.

Sam gave him a withering look. Meetings always took too long. A minute was too long, and this one was sure to be longer than that. "Start digging into Brett Haverson, the investor who tipped the FBI. We'll start with him after the meeting. The rest of you hit the street with the other investors. Call in any updates."

When she was alone in the office, she reached for the clip on the desk that kept her hair out of the way when she was working and put her hair up. The FBI meeting had been looming for more than a week now, and it still made her feel sick to think about the reasons for it and her involvement in the criminal prosecutions of three high-ranking members of the department, all of it far too close to her for comfort.

Former lieutenant Leonard Stahl had recently been convicted on charges of attempted murder and kidnapping stemming from the day he'd taken her hostage, wrapped her in razor wire and had nearly succeeded in setting her on fire. A renewed investigation into the unsolved shooting of her father had led, shockingly, to Deputy Chief Conklin, Skip Holland's close friend. The kicker had been discovering Patrol Captain Hernandez had known about Conklin's involvement and covered it up. The uproar had been fierce and relentless, thus the FBI inquiry.

Since the District wasn't a state, there was no state police to lead the investigation, so the Feds had been called in by the mayor. On the plus side, Sam trusted Avery Hill to oversee a fair process.

She grabbed her notebook and pen and headed for the conference room attached to the chief's suite of offices. The office next to the chief's that had once belonged to Conklin was now dark and the door closed. A fresh wave of grief assailed Sam when she recalled her father occupying the deputy chief's office, next door to his best friend, Joe Farnsworth.

Grief was such a weird thing, attacking as it did out of nowhere, on a perfectly ordinary Monday morning, nearly five years since that office had belonged to her dad. She stood in the hallway staring at the closed door, the buzz of voices from the conference room in the background.

"Sam."

She blinked and turned to look up at the chief, the man she'd called Uncle Joe as a child.

"Are you all right?"

"I, ah... Yeah. I'm fine."

"I still look for him in there too. Even when Conklin was deputy, I'd walk in there expecting to find Skip."

"It was such an inconvenience to me that he was deputy chief." Sam offered him a small smile as she recalled the early days of her career. "Everyone assumed I got special treatment because he was my father, when he actually went out of his way to avoid anything that smacked of favoritism toward me."

"He always held you to a higher standard than anyone else."

"Believe me, I know. And then I'd walk into O'Leary's to meet him for a beer after work, and he'd hug me and kiss me and call me 'baby girl' in front of the guys. I wanted to stab him." As she laughed at the memory, her eyes filled with tears that she refused to allow at work. She blinked them away and took a deep breath, determined to push through the way she always did, even when her heart was broken.

"He loved you so much and was so damned proud of you." He kept his voice low so they couldn't be overheard. "That goes for both of us."

"Means a lot. Thank you—and P.S., back atcha."

He glanced at the conference room. "Let's get this over with, shall we?"

"Yes, please. I've got a new vic that needs me."

"Heard about that. The woman who scammed her friends and family."

"Yep, and left me with nearly five hundred people with motive, not to mention their families and friends. Good times."

"I have no doubt you'll get to the bottom of it."

"We shall see. Please make this ordeal as short as possible."

"Wish I could, but it's not my meeting." His gaze shifted to Avery Hill as he approached them. "Morning, Agent Hill."

"Chief, Lieutenant, how are you this morning?"

"We'll be better after this meeting," Sam said.

Avery laughed, which made the handsome devil even more so. "Duly noted. Shall we?"

CHAPTER SIX

A very gestured for them to precede him into the conference room, where the other division commanders and department leadership had already gathered, along with Avery's deputy, George Terrell.

Sam's direct supervisor, Detective Captain Jake Malone, came rushing in, apologizing for being late, even though he wasn't late.

Sam took a seat at the far end of the room, tucking herself into a corner so she could observe without being observed. All the cases they were here to discuss involved her in some way or another, and the last freaking thing she wanted was anyone checking her reactions.

Speaking of handsome devils, Lieutenant Archelotta, head of IT, caught her eye and lifted his chin, offering silent support that Sam appreciated from the only other officer she'd ever dated after her marriage to Peter shit the bed. Although, calling what she'd done with Archie "dating" was a stretch. Mostly, they'd had sex, but that was ancient history now that she was happily married to Nick. Archie remained a valued friend and trusted colleague.

"Thank you all for being here." Avery stood at the head of the long table around which the MPD's top brass had gathered. "I understand and appreciate this is an intrusive and unwelcome process. It won't be quick or painless, but our goal is to make it as efficient as possible for all of you while providing the public with an accounting of what happened, who was involved and where we go from here. A few ground rules. First, we expect you to make yourself and your officers available to us as needed. Second, we expect you and the others on your team to be truthful with us. This will go a lot faster if we're all on the side of getting to the truth. If we later prove that members of this department lied to us, we'll file charges."

Sam noticed no one was looking at Avery as he spoke. Rather, everyone focused on the table or their own hands or some other random thing. It never came naturally to police officers to be investigated, but recent events had led to this day of reckoning that was sure to impact them all in some way.

Avery went through the list of interviews they planned to conduct. Homicide was far enough down the list that she shouldn't have to worry about the Feds for a few days, which was good. She had better things to do, with Ginny McLeod's murder to investigate.

After reviewing the schedule, Avery asked if there were questions.

Captain Roback from Vice raised his hand. "I'd like to know why we need this when we know who the criminals are, and all of them have been charged and put into the system."

"If I may?" the chief said.

Avery gestured for him to go ahead. "I hear what you're saying, Captain Roback, and at first, I felt the same way. In my mind, we've done a good job policing our own team and weeding out the people who don't belong here. But if there're others, I want to know who they are, and I want them gone before they can further sully the reputation of this department. We all know there are more hardworking, dedicated officers in this department than there are criminals. I welcome this investigation and fully support it. I expect all of you to do the same."

"Thank you, Chief," Avery said. "Any other questions?"

When there were none, he thanked them for attending the meeting. "We'll be in touch with each of you over the next few weeks."

That wasn't bad, Sam thought as she hung back, waiting for the others to leave the room before her. *Fourteen minutes.* She was on her way to the pit when someone called her name from the lobby. Turning, she was shocked to find Lenore Worthington, the stunning Black woman Sam had met during her first year in Patrol when she'd responded to a call for help and found Lenore's son, Calvin, shot to death outside their Southeast home.

Sam walked toward Lenore and hugged her. "It's so nice to see you."

"You too. I'm sorry about your dad."

"Thank you. You look gorgeous, as always." Lenore was always dressed to the nines, her nails done and her makeup perfectly applied. Sam recalled feeling like a slouch next to Lenore when she'd first known her.

"You're too kind."

"How've you been?" Sam asked.

"Oh, you know..." Lenore shrugged. "It's been almost fifteen years, but it doesn't ever get any easier. Calvin would've been thirty next month, which is so hard to believe. I have trouble picturing him as a thirty-year-old. He's frozen forever at fifteen."

"I'm so sorry."

"Do you have a minute?"

She didn't, but she'd make time. Sam had never forgotten Calvin Worthington or his mother's gut-wrenching grief. "Come on in." She led the way to her office in the pit and gestured for Lenore to go ahead of her.

When Freddie caught her eye, his brow lifted in inquiry. Sam raised her index finger to let him know she needed only a minute, and then they'd hit the streets.

"Have a seat." Sam went around to sit behind her desk. "What can I do for you?"

"I read about how you solved your dad's case after almost four years, and I know fifteen is a lot longer, but I wondered if maybe you might be willing to take another look at Calvin's case. There were so many things that didn't make sense, and I just thought that you..." Her voice broke, and she looked down. "I've followed your career. I know you're the best." She looked up at Sam, her chin quivering. "Doesn't my Calvin deserve the best?"

Sam swallowed the lump in her throat. She'd thought of Calvin often over the years. When he'd been killed, he was just two years older than Scotty was now. "He does. Of course he does."

Lenore's eyes brightened with hope. "So you'll look at it?"

"I'll mention it to my commanders and ask if we can put some people on it. It'll completely depend on what they say. If it were up to me, I'd do it in a second, but it's not."

"I understand," she said with a sigh. "I appreciate anything you can do. You were always so kind to me and my family, and it meant a lot to us. Even if there's nothing you can do, we won't forget that."

Sam had stayed with Lenore, her mother and daughter for two hours while they waited for the medical examiner to arrive. She'd made herself available to them in the days that followed and had spoken with Lenore several times over the years at events for victims. "I'm starting a new grief group for people who've lost loved ones to violent crime. I think it would mean a lot to people starting out on this journey to have your voice in that group. It would mean a lot to me."

"Tell me when and where, and I'll be there."

Sam handed her a flyer Dr. Trulo had made that included the details of the grief group's first meeting.

"Thank you."

"I'll consult with my command about a fresh look at Calvin's case and let you know. Is your number the same?"

She nodded. "It'll never change until I get the call that they've found my baby's killer. I'd be afraid to miss that call."

"I'll get back to you. It may not be this week, but as soon as I can."

"I'll look forward to hearing from you, and I'll be at the grief group."

"It was good to see you, Lenore."

"You too. I was so, *so* happy to read that you'd nailed the guys who shot your dad."

"Thank you. It was a relief to finally know, even if the answers were shocking."

Lenore stood to leave. "I can only imagine. But at least now you know."

"Yes, we do. I'll be in touch."

"Thank you for your time."

A minute after Lenore left the office, Freddie appeared in the doorway. "What was that about?"

"A homicide from my first year on the job. I was in Patrol, took the call for a shooting in Southeast. Calvin, a fifteen-year-old, was already dead in the driveway when I got there. That was his mother."

"Oh, wow. Did you remember her?"

Sam nodded. "I've never forgotten her."

"Did we get whoever did it?"

Sam shook her head. "The case was never closed. That's why she was here. She heard we closed my dad's case and wondered if we might take another look at Calvin's."

"What'd you tell her?"

"That I'll run it up the pole, which I will." She stood, gathered her keys, phone and notebook and put on her coat. "Let's hit it." As they walked toward the morgue, Sam said, "Talk to me about Haverson."

"He's the president of a community bank in Bethesda."

Sam groaned. "So we have to drive to freaking Bethesda?"

"We do."

"Why did I know you were going to say that?" Sam asked, resigned to an hour in the car. Nothing chapped her ass more than wasting time. Well, receptionists chapped her too. And needles. And flying. Her ass was chapped a lot, if she were being honest. And what did that even mean? Chapped the ass. She huffed out a laugh at the direction her thoughts had taken.

"Do I dare ask what's so funny?"

"I'm thinking about things that chap my ass."

"I withdraw the question due to lack of interest in the things that chap your ass, or anything involving your ass."

"I have a very fine ass. Just ask Nick."

"Stop it right now."

Sam cracked up laughing at his testy tone. She loved nothing more than to drive him crazy any way she could. When they were in the car, she said, "Tell me more about Mr. Haverson."

"He's fifty-four, married with three college-aged kids. Lives in Gaithersburg."

"How did he know Ginny McLeod?"

"I'm still trying to figure that out. I did a deep dive on her social media accounts but didn't see anything connecting her to him. That's at the top of my list of questions for him."

"So you have a list of questions. That's good. One of us should."

He shook his head and released a long-suffering sigh. "You're lucky you have me around to make you look good."

"Indeed, and I know it. Cam is making me look pretty good lately too. He did a shit ton of work yesterday that saved me from being up all night, which saves you from dealing with Cranky Sam today."

"Thank God for that. He's one of the best detectives I've ever worked with. I learn from him every day."

"Not as much as you learn from me, though, because if you say it's more, we're done."

"You continue to amaze and inspire me on a daily basis, Lieutenant."

"Are you being sarcastic? It pisses me off when I can't tell for sure."

That made him laugh—hard. "I like to keep you on your toes."

It took more than an hour to get to Bethesda, by which time Sam was on the verge of full-on rage at the waste of valuable time. "I'm ready for George Jetson travel anytime now."

"You'd be a psycho in one of those flying cars."

"People would get the hell out of my way. I should've used the lights." She tended to save them for actual emergencies, and last she checked, her time being wasted wasn't an actual emergency to anyone but her.

Inside the First National Bank and Trust on Arlington Road, Sam was greeted by one of her favorite things—a receptionist. Even better, this one did a double take when she recognized Sam.

"Mrs. Cappuano," she said, practically sputtering. "Welcome. What can I do for you?"

Sam flashed her badge to remind the woman what *Mrs. Cappuano* did for a living. "I need to see Mr. Haverson, please."

"Do you have an appointment?"

That was one of Sam's favorite questions. "Nope. What I do have is a dead body and a homicide investigation. Tell him I'm here, and I'd like to speak to him."

Her eyes went wide as she got up to see to Sam's directive.

"I like when people do what I tell them to."

"I like when they ask the appointment question. In my head, I'm counting down. Five, four, three, two..."

Sam laughed to herself at what an absolutely perfect partner he was, not that she could ever let him know that. He was already borderline unmanageable.

The receptionist returned a minute later with a gray-haired man wearing a dark suit and a scowl on his face. "What do you need?"

"Lieutenant Holland, Detective Cruz, Metro PD. We need a minute of your time. Either here or at our place. Your choice." No one ever chose their place, which was a crying shame. She loved nothing more than taking smug, entitled people into custody and didn't get to do it nearly often enough. "What's it going to be?"

"Come in."

Figured you'd say that.

Sam and Freddie followed him past cubicles of workers who reacted with surprise when they recognized her. Haverson's spacious office in the back had glass walls so he could see the goings-on in all corners of his little kingdom.

Freddie closed the door, and they both sat in the visitor chairs while Haverson settled behind his desk.

Sam glanced at Freddie and lifted her chin to tell him to get things started.

"How do you know Ginny McLeod?" Freddie took the baton and ran with it the way she'd taught him.

Haverson grimaced ever so slightly at the mention of Ginny's name. "She was my wife's high school classmate. They were close all through school and after. She and her husband were our friends."

"Were. Past tense."

"Hell yes, past tense. She ruined my life."

"How so?" Sam asked, wanting to hear the story in his words.

He stared at Sam as if he couldn't believe she was actually asking that question. "She stole more than two hundred thousand dollars from us."

"How did she do that?" Sam asked.

Continuing with the stare, he said, "Surely you've taken the time to review the details of her scam before you came to my place of business to interrogate me. It's all in the FBI reports."

"Mr. Haverson, I'm not appreciating your tone. We have a murder victim, which gives us the right to ask any questions we see fit."

"Good luck finding anyone who cares that she's dead. You'll have a long line of people celebrating her demise."

"Including you?"

"Fuck, yes. I'm glad she's dead. Did I kill her? No, but I'm glad someone else did. She had it coming."

"No one has murder coming," Sam said.

"They do when they steal someone's life savings so they'll never be able to retire or help their kids through college. People like her deserve anything and everything they get."

"We'll have to agree to disagree on whether anyone *deserves* to be murdered. Tell me how the money was transferred. I can read the reports, but I'd prefer to hear it from you."

Seeming to realize he was going to have to tell her what she wanted to know, he began to speak in a tightly controlled tone that seemed almost practiced, as if it was something he'd taught himself to get through the retelling of this story.

"She came to my wife, Clarissa, with an 'opportunity' that she felt we'd be interested in. She was putting together a group of investors to purchase an abandoned building in Gaithersburg and turn it into high-end condos, shops and restaurants. She had prospectuses, charts, graphs, everything you'd need to believe it was legit. We toured the building with a Realtor, who gave us even more information about how the place would be a gold mine once the renovation was finished. They were looking for two hundred highly motivated investors who would each own a piece of the pie and reap the benefits, which were touted to be sizable."

He took a deep breath and released it, sagging a bit as his tale unfolded. "My wife and I were intrigued. Ginny and Ken had done well. Really well. They had the fancy house and the fancy cars and the fancy vacations, while we were slogging away at well-paying jobs without really getting ahead. We wanted what they had, and we felt like she was showing us how to make that happen. So I cashed in a chunk of my 401(k), took a huge hit on taxes and early-withdrawal penalties and sent her a check."

"What happened then?"

"Nothing for a while. We kept hearing she was still working out the purchase details. These things are highly complex, she'd say when Clarissa asked for updates. I tried to stay chill about it, because investing is always about patience. When six months went by without anything happening, I started getting worried, especially when I saw on Facebook that Ginny and Ken were on a trip to Greece while I was waiting to hear that our investment was moving forward."

Sam took notes as he talked, processing the details and turning them over in her mind. "When did you start to fear you'd been scammed?"

"When the building we were supposedly buying sold to someone other than Ginny."

"How did you find that out?"

"I keep an eye on real estate transactions in our area, just out of curiosity about what's selling and for how much. The building we were supposedly investing in sold for two point two million about eight months after we gave Ginny the money."

"What did you do when you saw that?"

"At first, I couldn't believe what I was seeing. I went online to confirm the building was actually the same one. After I confirmed that it was, Clarissa and I went to their house. Their cars were in the driveway, but no one answered the door. That's when I first started calling my friend with the FBI. It took my friend four weeks to get others at the FBI to take it seriously and another four weeks after that before they started to actively investigate.

"Her scheme began to unravel when the FBI brought in the IRS. With the two agencies on the case, we quickly learned the whole thing was probably a scam. She never intended to buy or renovate that building, and apparently, she's been doing this shit for years and getting away with it by robbing Peter to pay Paul. At least I get now how she swings the house, the cars, the vacations."

"What I don't understand is how it took years for her investors to get suspicious."

"She was giving others small dividends on the investments, which pacified them. Those dividends came from new investors like us."

"But she didn't do that for you?"

He shook his head. "We never saw a dime or a report on our investment or anything after we gave her the money. In fact, with hindsight, Clarissa realized she barely heard from Ginny at all after we gave her the check. Everyone's busy, so it wasn't unusual for a few months to go by between get-togethers, but it was unusual for Clarissa to not hear from Ginny at all. Later, when we put the pieces together, we realized that Ginny's mother, to whom she was always exceptionally close, fell ill shortly after we invested, which probably meant she had less time to bring in new people to provide enough dividends to keep us from raising the red flag."

"Where were you on Sunday afternoon?"

He gave her a blank look, as if he couldn't believe she was asking him that.

"I told you I didn't kill her."

"I heard you, but you see, it's like this. People tell us all the time they didn't kill someone, and then we later find out they actually did. That's why we ask people to tell us where they were at the time of the murder and make them prove it. Saves us a lot of time in the end. So where were you on Sunday afternoon?"

Through gritted teeth, he said, "With my son in College Park. He's a freshman at Maryland. My wife and I took him to lunch. He can confirm it, and I can provide a receipt from the restaurant."

"If you could give us his phone number and a copy of that receipt, that's all we need."

He glared at her before reaching for his phone, getting the

number from his contacts and reciting it. From his wallet, he produced a receipt that Freddie took a picture of with his phone.

"Don't tell your son to expect a call from us," Sam said. "We check those things too."

"I didn't kill her, but good luck finding anyone on her list of investors who didn't want her dead once they found out she'd been scamming us. I mean, who does that to people they've known all their lives? She and my wife had been friends for years."

"It had to be extremely shocking."

"You have no idea. Sometimes, I still can't believe it, and I've known the truth of what really happened for months now. I still can't wrap my head around the fact that she actually stole from us."

"Besides yourself, who else was instrumental in helping the FBI and IRS to make a case against her?"

"There were two of us who did the heavy lifting. The other was Ginny's cousin, Alison Enders, who lives in Germantown."

"Do you have an address and phone number for Alison?"

"Yeah." Again using his phone, he wrote down the requested information.

"What was your sense of Ken's involvement in the scheme?"

"He was broadsided the same way the rest of us were, or so he said. Some people think he knew, others believe he didn't. It just depends on who you talk to."

"How would she have explained to him where the money was coming from if he didn't know?" Freddie asked.

"That was my question too. But from what he told investigators, he assumed it was proceeds from her various investments."

"And he was believed?"

"Ken passed a polygraph." He handed over the paper with the name, address and phone number of Ginny's cousin Alison.

"Did you ever have contact with someone involved in the scheme who talked about wanting to kill Ginny?"

"*Everyone* wanted to kill her. People said if she was dead, we might benefit from her life insurance, if she had it. You'll be hard-pressed to find anyone who was defrauded by her who didn't want her dead."

He leaned in, expression intense, eyes full of fury and maybe hurt too. "You have to understand, Lieutenant. She *ruined* our lives. She destroyed our faith in humanity. I mean, if a friend can do this to you... My wife and I had a solid relationship before this. And now..." He blew out a deep breath. "I made the mistake of blaming her for what Ginny did. She was Ginny's friend, after all. But it wasn't Clarissa's fault. We decided together to invest, and it was wrong of me to blame Clarissa. I never should've done that, and now I'm left to wonder if she'll ever forgive me."

"Where would we find your wife?" Sam asked.

His expression went completely blank. "Why do you need to talk to her?"

"For the same reason we wanted to talk to you. She was a victim of Ginny's scheme, and I'd like to gain her perspective."

"Her story would be very similar to mine."

"Good to know. Where can we find her?"

Seeming to realize he couldn't talk her out of speaking to Clarissa, he said, "She's a yoga instructor and teaches classes at night. During the day, she's at home."

Sam handed the paper he'd given her back to him. "Please write down your home address and your wife's phone number."

He did as she asked and gave the paper back to her. "Are you going there to see her?"

"We are, and we'd rather you not tell her we're coming."

"Why?"

"Because I asked you not to."

Oh, he didn't like that, but wisely refrained from saying so.

Sam stood, and Freddie did the same. "If you think of anything else that might be relevant to our investigation, please let me know." She handed him her business card. "I understand you have no incentive to help us figure out who killed her, but we'd appreciate your cooperation anyway."

"I've told you what I know. The rest of the details are in the court filings."

"Thank you for your time."

Sam led the way through the bank lobby. Every set of eyes in the place landed on her as she headed for the exit. Once outside, she took a deep breath of fresh, cold air that settled her. Being recognized everywhere she went was unnerving, especially in light of her job locking up criminals. She never knew when she might encounter someone she'd arrested years ago who'd recognize her due to her increased notoriety and love nothing more than to make something of her newfound role as second lady. That was a thought she was better off not entertaining.

"Where to?" Freddie asked when they were back in her car.

She handed over the paper Haverson had given them. "Let's go see Clarissa."

CHAPTER SEVEN

The Haversons lived in a brick-front colonial with black shutters and fancy iron work around a balcony on the second floor.

"How many brick-fronted homes do you think there are in the capital region?" Sam asked.

"Is that a rhetorical question?"

"No, I'm actually wondering how many you think there are."

"Tens of thousands?"

"Probably a good estimate."

"Is there a reason you're counting bricks?"

"Just curious." She pressed the doorbell and listened to the loud chiming that echoed inside the big house.

"I know what you're going to say."

"I don't get it with the nuclear-bomb doorbells. Wouldn't that scare the shit out of you every time it goes off?"

"I imagine it'd be rather startling."

"Rather." Sam looked in the window on the right side of the black front door. "If Haverson tipped her off that we were coming, I'm going to arrest his ass."

"No, you're not."

"Yes, I am."

"Then you can do the paperwork."

Sam cupped her hands around her eyes for a better view

inside. "I don't do paperwork. That's why I have you." She rang the bell again. "Wake up, Clarissa." Movement on the second floor had Sam looking up in time to see a blonde woman coming down the stairs with... *a fucking gun pointed at the door.*

Sam grabbed Freddie and pulled him back while simultaneously drawing her own weapon. At least they could say with reasonable confidence that her husband hadn't tipped her off. If he had, she was insane for greeting cops with a gun.

"What're you doing?" Freddie asked as he shook her off.

"She's got a gun, and it's pointed at us."

"Who is it?" Clarissa asked from inside.

While remaining out of sight of the window, Sam held up her badge. "Lieutenant Holland, Metro Police Department. We want to talk to you about Ginny McLeod." She spoke as loud as she could so the woman could hear her.

A series of locks disengaged before the door swung open.

Sam held her weapon in front of her so Clarissa could see it. "Put down your weapon and step back from it, hands up."

"This is my house. You don't get to tell me what to do in my own house."

"Detective Cruz, would you please inform Mrs. Haverson of her rights in this matter?"

"You have the right to remain silent. You have the right to an attorney—"

"Wait a minute. You're *arresting* me?"

"We aren't talking to you while you're armed," Sam said, "so if you're unwilling to put down your weapon and step away from it, then yes, we're arresting you and taking you to MPD Headquarters to have the conversation we wish to have with you. Any other questions?"

She glared at Sam. "I'll put down the weapon."

"Excellent." Sam continued to train her weapon on the woman until she had placed the gun on a front hall table and returned to the doorway with her hands up.

Sam stashed her gun in the holster she wore on her hip. "I assume I'd find that gun is registered if I happened to check?"

"It's registered. There were a series of B&Es in this

neighborhood a few years back, which is when I got it. No one ever comes here without texting first. I'm here alone during the day. A woman can't be too careful in this world."

"May we come in?"

"I guess. I'm not sure what you want with me. I didn't kill Ginny, even though I'm glad she got what she deserved."

That, Sam realized, was going to be a common refrain in this investigation.

Sam picked up Clarissa's gun, made sure the safety was on, removed the bullets and handed the weapon and ammunition to Freddie to safeguard while they were in the house. "We've just come from speaking to your husband."

Clarissa appeared surprised to hear that.

"We told him not to tell you we were coming."

She led them to a seating area off the dining room. "Oh. If you've talked to him, what do you need with me?"

"Talk to me about how Ginny first approached you with the investment idea."

Clarissa's expression hardened as she thought about that. "It was at a cookout at the home of mutual friends two summers ago. We were talking about vacations we'd taken or had planned, and as always, Ginny's vacations were way better than anyone else's. She and Ken had been to Bora Bora and stayed in one of those over-the-water huts they're famous for. Do you know what I mean?"

Sam held back a smile at the reference to the place where she and Nick had spent their honeymoon and celebrated their first anniversary earlier in the year. "I do."

Freddie coughed, as if hiding a laugh.

"I went to Bermuda, and she went to Bora Bora. The year before, it was Tahiti, and before that was Bali. I'll admit I was jealous of her and how well she and Ken were doing in their careers. I was driving a ten-year-old Honda Accord, while she was tooling around in a new Mercedes SUV. Her house was amazing. Her life was amazing. I made a joke about wanting to be her when I grew up, and then later, when no one else was around, she said something to me about an investment opportunity she was working on that might get me to Tahiti."

"You were intrigued?"

"Hell yes, I was intrigued. I felt like she was giving me the insider edge on the secret to her lifestyle. Brett and I work *all the time*, but with three kids to put through college and a big mortgage, we don't have a lot of extra money lying around. So when she told me about the investment group she was heading up, I was all in from the get-go." She looked down at the floor, her shoulders sagging. "I remember driving home that night and telling Brett about it and how we had to do it because it might be the thing that changed the game for us."

Bitterness crept into her every word, and when she looked up at them again, Sam saw the hurt too.

"She knew how hard we work for everything we have, how proud we are to put our kids through good schools without saddling them with debt. But she also knew how much having three kids in college at the same time hurt us financially. She *knew* that." Clarissa blinked back tears. "That's the part I can't get over. I told her how strapped we were after paying tuition for years, and she screwed us anyway. I thought it might be a way to jumpstart an early retirement. Instead, she's made it so we'll be working for the rest of our lives."

Sam waited to see if she would say more.

"The money she took... It was most of what we had left after we finish paying for college for our kids. It was our nest egg. And now it's gone, and the FBI told us from the outset that it would be a huge longshot to ever recover the money."

The woman's heartbreak was palpable.

"It just never occurred to me that someone I've known most of my life would steal from me."

"Why would it?" Sam asked. "No one would expect that from a lifelong friend. That's the part I'm having trouble wrapping my head around. What did she think would happen when people found out there was no development? That the money was gone? What do you suppose her end game was?"

"I don't know. I've had that same conversation with other

people she stole from, who were also close to her or Ken or both of them. No one knows how she expected this to end, but in the meantime, she appeared to have the time of her life spending other people's money."

"And none of you thought to question where she was getting the money to fund her lifestyle?"

"*No.*" She bristled at the question. "She always lived large, so it wasn't like this was something new. And she was my *lifelong friend*. Why in the world would I think she was using *my* money to pay for her lifestyle?" She looked down, her shoulders rounded with defeat. "I blame myself, and Brett blames me too. I was so caught up in the idea of having what Ginny had that I talked him into gambling our security, our future. It's my fault."

"Of course you know it was actually the fault of the person who scammed you."

"I was the one who wanted to invest. I wanted what she had, and now... Not only are our finances in a shambles, so is our marriage."

"In all your communication with other people who were defrauded by Ginny, did you ever hear anyone say they wanted to harm her?"

"*Everyone* has said it at one point or another. Remember, we were not only dealing with the shock of losing our money, but also grappling with the realization that our sibling, friend, cousin, neighbor, colleague had *stolen* from us. It was a double whammy for everyone involved." She glanced directly at Sam. "Have you talked to her cousin Alison yet? She got a second mortgage on her house to go in on the investment. She's in danger of losing her house. You should talk to her."

"Where will we find her during the day?"

"She works for an interior design firm in Germantown. Let me grab my phone to get it."

While she left the room to do that, Sam looked to Freddie. "Impressions."

"Motive everywhere we look."

"Finding this killer will be like locating a needle in the proverbial haystack."

"Unless we get lucky with prints that are already in the system."

"I don't think we will. I think this might've been a first-timer in the heat of the moment. Maybe the person who did this didn't go there intending to kill her. Maybe they just wanted their money back, and when Ginny told them that wasn't possible, they snapped and reached for the first thing they could find and went for her. This was months of impossible stress boiling over into a single moment. It's possible our killer has no record, maybe has never had so much as a speeding ticket."

"You're good at this. You should consider a career in law enforcement."

He was too funny—and he knew it. "So you like my theory?"

"I do, and I agree it was most likely heat of the moment after a long buildup once the scheme came to light."

Clarissa returned with a piece of paper that she handed to Sam. "That's the name of the company Alison works for."

"Got it, thank you." Sam gave her a business card and stood to leave. "If you think of anything else we should know, please give me a call. And for what it's worth, I'm sorry this happened to you."

"Thank you."

Clarissa walked them to the foyer. When they reached the door, Freddie returned the weapon and ammunition to her.

"Take the gun and go upstairs," Sam said. "We don't turn our backs on weapons. We'll see ourselves out."

Clarissa took the gun and went up the stairs.

Only when she was out of view did Sam open the door.

"She can still nail us from an upstairs window," Freddie said as they made their way down the front stairs.

Sam cast an uneasy glance at the second-floor windows, but didn't see Clarissa. However, she did walk a little faster than she normally would have to get back to the car. She was putting on her seat belt when her phone chimed with a text from Nick.

Can you do 1 p.m. at WKLA?

Sam checked the time, saw that she had enough to get to Germantown and then back downtown by one. *See you then.*

Can't wait.

She smiled at the way he managed to make her feel loved even with a two-word text.

"What're you smiling about?"

"A nooner with my husband."

"Ew."

"Not that kind. The kind where we pay a visit to the WKLA reporter who asked when we're going to have 'children of our own' to tell her how our thirteen-year-old wants to know what it means to be a 'real' child because some kids in school apparently told him he isn't one."

"Come on. No way."

"Way. So we're going there to have a talk with her."

"Does she know that?"

"Nope."

He laughed. "Can I please come and watch and bring popcorn? I promise to be so quiet, you won't even know I'm there."

"Sure," she said, laughing with him. "Knock yourself out."

"This is gonna be epic."

Nick had texted retired senator Graham O'Connor, his political mentor and adopted father figure, as well as Brandon Halliwell, chair of the Democratic National Committee, asking them to come to the White House as soon as they could. Graham arrived first and was shown into Nick's office and offered coffee.

"I'd rather have bourbon," Graham said, "but coffee will work if bourbon isn't an option."

"Coming right up, Senator," Tanya, one of the receptionists, said. "For you too, Mr. Vice President?"

"Yes, please, Tanya. Thank you."

"Of course."

Graham had actually combed his thick white hair before leaving his farm in Leesburg to come into the city. "I hope you've got good news for me, Nick."

"I have news, but I'm not sure you're going to like it."

Graham's face fell. "Are you going to break my heart, son?"

Nick loved that Graham considered him a son, not that he could ever replace John, the son Graham had lost. Senator John O'Connor had been Nick's best friend and his boss. His murder had been one of the most devastating things to ever happen to Nick. "I'm afraid so."

The older man grimaced but held his tongue when Tanya returned with coffees she set on the table in front of Graham. "Please let me know if you need anything else."

"Thank you, Tanya," Nick said. "Send Mr. Halliwell in when he arrives, if you would."

"Yes, sir." The door closed behind her with a faint click.

Nick got up from behind his desk and went around to sit across from Graham on the other sofa.

"Why?" Graham asked softly. "It's within reach. All you have to do is toss your hat in the ring. You'd barely have to campaign."

Nick took a sip of the coffee. "I don't want it. That's the God's honest truth. We both know I'd have to campaign—hard—for eighteen months. I don't want to be away from Sam and the kids. I also don't want to be surrounded by security for possibly the rest of my life. My term would encompass high school and college for Scotty. I don't want that for him. I don't want it for any of us. Until you've lived with round-the-clock Secret Service protection, you can't begin to know how confining it is."

Graham drank his coffee while listening intently.

"I know how badly you want this for me, and I love you for that and a million other things over the last twenty years. You're the primary reason I'm sitting in this office right now, and I don't want you to think I'm not grateful for all of it. I am."

"I know you are," he said with a sigh. "One of the proudest days of my life was seeing you sworn in as vice president. I have no doubt whatsoever you'd run away with the election."

"I appreciate your faith in me. I always have."

"It's not faith, Nick. It's certainty. You'd win."

"Maybe so, but I think the American people deserve a president who really and truly *wants* the job. That's not me. Don't get me wrong. If I had to do it in an emergency, I would without hesitation. But to spend eighteen months campaigning? I'm not doing that."

Graham put his cup on the table and leaned in. "Hear me out on this… What if you didn't do the usual amount of campaigning? What if you gave it one weekend a month or something through the primaries? I think people would appreciate that you've got your priorities straight and are keeping the focus on your young family."

"I don't want to miss even one weekend a month with my kids, Graham."

"Take them with you. Show them life outside of DC."

"And when Scotty doesn't want to go because his friends are having a sleepover or a birthday party or fill in the blank? It's not that simple. They have lives too, and I've disrupted Sam's and Scotty's lives enough. The twins are just starting to feel comfortable with us. I can't disappear from their lives for days on end when they're used to having me around. It wouldn't be fair."

Graham let out a loud groan. "You're killing me."

"I know. I'm sorry. But my mind is made up."

"About what?" Halliwell asked when he came into the room, a ball of nervous energy, as usual.

"He's not going to run."

CHAPTER EIGHT

Halliwell stopped short a few feet from where they were seated, his face losing all expression. "You gotta be shitting me."

"I'm not."

Halliwell looked to Graham, who only shrugged. "All due respect, but what the fuck, Mr. Vice President? Have you lost your mind?"

"Um, not that I know of."

"He doesn't want to be away from his family," Graham said, sounding resigned now that Nick had explained it to him.

"Take them with you!"

Nick looked the other man dead in the eye so there could be no misinterpretation. "I'm not going to run, Brandon."

Halliwell pushed a hand through his hair, seeming to take a minute to get himself together. "There's nothing we can do to change your mind?"

"No. I'm sorry. I wanted to give you plenty of notice so you can make other plans." While the election was three years away, the primaries would begin in just over eighteen months, so they had the time to figure out their options now that he was out of the mix.

Brandon sat in one of the other chairs, looking as if he'd had the wind knocked out of him.

"Surely you aren't entirely surprised," Nick said. "I haven't exactly been jumping for joy at the thought of running."

"No, you haven't," Brandon said. "But I thought when push came to shove, you would. I mean, no one has poll numbers like yours. People are going to be very disappointed when they hear this news."

"They'll move on to the next guy before we know it. It'll be fine, and of course I'll do everything I can to get our candidate elected."

"I came in here hoping to get a green light, and instead..."

"I know how you feel," Graham said. "But having known Nick since he was eighteen, I also understand his reasoning. He has what he's always wanted, his own family, so of course that's more appealing than traveling all over the country without them, doing something he hates doing."

Nick sent Graham an appreciative smile. It meant the world to him that Graham understood, even if he was disappointed. "I met with my team this morning to tell them my decision. Trevor is working on a statement now. I'd like to put it out as soon as possible, but I wanted to coordinate with you before we do it."

"We've invested a lot of time and effort into getting you where you are now," Brandon said. "You were chosen to be VP as the potential future leader of the party. The American people need you, Mr. Vice President. Without you, we could lose the White House. The ramifications of this decision are much bigger than your family. We're talking about the well-being and stability of the entire republic."

"As you well know, the Democrats have a diverse pool of extremely qualified men and women who could rise to this moment," Nick said. "Everyone is replaceable, Brandon."

"I don't know if you're as replaceable as you think you are." Seeing that Nick wasn't budging, Brandon took a deep breath and let it out, sagging into his chair. "This puts us back to square one."

"I realize that, and I'm sorry."

"We'll figure it out." Brandon turned his formidable gaze on Nick. "Are you sure there's nothing we can do to change your mind?"

"I'm very sure. There's one thing I want to be clear about in the messaging on this decision. I've directed Trevor to include this in the statement we're going to release. As vice president, I remain ready, willing and able to step up to serve my country should the need arise. I will not, however, seek the office of president in the next election. I don't want anyone to think I'm flaking out as VP. I've got this job for three more years, and I intend to do it to the best of my ability."

"Are you prepared for the firestorm that'll erupt when you release that statement?" Brandon asked.

"What firestorm?"

He huffed out a laugh tinged with disbelief. "People will be *crushed*, Mr. Vice President. They've pinned their hopes on you as a beacon of youthful energy and enthusiasm for the future."

"I'm sorry to let them down, but they should have a president who truly wants the job more than anything. The jobs I most want are dad and husband."

"I won't lie to you," Brandon said. "This breaks my heart. I was so looking forward to a Cappuano administration. But I do admire your priorities." He stood and leaned in to shake Nick's hand. "I'll be in touch."

"Thanks for everything, Brandon."

Nodding, he released Nick's hand and strode from the room with slightly less pep in his step than he'd had coming in.

"He's devastated," Graham said when they were alone. "As am I."

"I'm sorry."

"Don't be. Like he said, I admire your priorities. Maybe things would've been different for my son if I'd had mine straight when he was growing up and fathering a child and..." His shrug belied a world of heartbreak when it came to John, his youngest son.

"We do the best we can, Graham. That's all anyone can ask of us."

"I could've done better. I'm not without regrets when it comes to my family. Terry and all his troubles... Being around Lizbeth's kids reminds me of what I missed with my own while I was chasing almighty ambition. It's a rare man who can put aside his own desires for the betterment of his family."

"My fondest desire is to be with my family. You were always far more interested in me being president than I've ever been."

"I can't deny that," Graham said with a chuckle. "You've fought me every step of the way. And I know that's in large part because you feel you have this career because we lost John."

"I *do* have this career because we lost John. But I'd like to think we've made him proud in the nearly two years he's been gone."

"He'd be proud of you, for sure. He always said you were the brains of the operation."

"We were a good team. I miss him all the time."

"I know you do."

"He'd be proud of you too," Nick said. "He always was."

A knock on the door interrupted them. "Come in," Nick called.

His communications director, Trevor Donnelly, came in. "Pardon the interruption, Mr. Vice President, Senator."

"Come in," Nick said to his curly-haired aide.

"I've prepared the statement you requested." He handed a printed page to Nick, who scanned it.

Today I'd like to inform you of my decision not to seek the office of president in the next election. I have given this decision careful thought, and while I'm delighted to serve as your vice president—and ready, willing and able to step up should the need arise—I plan to devote my attention and time to my young and growing family once my current term ends.
As many of you know, I was the product of young parents and raised by my grandmother. All my life, I've yearned for the family I have now, and I don't want to miss a minute with my wife, Samantha, or our children Scotty, Alden and Aubrey as well as the twins' older brother, Elijah, who's also become part of our family. This was not an easy decision or one that I took lightly. I'm aware that many of my fellow Americans were hoping I would run and were prepared to support my candidacy. I appreciate the faith you have in me as vice president and the support you would've given my campaign. However, I wanted to give the DNC plenty of notice so they have the necessary time to plan for the next election cycle. I'm fully prepared to support the

eventual Democratic nominee and will, to the best of my ability,
offer advice and counsel to whomever that nominee may be.
It's the greatest honor of my life to serve as your vice president,
and I look forward to the next three years with enthusiasm and
excitement.

"This is perfect, Trevor. You captured exactly what I was looking for."

"Thank you, sir."

"I suppose the next step is for me to inform the president of my plan to release this statement imminently."

"I'll let you get to that," Graham said as he stood and offered a hand to Nick.

Nick took his hand and then stepped in to hug the older man who meant so much to him. "Thank you for understanding."

"Love you, son."

"Love you too."

"Bring the kids out to the farm to ride soon. It's been too long."

"We'll do that."

"I'm going to see my other son now," Graham said as he headed for Terry's office, no doubt to commiserate with him about Nick's decision.

That was fine. Nick had expected disappointment from his closest supporters and had mentally prepared for that.

Taking the statement Trevor had prepared with him, he walked the short distance to the president's suite and asked if President Nelson had a minute for his vice president.

"Of course, Mr. Vice President," one of the assistants said. "Go right in."

"Thank you."

Nick knocked on the door to the Oval Office and stepped inside. "Pardon the interruption, Mr. President."

"Come in, Nick." A handsome man in his late sixties with silver hair and sharp blue eyes, Nelson had aged noticeably in the weeks since his wife had left him to return home to South Dakota after his affair with Tara Weber became public.

The president had become much more cordial and friendly to

his vice president after surviving two scandals that'd rocked his administration to the core. He was lucky Nick and everyone else who worked in the West Wing hadn't quit when they found out he'd had the affair while his wife, Gloria, was going through cancer treatments she'd kept private during the last campaign. That news had revolted Nick and many others.

Nelson came around the Resolute desk and gestured for Nick to have a seat on one of the sofas in the middle of the Oval Office. "What can I do for you?"

"I wanted to let you know I'll be releasing this statement today."

Nelson took the paper from Nick and quickly read it, before looking up at him with a stunned expression. "I have to admit I didn't see this coming."

"I understand it's a surprise, but I've been coming to the decision for quite some time now, and I thought it was only fair to give the DNC and other potential candidates as much time as possible to make their plans."

"You have to know many people believe you would've walked right into this office if you wanted it."

"I don't know about that, but the truth of the matter is I don't want it."

"Because of me, right? Because of what happened with Christopher and Tara." His son had resorted to murder to try to discredit Nick—and Sam by extension—to feed his own political ambitions. "I ruined it for you, didn't I?"

"Those were difficult situations, to be sure, but the truth of it is in the statement. It's because of Sam and the kids. My older son will be in high school and college over the next eight years. Surrounding him with Secret Service during those years is a big ask, and it's not what I want for him. The twins have just lost their parents, and we're doing our best to give them a stable, loving home. How do I do that when I'm gone more than I'm home?"

"For what it's worth, I think you're doing the right thing. Your kids will grow up fast, and you won't want to have regrets."

"I already missed the first eleven years of Scotty's life. I don't want to miss anything else."

Nelson handed the statement back to Nick. "I appreciate the heads-up."

"Of course, Mr. President."

"What'll you do with yourself professionally after we leave office?"

"I'm not sure yet, but I've got three years to figure it out."

"You'll be overrun with more offers than you can handle."

"I guess we'll see what happens." Nick stood to leave. "I appreciate your time."

Nelson stood to shake his hand. "I appreciate yours. Let's put a lunch on the books to go over plans for the next few months. I've got a few things coming up I'd like you to be involved in."

He would believe that when he saw it since Nelson rarely included him in anything major, even after promising he would. "Sounds good. Have a good day, Mr. President."

"You do the same."

Nick returned to his suite, knocked on Trevor's door and handed the statement to him. "Green light to release it. Just wait until about three o'clock, if you would. I have something I need to do at one, and I don't want this to be a distraction."

"I'll take care of it, Mr. Vice President, and for what it's worth, I understand why you're doing this, but I'm sorry we won't work together anymore after we finish this term."

"I'm sure we'll still work together in some form or another, Trevor."

"I hope so, sir."

Terry came to the door. "You've broken my father's heart."

"I know. I feel bad about that."

"He'll get over it. He understands. We all do. We see how happy Sam and your family make you. I wouldn't want to be away from Lindsey either. It's all good."

"I'm sure we'll find something else to do when we leave office that'll allow us to keep working together," Nick said.

"That'd be nice. Brant asked me to tell you he's worked it out to leave for your one o'clock at twelve forty-five."

"Excellent," Nick said, relishing the plan for a showdown with the rude reporter and relieved to have shared his decision with the people closest to him.

GINNY'S COUSIN ALISON ENDERS WORKED AT AN UPSCALE INTERIOR design company off 118 in Germantown. She had dark hair cut into a bob, sharp hazel eyes and wore a navy power suit with sky-high heels. Sam loved a good shoe but drew the line at anything higher than three inches out of self-preservation.

Sam followed Alison to the offices at the back of the showroom.

"I didn't kill her," Alison said the second the door closed behind Freddie. "But I'm not surprised someone did. A lot of people were devasted by her scheme."

Every word reverberated with barely contained rage. "We grew up together, had sleepovers, double dates and vacations. We raised our children together, called ourselves 'best cousins.'" She sniffed out a huff of disdain. "And then she ruined *everything* by *stealing* from me." Gesturing for Sam and Freddie to sit in her visitor chairs, Alison sat behind a desk stacked with file folders, fabric samples and paint chips.

"Can you tell me how she sold you on the investment opportunity?"

"My husband, Tom, and I were on vacation with her and Ken. It was a trip we took every year to the Caribbean to get away from the winter blahs, as we called them. She was on the phone a lot, and when I asked her why, she told me she was working on the most exciting project of her career. It was a restored mill in a hot part of Gaithersburg that she was going to renovate and turn into condos and retail. When she talked about it, her eyes glittered with contagious excitement. In hindsight, I realize that was all part of the scam. Spread the excitement, get others excited and then separate them from their money."

"How much did you give her?"

"Three hundred thousand," she said on a deep sigh.

Sam nearly swallowed her tongue. Who had that kind of money just sitting around? "When did you realize it was a scam?"

"I was slow on the uptake because it never occurred to me that my own cousin would steal from me. Tom started getting worried about it a few months after we gave her the money, when there was no information about the development or what was happening. He started texting her every day for updates, and for a while, she responded with just enough info to keep him pacified. But after a few weeks of daily requests for info, she stopped responding to him—and to me when I'd text her."

"And that was unusual?"

"Very. Ginny wasn't only my cousin, she was one of my closest friends all my life. We talked almost every day, even when we were in college in different states. Long after everything that's come to light, it's still inconceivable."

"When was the last time you saw her or talked to her?"

"I was at her arraignment."

"Did you speak to her that day?"

"I did not. I hadn't spoken to her since the day before she was charged, when I called her."

"And what did you talk about that day?"

"I told her there was still time to make this right, to give back the money. She said it was all a big misunderstanding and not to worry, that the money was safe."

"Was it?"

"I have no idea. We think there might be some stashed in offshore accounts, though we've been unsuccessful thus far in finding any such accounts. And that's assuming she didn't spend it all. As Tom said, do you know what kind of effort it'd take to spend twenty million dollars?"

"Did you receive an accounting of what it was used for?"

"Vacations, cars, clothes, jewels, college tuition for their daughter, luxury cars for the kids, an Alaskan cruise for Ginny's parents, the list goes on and on. But it wasn't close to the full amount."

"Do you have any theories on who might've killed her?"

"Do you want the whole list or just the top five hundred most likely culprits?"

Sam appreciated sarcasm as much as the next person. "Our list of people with motive is incredibly long. We're trying to narrow it down. If there's anything that stands out in your mind as concerning, that would help."

"I understand and appreciate that your job is figuring out who killed her. You'll also understand that I don't give a flying fuck who did it. In fact, when I find out who it is, I'd like to buy them a beer to thank them."

"Were any other members of your family scammed by her?"

"One of Ginny's brothers, one of my brothers and another cousin were also scammed. The four of us are filing a civil suit against her estate, which is another way we hope to recoup some of what we've lost. But that's going to take years. So rather than anticipating retirement, we're looking at many more years of work unless we get lucky with the lawsuit. That's what she's condemned us to. And personally, I hope she's roasting in hell today. It'd be the least of what she deserves."

"Do you believe Ken or her children knew anything about what she was doing?"

"I've gone round and round about that, asking myself how could they *not* know. But she was good at hiding the truth, so I honestly don't know."

"Can you tell me where I could find her children?"

"Her daughter, Mandi, is a senior at Catholic University, and her son. Ken Jr., works in the defense community. I'm not sure where, but Ken Sr. would know."

"That helps. Thank you." As always, Sam handed over her card. "If you think of anything else we should know, please give me a call."

Alison took the card.

"Have you heard anything about funeral arrangements?" Sam asked.

She shook her head. "I'm not going, so it doesn't matter to me."

"Thank you for your time. We'll see ourselves out."

When they were outside, Sam blew out a frustrated breath. "I hate this woman, and I hate this case."

"Right there with you. It's really hard to be empathetic toward someone who'd rip off the people closest to her. I almost want her killer to get away with it."

"So do I, but we can't say that to anyone else. Ever."

"Understood. What's our next move?"

"After I meet Nick for the nooner, let's find Ginny's daughter at Catholic and find out what she knew and when she knew it. See if you can figure out where she is on campus."

As they got into the car, he said, "I'll do that if we can stop calling the meeting with Nick a *nooner*."

"You'll do it because I told you to, and anytime I get to see my sexy husband in the middle of the day, it's a *nooner*. End of conversation."

"It's not the end of the conversation. I have rights in this relationship."

"No, you don't, and we're not in a *relationship*, you freak."

"Now you're resorting to name-calling? I have so much dirt on you that you'd think you'd be nice to me just to keep me quiet."

"I could cut your tongue out with my rusty steak knife. That'd keep you quiet too."

He grunted out a laugh. "It always comes back to the steak knife with you, doesn't it?"

"It does, and you'd be wise to remember that."

CHAPTER NINE

As Sam drove to the TV station downtown, she puzzled through the McLeod case from every angle, realizing they were no closer to answers than they'd been the day before. Her phone rang, and she took the call from Captain Malone on the Bluetooth, which was a nice feature on her new phone. "Lieutenant Holland, hands-free while driving. May I help you?"

"She's finally joined the twentieth century twenty years into the twenty-first, and she wants us to have a party," Freddie said.

"Young Freddie is particularly mouthy this morning," Sam said. "We may need to do something about that at some point."

"Whatever," Freddie said.

"If you two are finished," Malone said, sounding amused, "what's up with McLeod?"

"The whole world wanted her dead, and no one is sorry that someone actually killed her. Other than that, we've got jack. What're you hearing from Crime Scene on the search for a murder weapon?"

"Nothing yet. I'm hearing we're looking for a Garden Weasel or some such thing?"

"Yep."

"Ouch."

"Right?"

"What's your theory?" Malone asked.

"Heat of the moment. Someone confronted her in the garage, they argued, it got heated, the perp reached for the first thing he or she could find and swung for the neck, scoring a direct hit."

"If they took the thing with them, we might never find it."

"I know, and there's also the very good possibility that if we do find it, we won't get squat from it, because we're probably looking at a first-timer with no prints in the system, rather than a career criminal."

"True."

"Let me tell you, Cap. This woman had it coming. Her scheme was so brazen as to be impossible to comprehend."

"I read about it in the paper yesterday."

"No one in her life was immune. Her own siblings, cousins and closest friends... It's unreal. It'd be like me scamming you guys, my sisters, Shelby."

"I'm not giving you my money," Freddie said. "It's enough that I've already turned over my soul to you."

"Do you see what I mean about young Freddie?" Sam asked the captain.

He replied with wheezing laughter.

"It's not funny!" Sam said.

"Yes, it is," Freddie and the captain said together.

Freddie shot her a smug look.

"I can end this call with the push of one button."

"She has no idea which button," Freddie said, "so that's an empty threat."

It was a relief, in a way, to be getting back to some semblance of normalcy after the shock of her father's death and the compounding shock of Conklin's culpability. The levity was a welcome respite from the pervasive grief that'd touched everyone who'd loved Skip Holland, including Freddie Cruz and Jake Malone. "Remember the good old days when he was afraid of me?"

"I do," Malone said, "and I think I like this better."

"Me too," Freddie said. "She's taking me on a nooner with her husband. I shouldn't be subjected to these things."

"Uh... I don't know how to reply to that."

"Nick and I are going to have a chat with the reporter who asked if we're going to have kids 'of our own.'"

"Oh damn. Really?"

"Yep."

"Does she know you're coming?"

"Nope."

"I'll take video," Freddie said, "so we can all enjoy it."

"Do I need to warn you to tread carefully so we don't attract more negative publicity?" Malone asked.

"Nick will be with her to keep her under control," Freddie said.

"That's true," Malone said, chuckling.

"If you two are quite finished, there's something else I wanted to tell you, Cap," Sam said. "Lenore Worthington came to see me this morning."

"I heard that. What's up there?"

"She heard we closed Dad's cold case and asked if I'd be willing to take reopen her son Calvin's case."

"How'd you leave it with her?"

"That I'd run it up the flagpole. You're the flagpole."

"I'll pull the files and take a look."

"Thanks, Cap. I don't want to leave her hanging. I told her I'd get back to her."

"Understood. I remember that case. Stayed with me for a long time. We never had so much as a lead or a thread to pull, as you would say."

"I'd love to dig into it after we close McLeod. *If* we close McLeod. Are we required to give despicable people the same level of effort we give innocent victims?"

"Unfortunately, yes."

"There oughta be a law that says horrible people don't get investigations when someone does the world a favor and ends them," Sam said.

"Of course you didn't actually say that out loud," Malone replied.

"Of course I didn't. But let it be said for the record, I'd much rather be taking a fresh look at Calvin Worthington's murder than hearing about all the ways Ginny McLeod deserved a rototiller to the neck."

"Duly noted," Malone said. "I'll check with Haggerty and the lab to see if they have anything helpful."

"Keep me posted."

"Will do. Enjoy the nooner. That reporter won't know what hit her."

"That's the plan. Later, Cap." She pressed a button to end the call and gave Freddie a smug look. "Check me out. Pressing buttons and getting it done."

"Um, you put the hazards on."

"I did not!"

He cracked up. "Made you look."

"Oh my God. You're a pain in the *ass* today."

"I do what I can for the people."

"That's my line, and it's trademarked, which means you're not allowed to use it without my permission. Did you find the McLeods' daughter at Catholic?"

"Duh, yes. Took me all of two seconds."

"Now you're just being cocky."

"If the truth hurts..."

Sam found a parking space near the studio to wait for Nick's motorcade to arrive. "We're doing the right thing confronting that reporter, right?"

"Hell yes. If nothing else, that reporter needs to be taught some basic manners. And it'll be good for her to hear how her ignorant question was repeated back to your son in freaking middle school, which is hellish enough without that."

"You said 'freaking.'"

"Don't you think this situation deserves a good 'freaking'?"

"I do."

"What she did is horrifying, Sam, and she deserves to be humiliated in front of her colleagues."

"I don't like to intentionally humiliate people, unless they're murdering scumbags."

"This is an exception worth making."

"I'm glad you think so."

"Anyone who isn't an asshole would think so."

"Wow, you're on a tear today."

"I love Scotty like a nephew. I hate that he heard about it and that you guys had to deal with explaining it to him."

"I know, and thank you for loving him like a nephew. That's sweet."

"It's true. I don't have siblings. I have you and your family and Gonzo and Jeannie and the family we've created together."

"I love that family."

"I do too, and when someone comes for one of us, they come for all of us."

A flash of light caught Sam's attention. She glanced in the rearview mirror and saw the motorcade pull onto the street. Her heart gave a happy lurch at knowing she'd see Nick in a minute. "Here comes the cavalry."

They got out of Sam's car to wait on the sidewalk.

Brant was the first one out of Nick's car. The handsome young agent took a good look around, nodded to Sam and Freddie and then opened the door for Nick. Other agents swarmed the area, and some went inside ahead of them. They had this down to a well-oiled routine they never deviated from, which was what kept Nick as safe as he could be under the circumstances.

And then there he was, gorgeous in a dark navy suit, a steel-blue tie and a crisp white dress shirt. His handsome face lit up with delight when he saw her waiting for him. He held out a hand to her, and Sam went to him, oblivious to anyone else.

He put his arm around her and kissed the top of her head. "How's my cop?"

"Frustrated and annoyed until right now."

Smiling down at her, he said, "Why? What happened right now?"

"You happened."

"What do you say we go make Kayla's day?"

"I say that's a fine idea."

Holding hands, they walked into the building, where a shocked receptionist greeted them.

"Allow me," Sam said. "I have a way with receptionists."

"Have at it, babe."

Sam showed the woman her badge. "We'd like to see Kayla Owen, please."

"I, um, does she know you're coming?"

"She doesn't, and we'd prefer to surprise her. Can you make that happen?"

Rattled by Sam's unblinking stare, the woman made a call that brought another woman to the reception desk a few seconds later.

"Please take Vice President and Mrs. Cappuano to Kayla Owen's office," the original woman said to the second one.

The second woman stared at them for ten full seconds before she blinked and seemed to recover herself. "Right this way."

With the Secret Service surrounding them and Freddie somewhere in the scrum, Sam and Nick followed the woman up a flight of stairs and through frosted double doors bearing the WKLA logo. Inside, they found yet another receptionist, who stood, her mouth falling open in shock. Thankfully, she didn't say anything to impede their progress as their guide took them around the reception desk, through another set of doors and past full-length windows behind which on-air talent watched them go by with stunned expressions.

"This is really, really wicked fun," Sam whispered to Nick as she noticed every eye in the place fixed on them as they walked by cubicles, leaving a trail of shocked people in their wake.

"So fun and about to get more so."

"We're bad, *bad* people to be enjoying this so much."

"Nah. We're just pissed-off parents."

Leave it to him to perfectly sum it up.

The woman leading them pointed to a group of offices at the end of a long corridor. "Third door on the right."

"Thank you very much," Nick said as they followed the two Secret Service agents leading the way.

At the doorway to Kayla Owen's office, the agents stepped aside to allow Sam and Nick to go ahead of them.

Nick knocked on the door. "Sorry to disturb your work, Ms. Owen."

The pretty young dark-haired reporter, her face covered in a thick layer of camera-ready makeup, looked up from her computer, double-taking as shock registered in her expression.

"My wife and I would like a minute of your time." Nick sent Sam in ahead of him and closed the door behind them.

Sam would've left the door open so people could hear what they had to say to Kayla, but Nick was always the classier of the two of them.

"I... I've been meaning to reach out to you about the press briefing last week."

"That's why we're here. We'd like to introduce you to our children." Nick pulled the kids' recent school photos from his suit coat pocket and placed them on Kayla's desk.

Sam loved that he'd come prepared. Of course he had. He was nothing if not thorough in everything he did. She decided to sit back and allow him to speak for both of them, because he'd get it just right, when she'd be tempted to rip the woman's head off and then stab her with a rusty steak knife to make sure she was really dead.

"This is Scotty. He's thirteen. His biological mother and grandfather died months apart when he was very young, leaving him a ward of the Commonwealth of Virginia. I met him two years ago at a state home in Richmond when I was a senator. Our bond was immediate. Sam and I made him part of our lives and later adopted him. He's since become the center of our world and the best part of both of us. The only regret we have where he's concerned is that we didn't meet him sooner, because we love him so much.

"This adorable young man is Alden, and this is his equally adorable twin sister, Aubrey. They recently came into our lives when my wife met them during the investigation into a home invasion in which their beloved parents were tortured and murdered. Alden witnessed some of the horror his parents endured. When they needed a place to stay after that nightmare, we happily provided them a home that's since become permanent, as their older brother and legal guardian is in college and not able to care for them. Nothing has made us happier than to fill that role for them and to help all three of them through the traumatic loss of their parents and home." He added a photo of Elijah with the twins, taken during a recent weekend visit.

Kayla stared at the photos with big, haunted brown eyes that shimmered with unshed tears that made Sam want to throat-punch her. The emotional reaction was a little too late.

"Every night, Alden and Aubrey play chase with Scotty until he eventually lets them catch him. Their screaming laughter and happy smiles are the best part of our day. Scotty loves baseball and sports and spaghetti more than anything, but he's an incredible big brother. Aubrey can sing—in Italian—so beautifully, it'd make you weep. Alden is fiercely protective of his sister and always lets her pick their bedtime story. They're going to be six soon, but he's already somehow more of a man than many of the actual men I've known in my life. Their older brother, Elijah, is in college at Princeton and plans to move home to DC after he graduates so he can live close to his siblings and see them all the time. They worship him, the last remaining tie to the family they once knew.

"These are our *own* children, Ms. Owen. They're as real to us as any children can be, and when our son comes home from the hellscape known as eighth grade and asks us what it means to be a child of our own, that breaks something in us, because that tells us the kids at school have weaponized those words against an innocent boy who's already had more than enough pain in his young life. He just lost his beloved adoptive grandfather. His father is the vice president and his mother a decorated homicide detective. The poor kid is surrounded at school and everywhere else by Secret Service. He has enough to deal with without a reporter blindsiding his mother with such an ugly question."

Tears spilled down her cheeks. "I... I'm so sorry."

Sam rolled her eyes. "Now you're sorry. When I gave you the opportunity to rephrase the question, you dug in deeper."

"I didn't mean to..."

"We know you have a job to do, Ms. Owen," Nick said, "and we appreciate that your job can be difficult. However, we encourage you to work from a place of common decency and an understanding that words matter. You'll go further in your career if you begin there. That's all we wanted to say."

Sam had more she'd like to say, but she bit her tongue and let him nudge her toward the door. He was the only person alive who could nudge her in any direction he wanted her to go.

"Wait."

They stopped and turned to the reporter.

She looked frazzled and undone. Good. Sam hoped she'd never forget this.

"That's why I've wanted to reach out to you, to sincerely apologize for my thoughtless question. I've been very well schooled over the last week about adoption and what's appropriate and inappropriate, and I'm... I'm sorry."

"We accept your apology," Nick said. "And we'll hope you'll do better in the future."

"I will. I promise. In fact, if you'd like to sit for a quick interview while you're here, we could talk about what happened and what's been learned from it, by me and others."

Sam had to give her credit for thinking fast on her feet. She glanced at Nick to gauge his interest in an interview.

"I wouldn't be opposed to that," he said.

"Really?" Kayla was nearly breathless with excitement.

"Yes," he said, "but only because I believe your apology was sincere. Otherwise, we wouldn't even consider it."

"It's completely sincere. It breaks my heart to hear about kids harassing your son because of my ignorant question."

When he looked her way again, Sam shrugged, as if she had all the time in the world to be interviewed. She could take another few minutes, because she'd get to spend those minutes with him.

"In that case," Nick said, "we'd be happy to do a quick interview about adoption, the proper way to speak of and about adopted kids and how important it is for people who have room in their homes and hearts to step up for kids who need loving families."

"Give me five minutes, and we'll make that happen."

CHAPTER TEN

Sam and Nick stepped aside so she could all but sprint from the room to tell her bosses she'd landed a rare exclusive interview with the second couple.

"You're so hella sexy when you go into protector mode," Sam said to Nick after he'd collected the kids' photos from Kayla's desk.

Grinning, he said, "Is that right?"

"That's right. In fact, if I didn't have a body cooling in the morgue, I'd want to take you home and show you just how sexy I find you when you're defending our family."

His lovely hazel eyes heated with desire. "Could you maybe show me later?"

"I'm sure something could be arranged."

Sam stepped closer to him, flattened her hands on his chest and looked up at him. "Those kids are so damned lucky to have you on their side."

"I'll always be on their side."

"Are you really going to give the woman who asked me such an awful question an interview?"

"Is it okay if I do? I figure it's a good chance to influence the way people speak about adoption and adopted kids."

"Look at you, always one step ahead of me."

"Not always."

Sam relaxed into his embrace, stealing the time with him while she could. "Most of the time, but that's okay. We don't want me doing the thinking for this operation."

A knock on the door had them separating.

"Pardon the interruption, Mom and Dad," Freddie said, "but I just heard from Malone that Crime Scene might have something for us."

Sam had almost forgotten her partner was waiting for her. "We're going to be another few minutes. The VP has decided to give our reporter friend an interview so he can take advantage of this opportunity to do some educating on adoption terminology."

"Wow, that's cool. So I take it your convo went well with her?"

"We made our point and accepted her apology," Sam said. "Or at least he did. I'm still holding a grudge."

"She does that," Nick said.

"Believe me, I know," Freddie replied. "She loves a good grudge."

"Can you two please quit talking about me behind my back in front of my face?"

"Why do we have to?" Freddie asked. "It's so fun."

The return of Kayla Owen saved Sam from having to come up with a witty retort. "We're ready for you if you'd like to come with me." She glanced at Freddie.

"This is my partner, Detective Cruz. Freddie, this is Kayla Owen."

He nodded to her because he was too polite not to. But since he was still pissed about what she'd said, he wasn't overly friendly.

They followed her to a studio where several people waited for them. Kayla introduced them to a producer, sound technician and cameraman, all of whom fell over themselves to shake their hands, welcome them to the studio and thank them for the interview. By the time they were mic'd up and seated, Sam was over the whole thing.

"We're here today with Vice President and Mrs. Cappuano for an exclusive interview. We may as well be truthful—you're doing me a big favor after teaching me an even bigger lesson. Last week, I made the mistake of asking what I now know was a highly inappropriate question during Mrs. Cappuano's press briefing in her position as a lieutenant with the Metro PD. I asked if the Cappuanos plan to have children of their own. In light of the fact that the second couple has adopted one child and is foster-parenting a set of twins who recently lost their parents to murder, they rightfully found my question offensive and came to my office today to tell me so. I invited them to sit for this interview so they could discuss the role adoption has played in their family and the proper terminology to use when talking about adopted children. Thank you for being here today, Mr. Vice President and Mrs. Cappuano."

"Thank you for having us and for your sincere apology," Nick said. "We appreciate it as well as this chance to share what adoption has meant for our family."

"Your thirteen-year-old son, Scotty, is adopted, correct?"

"He is, and he's the best thing to ever happen to us." Nick glanced at Sam.

She nodded. "He made us parents, and we couldn't love him more. He's everything to us."

"You've also taken in a set of five-year-old twins. Can you discuss your decision to add to your family with the twins?"

"It wasn't really a decision," Nick said, "so much as fate that brought Alden and Aubrey to us. Sam met them in the course of investigating the murders of their parents, and when they needed lodging late at night, she offered to bring them home since we're licensed foster parents from when we first had Scotty with us. That's evolved into them living with us while their older brother is in college."

"Do you plan to adopt the twins?"

"No," Nick said. "But we do plan to keep them with us until they're of age. Their brother has made us co-guardians, and we all agree that keeping them with us makes the most sense as he finishes college and begins his career. He hopes to end up in DC so he can live close to them and see them often. Obviously, none of this was planned, so we're making it up as we go with Alden and Aubrey's best interests foremost in our minds."

"It's important to mention that the twins have very quickly become part of our family," Sam said, "as has their brother, Elijah.

I understand people who've heard me speak about my struggles with infertility are curious about whether we'll add to our family the old-fashioned way, but for now, we're very content with the three and a half kids we have. There're so many children of all ages in need of good homes."

"When we first met Scotty, one of the things he said has stayed with me ever since," Nick said. "He told me, rather matter-of-factly, that older kids like him didn't get adopted because everyone wants babies. He was so resigned to never again having a family of his own, which broke my heart and made me even more determined to make him part of our family. That was the best thing I ever did, right up there with marrying my gorgeous wife."

Sam felt her face flush with embarrassment that infuriated her. She didn't need to be seen blushing over a compliment from her husband on TV. He'd pay for that later.

"When people speak to and about adoptive families, what are some things to avoid?" Kayla asked.

Nick glanced at Sam.

"Referring to 'real children' or 'children of our own' to adoptive parents is unacceptable," she said. "We have real children who are very much our own. The fact that they aren't our biological children doesn't matter to us. We don't look at them and think, 'I so wish I'd given birth to him or her.' They're everything we could ever want and more than we ever dreamed possible."

"Congratulations on your beautiful family, and thank you for educating me and our viewers on how best to speak about adoptive families. Before I let you go, the other thing my bosses want me to ask you, Mr. Vice President, is whether you've made a decision about running for president in the next election."

"I have," Nick said. "The White House will be releasing a statement later today announcing that I don't intend to run because of the same family we've been discussing. I want to be an active, hands-on father to our children, and I can't do that if I'm off on the campaign trail."

Kayla seemed staggered by the huge exclusive she'd been handed. "People will be disappointed."

"I'm aware of that," Nick said, "but my priorities are with the people most important to me—my wife and our kids. I've absolutely loved being vice president—"

Liar. Sam had to hold back a giggle as the word popped into her head.

"—and I'm thrilled to serve the American people in this capacity. But I'm not going to run."

"Thank you for your time and for being here today. I promise not to forget what I've learned from this incident."

"Thank you for having us," Nick said.

"And we're out," the producer said. "Holy shit. Did you just give us an exclusive, Mr. Vice President?"

"I did."

"Thank you so much, and may I be among the first to say I'm very disappointed we won't see you in the Oval Office. I think you'd make an amazing president."

"That's nice of you to say, but I'd much rather be an amazing dad."

Whoa, he's really racking up the points, Sam thought. He'd be richly rewarded for being the best husband and father ever as soon as they got a minute alone.

"I gotta go, babe," she said.

"I know. I'm with you."

They walked out together, his arm around her shoulders as everyone in the newsroom watched them go, with Freddie bringing up the rear.

"The goldfish are on display again," she said to Nick.

"A few more years, and then we'll be done."

"Years? As in more than one?"

"Three, actually."

"Now you're just being mean."

His laughter was one of her favorite things in the entire world.

"On a scale of one to lame, I've had better nooners," she said.

"I'll make it up to you very soon. We'll kick everyone out and take a full day off together while the kids are at school."

"Promise?"

"Close your new case, and it's on, baby."

"I'm never going to close this case. Everyone she knew wanted her dead, or so it seems."

"You'll figure it out. You always do."

"This may be the one that stumps me."

"Nah, my money is on you." He stopped at the door to the SUV, where several Secret Service agents waited for him to get in. "Are you working late?"

"Not sure yet. I'll let you know."

He leaned in to kiss her, oblivious to the eyes always trained on them. "I'll see you soon. Love you."

"Love you too."

"Be careful out there this afternoon."

"Always am."

She could tell he'd much rather stay with her than return to the fortress known as the White House, but he got into the car, and the door closed behind him.

Freddie leaned against her car, scrolling through his phone. "Ready?"

"Don't scratch my paint." Sam unlocked the car and got in. "What's the deal with Crime Scene?"

"Haggerty wants us to come by the lab when we can."

"Should we do that before we see the McLeods' daughter?"

"Probably. Malone said they have something interesting."

"All right. We'll go there first."

"With a stop for lunch on the way?"

Delays annoyed her, and this day had already had too many of them, although the time with Nick didn't count as a delay. The interview had been unexpected, but for a good cause if it made one person think differently about how they spoke to adoptive parents or about adopted children. She also wondered how big of a story Nick's decision not to run for president was going to be. Hopefully, it'd be one news cycle, and then something else would take the stage.

Even as she had that thought, she had a sinking feeling it might turn out to be a bigger deal than either of them was anticipating.

~

AT THE LAB, LOCATED IN THE CITY'S SOUTHWESTERN QUADRANT, SAM found Haggerty in the office he used when he was there.

He stood when he saw them in the doorway. "I just heard the news that your husband's not going to run. Gotta say I'm shocked. I figured he'd be a shoo-in."

"Turns out he's not interested." She shrugged as if it was no big deal.

"It's somewhat refreshing to hear a guy put his family ahead of his ambition. Good for him."

"Good for all of us."

They followed Haggerty to a locked room. He used a key to open the door. "Come in." On a table inside the room, a series of yard implements had been laid out. Each of them had been tagged.

"Per the info you provided from the ME, we looked for anything that could make a ragged wound like the one in Mrs. McLeod's neck. We narrowed it down to these."

"I assume you've had them analyzed."

"We did, and while they all had grass and dirt and other refuse on them, only this one was wiped clean." He pointed to an object with a long handle and sharp points on the end. "Unfortunately, every part of it was wiped clean. Even the handle."

"Figures. It can never be that easy."

"But I'd guess that's your murder weapon."

"Where'd you find it?"

"In a closet in a basement bedroom."

"So the person who killed Ginny, possibly in a fit of rage, had the presence of mind to thoroughly clean and stash the implement he or she used to do the deed."

"We're pulling the drains from the downstairs bathrooms and the kitchen and taking another look at the outdoor hoses."

"Thanks for the info." To Freddie, she said, "Take a picture of that, will you?"

He withdrew his phone and snapped the photo they'd add to the murder board.

"Let me know if the drains yield anything new," Sam said to Haggerty.

"You'll be the first to know. I was reading about the fraud case. You got motive all over the place, huh?"

"You know it. Almost everyone who knew her wanted her dead."

"I don't envy you this one."

"Do you envy me the others?"

Haggerty laughed. "Nope, but they do keep us in business."

"Unfortunately, yes, they do. Let's hit it, Detective Cruz."

When they returned to the car, Sam called Jeannie McBride and asked her to do another canvass of the McLeods' neighborhood to determine if anyone saw someone cleaning something with the outdoor hose on Sunday afternoon.

"I'll call you if I get anything," Jeannie said.

She no sooner ended that call when her phone rang with another from Darren Tabor, her favorite reporter from the *Washington Star*. "What's up?" Sam asked when she took the call.

"*Seriously*, Sam? You handed the exclusive of the year to that hag who asked you that awful question last week?"

"First of all, I didn't hand anything to anyone. That was my husband's scoop to give to whomever he wanted. It was his call, not mine."

"Still... I'm disappointed."

"Sorry to disappoint."

"You could make it up to me with a scoop on the McCleod investigation. A lot of people are talking about that after what she did."

"I haven't got anything yet."

"But when you do?"

"I'll keep you in mind."

"Gee, thanks."

"Gotta go." She quickly closed the phone before he could say anything to that and drove toward Catholic University on Michigan Avenue, with a detour to one of Freddie's favorite sandwich shops. Sam ordered a veggie pocket, while he got a large steak bomb full of onions, peppers and cheese. The smell made

Sam's mouth water and probably added five pounds to her ass by osmosis. He downed the entire thing as well as two bags of chips and a large cola.

Sam was living for the day when his metabolism slowed down and his horrendous dietary choices caught up to him. With her luck, she wouldn't live to see that day.

"I hope you have some gum or something so you don't kill anyone with your onion breath. Namely me."

"I've got gum."

"Congratulations, you've made it so we both smell like grilled-onion BO."

"Maybe that's what you smell like, but I'm like a fresh spring day over here."

She snorted with laughter. "Sure you are."

After arriving at the Catholic campus, Freddie directed her to park outside one of the residence halls. "She's in room 311."

"I don't even want to know how you found that out."

"It's better if you don't ask."

"I'd wonder what she's still doing here when her mother was just murdered, but knowing what I do about the mother, I suppose I shouldn't be surprised."

"True."

They followed a group of young people through the main door but were stopped from proceeding to the elevator by a security guard. "May I help you?"

Sam and Freddie showed him their badges. "We're looking for Mandi McLeod in 311."

"I can call her to come down."

"We'd prefer to go up."

They engaged in a visual standoff before the guard finally blinked. "I know who you are."

"That's nice. Can you get out of my way now?"

He frowned but stepped aside.

In the elevator, Sam said, "For fuck's sake. Why do people waste my time telling me they know who I am?"

"Because seeing someone famous makes their day."

"Ugh. Shut up. I'm not famous."

"Whatever you say."

"I say I'm not famous, so that's the end of it."

"Okay."

"Stop being insubordinate."

"I can't. It's too much fun."

She glared at him on the way out of the elevator and followed the signs to room 311. "She'd better be here, or I'm gonna be pissed."

"You'll be pissed either way."

"True." He amused the hell out of her, not that she could ever let him know that when he was already out of control. It was her own fault, but she wouldn't have him any other way.

CHAPTER ELEVEN

S am knocked on the door of 311, where a dry-erase board announced that Mandi and Sarah lived there.

A young woman with wet dark hair came to the door, her eyes bugging when she recognized Sam.

"Famous," Freddie whispered under his breath, earning an elbow to a gut full of steak bomb.

Sam showed her badge. "Lieutenant Holland, Detective Cruz, MPD. We're looking for Mandi McLeod."

"I'm Mandi. Is this about my mom?"

Sam thanked her lucky stars that they'd gotten lucky to find Mandi somewhat easily. "It is. Could we come in for a minute?"

"Sure."

She stepped aside to admit them into a cluttered space with clothes and towels strewn about, books stacked on desks and colored lights strung on the wall. Mandi pushed aside a pile of clothes and gestured for them to sit on one of the narrow beds.

Sam had commuted to school, so she'd missed this part of college life, which was fine with her. Communal living had never appealed to her.

"Did you figure out who killed my mom?" Mandi asked.

"Not yet. I'm somewhat surprised to find you still at school. I'd think you'd be with your family."

"I hadn't spoken to either of my parents in months, not since I found out what they did."

"They?"

"My brother and I believe my dad knew what she was doing. How could he not?"

That was an interesting development. "How did you find out about the scam?"

"When the FBI and IRS began investigating her and word started getting out that she might've stolen from people we know."

"Before that, you had no idea?"

"None. And then the list of people she stole from began to go public... Friends, friends' parents, our godparents, aunts, uncles, neighbors, people my brother and I have known all our lives. We were shocked and disgusted and... We were so *hurt*. How could she do this to people we love? People who loved her? Our entire lives *imploded*, Lieutenant. Everyone turned on us. It's been a nightmare."

"Have you been in touch with any of those people?"

She shook her head, her eyes filling. "My own aunts and uncles won't take my calls. The girls I played soccer with in high school hate me because my mom stole from their parents. It's the same for my brother. None of the guys he played baseball with will talk to him. He and I have been frozen out by everyone who matters to us, even those who weren't scammed. We're guilty by association, I guess. I'll have to get loans to finish my senior year of college."

"Your parents don't help you?" Freddie asked.

"Their assets were frozen by the government. And besides, after this, I don't want anything from them. I'm working two jobs and holding down eighteen credits while everyone I care about, except my brother, acts like I'm dead to them. That's my life now." Hurt and bitterness crept through every word she said. "My mother was dead to me before yesterday."

"How did you find out about her death?" Sam asked.

"My father called late yesterday afternoon, a few hours after he found her. I couldn't imagine why he'd be calling me. I knew something bad must've happened for him to reach out. He knew I wanted nothing to do with either of them."

"I'm surprised you took the call," Sam said. "Or that you hadn't blocked them both."

She blinked but failed to stop tears from spilling down her cheeks. "I should've blocked them, but I couldn't bring myself to do it. They're still my parents. And when he called me, I just wanted to hear his voice."

Freddie got up to get her some tissues from a box on the bedside table and handed them to her.

"Thank you." She wiped her face. "I know it was weak, but I love my parents and hate them too. I hate what they did and how they ruined our lives with their greed."

"Do you know of anyone who might've been angry enough with your mom to kill her?"

"I know tons of people who are that angry. If you're asking if I know who actually did it, I don't. I'm sure I'd be among the last to know. Many people think my brother and I knew what they were up to, but we didn't. No one believes that, though."

"You've said 'they' and 'them' several times," Freddie said. "You're convinced it was both of them?"

"She's the one the government charged, but I just don't believe he didn't know. How could he *not* know? He swore to us that he didn't and passed a polygraph, but we don't believe him."

"Has he lied to you before?" Freddie asked.

"Not that I know of. But if you'd asked me if my mom was capable of stealing from our closest friends and family members, I would've said no way. So who knows if they lied to us about other stuff?" She wiped away more tears before adding softly, "This has ruined my life, and I'm only twenty-one."

"We're sorry for what you've been through," Freddie said, always the empathetic one.

"I have to ask where you were yesterday," Sam said.

"I was here all day. I had study group in the morning. I was here by myself the rest of the day."

"Can anyone verify that?"

"My roommate was here in the morning, but she left around noon and was gone when I got back from study group. She didn't come back until this morning."

"And you didn't see anyone else for the rest of the day yesterday?"

"No, after my dad called, I stayed by myself. I didn't want to see anyone."

Sam gave Mandi her card. "If you think of anything else we should know, call me."

"Did you talk to the Realtor? Cheri Clark?"

"Not yet. What about her?"

"She was in this thing up to her neck with my mother, even though she wasn't charged. Without her showing the properties, no one would've taken the bait. I believe my mom was paying her kickbacks, but the Feds haven't been able to make a case that she knew what my mom was doing."

"Do you know where we'd find her?"

"Chevy Chase."

Sam bit back a groan at the thought of more time wasted in traffic as they returned to the same area where they'd been that morning. "And your brother? Where is he this time of day?"

"Downtown."

As Sam and Freddie made their way out of the dormitory, several students called out to Sam.

"I can't believe your husband isn't going to run."

"How can he do this to us?"

"We need him."

"Ugh," she said when she and Freddie were outside. "Why do they gotta yell at me about him?"

"Um, because you're sleeping with him and can deliver their messages?"

"That was a rhetorical question. You should know the difference by now."

"Apologies."

"Not accepted. Flip a coin. Heads, we go to Chevy Chase. Tails, we go downtown."

"Why can't there be a third choice of neither?"

"I know." Even the walk to the car was annoying her because it took ten full minutes.

"I need a snack."

"You just ate lunch!"

"That was, like, two hours ago."

"It was forty-five minutes. No snack."

"You're mean when you have motive everywhere you look."

"I'm mean all the time. All this motive just makes me cranky on top of being mean."

"That's true."

When they were in the car, Sam said, "I want to bring the husband in for a formal interview."

"I was going to ask about him."

"No, you weren't."

"Yes, I was! I was going to say we need to talk to the husband again."

"Whatever you say, rock star."

"I was gonna!"

"Shut up, call Patrol and ask them to pick him up at the brother's house. You still got the address from yesterday?"

"Yes, I still have the address," he said, sounding annoyed that she'd even ask.

"All right, then, get on it." She directed the car toward Chevy Chase, full of resentment for the next hour on the road when she had far better things to do than drive through hideous traffic to get to the far northwestern part of the city.

Freddie made the call to Patrol and gave them the address of where Ken McLeod was staying. "They're on it." He looked over at her. "Speaking of Patrol, I still can't believe Captain Hernandez knew about Conklin's role in your dad's shooting. I can't even imagine what that must be like for you and your family."

"I can't believe the people who stayed quiet when two of their own had been murdered." The men Conklin had protected had also been tied to the murder of her father's first partner, Steven Coyne, decades ago. "I'll never get over that, but I'm thankful they're getting what's coming to them. As for Hernandez, it was his own stupidity that did him in. Sending me a note, written in his own hand, that the answers were closer than we realized... He screwed himself."

"And thank God for that. Otherwise, we never would've known he was involved."

"I just wonder who else knew."

"You think there're others?"

"I'd bet my life on it."

"Seriously?" He shook his head. "How's that possible?"

"The same way it was possible that Conklin and Hernandez knew. The same reason Ginny McLeod did what she did. It's about greed, pure and simple. Money makes the world go round, young Freddie, and people will do anything to get more of it, even sell out a friend or allow that friend to nearly be murdered to protect their cash cow."

"It's disgusting."

"Yep, but it's reality."

"How can you be so matter-of-fact about fellow officers selling out your dad for money?"

"Because if I truly let myself go there, I wouldn't be able to do the job anymore."

"Yeah, I can see that."

"Karma is a bitch. Look at Conklin and Hernandez. They had it all. Deputy chief and captain, big pensions and all the perks of being high-ranking officers. Now they're charged with felonies that'll put them in jail for decades."

"I want them to lose their pensions too."

"We're working on that. The chief has the same goal, believe me."

"What do you think the FBI investigation will show?"

"That there's still some rot in our department that'll need to be weeded out. We're going to learn things about ourselves we might not like, mostly that we need to do better on a number of levels. Introspection is almost always painful."

"I want to know who else knew."

"We may never grasp the full extent of it, so I take comfort that they're probably shitting themselves, especially with the FBI peeling back the layers."

"I never thought I'd actually welcome the FBI investigating us."

"I know. I feel the same way, but that's a thought we should probably keep to ourselves, especially since the investigation will take a while."

"True. Have you heard any more about Gonzo's situation?"

"Nothing more than the chief is talking to the U.S. Attorney about it. He may have no choice but to charge Gonzo, especially since he's admitted to what he did. That's another thing we might have to suck up and deal with. As much as I hate this for him, in the end it's his call."

"I hate a lot of things lately."

"You can't let it make you bitter," Sam said. "Not if you want to continue to do this job, and I think you do."

"Of course I do, but it's infuriating. We're supposed to uphold the law, not break it. How am I supposed to feel as a lowly detective when my deputy chief and one of the most senior captains of the MPD are charged with covering up the circumstances of the attempted murder of our former deputy chief?"

"You're supposed to feel furious," Sam said.

"And then one of the best cops I've ever known is going to be charged for something he did in the throes of addiction brought on by trauma on the job. How's that fair?"

"It's not. None of it is fair. But it's life. People are flawed. They do stupid things. They get greedy. They look out for themselves first and foremost. That's just how it is, as much as we wish it wasn't. Take our friend Ginny. Look at what she did to her family and friends, what she did to her *kids*."

"It's gross."

"And for what? So she could take a few more vacations every year and buy more stuff? What good does any of that do her now? She couldn't take any of it with her."

"You know what's bugging me?" he asked.

"What's that?"

"She spent a lot, but twenty million? There has to be some cash left somewhere."

"We pulled the financials, right?"

"Yeah, Cam did."

"Let's give him a call."

Freddie made the call on his phone and connected it to her Bluetooth.

"Do I even want to know how you did that?"

"Never mind."

She ought to tell him to stuff his never mind up his—

Cameron picked up the call. "Hey, what's up?"

"The LT and I are talking about how one goes about spending twenty million. We imagine that'd take some doing."

"It would, for sure, and from what I can see, she spent only a fraction of it."

"Then where's the rest?" Sam asked.

"A very good question and one the Feds have been chasing for more than a year. The theory is offshore accounts, but no one has been able to locate them, and Ginny wasn't talking. They even offered her lesser charges if she came clean on where the money was stashed, but she never said."

"She would've had to have help setting that up," Sam said. "Most regular people wouldn't know how to open offshore accounts."

"The Feds worked that angle hard and never found anyone. The theory is that Ginny communicated only in person and never on the phone or electronically so there wouldn't be any kind of paper trail."

"Ugh," Sam said. "This woman is pissing me off."

"You met with her daughter?" Cam asked.

"We did. The kid is devastated, but not because her mother is dead. Because she ruined their lives before someone killed her. She scammed the parents of the daughter's friends."

"Harsh."

"No one was immune, including her own siblings, cousins and close friends."

"What was her plan?" Freddie asked. "After she screwed everyone in her life, including her own kids, what then? And how did she think she'd get away with it?"

"She did get away with it until Haverson alerted the Feds,"

Cam said. "That was the first domino to fall. Personally, I think she planned to be long gone by the time she got found out."

"Which means there could be a fake passport and other documents somewhere. Cam, call Haggerty and ask him to go back and look again for hidden safes. I want every piece of paper currently in that house and everything that was taken during the federal investigation."

"I'll get on that," Cam said.

"Tell them to bring it to our conference room. We'll start from scratch in case the Feds missed something."

"And doesn't that sound like fun?" Freddie asked.

"The devil's in the details, my young friend," Sam said.

"Where're you heading now?" Cam asked.

"To see the Realtor who enabled Ginny's scam."

"Where is she?"

"Chevy fucking Chase."

"Ugh."

"You said it. Back to the outer reaches of Northwest for the second time today."

"Better you than me. You should know this place is on fire with the news that Nick isn't running. The press corps has tripled outside."

Sam groaned. "What the hell do they want with me? I never give them anything. What makes them think I'm going to start now?"

"Hope springs eternal," Cameron said. "What's next after the Realtor?"

"The son, and then we're coming back in to talk to the husband. We had Patrol pick him up. They should be bringing him in soon. Have him sit in interrogation until we get there. If he asks for a lawyer, get him one."

"Will do."

"We'll be there as soon as we can, but probably three days from now with the way this traffic is looking."

"I'll hold down the fort for you."

"Thanks. Let us know if anything pops."

"Will do."

Freddie ended the call.

"Get your phone off my Bluetooth."

"Your Bluetooth likes my phone. They're in a relationship."

"Their relationship is over."

"It's just getting started. They had sex last night."

Sam cracked up. "Your phone moves a lot faster than you did."

"Don't slut-shame my phone, Sam. That's not a good look on you."

"I'm trying to figure out where you went so wrong."

He looked at her, incredulous. "You are? Really? I believe it happened the day Stahl said, 'Cruz, you're with Holland.'"

Sam had almost forgotten that Stahl had been the one who first assigned them to work together. "I guess we should thank him for that much."

"Nah, we still hate his guts, but he did put us together."

"You were such a nice boy then. So unspoiled, with sparkling principles."

"My principles are still sparkling."

"They're a little dingier than they used to be."

"That is not true! My principles are sterling. It's the rest of me that's a little dingier, thanks to you."

"Admit it. I made a man out of you."

"Oh my God. Shut up, will you?"

"That's my story, and I'm sticking to it."

"You do that."

"Thank you, I will."

He was one of the only reasons she could stand to do this job day after day. No matter what they were dealing with, being with him was always fun and funny and entertaining. Sam had long ago realized that she'd lost all perspective and any impartiality she might've once had where he was concerned. He was family to her. Period. In light of that, she should probably reassign him, but that wasn't going to happen.

She needed him too much.

CHAPTER TWELVE

It was nearly three o'clock when they arrived in Chevy Chase.

"I used to envy the kids that lived out here," Sam said.

"How come?"

"I thought they were lucky to live in real neighborhoods outside the city, but now I know we were the lucky ones because we had access to everything close by. They had to take a long Metro ride to get to anything good."

"I always thought it was weird that there are two Chevy Chases."

"Right? And don't mistake them. There's the DC Chevy Chase and the Maryland Chevy Chase."

"And they're right next to each other. Bizarre. And we're coming to see Cheri Clark in Chevy Chase. It's a double-C kinda day."

"I got a lotta words I can think of that start with C that describe this day."

"But you're not going to share them."

"Dingier Freddie loves my dirty words."

"No, he doesn't."

"Cock, cocked—"

"Sam! Shut up."

While she laughed at her own joke, she found a parking space three blocks from Clark's office on Connecticut Avenue. They fought against a chilly headwind as they walked.

"That's the second lady," a guy said to his friend when they passed him on the sidewalk. "Hey, tell your husband he needs to run. There's no quitting in politics!"

"Am I allowed to shoot him?" Sam asked Freddie.

"I'll pretend not to see anything, as long as I don't have to do the paperwork."

Thankfully, the loudmouth didn't pursue her, so she didn't have to shoot him. They stepped into the lobby of a three-story office building, found Cheri Clark Real Estate on the directory and hoofed it to the third floor.

"They need an elevator in this place," Sam said when they reached the third floor.

"Or you need to work out more."

"Shut your face."

His snicker would've made her mad if she wasn't so winded. He might be right about needing to work out if climbing two flights of stairs made her feel like she was going to die. Not that she planned to tell him that.

The lights were off in Cheri's office, and when Sam tried the door, it was locked. "Mother effer. If she's not here after we drove all this way, I'm going to arrest her for wasting my time."

"No, you're not. I'm definitely not doing that paperwork."

"You'll do it if I tell you to. Find out where she lives."

Freddie got busy on his phone and had an address within two minutes. "It's about a mile from here."

"Let's go." Back down the stairs they went, Sam lamenting that she'd climbed them for nothing, and now she knew exactly how out of shape she was. "Is there a picture of this woman?"

Freddie handed over his phone.

Sam took a good long look at a perky woman with shoulder-length blonde hair and perfect teeth highlighted by red lipstick and handed the phone back to him. "I'm glad I don't have a job that requires me to wear lipstick all the time."

"We're all thankful for that."

"You're in rare form today, Frederico," Sam said as they walked back to the car.

"Don't call me that. You sound like my mother."

"How is my friend Juliette?"

"She's driving me crazy asking when I'm going to make her a grandmother."

"Ah, the eternal question of mothers everywhere. You get a month, maybe two, after the wedding before the questions start."

"It's annoying. Elin and I aren't in any rush to have kids, and I'm not letting anyone pressure me into it, even my mother."

"That's the way. Stay strong, grasshopper."

"I'm trying, but the struggle is real. Hey…" He pointed.

When Sam saw the woman he was pointing at, she took off running.

The woman saw them coming, blanched and then spun around, attempting to run on three-inch heels. To say they had the advantage on her would be putting it mildly.

Sam caught her easily and had her handcuffed before Freddie reached them.

Because he was the less winded of the two of them, she let him take care of reciting the woman's rights. Sam really needed to get back to the gym, or actually join a gym in the first place.

Cheri struggled against Sam's tight hold on her. "I haven't done anything!"

"If that's the case, why'd you run?" Sam asked.

"I was scared. Everyone knows how you are."

"How am I?" Sam asked as they perp-walked her to her car.

"A hard-ass bitch."

"Oh, that's so mean! I'm hurt! Aren't I hurt, Detective Cruz?"

"It's too bad that people don't realize you take that as a compliment."

She loved him so much. He was the absolute perfect wingman. "I know, right?"

"I want a lawyer."

"It's funny, isn't it, Detective Cruz, how often 'innocent' people lawyer up at the first sign of cops?"

Cheri glared at her. "I'll tell you the same thing I told the Feds:

I had no idea what Ginny was doing when she asked me to show properties to people. I was just doing my job."

"And if we were to pull your financials, we'd find that you never received any payments for doing dirty work for her, right?"

"Of course she paid me for what I did for her company. I don't work for free. Do you?"

"I thought Realtors got paid when something sells," Sam said, "not when they show properties. But you must be unique."

"We had an arrangement. I showed properties, and she paid me. How is that illegal?"

"We'll talk about that when your lawyer shows up."

Sam drove them back to headquarters in traffic that'd gotten worse while they were in Chevy Chase. By the time they arrived at HQ, she was feeling extremely cranky and out of sorts. "Get her processed," she said to Freddie.

"Processed?" Cheri said on a screech. "You can't charge me for showing properties!"

"Nope, but we can charge you for hampering a homicide investigation and resisting arrest."

Her face lost all color as her mouth fell open. "*How* did I hamper a homicide investigation?"

"You made us chase you." Sometimes, this job was actually fun. Giving entitled people like Cheri a comeuppance was Sam's kind of fun. "Take her to Central Booking, Detective Cruz."

"You can't actually charge me with anything."

That made Sam laugh out loud. "You want to set her straight on that, Detective?"

"I'll take care of it." Freddie led the woman toward the entrance while Sam hung back for a better view of the massive media presence outside the main door.

"Jesus," she muttered, unnerved by the intense interest in Nick's announcement.

Speaking of the devil… Her phone rang with a call from him.

"I'm not sure if I should continue taking your calls."

"You absolutely should."

"What's up?"

"The whole world has gone *mad* over the announcement."

"I'm seeing that in a massive media presence at HQ." Sam's anxiety spiked into the red zone. "In what way are you seeing it?"

"In the say-it-isn't-so way. Brant was just in here, and they'd like to put a couple of agents on you, just for the next few days until it dies down."

"No."

"Sam, *please*? This is the kind of thing that brings out the lunatics. You have to let me protect you."

"I'm fine. No protection needed. But please pass along my thanks to Brant for his concern."

Her comment was met with dead silence.

"Hello?"

"I'm here," he said in a tense tone.

"You're pissed."

"Kinda."

"You know how I feel about being followed by security, Nick. I *am* security."

"And you know how I feel about you. What if someone decides to kidnap my wife and hold her hostage because I decided not to run for president?"

"No one would do that. I know you're popular, but that'd be crazy."

"If you could see some of the emails my team is getting, you'd know it's not so crazy. They're being super hateful about me choosing not to run. Brant was a bit upset I didn't give him a heads-up before I released the news. In fact, it never occurred to me it would matter to them. The Secret Service has doubled the kids' details."

Hearing that, Sam felt sick. "Seriously?"

"Dead seriously. Please, Sam... Just this once, please do what I'm asking you to do."

He sounded so stressed that her overwhelming resistance became less important than his peace of mind. "Fine. One agent who stays the hell out of my way."

"They work in teams. You get two, and I'll pass along your request."

"This is a one-time thing, Nick. And only until the story dies down."

"Thank you."

"I must really love you."

"God, I hope you do, because at this rate, we're going to end up back in the Secret Service bunker."

"Don't even say that." Sam cringed, recalling being stuck in the underground bunker for days while the Secret Service assessed a credible threat against their family.

"I'm not the one saying it. I had no idea people were this invested in me running. I'm truly shocked by the reaction."

"I hate to say I told you so, but…"

"You love to say you told me so."

"Yeah, I kinda do. It's even more fun to say to Freddie."

Nick laughed. "Poor Freddie."

"Poor you. Are you okay?"

"I guess. It's just bizarre to be the subject of this kind of attention."

"I assume if they doubled the kids' details, they doubled yours too?"

"Tripled."

"God, Nick…"

"It's fine, babe. They're on it, and everything's okay as long as you and the kids are safe."

"And you. Please don't take your own security lightly. People are nuts."

"Trust me, I know. Where should I send your detail?"

"HQ, but tell them to stay outside. I'll be here for a while. Tell them I'll mostly ignore them, and they're to do the same to me, if they know what's good for them."

"Will do," he said on a soft chuckle. "Love you."

"You owe me big for this."

"I owe you big for a lot of things, and I swear I'll make it up to you."

"Can't wait. See you soon."

"Watch your back, babe. It's my favorite back in the whole world."

"Will do. See you."

"Bye."

Sam hated to end the call, but she had too much to do to hang inside the morgue door, talking to her husband like they were a couple of middle schoolers in the throes of first love. Even if that was how it felt. She'd been in love before him, but her feelings for him were on a whole other level than anything she'd experienced with anyone else. If you'd asked her before him if soul mates existed, she would've scoffed. Now she knew better.

"Everything okay?" Lindsey asked.

Sam realized her friend had been standing there for a minute, watching her.

"Uh, well, the world's gone mad over Nick's announcement, and now I've got a detail."

"No way. It must be bad for them to insist on that."

"I guess it is. Who knew that people would feel that he owes them something?"

"Jeez... That's insane."

"Yep."

"So you've got a detail."

"I've got a detail, but I told Nick to tell them to stay the hell out of my way."

"In those exact words, I presume."

"What other words should I have used?"

Lindsey's eyes lit up with silent laughter.

"I gotta go deal with Ginny McLeod's fake Realtor, who ran from us when she saw us coming but doesn't see how that impeded a homicide investigation."

"With the mood you're in, I presume you're going to enjoy setting her straight."

"You presume correctly, Doc. By the way, Haggerty's team found an implement that's most likely our murder weapon."

"Is that right? Ragged edges?"

"Super ragged, and the only one in the house that'd been wiped completely clean and then stashed in a downstairs bedroom closet."

"Ah, damn, so it's no help to you."

"It's something we didn't know before—that the perp took the time to clean the murder weapon thoroughly and hide it in the house while Ginny bled out on the floor. That makes it a little more cold-blooded than it initially seemed."

"I don't envy you any of your cases, but this one..."

"It's a bitch, and so was she. We met with her daughter, who was in tears telling us everyone in her life has turned on her. In addition to her own family, she scammed the parents of the kids' friends."

"Good Lord. She was a sociopath."

"Indeed. It's hard to work up the same level of enthusiasm for getting her justice that I usually feel."

"I don't blame you. Not that anyone deserves to be murdered, but..."

"Exactly. See you later."

"Let me know if I can help."

"Will do."

Sam made her way to the pit and went straight to Cameron Green's cubicle. "Could I please see the Fed reports about the role of the Realtor?"

"Yep." He sifted through meticulously labeled manila folders, found the one she'd requested and handed it to her.

"You make us all look like slackers."

The young detective looked up at her, seeming stunned. "I, um..."

"That was a compliment, Green." She rolled her eyes. "Sheesh. You're a very good detective."

"Oh, well, thanks. I enjoy it."

"That shows. Give me the highlights on our friend Cheri."

"She's a pretty successful Realtor in Northwest. Some of the biggest transactions in the last year were handled by her on both sides—buyer and seller. She's very active in civic organizations like the Rotary, chamber of commerce, etc. Her business is booming— or it was until Ginny McLeod's scheme was uncovered, and people started accusing her of being in bed with Ginny. She swore, under oath, that she had no idea what Ginny was doing when she asked Cheri to show properties to some of Ginny's clients."

"By the time Ginny had brought hundreds of people to see a run-down former warehouse, wouldn't Cheri have been a little curious about what was going on? Especially when no one ever bought anything."

"That's what the Feds wanted to know too, but Cheri said Ginny asked her to show the properties and paid her to do it. She didn't ask any questions about why."

"Do you find that hard to believe?"

"Extremely, and so did the Feds. But Cheri never deviated from her story over the months the Feds spent investigating both her and Ginny. I took a look at her recent financials, compared them to a year ago and found her business is down fifty percent year over year. The affiliation with Ginny has hurt her, despite her persistent claims that she had nothing to do with the scam."

"I hate these women," Sam said.

"A lot of people do."

"So many haters that finding a murderer in this crowd is going to be almost impossible."

"Something will break if we keep digging."

Freddie came into the pit, looking annoyed. "A pleasant lady, Ms. Clark is. She's processed and waiting in interview two."

"And the lawyer?"

"Has been called. Said he'd be here in the next couple of hours."

"That must've pleased her," Sam said.

"Not so much." Freddie ran his fingers through his hair. "She's furious and talking about calling the media to report harassment."

"Let her," Sam said. "We can tell the world how she ran from cops who just wanted to ask her a few questions. Last time I checked, innocent people don't run from cops."

"Truth," Freddie said.

"Green, do a deeper dive into Cheri's finances. If there's anything to find, find it."

Green nodded. "On it."

"While we wait for her attorney, let's get everyone in the conference room to go over what we have and next steps."

CHAPTER THIRTEEN

While they got themselves together, Sam went into her office for a quick look at her email and to check her messages. She gave out tons of business cards but rarely ever heard back from anyone who thought of additional information she ought to have, which was fine. She'd continue to give the cards in the hope that someday one might yield a tidbit that blew a case wide open.

She was scrolling through her email when Avery Hill appeared in her doorway. "Not now, Agent Hill. I'm knee-deep in a homicide investigation."

"The woman who scammed her family and friends, right?"

"That's the one."

"You must have motive coming out the wazoo."

"And every other orifice, which means I don't have time for you today."

"I was hoping you could find some time in the next day or two."

"Everything I know about Stahl and Conklin is already in the record."

"Everything?"

"Everything that matters."

"I'll bet there's a lot more you've forgotten that might come out in conversation."

"You'll understand I'm not eager to have conversations about either of them or Hernandez, for that matter."

"I do understand. I knew your dad, admired and respected him, and while I can't begin to know how you must feel to have the trail lead into your own department, I'm heartbroken for you that it played out the way it did."

"Thank you." She didn't want him or anyone else to be heartbroken for her, but she'd sound like a bitch if she said so. No one in the world could possibly understand the feelings of betrayal she carried now that she knew the truth. That people within the department she and her father had served for more than four decades combined could've let them down the way Conklin and Hernandez had. "The only thing I want is to find out who else knew the truth."

"You believe it went beyond Conklin and Hernandez?"

"Hell yes, I do. The money would've been tantalizing to more than just the two of them. We can work overtime and extra details until we're blue in the face, but we can only make so much money as cops." Another thought occurred to her. "Remember when we busted the prostitution ring that took down the Speaker of the House?"

"How could I forget?"

"Think about how many high-level officials were implicated there. I don't care what you do for a living, easy money is easy money. And cops aren't immune to the siren's song, even if we'd both like to think they are."

He came in and took a seat. "Do you have any names in mind?" His lyrical South Carolinian accent had become so familiar to her in recent years. There'd been a time when his unrequited interest in her had made her exquisitely uncomfortable, but that was long in the past now that he was happily married to Shelby.

She was still thinking about Avery's question when Sergeant Ramsey appeared at her door, interoffice memo envelope in hand, his face bright red with rage that made his mean eyes bug.

"What the fuck are you doing, Holland?"

Avery stood and turned toward the door.

"I'm sorry, what?" Sam said.

"You know exactly what I'm talking about, you fucking cunt."

"Hey," Hill said. "Watch your mouth."

"Shut up. I don't work for you, you fucking Fed."

"I'm not sure what's crawled up your ass and died this time, Ramsey," Sam said, "but I can assure you it has nothing to do with me."

"You're a fucking liar, and I'm going to prove it."

"Knock yourself out. Oh wait, you already did that when you went through the window in the lobby, right?"

"You think you're so fucking smart," he said, sputtering with outrage, "but you mark my words, Holland. I'm going to end you."

"You heard that threat, Agent Hill, right?"

"I did."

"If you think you can resort to blackmailing me to save your precious Gonzales—"

"*Whoa*," Sam said. "Someone's *blackmailing* you? If you're this pissed, they must have something awesome on you." She leaned in, hoping to project intense interest. "What's got you so hot under the collar?"

His eyes narrowed into a look of pure hatred. "Fuck you. You'd better watch your back."

Sam smiled at him as if nothing he could do would ever get to her. "Got it. Will do."

Ramsey stormed off.

"What the *hell*, Sam?" Avery said.

"That'd be my good friend Sergeant Ramsey. We go way back."

"He just threatened your life in front of an FBI agent. We could charge him."

"Eh, he's not worth it. I'm not worried about him, and you shouldn't be either. But if I should turn up dead, maybe you could mention what he said to Malone or someone who'd care?"

"Don't make jokes. That guy is unhinged. I wouldn't put it past him to come for you."

"Well, the good news is that as of about right now, I've got a Secret Service detail until people get over the news that Nick isn't going to run."

"I heard his decision isn't going over well."

Sam shrugged. "I get it. He's the best. I understand why people are disappointed, but he's not going to change his mind."

"I'll confess to being disappointed myself. I was looking forward to a Cappuano administration."

"Whereas he's looking forward to not missing a minute of the teenage years with Scotty or elementary school with the twins."

"I admire that. I really do."

"It's the most important thing to him, and, selfish cow that I am, I'm thrilled to know he's not going to be off campaigning for months on end." The thought of that gave her angina. "I don't think single parenthood would look good on me."

"You could do it if you had to."

"Thank God I don't. I've got my team waiting in the conference room. I'll give you some time tomorrow afternoon, later in the day if that works."

"I'll take what I can get. Thanks, Sam."

"I'd say it was no problem, but this whole thing is a huge problem to me."

"I can only imagine."

"I'm making an effort to not let it ruin a job and a career I've loved, you know?"

"I get it. But the betrayal strikes deep."

"As deep as it gets. And to answer your question from before Ramsey rudely interrupted us, I don't know who else might've been aware of the gambling ring. I'm still shocked that Conklin, of all people, knew and never said a word while pretending to be my dad's close friend. Hernandez was another huge shock."

"I'm sure."

"My dad was a great cop. One of the best I've ever known, and I'm not saying that just because he was my dad."

"Everyone says that."

"That's nice to hear. He raised me to always try to do the right thing, even when it's the hard thing. That was the credo he lived by and instilled in me and my sisters. I hope that, despite what we've uncovered since he died, people will remember him for how he lived and did the job and not for the way he died."

"They will and they do. I promise you. People remember."

"That's good to hear. Protecting his legacy is really the only thing that matters to me when it comes to this whole mess."

"I understand. I'll let you get back to work and check in with you tomorrow."

"Thanks, Avery. I know I'm supposed to rail with every fiber of my being against the Feds investigating us, but I've got to say I actually kind of welcome it this time. If there are others who knew…"

"We'll find them," Avery said, his expression fierce. "We will *find them*, Sam."

She nodded, her throat tightening around a hot knot of the emotion that still caught her off guard weeks after her father's sudden death. Not to mention the horror that'd followed when the newly reinvigorated investigation into his shooting had led to their own deputy chief, among others.

"I'll see you tomorrow," he said.

"I'll be here."

At the doorway, he turned back to face her. "You know… A lot of people would've said fuck it after they uncovered this kind of betrayal. I give you a lot of credit for continuing to show up and do the job."

"What choice do I have? It's the only thing I've ever been any good at, the only thing I know how to do."

"You're exceptionally good at it, and it's what you should be doing."

"Now that the fear of my husband becoming president has been taken off the table, I can exhale a bit about my own future. Looks like I'll be spending it right here, so if you could get rid of any of the remaining scumbags in our ranks who knew who shot my dad and didn't say anything, I'd consider that a personal favor."

"We're working on it. People are less than forthcoming, but we're not going to be deterred by stonewalling."

"Go get 'em."

"Good luck with the fraud case."

"Ugh, I'm going to need it."

"You'll figure it out." He waved as he walked away to continue plumbing the depths of the MPD for scumbags.

Once upon a time, she'd been under the illusion that everyone in the department viewed the job the same way she and her father did. Those illusions had been shattered a long time ago. Whenever she'd talked to Skip about it, he'd advised her to continue to stay on the side of right, do the job the best way she knew how and she'd be fine. "You can't control what others do," he'd said. "Only what you do and how you react."

As she gathered what she needed for the meeting, she let the soundtrack of his voice play in her mind. She'd known him as well as she knew herself and knew exactly what he'd say to any comment or question. That was a huge comfort to her now that he was no longer physically present. Knowing what he'd say about any topic would keep him present to her for the rest of her life. And for all the life she had left, she'd fight for justice for him, even if it meant seeing colleagues she'd worked with for years taken down. If there were others, she hoped they were freaking out with the FBI crawling all over HQ.

She went into the conference room where her detectives had gathered. While they waited for her, they'd updated the murder board with additional information, including photos of Ginny alive and dead, the garden tool they assumed was the murder weapon, a list of the people they'd talked to and others who'd been scammed.

"How did you order the list of her victims?" Sam asked.

"By dollar amount invested," Jeannie said. "The ones at the top put in the most. The thought is to start with them and work our way down."

"Tell me we aren't going to have to talk to all of them."

"Uhhh, well," Jeannie said with a smile and a shrug.

"I hate this woman, and I hate this case," Sam said. "If you were wondering."

"We weren't wondering," Cameron said, smiling. "But thanks for confirming."

"Of course even vile people deserve justice when their lives are taken," Freddie said. "But sometimes it's hard to feel bad for them when it seems like they had it coming."

"Indeed," Sam said, "but we will get justice for her just the same, whether she deserves it or not. What're we seeing in the financials?"

"Nothing that would lead you to believe that the woman had twenty million floating around," Cameron said.

Detective Matt O'Brien, the newest member of their team, distributed a printed summary of the McLeods' financials, which consisted of several brokerage accounts, bank accounts with several thousand in each and retirement funds. "As you noted, we suspect the bulk of the funds were stashed in offshore accounts that haven't been located."

A knock at the door sounded.

"Enter," Sam called.

Patrolman Clare, whom Sam had met at the scene of Tara Weber's murder, ducked his head into the room. "Pardon the interruption, Lieutenant, but per your request, we've put Ken McLeod in interview one."

"Thank you, Officer Clare."

"You should know he's furious to have been detained and is screaming for a lawyer."

"I assume you allowed him to make that call?"

"Yes, ma'am."

"Good work. Thank you."

He nodded and left the room.

"So we've got another member of Ginny's posse, who says he had nothing to do with the scam, screaming for a lawyer," Sam said as a headache formed between her brows. "What do we make of that?"

"I want to dig deeper into his alibi," Freddie said. "We've learned—recently—that alibis can be fabricated." He referred to the Weber case, in which an airtight alibi had proven to be full of holes upon closer examination.

"Good point," Sam said. "McBride and O'Brien, head out to the Potomac Country Club where McLeod said he played eighteen holes on Sunday and see if you can find people to confirm he was there the whole time. Also, talk to the three people who were part of his foursome." Sam handed them the piece of paper from her pad where McLeod had reluctantly written down the names and numbers.

"Will do," McBride said as she and O'Brien got up to leave the room.

"I want to talk to Dan and Toni Alino," Sam said. "McLeod told us they were his and Ginny's closest couple friends. Both of Dan's parents have Alzheimer's, and she took their money knowing that."

"This woman gets more despicable with everything new I hear about her," Cameron said.

"Agreed," Sam said. "And then there are people like Lenore Worthington, still waiting fifteen years later for justice after her teenage son was gunned down in his own driveway. I'd much rather be taking another look at that case than dealing with this one."

"Me too," Cam said. "Maybe after this one is closed?"

"That's my hope. I'm waiting to hear from Malone that we're authorized to revisit that investigation. In the meantime…"

"We have to figure out who killed Ginny McLeod," Freddie said.

"Right," Sam said. "Let's go find the son, and we'll start in the morning with the Alinos."

Freddie glanced at the clock on the wall. "More likely to find the son at home than at work at this point, I'd imagine."

Sam was surprised to see it was already five thirty. "Let's give that a try." Mandi had given them her brother's addresses at home and work, as well as his phone number.

"What about Cheri and Ken?" Freddie asked.

"Are their lawyers here yet?"

"Let me check." He left the room for a few minutes before returning, shaking his head.

"Then I guess they're going to be our guests for the evening."

"That ought to make them happy."

Sam shrugged. "Not my problem. Have them escorted downstairs, and let them know we'll speak to them after their attorneys arrive tomorrow."

"I get to do all the fun stuff around here," Freddie muttered as he went to see to her instructions.

Keeping Cheri and Ken on ice for the night filled Sam with a perverse feeling of pleasure, since they'd both been so agreeable to begin with.

When Freddie returned to the pit fifteen minutes later, he looked frazzled. "Pleasant folks."

"I take it they're not happy to be the guests of the District for the night?"

"You'd be correct, but as I mentioned to them, once they ask for an attorney, we have no choice but to wait for the attorney to arrive, and since our shift is ending…"

"What can we do? We can't force the lawyers to come in after hours."

"Exactly."

"Let's go to Arlington." Rush-hour traffic out of the District would be hideous.

"Traffic is gonna suck."

"You read my mind."

As they went outside, Sam took note of the black SUV with the dark windows parked behind her car, making it so she couldn't leave unless the SUV moved.

She walked around the SUV and unlocked her car.

"Mrs. Cappuano—"

Spinning around, she confronted the two agents, one of them an older Black man wearing a sharp suit and dark sunglasses, the other young, blond and fresh-faced. "It's Lieutenant Holland, and here's how this is gonna work. You're going to stay out of my way, and don't talk to me. Got it?"

"Yes, ma'am," the younger agent said. "Lieutenant, ma'am."

"It's so nice to meet you," the older agent said with a sarcastically polite tone that Sam respected. "I'm Vernon, and this is Jimmy. It's our pleasure to offer you protection."

"Fuck me to tears," she whispered as she got into her car, started it and began backing up, giving them seconds to move the SUV before she hit it.

CHAPTER FOURTEEN

"I'll pass on that, but what's this about?" Freddie asked.

"People are going apeshit since Nick's announcement went public." Sam gestured toward the unusually large gathering of reporters outside the main door to HQ. "And now I've got a temporary detail."

"Holy crap. You actually agreed to it?"

"My husband asked me nicely, and since he sounded incredibly stressed by the fact that they'd already doubled the size of the kids' details and tripled his, I agreed to it."

"Damn. So people are making threats over him deciding not to run?"

"Something like that. He said Brant was pissed that Nick didn't give the Secret Service a heads-up before the announcement. But like he said, why would he think they'd need to know?"

"Because people are crazy, and they're going to be disappointed he's taking himself out of the running."

"Why would anyone feel he has an *obligation* to run for president? That boggles my mind."

"I think it's more that they wanted him to run so badly, they're devastated he's not."

"Devastated to the point they'd threaten his wife and children with harm?"

"Like you said, people are crazy."

"They're just proving he did the right thing by getting the hell out of there. Being VP is bad enough. I can't imagine what it'd be like for him to be president and have to put up with a whole other level of crazy."

Twenty minutes later, while they sat in standstill traffic on Memorial Bridge, Sam gazed toward Lincoln, her favorite of the memorials. She often went there when she needed to think. In the distance, the eternal flame marking President Kennedy's grave at Arlington National Cemetery stood out in the encroaching darkness, a stark reminder of the sacrifices some past presidents had made in service to their country. The sight of that flame made her even more grateful that her beloved wouldn't be joining their ranks.

"I hate how early it gets dark this time of year," Sam said.

"I know. It's depressing."

"So is this traffic. I don't know how anyone can stand to commute around here and have to deal with this every day."

"Agreed. We're lucky to live in the city."

It took almost an hour to get to the neighborhood where Ken McLeod Jr. lived in a brick-faced townhouse. More bricks.

Sam eyed the clock to gauge whether she'd make it home in time to see the twins before bedtime. It wasn't looking good, which made her ragey. "He'd better be freaking home."

"I hope so. Lights are on, so that's a good sign."

Ignoring the agents, who'd gotten out of their SUV, Sam and Freddie went up the stairs and rang the doorbell. A young man who shared his father's light-brown hair came to the door wearing a Georgetown T-shirt and basketball shorts.

Sam showed her badge through the storm door. "Lieutenant Holland, MPD. Could we have a minute of your time, please?"

He opened the door. "My sister said the second lady wanted to talk to me."

"Right now, I'm not the second lady. I'm the homicide detective investigating your mother's murder."

"Come in."

Ken led them to a family room at the back of the stylish house where the TV was set to ESPN. Judging from the smell, he was cooking dinner.

Sam's stomach growled.

Using the remote, he reduced the volume and gestured for them to have a seat on a gray leather sofa. "Let me just turn down the stove." When he returned, he sat across from them in a recliner. "What can I do for you?"

"We're investigating your mother's murder and wondering if there's anything you can tell us that might help."

"Why would I want to help when she ruined my life and my sister's?"

"Because no one deserves to be murdered."

He let out a harsh laugh. "Some people do, and she's one of them. She got exactly what was coming to her, and I hope her final moments were as horrible as she's made my life and Mandi's since her scheme came to light. My closest friends won't return my calls or texts because she scammed their parents. They can't believe I didn't know what she was doing, but I didn't. Why would I? I haven't lived at home in years. How would I know what she does?"

"Were you close to your mother before this?"

"Close as in talked every day? No, but we saw each other, had dinner occasionally, did holidays, the usual stuff. I'm busy. She was busy." He shrugged. "It wasn't all the time, but we weren't estranged or anything."

"But you were after you found out about the investigation?"

He gave her an incredulous look. "*Yes*, we were estranged after I found out what she did."

"Did you talk to her about it?"

"What was there to talk about? After seeing the list of victims, I was too busy throwing up to talk to my mother. Everyone close to us was on that list. Can you imagine what it would be like to find out that your own mother scammed the people closest to you? Your friends' parents? Everyone thinks their money bought me this place, when that's not the case. But who would believe that with more than twenty million gone missing? And the Audi R8 she gave me for Christmas? I refuse to drive it, and when I sell it, the money is going toward restitution."

"Where were you on Sunday afternoon?" Sam asked.

He gave her a blank look. "Are you asking if I killed my mother?"

"Did you?"

"No, but I'm not surprised that someone else did. And I was with my flag football team all afternoon. I can give you twenty people who can verify that."

"Two will be good. Were you sad to hear she'd been killed?"

After a long hesitation, he said, "I'm sad to have lost the mother I used to think she was, the mother who raised me and cared for me and gave me birthday parties and came to my baseball games. I'm very sad to have lost that mother, but apparently, I lost her quite some time ago and didn't know it until recently. Am I sad that the woman who scammed the people closest to us is dead? Absolutely not. That woman was a monster."

"Do you have any idea who might've been angry enough to murder her?"

"A lot of people were and with good reason. She ruined their lives."

"Anyone specifically that you know of?"

He shook his head. "Even if I did know exactly who did it, I'm not going there. People have suffered enough because of my family. Whoever took her out did us all a favor. At least now we don't have to be dragged through a trial." Taking a breath, he released it and seemed to sag somewhat. "I'm not a heartless bastard, in case you're wondering. There was a time, not that long ago, when the thought of my mother being murdered would've been horrifying. But after what she did..." He grimaced. "I just don't care."

"Have you spoken to your dad?"

"Briefly."

"What's your feeling on what he knew and when?"

"I think he knew all along, but he swears that's not the case, and the polygraph supported his claims. Who knows what to believe?"

As always, Sam handed over a business card. "I understand how difficult your situation is, but if you think of anything that might help our investigation, please give me a call. My cell number is on there."

"Have you heard anything about whether there's going to be a funeral for my mother?" he asked.

"I haven't, but I presume your father would know that."

"He's not answering his phone."

"That's probably because he's currently in a jail cell at MPD HQ."

His mouth fell open. "He's in *jail*? Why?"

"We wanted to talk to him. He wanted his lawyer, and the lawyer didn't get there before our shift ended. So he's spending the night."

"His attorney probably isn't coming. The guy he would've called was on the list of people my mother scammed."

"Wouldn't he know that?"

"He might've thought his old friend would come anyway. He won't."

"That's good info to know. Thank you for your time."

Sam gestured for him to lead the way to the door. She never turned her back on anyone during an investigation, even someone she didn't suspect of murder.

At the door, he glanced at her. "Will we be notified if you catch our mother's killer?"

"Do you wish to be?"

He thought about that for a second. "I guess."

"Then we'll make sure to update you if or when we close the case."

"Thank you."

They stepped outside into cold, dreary darkness that depressed her.

"I freaking hate this time of year," she said, glancing at the rearview mirror and seeing the two Secret Service agents getting back into their SUV.

"Me too. Except for the part about eating my body weight in turkey. I like that day a lot."

"You would. You're a bottomless pit."

"I'm a growing boy."

"I can only hope you start growing in the wrong direction. Nothing would make me happier."

"You're being a nasty cow."

"I'm always a nasty cow." Sam laughed, relieved, as always, for the rapport she shared with him. It made the unbearable bearable on a daily basis. "Am I dropping you back at HQ?"

"Nah," he said. "I'll take the Metro. It'll get me home faster."

"Lucky you."

"I'll be super lucky when I get home."

"Do you two newlyweds ever take a night off?"

"Do you?"

"None of your business."

"And yet my sex life is your business?"

"You made it my business when you turned your phone off to get lucky the first time."

"Oh my God, seriously? Did you really just bring that up? That was almost two years ago."

"Some things never get old, like you finally getting laid and then getting yourself shot."

"That was a hundred percent your fault for being a nasty cow."

"No, that was me teaching you a lesson that you had to go and learn a little too well."

"You were scared I was going to die."

"No, I wasn't."

"Yes, you were."

Sam pulled into the closest Metro station and brought the car to an abrupt stop. "Get out."

"Love you too."

"If you're still talking, you're not doing what you were told."

"Have a lovely evening, Lieutenant."

"Yeah, yeah, you too. Don't sprain anything."

"It does get rather athletic at times."

"Out!"

Still laughing, he got out of the car, shut the door and took off jogging into the station.

"Freaking pain in my ass," she muttered as she pulled out of the station and back into traffic, paying no mind whatsoever to whether her detail was following her. Keeping up was their problem, not hers. The phone rang, and she took the call from the department shrink, Dr. Trulo, on the Bluetooth.

"What's up, Doc?" she asked, amusing herself.

"Checking in about our first meeting tomorrow night."

"Ahhh..."

"Honestly, Sam. Don't tell me you actually forgot."

"I didn't forget."

"Liar."

"Everyone is a comedian today. What's the plan?"

"I've reserved the lieutenants' lounge for seven o'clock for the grief group meeting."

Hearing that, Sam wanted to scream at realizing she'd miss another night with her kids, even if it was for a good cause. "I always forget we have a lounge."

"You do, and you were supposed to reserve it. It's a good thing I checked."

"One thing you need to realize about working on a special project with me, Doc, is that you always have to check."

His laughter rang through the car's speakers and made her smile. Where she'd once resisted his attempts to shrink her, he'd since become a trusted friend and colleague. "I figured that out a while ago, which is why I also called all the people on your list to let them know our first meeting is scheduled for tomorrow night."

"You're nothing if not thorough."

"You've got a lot on your plate. I don't mind doing a little extra. The only one on your list I couldn't get in touch with was Roni Connolly."

"And she's the one I most wanted to get there." Sam sighed, resigned to another delay in getting to her family. "I'll stop to talk to her on the way home. See if I can convince her to join us."

"Will I need to remind you tomorrow that you have somewhere to be tomorrow night?"

"Might not be a bad idea."

"You'll be glad to know that your friend Officer Charles has agreed to help with the administrative aspects of our group."

"Is that so? Well, that's awesome news." The young officer had impressed the hell out of Sam with her attention to detail in planning the police funeral for her father. She'd pleaded with the chief to share Officer Charles with her and was thrilled to know she'd be involved in the grief group.

"It is indeed. She can't make the first meeting because she's on duty, but she's going to be helping behind the scenes. You should talk to her about her own history with violent crime and how she came to be a police officer. Fascinating young woman."

"I'll do that, and yes, she is."

"All right, then. I'll talk to you tomorrow."

"Thanks for all you did to get this off the ground, Doc."

"It was your idea. I just took the ball and ran with it."

"I appreciate it."

"Have a good evening, Lieutenant."

"You too."

Though everything in her desperately wanted to get home to her family, she took a detour back into town and parked outside Roni Connolly's building. In the vestibule, she pressed the button for 3C and waited for a response. When there was no answer, she pressed the button a second time.

"Yes?"

"Roni, it's Sam Holland. Could I come up for a minute?"

"Um, sure." She buzzed her into the building, and Sam went inside, letting the door slam behind her.

Hearing pounding on the door had her looking back to see the two agents glowering at her. She went back to let them in. "See if you can keep up, gentlemen." Without waiting for them to reply, she spun around and took the stairs to the third floor two at a time. Outside 3C, she knocked.

Roni opened the door and stepped aside to invite Sam inside.

Sam held up a hand to the two agents, who'd followed her up the stairs. "Wait here."

She could tell Vernon wanted to object to being told to wait outside, but Sam didn't stick around to hear his concerns.

"This is a nice surprise," Roni said in a dull, flat tone that was in direct contrast to the woman she'd been before Sam had shattered her world with the news of her young husband's senseless murder. She'd known her for two minutes before she'd had to deliver that news, and even she could see the difference.

Roni had dark hair that fell to below her shoulders, and while her brown eyes were still sad, they'd lost some of the shock that'd been so present the last time Sam saw her.

Sam followed her to sit on the sofa. "How've you been holding up?" She hated herself for the stupid question. How did she think the young widow was holding up?

"Good minutes, bad minutes." Roni shrugged. "You know how it is. You just lost your dad."

"I do know, but my dad was a lot older than Patrick..."

"A loss is a loss, no matter when it happens."

"True. Remember that grief group I mentioned a while back?" Roni nodded. "What about it?"

"The first meeting is tomorrow night at MPD HQ. I have no idea if the group will be any help at all, but I'd really like to invite you to come if you're able to. I have to believe it'll do some good, you know?"

"Maybe. I'm back to work, and some days are busier than others. I'll have to see how I am tomorrow, but I do appreciate the invite."

"Of course."

"It's really nice of you to come by to check on me. Darren has told me you've asked about me, and that's just such a huge honor with all the people you must deal with." Roni wrote obituaries for the *Washington Star*, where Darren worked.

"I've thought of you so often."

"It means a lot."

"Listen, I'm going to be honest with you. Maybe too honest."

"Um, okay..."

Sam was gratified to see a hint of amusement in the younger woman's eyes. "I'm a shit friend. I'm busier than a one-legged man in an ass-kicking contest. I've got no time for anything. I have no idea what I'm even doing here, but I like you. I'd like to be your friend if you could use an extra one. And I'd totally understand if seeing me is too much of a painful reminder of the worst day of your life. Wait... Are you *laughing*?"

Roni waved a hand in front of her face. "Sorry, but that was funny. I'm a shit friend, but I'd really like to be friends with you. Way to sell yourself, Lieutenant."

"My friends call me Sam."

"Sam," she said with a small smile. "And I'd be honored to be friends with a woman I admire so much."

"Oh jeez. Don't do that. I'm a red-hot mess."

"Well, you'd never know it from the outside looking in."

"If I let you into the inside, you have to promise to not look too hard at the messy parts."

"I promise. Can I tell you something?"

"You can tell me anything. We're friends now."

"Some of my closest friends from before Patrick died have disappeared off the face of the earth. I never hear from them or see them."

"People don't know what to do with other people's grief. I've seen that in my own life."

"It's just that I want you to know, as my new friend, it means a lot to me that you went out of your way at the end of what was probably a hideously long day to come by and see me. You're already doing way better than most of my longtime friends, which is admirable for a shit friend."

"I like you," Sam said, laughing.

"So you said."

"If I pick you up tomorrow night around six forty-five, would you be more or less likely to attend our meeting?"

"Slightly more likely."

"Then I'll be outside tomorrow at six forty-five. Come if you want. Don't come if you're not up to it. I'll come every Tuesday until you decide you might be ready."

"That's a lot to ask of a new friend."

"Maybe you can help me change my track record for being a shit friend."

"Maybe so. Tell me this, girlfriend, what's up with your husband deciding not to run for president?"

"Heard about that, huh?"

"Safe to say the whole world has heard. It's the only story cable news is covering."

"Oh joy."

"Is that why you've got a couple of big dudes following you around?"

"Yep. Nick asked me nicely."

"Just so we're straight—I'm devastated he's not running. I think he'd be a remarkable, inspirational leader."

"Thank you. I think so too, but between us friends, I'm thrilled he's going to be a remarkable, inspirational father to our kids instead."

"I get that, and I respect it, but damn... Other people are *losing* it."

"So I've heard. I try to stay away from that crap so I can act like it's not happening."

"Good plan. Don't turn on the TV tonight."

"Thanks for the advice. I'd better get home so I can see my little ones before they're asleep for the night."

"I'd love to meet my new friend's family at some point."

Sam stood to leave. "That can be arranged. Maybe I'll see you tomorrow. Maybe I won't. Either way is fine."

Roni walked her to the door. "Am I allowed to hug my new friend?"

"Very briefly."

Roni laughed as she hugged Sam. "Thank you so much for the visit, for being my new shit friend, for all of it."

Sam hugged her back. "You may live to regret this friendship."

"I don't think I will."

Sam handed her one of her cards. "My number's on there. Use it anytime you need a shit friend."

"I will. Thanks."

Feeling good about the visit, Sam left the apartment and went down the stairs, hearing the heavy footsteps of the agents behind her. Outside, cold air reminded her that the long winter was coming, and while the winter used to drive her crazy with its endlessness, now it was a chance to hunker down with her love and their kids. Winter didn't piss her off anymore, but plenty of things still did. Such as the agents following her.

She felt good about the conversation with Roni and to see the young woman doing slightly better than she'd been the last time Sam saw her. She hadn't gone in there planning to offer friendship. That'd been spontaneous, but it had felt good to make that overture and to have Roni accept it. She wasn't someone who ran around making new friends on the regular, but she suspected Roni would be worth the effort. From the first day Sam had met her—on the worst day of Roni's life—Sam had felt a connection with her, and she was glad they'd be keeping in touch.

CHAPTER FIFTEEN

It was nearly eight by the time Sam turned onto Ninth Street, which was completely overrun with media and the largest Secret Service presence she'd seen yet since Nick became vice president. "Christ have mercy," she muttered as the agents worked to clear a path for her to get to the checkpoint. Ten minutes later, she parked in her assigned spot outside their home.

She was about to get out of the car when her phone rang with a call from Gonzo's fiancée, Christina Billings. Groaning at yet another delay, she took the call because that's what Gonzo would do for her in the same situation. "Hey."

"Sam! You have to do something!"

"About?"

"You can't let him plead guilty to charges that'll kill his career!"

"I tried to tell him that, but he seems very determined."

"So *talk him out of it.* This is crazy! He was sick when he did what he did. He'd never have done that in his right mind. You know that as well as I do."

"I do know that, but it's not that simple, Christina. Somehow, people in the department found out, and now it's not possible to put the genie back in the bottle."

"People listen to you, Sam. You could fix this for him. *Please.* He's worked so hard on his recovery. Even though he seems resigned to pleading, something like this could wreck him."

"I know," Sam said, sighing. "I've had the same fear, and I've raised it with the commanders. The chief was planning to talk to USA Forrester about it, and I'll follow up with him tomorrow to see where we are."

"Thank you," Christina said, sounding relieved. "He may not be strong enough to fight back on this, but I'm strong enough to fight for both of us."

"Good. He's going to need that."

"Please, Sam. Please don't let this happen."

"I'll do everything I can. I promise."

"Okay. I'm sorry to call you in a panic, but I just now heard of his plan to plead out."

"I would've thought he'd talked to you about it."

"He didn't because he knew what I would say." Christina paused before she continued. "We're finally getting him back. A hit like this... I just don't know if he'd survive it, Sam. He's being so matter-of-fact about it, but you know how he really feels."

"I do, and I've been as upset about it as you are. Any word on a release date?"

"In time for Thanksgiving."

"That's great. I'm so glad to hear that."

"Me too. You have no idea..."

"We're all going to be there for him and for you."

"Thank you."

They said their goodbyes, and Sam closed her phone without the usual smack that gave her such satisfaction. After pondering the situation for a few minutes, she decided to do something she rarely did and called the chief on his cell phone. She saved that card for only the most critical of situations. This certainly counted.

"Hey," he said when he answered. "What's up?"

"This is your niece Sam calling her uncle Joe for a work-related personal favor."

He huffed out a laugh. "Have the zombies arrived and no one told me?"

That made her laugh too. "Not yet, but I'll let you know if they do. This is about Gonzales."

"Ah, yes, and the plea deal, I presume?"

"That deal is total bullshit. He was suffering from PTSD after his partner was murdered right in front of him. Rather than charging him with a crime, we ought to be thanking him for his service."

"You know I completely agree with you, but people found out about it, and now it's out of my hands."

"People meaning Ramsey, who's been digging for shit on my team because of his beef with me."

"I never heard where the info came from, just that it was credible. It was sent anonymously to the USA's office. By the time I heard about it, there were already charges pending."

"Call USA Tom Forrester, Chief. Remind him that Arnold was killed three feet from Gonzo after he let him take the lead for the first time. Gonzo believes he should've taken the bullet himself. We have to at least *try* to fix this."

"I've been talking to Tom and doing what I can. No guarantees."

"I appreciate the effort. Here's what I'm thinking: We have Gonzo make a statement, owning what he did and why and going public with the struggles he's endured since his partner died. It'll be a big ask of him after everything, but I think he'd do it. So he owns what he did and understands that as a law enforcement officer, he should've done better. I think we could spin it in conjunction with Forrester, who could say, in light of Sergeant Gonzales's long stint in rehab and his distinguished career, as well as the circumstances of his partner's murder, he's declining to pursue charges because no one was hurt by what Gonzo did except Gonzo."

"It's a good idea. I'll pitch that to Tom and see what he says."

"Gonzo might object to playing the sympathy card to avoid charges, but I say it's worth a shot. I can probably talk him into it."

"If anyone can, you can."

"Thank you. I think. And thank you for trying."

"Anything for you, kid, as long as you never tell anyone I said that."

"Said what? Have a good night."

"You too."

Sam closed the phone and got out of the car as Nick came down the ramp toward her.

From the checkpoint, reporters began shouting questions at them.

"Why aren't you running?"

"Tell us the truth. Why don't you want to be president?"

"Any chance you'll change your mind?"

"Is it because of the Nelson scandals?"

Nick put his arm around Sam and escorted her up the ramp and into the sanctuary of their home.

Sam nodded to Nate, the Secret Service agent working the door, while wondering if her detail would go home for the night or stay outside. She didn't care enough to ask.

"I was worried when you didn't come in," Nick said.

"I was on the phone. Christina called about Gonzo's plea bargain, asking me to do something to stop it. I called the chief, and he's going to talk to Forrester again tomorrow."

"I hope they can work something out, because it's screwed up that they're even considering charging him."

"Agreed."

"What do you want first? Kids or food?"

"Definitely kids. Are the Littles still awake?"

"Yep. Scotty is reading to them."

"Let's go." As she led the way upstairs, Sam said, "After I close this case, I want a full day with my family. We'll take them to the farm."

"Graham was just saying we haven't been there in too long."

"Maybe we'll sleep over at the cabin." John O'Connor had left Nick a small cabin located a few miles from Graham and Laine's place in Leesburg. They used it as a getaway from time to time. "I hate that I have so little time with the kids on days like this one."

"You give them plenty on the other days. Don't worry. They're very well loved, and they know it."

"Keep telling me that."

"Anytime you need to hear it."

At the doorway, they stopped to watch as Scotty read to the twins, who were snuggled up on either side of him. Seeing the three of them together always made her heart feel too big for her chest, and never more so than when Scotty was in big brother mode.

"One more," Aubrey said when they finished the story.

"No more. You two are up way past your bedtime."

Sam held back a laugh at how much he sounded like his father. She stepped into the room and took Scotty's place between them after he got off the bed. "Snuggle me, little people. I missed you so much today. Tell me everything that happened."

She listened to stories from the front lines of kindergarten, about how Maisy had put glue up her nose, and Taylor got glitter in her eye, and Billy's mom had brought in cupcakes with green icing that turned their tongues green. They had her laughing and nearly crying over how sweet and cute and funny they were. She stayed with them until she could tell they were ready for sleep and then kissed them both good night.

"Cuteness overload," she said to Nick when she rejoined him in the hallway. "And I need to take cupcakes to their class."

"You don't have to."

"I want to."

"Um, where will you get these alleged cupcakes?"

She glared at him as they went downstairs. "I'll make them."

"Oh. Um. Well, do you know how?"

"Yes, I know how. What do you take me for?"

"Is that a rhetorical question?"

"You're full of beans tonight, Mr. Vice President." Sam peered into the oven to see what Shelby had left warming. Enchiladas. Yum. "Is that because you've got the whole country losing its collective mind over your decision not to run?" She grabbed pot holders from the counter and retrieved her dinner.

"I can't believe the way this went down. It never occurred to me I'd be told I was obligated to run. We have people working overnight in the office to handle the phones. It's madness. And Trevor says I need to give another interview because people have more questions."

"Are you melting down on the inside?"

"Not really. I'm in full-on denial mode that this has turned into a much bigger deal than anticipated. Derek also hinted to me that Nelson isn't happy I owned the news cycle today."

"Too bad. When he owns the news cycle, there's murder and extramarital affairs while his wife is being treated for cancer."

"True," Nick said, pouring her a glass of chardonnay and bringing it to her.

"Nothing for you?" she asked, taking a bite of the delicious enchiladas.

"Not tonight. I want to be able to sleep. I'm actually tired."

"The decision has been weighing on you, and now that it's made and set in motion, you can relax. The reaction has nothing to do with you or us. Of course people who like you are disappointed, but that's not our problem. You don't owe them anything more than what you've already given, which is way more than some people ever give to their country."

"I might need some *help* relaxing." He punctuated the statement with waggling brows and a wolfish grin. "My nerves are stretched rather *tightly*."

"Are you, by any chance, using this situation to get lucky?"

"Hell yes, I am, and P.S., my wife is kinda easy that way. I don't need to resort to trickery to get lucky."

"Your wife is *so* easy, but only with you. No one else in this world thinks she's easy, and she likes it that way."

"Speaking of you being a pain in the ass, how'd you make out with the detail?"

"Fine. I told them to leave me the hell alone, and they left me the hell alone."

His lips quivered with amusement. "Thank you for tolerating them and giving me peace of mind."

"I'm tolerating them *temporarily* this *one* time."

He refilled her wineglass and took a sip from his glass of ice water. "Duly noted, my love."

"I officially made a new friend today."

His brows lifted. "For real?"

"Yes, for real."

"You hate people. You don't make new friends."

Sam nearly sneezed wine out her nose at how accurately he summed her up. "I've made a rare exception for Roni Connolly."

"The one whose husband was hit by the stray bullet?"

She nodded. "That's the one."

"Why her?"

"You know, I have no idea, but from the minute I met her and had to give her the most devastating news of her life, I've felt this strange connection to her and a desire to make sure she's going to be okay. Somehow. I can't explain it."

"It's very sweet of you to look out for her."

Sam scowled at him. "Call me a bitch if you must, but do not say I'm *sweet*."

"Sweetest bitch I've ever known."

"Ugh. Next, you'll be telling me I'm *nice*."

"I'd never insult you that way."

God, she loved this man with every fiber of her being.

"But I am kinda concerned about you making a new friend *and* deciding to make cupcakes in the same day. Who are you, and what've you done with my Samantha?"

"I haven't made the cupcakes yet, so don't get too excited."

"If you're around, I'm excited. That's just how it goes."

Scotty came into the kitchen in time to catch that comment and made a loud groan. "Dear God. Does it ever end? Is there ever a time when you're not talking about *that*?"

"We weren't actually talking about *that*, if you must know," Nick said. "We were actually talking about cupcakes."

"Is that, like, a metaphor? We learned about them in English class. It's when you use one word when you mean something else altogether. And with you two, it's always about the something else."

Sam, who'd been trying to hold it together, lost it laughing. She loved him as much as she loved his father.

"It's not funny," Scotty said. "A man ought to be able to get a bowl of ice cream in his own house without having to put up with this nonsense."

Nick bit his lip, clearly trying not to laugh hysterically.

Scotty made a big production of getting out a bowl, a spoon

and the ice cream. "Anyone want some? You could use some cooling off."

"I'll have some," Sam said.

"Make it a double," Nick added.

Scotty served up cookies-and-cream ice cream to the three of them and sat with them at the table. After his second bite, he glanced at them. "I heard what you did today."

"What did we do today?" Sam asked, glancing at Nick. She wanted to hear the details in Scotty's words.

"You went to see that reporter who asked the offensive question, and then you gave her an interview about adoption and proper terminology."

"Oh," Nick said. "That."

Scotty shot him a withering look. "You knew what I was talking about." He took a huge bite of ice cream, and, talking with his mouth full, he said, "It was cool that you did that."

"It was kind of fun," Sam said. "You should've seen the looks we got when we walked into that newsroom unannounced."

"You didn't tell them you were coming?" Scotty asked.

"Nope. We just showed up."

"Holy crap. Imagine minding your own business at work and the VP and his wife come walking in. That reporter must've been shitting a brick."

"I'm supposed to tell you not to talk like that," Sam said.

He rolled his eyes. "Whatever."

"I'm also supposed to tell you it's fresh to say 'whatever' to your mother."

"What*ever*," he said, eyes dancing with glee.

To Nick, Sam said, "Are we going to look back at this as the moment we lost all control of him?"

"I think that might've happened when you encouraged him to blow off eighth-grade math," Nick said.

"That was her finest moment as a mother," Scotty said, offering her a fist bump.

Sam gave him the bump. "Thank you. I thought so too."

"Where are we with the dog conversation?"

"About the same place we were this time yesterday," Sam said.

"That's not progress. We need some progress."

"Christmas is coming," Nick said. "Make a list."

"Here's my list: dog. Any questions?"

"Isn't it your bedtime?" Sam asked.

"Not for another ten minutes, which gives us plenty of time to discuss this dog we're going to get for Christmas. What kind should we get?"

"If we were to get a dog," Sam said, "I'd want it to be a rescue."

"What does that mean?" Scotty asked. "A rescue?"

"That's what they call dogs who are taken in by shelters."

"Oh, like foster kids."

"Not like that at all, because hello, dogs," Sam said. "Not children."

"You know what I mean. They're little people in need of a good home, which means I'm down with adopting a rescue. Can I help to pick him out?"

"If we decide to get a dog, you can help to pick him out," Nick said.

"I can't wait." He took all three of their bowls to the sink, rinsed them and put them in the dishwasher. Then he came to the table and hugged them both. "Thanks again for what you did with that reporter."

"Anything for you, kid." Sam echoed the chief's words to her earlier. "It's what family does for family."

"I'm glad you're my family, even if you're always talking about *that*."

"Not *always*," Nick said, grinning.

"What*ever*." He walked out of the room, letting the kitchen door swing closed behind him.

"What*ever* I did to deserve that kid, I'm going to be eternally thankful for it," Nick said.

"Ditto. He's amazing, even when he's being a cockblocking ass pain who's not letting the dog thing go."

"No, he isn't. We're gonna have to deliver on this, aren't we?"

"I believe we are. But are you sure we're not setting a horrible precedent by letting him wear us down?"

"I'm not sure at all, but I want him to have a dog as badly as he does."

"Same."

They got up, finished the dishes and shut off the lights before heading upstairs.

"How do we know if we're setting a bad precedent?" Sam asked after they'd looked in on the twins and then closed their own bedroom door for the night. "Like, what comes next? A car?"

"He'll want a car when he's old enough to drive, and we'll probably get him one since it'll be easier for us. Not because he thinks he deserves it. He's not that kind of kid."

"True."

"Remember how excited he got when I got him a game console to use when he was visiting us? You'd have thought I'd given him a million dollars, because he'd never had one of his own. He's not so far gone from that life that he's forgotten what it was like. I don't think he'll ever forget where he came from."

"I love him unreasonably. I'm afraid I'd spoil him rotten if you weren't here to stop me."

"Same. If he ever finds out that all he has to do is ask us for anything he wants..."

Sam laughed. "We suck at this."

"Maybe so, but he never doubts how much we love him. We made a rather public statement today to that effect."

Sam raised her hand for a fist bump. "We did good work there."

He wrapped his hand around hers and gave a gentle pull, bringing her into his arms. "Some of our best work."

"You mess with our kids, we're coming for you," Sam said.

"That's right."

"Am I allowed to be silly excited that the whole world knows you're not going to run and that I get to keep you all to myself forever and ever?"

"You're definitely allowed. Feel free to celebrate in any way you see fit."

Sam loved the way his eyes went wide and his mouth fell open when she dropped to her knees in front of him and began working on his belt.

"Always a good choice."

She laughed as she worked her way into the navy suit pants, unzipping him over a suddenly huge bulge. "Why, Mr. Vice President, a girl might think you're happy to see her with this kind of reception."

"I'm very happy to see you. Always."

"So I see—and feel."

"Feel free to do more feeling."

Could he be any more adorable or sexy or perfect for her? Nope. Not possible. Just as she was about to take things to the next level, his cell phone rang with the tone he'd programmed for his chief of staff, Terry O'Connor.

Nick let out a tortured groan. "I have to get that."

CHAPTER SIXTEEN

S am released him and sat back as he fished the phone out of his pocket.

"What's up?" he asked in a gruff tone that probably told Terry exactly what he was interrupting.

Only because she was watching him so closely did she notice shock register on his face. *What now?*

"Are you freaking kidding me?"

His entire body tightened with tension that pissed her off. She'd had him on the way to relaxed.

To Sam, he said, "Turn on the TV. Channel 26."

Sam was almost afraid to do as he asked, but she got up to find the remote. And when she turned on the TV, she had to blink twice in rapid succession to believe what she was seeing. Nick's estranged mother was giving an interview about his decision not to run for president. What the actual fuck?

The caption at the bottom of the screen read, "Nicoletta Bernadino, mother of Vice President Nick Cappuano."

Nick sat on the bed and put the phone on speaker as he stared at the face of his mother, who'd been told all her life she resembled actress Sophia Loren.

Sam sat next to him as they listened to Nicoletta talk with authority about the vice president as if she spoke to him regularly.

She didn't.

When Sam looked at her mother-in-law, she didn't see the serene beauty of Sophia Loren. She saw a shameless user who'd neglected her son all his life and now wanted to capitalize on his success.

"He very much wants to be president, but just not now," Nicoletta said.

"Did you tell her that?" Terry asked.

"I haven't talked to her in months, since I threatened her with legal action if she didn't stay out of my business."

"Might be time to take that legal action to shut her up."

"It's apparently overdue," Nick said, sounding incredulous.

Sam wished she could get her hands on the woman so she could wring her neck. Hadn't she hurt him enough during a childhood full of broken promises? Anytime she crawled out from under her rock, she made trouble for Nick, and Sam wasn't having that.

"Let's not watch this train wreck." Sam shut off the television. "Terry, will you please issue a statement for the vice president?"

"Of course."

"Have it say this: Vice President Cappuano is not in contact with his mother. She has no inside information about his deliberation process and speaks with no authority about or for him. She has been, at best, an occasional walk-on character in his life, which was entirely her choice from the beginning. Anything she says about him, his family or his career should be taken as complete fiction. You got that?"

"Got it."

"Good. Issue it immediately."

"Will do. I'll speak to you in the morning, Mr. Vice President."

"Thank you, Terry," Nick said as he ended the call.

"Now," Sam said, dropping back to her knees in front of him and placing her hands on his thighs. "Where were we?"

He twirled lengths of her hair around his fingers and smiled down at her. "Remind me never to cross you."

The sadness she saw so plainly in his eyes infuriated her. She'd love five minutes alone with her mother-in-law, but there'd probably be blood and paperwork to contend with afterward. "Is it okay to say I hate your mother?"

"It's okay."

"Can we get back to what we were doing before we were so rudely interrupted?"

"You know I never say no to one of your superdeluxe treatments, but would it be okay if we just did this instead?" He gave a gentle tug to bring her to her feet, then wrapped his arms around her waist and leaned his head against her.

Sam wanted to rage over the way his mother continued to hurt him. She ran her fingers through his hair and held on tight, giving him as much love as she possibly could.

"That statement you drafted on the fly was perfection," he said after a long period of quiet.

"I do what I can for the people."

He pulled back to gaze at her. "Thank God I have you and our family."

"You'll always have us. You're our hero, and we love you more than anything."

"Thank you for loving me."

She smiled at the reminder of their wedding song. "Easiest thing I've ever done."

SAM CARRIED THE INCIDENT WITH NICK'S MOTHER AND HIS shattered reaction to it with her as she left the house the next morning after having breakfast with him and the kids. He'd put on a good front for the kids. They probably hadn't noticed the sadness in his eyes, but Sam had seen it and continued to be furious by what his mother could do to him with her selfishness. No doubt the network had paid her to come on and spread her bullshit.

Sam glanced toward the checkpoint, her eyes bugging at the massive media presence, and then groaned when her detail approached her.

"Mrs. Cappuano," Vernon said, "we'd like to drive you today."

"That's not happening. Anything else?"

He started to say something, seemed to think better of it and then shook his head.

"Good, now can you please get me out of here? I've got to get to work."

"Yes, ma'am."

It took her two agents working with six others at the checkpoint to get her through the crowd that shouted questions at her as she drove past them. She picked up bits and pieces of what they were saying: "convince him to run," "his mother," "want to be president," "because of Nelson."

Did they think she was going to stop, roll down her window and suddenly get chatty with them about her husband's career when she'd never said a word about it or him in all the months he'd been in office? Not going to happen in this or any other lifetime. But she was curious about what was being said about them, so she turned on WTOP and caught the broadcast in the midst of covering Nick's decision and the subsequent fallout.

"The vice president's office immediately issued a statement that discredited Ms. Bernadino and referred to the apparent estrangement between Vice President Cappuano and his mother. According to sources close to the vice president, he's never had a relationship with his mother, who was largely absent from his childhood. Ms. Bernadino has given several interviews since her son became vice president, but each time, the vice president has reaffirmed the fact that he's not in contact with her. Last night's statement was the most pointed one yet on the topic of his mother.

"In other news, after the announcement from the vice president that shook Washington's halls of power yesterday, the Democratic National Committee finds itself back to square one with the party's assumed frontrunner out of the race. We've got DNC chair Brandon Halliwell with us for an exclusive interview. Mr. Halliwell, when did you find out the vice president had decided not to run in the next election?"

"A little before the rest of the world heard the news."

"Was it a surprise to you?"

"Not completely. In hindsight, the vice president has been indicating for some time in private meetings and other deliberations that he might not run. I'll admit that I and others within the party leadership had fervently hoped he'd change his mind. That said, I do respect his reasons for sitting this one out."

"Did you expect the outpouring of disappointment and even anger since the vice president released his statement yesterday?"

"That didn't surprise me. I already knew how popular he has become, which is why I was so excited about his potential run. I was disappointed that he decided not to run, so I get why others are too."

They went on to talk about other potential contenders for the Democratic nomination, and Sam could almost feel the lack of enthusiasm in Halliwell's voice. She understood how he felt. No one but Nick Cappuano would do for her either. With her beloved husband in mind, she flipped open her phone and, while stopped dead in traffic, put through a call to Avery Hill. She hadn't yet figured out how to use the Bluetooth to make an outgoing call, but didn't want to admit that to anyone, especially Freddie. He'd take too much pleasure in mocking her.

"Good morning. Don't tell me you're blowing me off this afternoon."

"I reserve the right to blow you off later if my day spins out of control, but that's not why I'm calling."

"What's up?"

"I need an inappropriate personal favor."

"I'm a married man now, Sam. I don't give out those kinds of favors to other women anymore."

Sam snorted with laughter at how his suggestive words were dipped in the sweetest of honey thanks to his accent. "Very funny. This is about Nick's mom. Did you see her bullshit interview last night?"

"I might've caught part of it."

"We have to do something about her. If you could see what it does to him when she slithers out from under her rock... It's unbearable."

"Ugh. That sucks. What can I do?"

"Find her, send some agents to talk to her, put a scare on her?"

"Hmm, well, that might be considered an inappropriate use of government resources."

"Not if you're using your resources to protect the vice president."

"That's true."

"So you'll do it?"

"Where is she?"

"Last I knew, she lived in Cleveland, which is why I called you. I don't have federal jurisdiction like you do."

"I'll look into it. I can't promise you anything, but I will take a look."

"Thank you."

"Regardless of Nick's standing as the VP, this still counts as an inappropriate personal favor."

"Understood. I'll owe you one."

"Nah, it's fine. It'll be fun to scare her into shutting her mouth."

"Trust me when I tell you, almost no one I know is more in need of a scare from the FBI than she is."

"I'll see what I can find out and get back to you."

"Thanks, Avery. How's Shelby feeling? I haven't seen her in a couple of days."

"The mornings are rough, but the rest of the day, she feels good. She's just really tired. Her sister told her to expect this pregnancy to be tougher than when she was expecting Noah because she has to take care of him too."

"I'll check in with her to make sure we're not working her too hard."

"Sounds good. I'll see you this afternoon. Don't blow me off."

"I'll try really hard not to."

He laughed. "You do that."

"Thanks again, Avery. Seriously. I appreciate this, and I know Nick would too."

"We'll do what we can. Talk to you in a bit."

"Have a good one." Sam slapped the phone closed and zipped between two cars to gain access to the lane that was actually moving, earning her a horn blast and a middle finger from the driver she'd cut off. "Sorry. It had to be done."

Her phone rang, and she took the call from Captain Malone on the Bluetooth. "Morning, Cap."

"Morning. Checking in for the latest on McLeod."

"Ugh, I hate that case."

"I'm aware of that, but you still have to solve it, if you can."

"Do I really? We need to pass a law that Homicide resources should only be expended on people who deserve justice."

"I'll get right on that," he said dryly. "In the meantime, where are we?"

"We're working our way, slowly, through all the people who had motive. Today, we're talking to some of the bigger investors, figuring they'd have more motive. But honestly, there's motive everywhere we look. We've also got the husband and the Realtor in lockup, awaiting lawyers."

"I heard the Realtor is raising holy hell and talking about lawsuits."

"She lawyered up. Her lawyer couldn't get there yesterday. That's not our fault."

"Try telling her that."

"I will tell her that when I get around to her today."

"Nick's announcement bumped the twenty-four-seven coverage of the McLeod case out of the headlines. Jesus, Sam. We've never seen this many reporters at HQ."

She glanced in her rearview mirror for the first time since leaving home and was a tiny bit relieved to see the black Secret Service SUV following her. Not that she'd admit that to anyone ever. "Sorry about that. I don't know why they come to my workplace when I've never once given them anything about him."

"It's not your fault your husband crushed the world with his announcement."

"Ouch. You really gotta put it that way?"

"It's true. I've felt a little less optimistic about the future since I heard he's not running."

"Whereas the future is looking bright and rosy from my perspective."

He barked out a laugh. "I'll bet it is."

"I'm not going to lie to you. I'm so relieved. I would've

supported him no matter what he did, but I'm so much happier to support him as a private citizen than as president. VP has been enough of a drag for all of us, but especially for him. The security makes it *so* confining."

"I couldn't do it. I give him credit."

"I do too, but I'll be very glad when his term ends."

"What's he gonna do?"

"He's not sure yet. He's considering his options, but he's got a few years yet to figure it out."

"I'm sure he'll kill whatever he does."

"Thanks. I'm excited to see what comes next." It meant a lot to Sam that the people closest to her loved and respected her husband. That was another thing that had been missing during her first marriage, when her family and friends had done little to hide their contempt for Peter.

"The other thing I wanted to tell you was that I talked to the chief, and he's agreed to give you some latitude to take a look at the Worthington case, but no OT."

Sam felt a charge of excitement at being able to tell Lenore they were going to investigate Calvin's case again. "Thank you. That'll mean a lot to Calvin's mother. She's never given up on trying to get justice for him."

"I remember that case and how we never uncovered a single lead. It was frustrating."

"Who was the lead on it? Do you recall?"

"I think Stahl was. He was a detective then."

A trickle of unease rippled down her backbone. "If he was anything like he was as a lieutenant, I'm sure he left many stones unturned."

"I suppose we'll find out. Have you met with Hill yet?"

"This afternoon. You?"

"Yesterday."

"How was it?"

"Not too bad. Mostly, the Feds are looking to get a handle on roles and responsibilities and interpersonal issues."

"I'm sure my name came up a few times on the interpersonal issues."

"Once or twice."

"I hope you told them it's not my fault the men in our department can't handle a woman who's smarter than they are."

"Not all the men can't handle it, and they know that. I made sure to mention you've had a tough path with your dad being deputy chief when you were first with the department and then a revered injured officer in the later years."

"People like Stahl and Ramsey, and I'm sure others, are convinced the only reason I've ever gotten anywhere was because of who my daddy was. They refuse to believe it could've happened because of *me*."

"The people who matter know that, Sam."

"I know, but it still rankles to be dismissed by idiots who are always looking for someone else to blame for their own failures. It burns Ramsey's ass that I outrank him, but whose fault is that?"

"One hundred percent his. He's had disciplinary issues from the start."

"People like that shouldn't be allowed to go the distance in this career. If they're bad or corrupt, they ought to be drummed out."

"You're preaching to the choir, my friend. I've always believed that."

"So while I have you, Christina Billings called me last night. She's having a stroke over Tommy taking the plea. I called the chief last night, and he agreed to have a conversation with Forrester about it. We have to stop this if we can."

"I agree, but we may have trouble selling it to the rest of the department, including the aforementioned men who can't handle your success, yada, yada."

"I think Gonzo needs to issue a statement, owning it, citing the causes for his poor choice and tell the story of what his life has been like since his partner was murdered. In other words, play the sympathy card."

"I can't see him doing that," Malone said.

"As far as I can tell, it's going to be that or plead to a charge that'll stop his very promising career dead in its tracks."

"We'll have a talk with him when he's ready. In the meantime,

I'll text him and tell him not to sign anything until we can have that conversation."

"Thank you." Sam released a deep breath she hadn't realized she'd been holding as they discussed Gonzo. "It'll mean more coming from you, and it'll buy us some time to consider the options."

"That's the idea. I'll text him right now, make it sound like an order."

"That's perfect. Let me know what he says."

"Will do. So you and the doc have your first grief group meeting tonight, right?"

"That's what he tells me."

"You good for that?" he asked hesitantly.

"How do you mean?"

"Your dad and all that."

"Um, well, define 'good.'"

"I hope it helps you and others to talk about what you've been through," he said.

"You're welcome to come, Cap. Skip was one of your best friends. You have every right to be there if you'd like to be."

"I'll think about that. Thanks for the invite, and I really do admire you and Dr. Trulo for coming up with this idea. It'll help a lot of people."

"We hope so."

"I'll let you get back to work. See you at some point."

"Later." Sam slapped the phone closed and gave silent thanks for good friends who'd helped her through the toughest loss of her life. Knowing so many other people had loved her father and mourned his loss helped to lessen her own grief. His name came up every day, whether it be at work or at home, and the funny stories and sweet memories sustained her as she learned to navigate life without Skip Holland.

CHAPTER SEVENTEEN

Thinking about her father and the grief group had Sam putting through a call to her sister Tracy.

"Morning," Tracy said. "Did you catch the case of the woman who ripped off her friends?"

"Yep, and it's a beast."

"Your husband has the whole world going crazy over his decision."

Sam winced. "And I should've told you guys before it went public."

"Don't worry about that. You have enough to think about."

"Still... Common courtesy and all that."

"We're not sweating it, and you shouldn't either. Did you see his mother on TV last night?"

"Unfortunately, yes. She's so fucking gross. I might've asked Avery to do something about her."

"As in the FBI?"

"The one and only."

"Oh my God! That'd be freaking awesome!"

"That's what I'm thinking too. Put a little scare into her and shut her up. If you could see what it does to him when she reappears... It makes me so furious."

"I can only imagine how badly you want to stab her."

"With every fiber of my being."

"I'm sorry. For you and for him."

"Thanks. I try to tell myself it is what it is, but seeing him hurt makes me crazy."

"It makes me crazy, too, and he's not even my husband."

"Thank you for that. So I wanted to make sure to remind you that the grief group meeting is tonight if you guys still want to come."

"I'm hoping to get there with Ang and Celia. No promises, though. It's minute-by-minute for all of us."

"Trust me, I understand that. At least we'll have three people there besides me and Dr. Trulo." Sam still wasn't convinced she'd actually get Roni to go.

"You'll have more than just us. People need this so badly. I need it. I've been so… I don't know… *off*, I guess you'd say, since Dad died."

"I know what you mean. I feel extremely *off* myself."

"And with Thanksgiving coming… Ugh. I just want to forget it this year."

Thanksgiving had been one of Skip's favorite days of the year. He'd always said he'd eat the big turkey dinner every day if he could.

"He's supposed to be calling me nonstop to ask if I got the turkeys yet and to remind me he's paying for them," Tracy said, sniffling. "I keep waiting for that call."

Sam laughed even as she blinked back her own tears. "And every year, you'd have to tell him, 'Dad, they'll be rancid by Thanksgiving if I get them now.'"

"Right," Tracy said, laughing. "Every year. Same conversation."

"Remember the year you forgot to cook the giblets for him?"

"God, yes. I thought he'd disown me."

"So gross. Who eats that shit?"

Together, they said, "Skip Holland."

"I miss him so much, it makes me ache," Sam said.

"Same. I just had this conversation with Brooke," Tracy said of her nineteen-year-old daughter, "when she asked me how long it would take until it didn't hurt so badly anymore."

"What did you say?"

"I told her it would probably always hurt a little because there's a hole in our lives where he used to be, but he wouldn't want us to let the pain get too big. He'd say he had a good life, and he wants the same for us."

"That's really perfect. Mind if I use that if I need it with Scotty?"

"Go for it. It's the truth. I'm sure of it. That's what he'd want."

"It is."

"I know you're dealing with the added grief of discovering Conklin's involvement and that other officer. What's his name?"

"Hernandez."

"Yeah, him. That has to compound the loss for you."

"It doesn't help. That's for sure."

"I have no doubt that you and everyone involved will get justice for Dad."

"If it's the last thing I ever do."

∼

NICK TOOK THE MALAISE OF HIS MOTHER'S UNEXPECTED reappearance with him to work, dragging after a restless night of not enough sleep. He'd been plagued by old dreams of his childhood and the many days he'd sat by the window of his grandmother's small apartment, waiting for someone who wasn't coming. The scent of Chanel No. 5, the scent of his mother, had wafted through the dream, revolting him. He hated that scent and the reminders of disappointment that came with it.

What was she doing going on TV to talk about him when she hadn't talked *to* him in months? Not since the last time she'd surfaced like algae in a pond to stick her nose into his business during Christopher Nelson's reign of terror, which had led to the murder of Sam's ex-husband in a plot that had shocked Nick to his core. His mother's involvement had only made it worse. The person who should've been protecting him had once again let him down. He ought to be used to it by now, but he never had figured out a way to protect his heart from her cruelty.

It pissed him off that she still had the power to hurt him. By now, he should be long over her ability to crush him, but if last night was any indication, he was a long way from over it.

Terry was waiting for him with the morning security briefing and other matters that required his attention, which kept his mind occupied and off the thing he didn't want to think about. "So about that interview your mother gave last night," Terry said when they'd completed the rest of the items on Terry's usual morning list.

Nick braced himself. "What about it?"

"Trevor is juggling a bunch of inquiries for more information about your relationship with her after the statement from last night."

"Sam does some of her best work when my mother is involved."

"She does. I'm really sorry you have to deal with her like that."

Nick shrugged, as if his mother regularly devastating him was no big deal. "It is what it is. I learned a long time ago not to hope for her to change." His personal cell phone rang. "Ah, look who it is. My dad is probably in a rage today too." He took the call from Leo Cappuano, who had been just as absent as his mother when Nick was a child but had made a concerted effort to be better in recent years. "Hey, Dad."

Terry waved as he stepped out to give Nick some privacy.

"Nick..." Leo was sputtering, which was unusual. "I'm just *beside* myself. What the *hell* is she thinking?"

"I believe she's not thinking so much as profiting."

"Disgusting. I'm so sorry. I wish there was something I could do to make it stop."

"It helps that you called. Try not to let it upset you. That's what I'm doing. And I'm sorry I didn't call you before my decision went public. I should've done that."

"Don't worry about me, although I'll admit I'm a little disappointed I won't get to sleep in the Lincoln Bedroom."

Nick laughed. "I could probably make that happen now if you'd like."

"Nah, I'm just kidding. I hope you know that one of your parents is very proud of you for all you've accomplished and is looking forward to whatever comes next for you and your family."

"Thanks, Dad. I appreciate the call. We're looking forward to seeing you guys at Thanksgiving. Scotty got a new race car driving game he says the boys are going to love."

"We're looking forward to it too. We'll see you next week. In the meantime, take care, son."

"You too." Nick put down the phone and sat back in his chair, resting his head against the leather while wishing he had some control over the tangled emotions his mother stirred in him. He loved her and hated her and wished she were different while also wanting her to go away and leave him alone. He felt all those things in the span of a few seconds, the same things he'd felt all his life where she was concerned.

When he was a child, he hadn't yet figured out how to manage the emotional carnage she left behind. As an adult, he'd tried his best to avoid her and the mess that came with her. But the emotions... They were exactly the same as when she'd promise him a visit and then never show up.

Why was he even thinking about this shit when his life was so great now? Why did he let her suck up his mental energy? Without giving himself too much time to consider the implications, he picked up the phone and called her.

"Nick," she said, sounding surprised.

With one word from her, he realized he'd made a huge mistake. The sound of her voice made him feel like the love-starved child he'd once been, waiting for something, anything from the mother who couldn't care less about him. Then and now. "Why are you doing this? Why are you going on TV and talking about me like you know anything about me or my life?"

"You're my son! Of course I know about you and your life."

"When we haven't spoken in months, you have no right to go on TV and talk about me like you have some sort of inside info when you don't."

"That statement you released was very disrespectful."

"Are you for real right now? You want to talk about what's disrespectful? You wanting nothing to do with me until I became successful and famous, and now suddenly you want your little piece of the action."

"That's not true."

"Oh please. Don't make it worse by lying to me on top of everything else. I don't want to get ugly with you, but I will if you don't stay out of my life and my business. The next time I see you talking about me in any capacity, you're going to face legal action." He should've taken that action after she resurfaced during the Christopher Nelson investigation, but he'd refrained. That, he now knew, had been a mistake. "This is the only warning you're going to get before I play hardball with you."

"Maybe I should go public with my son the vice president threatening to play hardball with his mother."

"Do whatever you need to do. Just keep your mouth shut about me and my family. I won't hesitate to make your life as miserable as you've made mine."

She released a harsh laugh. "Your life has hardly been miserable. Look at where you work."

"No thanks to you. Leave me alone and keep your mouth shut about me. I mean it." He ended the call before she could say something that would further lacerate the heart she'd broken too many times to count. It infuriated him that his hands shook for five full minutes. He was thirty-seven, and she was still getting to him the way she always had.

Closing his eyes, he focused his thoughts on Sam, Scotty, the twins, the family they'd created with their children, Sam's family, his dad, their close friends. He thought of each of the people he loved—and who loved him.

He'd traveled a million miles from that apartment in Lowell, Massachusetts. He worked in the White House. Millions of people knew his name and were crushed he wasn't going to run for president. Why was he letting one miserable excuse for a human being get to him this way?

Gazing at the phone on his desk, he picked it up again and did something he should've done months ago. He called his lawyer friend Andy Simone to figure out how he could prevent her from doing this to him anymore.

Enough was more than enough.

Taking the largest ten investors in Ginny's scheme, Sam and her team hit the streets to start at the top with a plan to work their way down through the list until something popped.

"Most of the time, I feel pretty confident we'll figure out what happened, but not this time," she said to Freddie as they drove to Bethesda in traffic that thankfully wasn't as heavy as usual. They'd waited until after nine to leave HQ, hoping to avoid the worst of rush hour.

"I was saying that to Elin last night, how we have hundreds of people with motive."

The day had only just begun, and Sam already felt exhausted. She hadn't slept well after Nicoletta's performance and Nick's reaction to it.

"Christina called me last night, freaking out about Gonzo accepting the plea," Sam told him.

"She just found out about it?"

"Sounded that way. I talked to the chief, and he's doing what he can with Forrester. Malone was going to text Gonzo and tell him not to sign anything until he has a chance to talk it out with us. We agreed it'd be better coming from him."

"God, I hope he does what he's told."

"Me too. I can't bear the idea of him torching his career because of Ramsey's warpath against me."

"I heard Ramsey is losing his shit over something he got in the interoffice mail."

"I heard that too. Wonder what it was?"

"No idea, but it must've been bad if he's flipping out."

"Must've been." It was all Sam could do not to giggle like a fool. What goes around comes around, and when you're an asshole like Ramsey was, you had to figure there was plenty of shit to be found. They'd barely had to try to find it.

"Heard about Nick's mom spouting off on TV again last night."

"Yeah, she's nothing if not consistently awful."

"I hate that for him so much."

"Me too. You have no idea. It crushes him when she profits off her association to him, such as it is."

"It's disgusting," Freddie said.

"Sure is."

"Were we able to track down info about the Alinos, the friends with the parents with Alzheimer's?"

"Jeannie talked to Mrs. Alino this morning, and they've spent the last two days in the hospital with Mr. Alino's father, who has some sort of infection. Neither of them has left the hospital, and she said they have nurses who can attest to that. When Jeannie asked if there was anything she could add to the investigation into Ginny's death, Mrs. Alino said she had nothing to say."

"So that's a dead end."

"Jeannie is going to the hospital to confirm their alibi information."

"I keep thinking about Ginny stealing from friends who had parents battling Alzheimer's. That's sociopathic."

"Completely."

"Jeannie also said none of the neighbors noticed anyone cleaning something outside the house on Sunday."

"One dead end after another."

Their first stop was at the home of VocalExchange, a recording studio that occupied the top floor of an office building off Rockville Pike. Naturally, they had to contend with a receptionist to get to Mark Townsend, the studio's owner.

"Do you have an appointment?" the young woman asked.

"Do we have an appointment, Detective Cruz?" Sam asked with long-suffering patience.

"We don't need one," Freddie said. "We're cops investigating a murder. Tell him we can do it at his place or ours. His choice."

"Ah, just a minute," the receptionist said, scurrying through a set of double doors.

"Mean and scary," Sam said, chuckling.

"I've learned from the best."

"If only they knew what an empty threat that really is. Like we're gonna haul his ass all the way downtown in this traffic."

"Right? Not to mention the paperwork. How long you giving her before you go Sam Holland on her?"

"One more minute."

While they waited, Sam perused a brochure about the studio and learned they did a wide range of voice-over work for radio and TV commercials, audiobooks and a variety of other mediums.

The receptionist returned with seconds to spare. "Right this way."

CHAPTER EIGHTEEN

As they followed the woman through the double doors, Freddie flashed a smug smile at Sam.

Being mean and nasty didn't come naturally to him the way it did to her. It made her ridiculously proud to see him assert himself during an investigation.

Unlike most of the offices they visited, this one was mostly studios with glass fronts facing a main corridor. People were working inside several of the studios they passed on their way to Townsend's office, which was down another corridor. The receptionist gestured for them to go in.

"Thank you," Freddie said to her as he went by, always polite, even when trying to be mean and nasty.

Sam figured Townsend to be in his mid-fifties. He had salt-and-pepper hair and a harried way about him, as if he had more to do than he could possibly squeeze into his awake hours. She knew what that was like.

They showed their badges.

"Lieutenant Holland, Detective Cruz, Metro PD," she said.

He sat back in his chair, eyeing her with the curiosity she'd come to expect since Nick became VP—especially from men. They probably wondered why the VP "allowed" his wife to run around without a detail, solving murders. If only they knew no one "allowed" her to do anything. "What can I do for you?"

"We're investigating Ginny McLeod's murder," Sam said.

"I'm surprised anyone is wasting time or resources on her. Trust me when I tell you, she wasn't worth it."

"We've heard that from a few people, but our job is to get justice for her whether she deserves it or not."

"What about justice for the people she defrauded?" Bitterness dripped from his every word. "When do we get justice?"

"How did you know Ginny?"

"I went to high school with Ken. We've been friends since then. Or we were until his wife decided to put her mark on me. Do you have any idea how hard I've worked to build this business? To build a life for my wife and kids? I was five years from retirement, and now..." He shrugged. "I was going to turn the business over to my oldest son, but now I'll have to sell to have any chance of ever retiring. That's what she took from me. The legacy I'd hoped to leave my children."

"How much did you invest with her?"

"Three quarters of a million."

Sam held back a gasp. Yes, Ginny had been sinister in her plot, but her victims had been somewhat easily led to give up that kind of money for something that might or might not pay off.

"I can tell you're wondering what kind of fool invests that kind of money in something like this, but you had to know Ginny to fully appreciate how she managed to pull this off. She was very convincing that this was the opportunity of a lifetime, the chance to double my money without having to lift a finger. I kept thinking it was too good to be true, but for every question I had, she had an answer. My wife and I did our due diligence. We talked to other investors Ginny worked with who'd seen amazing results, or at least they said they had."

"Do you recall who the people were who attested to her investment success?"

"I gave all that info to the IRS as part of their investigation, but it didn't lead anywhere. The names were fake, the stories were fake. It was all fake, except for the fact that she took our money, and now it's gone. That's very real." He paused and then glanced at her. "Have you spoken to Tina Goss?"

"We haven't heard her name," Sam said, glancing at Freddie for confirmation.

He shook his head.

"Who is she?" Sam asked.

"Her husband, Jack, was one of the investors. He took his own life after Ginny's scheme was uncovered. You should talk to Tina." Townsend seemed to think better of giving her the info. "I don't know why I'm helping you. I don't care who killed Ginny. The person who killed her did us all a favor getting rid of her, except now, of course, we'll never know if she stashed the money somewhere."

"Where were you on Sunday afternoon?"

The question seemed to shock him. "You aren't asking if I killed her, are you?"

"I'm asking where you were on Sunday afternoon."

"I was right here, Lieutenant. Working, like I do seven days a week, because I don't have time to waste if I want to try to earn back some of what I lost. I work every day."

"Was anyone else here with you?"

"One of my sound engineers was here."

"Could we please speak to him or her?"

Though he was clearly pissed, he picked up his desk phone, made a call, asked the sound engineer to come to his office.

After a few uncomfortably quiet minutes, a knock on the door preceded a younger man into the room. "You wanted to see me?" He did a double take when he saw Sam.

She got that a lot these days.

"These MPD detectives are investigating the murder of Ginny McLeod. They're wondering where I was on Sunday afternoon."

"Uh, you were here. From about eleven to seven or so, when we finished up."

"And your name is?" Sam asked.

"Rob Heinke."

"Spell the last name for me." Sam wrote it down. "And your phone number?"

"Why do you need that?" Townsend asked.

"In case we have other questions."

"Like what? He told you I was here from eleven to seven. What other questions would you have for him?"

Sam glanced at the younger man, who seemed undone by the entire thing. "Your number."

He looked to Townsend before shifting his gaze back to her and reciting the number.

"Thank you," Sam said.

"You can go on back to work," Townsend said.

Heinke hightailed it out of there as if his ass was on fire. She had that effect on people.

"I don't know what else you would need from him."

"We've learned to gather all the information we might ever need," Sam said. "So we don't have to backtrack."

"I didn't kill her, but I'm glad someone else did."

"I've heard that from others."

"I'm sure you'll hear it a few more times before you're done."

"Where would we find Tina?"

Townsend seemed hesitant to provide the information, but pulled out his phone and scrolled through to find her in his contacts. "She works at home in Rockville." He gave them the address. "Please don't tell her I sent you. The poor woman has had enough to deal with without thinking I've turned on her too."

"Why would it matter if you turned on her?"

"Because we're friends. After what Ginny put us all through, some of us have become close in our shared agony."

"How close are we talking?" Sam asked.

He stared at her, all but simmering with rage. "What the hell is that supposed to mean?"

"You know what it means. Were you or *are you* more than friends with Tina?"

"I, uh, I don't have to answer that. My personal business is just that."

"Not during a homicide investigation, it isn't. Answer the question, or we'll take you in for a formal interview downtown. Your choice."

"How is this relevant to the investigation?" he asked, sounding incredulous.

"Everything is relevant when it involves a homicide, Mr. Townsend. We'd appreciate it if you'd answer the question and stop wasting our time."

"I... I became friends with both of them—Jack and Tina—after we started to fear we'd been scammed."

"How did you meet them?"

"They went to the press about their suspicions. This was when we were still trying to get the Feds to take us seriously. Long before the official investigation began. When I saw them quoted in an article about a potential real estate scam, I reached out to them, and we began talking. We had a lot in common."

Townsend paused, ran a trembling hand over a face marked by exhaustion and tension. "Jack... He was out of his mind over it. Everything he'd worked so hard for, just gone. And for a long time, no one seemed to care. We had what we believed was proof she'd stolen hundreds of thousands from us, and we couldn't get the FBI to take our calls or to listen to our complaints, even with one of us having a friend who was an agent. We filed reports with our local police departments, who gave the matter a cursory glance. It was all so frustrating, especially since Ginny was still living large while we were coming to the realization that we'd been totally fucked over by a *friend*. It was all so unbelievable."

Sam took copious notes as he spoke.

"We became friends and allies in our efforts to get justice for ourselves and what we knew had to be other victims. And then... Just when I thought it couldn't get any worse, Tina called me with the horrible news that Jack had taken his own life." Townsend's eyes filled with tears. "That news hit me like a fist to the gut. I couldn't breathe."

Sam gave him a minute to collect himself, waiting as patiently as she could for him to get to the point.

"I went to see Tina that night, to offer what support I could, and I started visiting her regularly, looking out for my friend's widow."

"Did your wife visit her too?"

He shook his head. "She chose to take more of a hands-off approach to the entire situation. She was upset about it, for sure, but she said she couldn't let it consume her the way it had me and Jack. And she blames me, of course, for the entire mess. I was the one who was gung ho to invest. She didn't think we should, and when she was proven right, well... Our marriage has been in name only since then."

"So you were visiting Tina alone?"

"Yes."

"Are you romantically involved with her, Mr. Townsend?"

"You have to understand what we've been through..."

Sam had to bite back the urge to scream. "Are you involved with her?"

"Yes! I'm involved with her! I'm in love with her. Are you happy? Does that help you figure out who killed Ginny?"

"No, it doesn't, but it helps us to understand who might've had motive to kill her."

"Tina didn't kill her."

"How do you know that?"

"Because I was with her Sunday night when we found out she'd been killed, and Tina was genuinely shocked. And dismayed, because we all know that with Ginny gone, it becomes that much more difficult to recover any of our money. We'll have to deal with her estate and all that. I doubt any of us will live long enough to see this tangled, twisted mess resolved. No one knows where the money is. Not even Ken, or so he says."

"Do you think he knew what she was doing?"

"Not at the beginning, but later on... I can't see how he didn't know. How would she explain the sudden windfall?" He glanced at Sam, seeming hesitant and uncertain. "Are you going to have to make my relationship with Tina public?"

"Not unless one of you had a hand in killing her or knows who did."

"We didn't."

"So you say. But we've had people with rock-solid alibis turn out to be murderers. Just happened recently, in fact. So you'll pardon us for remaining skeptical of everyone who had the kind of motive you did."

"Investigate me to your heart's content," he said with a shrug.

"You won't find me anywhere but here, with Tina and then at home on Sunday. All I do is work, and the only pleasure in my life is with Tina. My marriage is basically over because I made the huge mistake of investing with Ginny. I'd give anything to be able to have that decision to do over again. Anything at all."

Sam handed him a card. "If you think of anything else that might be relevant, or have any thoughts about who might've been angry enough to kill her, call me. My cell number is on there."

"The list of people angry enough to kill her is long."

"We're aware of that. Thank you for your time. Don't tell Tina we're coming."

"Why not?"

"Because I told you not to. We'll see ourselves out." On the way to the parking lot, Sam said to Freddie, "For fuck's sake. What part of 'don't tell her we're coming' does he not get?"

"The part where he has to do what you tell him."

She huffed out a laugh. "Men hate being told what to do by women."

"Just for the record, I don't mind it."

"That's because women rule your life at home and at work."

"And I wouldn't have it any other way."

"You were good in there with the receptionist. I like to see your assertive side coming out."

"Thanks. I think…"

When they were back in the car, Sam took a call from Malone. "What's up?"

"Lawyers for the husband and Realtor are here."

"All right. We'll be back soon."

"The Realtor's lawyer is making a huge stink about unlawful arrests and the usual nonsense."

"Nothing unlawful about us detaining a material witness in a homicide investigation."

"You know that, and I know that…"

"No worries. I'll take care of her when I get back."

"Where are you?"

"Bethesda."

"Oh damn. I'll let them know it's going to be a while."

"I've got one more stop to make, and then we'll be in."

"Got it."

Sam closed the phone and started the car, heading for the parking lot exit. "You got me an address for Tina yet?"

Freddie shot her a scathing look. "Of course I do."

"I had no doubt."

His GPS directed them to Rockville.

"Thank you for taking care of this before we go back into town."

"There was no way I was driving way the hell out here again if I could avoid it." And then she recalled the meeting she had scheduled with Hill. That was going to mess up her entire day.

Tina lived in a modest two-story home in a well-established neighborhood. The house was white with black shutters and mature landscaping.

"When I was a kid, I used to think it would be so cool to live in a place like this," Freddie said of the tree-lined streets with sidewalks and well-cared-for homes. "I thought people who lived in neighborhoods like these didn't have any problems."

"Now you know better. Everyone has problems."

"Right, and sometimes people with bigger houses have bigger problems. Take this lady, for instance. She had her life figured out. A long marriage with a man she probably still loved until they were taken in by a con, and it all went to crap. Now he's dead, she's financially devastated, and inside the beautiful house is a life in ruins."

"That's very profound, young Freddie. And sadly true."

"It's so sad. She thought she had it all until an unscrupulous con artist took it from her." He sighed. "I'd much rather be investigating Calvin Worthington's murder than Ginny McLeod's. He's the kind of innocent victim I wanted to seek justice for when I became a detective."

"Me too, but we have to remember that nothing is justification for murder, not even the most despicable acts."

"Keep reminding me."

"Will do." Sam pressed the doorbell and listened to it chime inside the house. "Another scary-ass doorbell."

"You love them almost as much as you love receptionists."

"I love them even more." She peered through the beveled glass beside the front door and rang the bell again. "Here she comes."

On the other side of the door, a woman said, "Who is it?"

Wary after the gun incident with Clarissa Haverson, Sam called out to her. "Lieutenant Holland, Detective Cruz, MPD."

They raised their badges to the window next to the door.

A series of locks disengaged before the door swung open to reveal a middle-aged woman with fading blonde hair, lines around her eyes and her mouth set in a tight, uncompromising expression. "What can I do for you?"

"We'd like to speak with you about the murder of Ginny McLeod," Sam said.

"I have nothing to say about her."

"I understand what you've been through—"

"No, you don't. Your young, handsome husband is very much alive. Your life hasn't been ruined by someone you thought was a friend. You have no idea what I've been through."

"I'm sorry, I only meant that I understand why you feel the way you do about Ginny, but our job is to figure out who killed her."

"It's a waste of taxpayer dollars. Whoever killed her did this world a huge favor. Now she can't ruin anyone else's life the way she ruined mine and my husband's and so many other people's."

"While we understand your dislike for her—"

"I don't dislike her. I *hate* her. I hate what she did to me and Jack and other people who worked their whole lives for what they had only to have it taken from them—by a supposed *friend*. I hate her."

"We're still required to investigate her murder. We can talk here or at our place. Your choice."

Glaring at Sam, she stepped back to let them into her house.

CHAPTER NINETEEN

Sam rolled her eyes at Freddie and followed Tina into the house that was as nice on the inside as it was on the outside. They were shown into a cozy living room where Sam and Freddie sat together on a love seat. She'd have to make a joke about that later.

"What do you want to know?" Tina asked.

"How did you know Ginny?"

"We went to college together."

"How did you and your husband decide to invest with her?"

"She made us an offer we thought would be stupid to refuse. She had all the answers, testimonials, financials. You name it, she had it. We were bowled over the same way everyone else was by a no-lose proposition. It was supposed to take twelve to eighteen months, and then we'd see a big return." She paused and glanced directly at Sam. "I know you have to be thinking how stupid we all are, but if you'd heard what we heard, you would've done the same thing."

No, I wouldn't have, Sam thought, but she kept that to herself. Her father, the cynical cop, had always told her and her sisters that if something seemed too good to be true, it almost always was. Usually he was referring to boys, but the lesson applied universally.

"When did you realize the investment was a scam?"

"When the twelfth month came and went without a word from her. She went completely silent on us, and later we found out she'd done the same to the other investors."

"What did you do when you couldn't get in touch with her?"

"At first, we panicked. She had most of our savings and *wasn't returning our calls*? How could that be? So we went to her house, and Ken said she wasn't home. He didn't know where she was or when she'd be back." Tina swallowed hard and seemed to fight tears. "I had to keep Jack from storming into the house. He was convinced she was in there, and Ken was covering for her."

"What did you do then?"

"We went to the Rockville Police Department, filed a report, met with detectives and were told they were going to look into it."

"Did they?"

"They said they did, but they weren't able to locate Ginny either. We asked them to get a warrant to search their house, and they said they'd try, but that never happened. So we started calling the FBI every day until we got through to an agent who took our report and promised to look into it. We never heard from him again."

Sam hated the way law enforcement had failed these people. "I'm sorry you had that experience."

"I am too, because in all the time that was wasted, Ginny had the chance to hide the money in places we'll probably never locate. We'll never get back all those months that could've been spent stopping her before one of the other victims finally got someone to take this seriously."

"Where were you on Sunday?"

"Why do you want to know?"

"We're asking everyone who had motive where they were when she was killed."

"I didn't kill her. Believe me, I wanted her alive so she could tell us what the hell she did with all that money. The IRS and the FBI went through everything and couldn't find where she spent more than a million of the twenty-two million she stole. So where's the other twenty-one million? Only she knew that, and now..." She shrugged with a helplessness that sparked sympathy in Sam. She could only imagine how frustrated and heartbroken Tina had to feel. She'd lost a lot more than her life savings to Ginny. "I was at my tennis club from eleven to two on Sunday. My club membership is the one thing I managed to hang on to after we lost the money."

"Is there someone who can confirm that?"

"My friend Celeste was with me the whole time."

"Can we please have her number?"

Glaring at Sam, Tina found the number on her phone and recited it.

Sam wrote it down, tore the page out of her pad and handed it to Freddie, who got up to go outside to make the call.

"Tell me about the day your husband died."

"Do I have to?"

"I'd appreciate it if you would."

Tina sagged into the corner of her sofa, arms crossed as she fixated on a spot behind Sam. "He'd been so upset. So, *so* upset. I suggested he play golf with some friends while I visited our daughter. She'd had a baby three weeks earlier, so I'd been spending a lot of time helping her. I think about that now and just wonder if I'd been around more, I might've known what he was planning. But I had no idea. I knew he was devastated over what Ginny did, but it never occurred to me that he would... I just didn't think..."

She blinked furiously and then swiped at tears. "How could he leave me to deal with this alone?" Shaking her head, she wiped more tears.

Sam made an effort to be patient and not rush her.

"I came home and couldn't find him. I checked upstairs and in the garage before going out to his woodshop when I noticed the door was open. He hadn't been out there in months, since before we realized Ginny had stolen our money, so I took it as a good sign. I vividly remember walking out there, feeling hopeful that maybe we were going to get back on track, that we would be okay."

Tina dropped her head. "But when I went in there, he... He was hanging from the rafters. I screamed and went to him and tried to get him down, but he was gone. Later, I found out he'd been there more than three hours by the time I found him. He waited until he knew I'd be gone awhile." Wiping away more tears, she looked up at Sam. "That's what she did to us, Lieutenant. She took our money, stole my husband's will to live, denied our daughter and grandson their father and grandfather. She took everything we had, and I blame myself. She was my friend, and I was excited to invest in her business. I talked Jack into it, and now he's dead."

"Do you know of anyone who might've specifically threatened her or said they wanted her dead?"

"Everyone involved joked about wanting to have her killed. No one meant it, of course. It was a coping mechanism."

"Did anyone seem to take it more seriously?"

She thought about that for a second. "Not that I ever saw. It was all talk that came from devastation and despair. If there's any silver lining to this nightmare, it's that I've made a lot of new friends."

"Including Mark Townsend?" Sam felt like a complete asshole for kicking Tina when she was already down, but she had to know if there was anything more to their association than two people seeking comfort from each other.

She blinked several times, clearly shocked. "What about him?"

"I understand the two of you are romantically involved."

"We... I... He's been a very good friend to me since Jack died."

"I'm going to be honest with you, Tina. We've already talked to him. We know it's more than just friends."

"He... He *told* you that?"

"He did, because he understands we're running a homicide investigation here, and the details matter. I'm honestly not looking to make anything worse for you. I promise. I just want to understand your relationship with Mark and figure out if it has any relevance to the murder of Ginny McLeod."

"It doesn't. We had nothing to do with that, but neither of us was sorry to hear she was dead. When you treat people the way Ginny did..."

"No one deserves to be murdered, Tina. Not even Ginny."

"Some people do," she said, her eyes flashing with fury. "Some people don't deserve to walk among the rest of us because they're so indecent, so morally bankrupt that the world is a better place without them."

"Maybe so, but murder is still illegal, and as such, it's our job to figure out who killed her. Tell me the details of how you became involved with Mark Townsend."

"I don't see how it's relevant."

"You don't have to. It's relevant to me, thus you have to answer the question."

"And if I don't?"

"We'll arrest you, take you downtown to be processed and hold you overnight to be arraigned."

She blanched. "On what charges?"

"Obstructing a homicide investigation."

"Because I don't want to answer personal questions that have nothing to do with Ginny McLeod?"

"Your relationship with Mark Townsend does have to do with her. Without her, you never would've met him. And as of right now, you're officially wasting my time, which is a secondary offense. So what's it going to be? Are we going to talk here or downtown?"

While Tina visibly fumed for a full minute, Sam counted down in her mind, giving her ten more seconds before she was going to be taken into custody.

"Fine. I'll tell you, but for the record, I still say it's none of your business."

"Noted."

Freddie came back in, handed Sam the paper she'd given him with the tennis partner's phone number that now had a big checkmark on it. He sat next to her.

"Tina is going to tell us about her relationship with Mark Townsend," Sam said.

"Ah, gotcha," Freddie said.

Tina glared at both of them as the words came out through a clenched jaw and tight lips. "Jack and I met Mark around the time we figured out Ginny had scammed us. We commiserated, spent time with Mark and his wife until she basically stopped speaking to him because she was so angry about him insisting they invest with Ginny."

Sam took notes as Tina spoke. She was now interested in speaking to Mark's wife, whereas she hadn't been before. This was why she forced people to talk about things they'd prefer not to discuss, because you never knew what additional tidbit would surface in the retelling from a different individual.

"Mark would talk to Jack and me about it, how it felt unfair to him that she was fully on board until it became clear they'd been scammed, and then it was all his fault. He said they had epic, screaming fights for weeks, until she finally quit talking to him altogether. That, he said, was a huge relief. He would come over, have a beer with Jack, commiserate on the latest with the investigation. The three of us became close friends. Like comrades in a war, of sorts. Our war against Ginny.

"And then, when Jack died, Mark helped me with everything— funeral arrangements, estate stuff, lawyers, all of it. He was just so there for me in a way my daughter and friends couldn't be because they were so devastated. I was so devastated. I found myself turning to Mark for comfort as well as support. And after a while, I realized I had genuine feelings for him. I was widowed, and he was basically estranged from his wife... There's nothing illicit about our relationship. We're two lonely, wounded people finding comfort in each other."

"Is there any chance his wife knows you're more than friends?" Freddie asked.

"I don't know what she knows. We don't talk about her. They don't have the money to get divorced, so they're forced to live together. From what Mark says, she stays in her part of the house, and he stays in his."

Sam couldn't conceive of living like that. It reminded her too much of her miserable first marriage during which she'd go days without actually speaking to Peter, usually when he was punishing her for some perceived transgression. Thinking about that horrible time in her life could always make her feel furious with herself about what she'd put up with for far too long.

"You're not going to make our relationship public, are you?" Tina asked.

"Not unless it plays into Ginny's murder in some way."

"It won't. Neither of us had anything to gain by killing the only person who knew where the money was stashed."

As she always did, Sam handed over her business card. "If you think of anything else that might be relevant, call me. No matter how trivial it might seem."

Tina took the card and got up to show them out.

"We appreciate your time," Sam said at the door. "And I'm sorry for your losses."

"Thank you."

When they stepped outside, the door clicked shut behind them, and the locks reengaged.

"Don't be envious of people who live in nice neighborhoods like these," Sam said to Freddie as they walked to the car. "The beautiful facades often hide the suffering within. People look at someone like Tina living in that beautiful home and think she has it made, when that's not true. Her life inside that beautiful home is in ruins."

"All because a friend talked her out of her money."

"I want to know if there's a video of Ginny's sales pitch, because if there is, I'd love to see what was so incredibly special about her that she could talk people into parting with their life savings."

"I'll check the federal files again to see if there's anything like that, but I didn't see anything the first time I looked."

"I just feel like my bullshit-o-meter would be registering in the red zone if she tried to get me to part with my money. Didn't anyone think, 'Hey, maybe this is a massive con'?"

"You would have because you're preconditioned to think the worst of people. Someone like Tina, she doesn't think that way. She hasn't seen what you have."

"True." Sam glanced at the clock, which inched closer to noon. When she thought of how many hours she had to get through before she could go home... Ugh. And tonight was the grief group too. *Double ugh.* "Me and my big ideas."

"Which big idea are we lamenting now?"

"The grief group."

"I thought you were excited about that."

"I'm as excited as it's possible to be about grief, but it's going to keep me at work late tonight, which means no time with the kids. I hate that."

"You've become such a mommy."

"Sometimes, I think I suck at it. I'm gone more than I'm home."

"You don't suck at it. You love them, and they know that."

"Still, I feel like they deserve better than what they get from me most days."

"Sam, come on. You have the kind of job that takes a ton of mental energy and time. They know that. They don't want anything more than your love, which is so much more than what many kids have. It's the most important thing you can give them."

"More important than my time?"

"They have what they need—a safe, loving home, and they're surrounded by people who'd do anything for them. They're lucky kids, and they know it."

"Scotty does. The twins had it better with their parents than they'll ever have it with us."

"Well, of course they did. They were their parents. They'll always be the A team. But you guys make for a damned good B team, if you ask me."

"That's nice of you to say. Thanks. I have a lot of insecurities where they're concerned. Their mother was incredible. She was the craft mom, the baking mom, the playdate mom, the room mom. And then there's me."

"You love them. That's all they need."

"I hope so."

"So what's our plan?"

Sam thought about that for a minute. "I want you to go find Mark Townsend's wife and interview her. I'll jump on the Metro back to HQ to do the interviews with Ken McLeod and Realtor Barbie."

"Ohh, Mom's letting me take the car."

"Don't let anything happen to it."

Rolling his eyes, he took the keys from her and got into the driver's seat. "You know it's going to be, like, thirty minutes on the train, right?"

"I'm aware of that, but thanks for letting me know."

"You could go with the Secret Service."

Sam had almost forgotten about her detail. "Ugh, no way. I'm not giving them the satisfaction."

"You realize there'll be actual *people* on the train, right?"

He was so fresh, but also so funny. "Yes, I've heard that others often use the Metro. But again, thanks for checking."

"And you understand that those people will be staring at you and wondering what the hell the second lady is doing on public transportation, correct?"

"For fuck's sake, Freddie. Shut up!"

He cracked up laughing. "Oh, to be a fly on that wall. Take the Red Line to Gallery Place and then the Yellow Line one stop to National Archives."

"How do you know this by heart?"

"Um, because I grew up here and have been riding the Metro my whole life?"

"I grew up here too, but I don't know the Metro map by heart."

"There's so much I could say to that, but I'll refrain out of respect for my superior officer."

"Good call, grasshopper."

"When do I get to graduate from grasshopper to murder hornet or something cool?"

"You're not there yet. You might be approaching mosquito status in the near future." Sam had to bite her lip to keep from laughing at her own joke. That was a good one, if she did say so herself.

"I can hear you trying not to laugh," he said.

Sam hated when people knew her so well that she couldn't get away with anything. "You gotta admit... It was a good joke."

"No, it wasn't."

"Yes, it was."

They bickered all the way to the Rockville station, where he pulled into the Kiss & Ride lot.

"Get out," he said.

She glared at him. "Watch your mouth, Detective Mosquito. You know what we're after with Townsend's wife, right?"

"Duh, yes, I think I can handle it."

"Bring me back a thread to pull, and I'll consider making you a yellow jacket."

He snorted. "Gee, thanks."

"I think yellow would look good on you, grasshopper. Don't get shot or anything when you're without supervision."

"I'll try my best not to."

Sam felt reluctant to leave him for some reason, which she immediately shrugged off as silly. He was a well-trained police officer, thanks in large part to her. He'd be fine. He'd better be, she thought as he drove off, and she headed inside to hitch a ride downtown on the Metro.

CHAPTER TWENTY

S he drove him to drink, but he loved her anyway, Freddie thought as he dodged through traffic on his way to Mark Townsend's home in Potomac, another of those communities that had sparked envy in him as a child. Since it would take him about twenty minutes to get there, he put through a call to his wife.

Weeks after tying the knot, he still loved to refer to the exquisite Elin Cruz as his *wife*. Having a wife was the best thing ever.

"Hey," she said when she picked up, sounding breathless.

Her breathlessness reminded him of things he had no business thinking of in the middle of a workday.

"Freddie? Are you there?"

"I'm here, babe. What's up?"

"Just working out. You?"

Picturing her sweaty and disheveled after a workout was another thought he shouldn't be having while at work. "On my way to Potomac in Sam's car, so I figured I'd say hi while I'm driving."

"Where's Sam?"

"She took the Metro back to HQ."

"She did? What's up with that?"

"Desperate times. We've been pounding a lot of pavement out

in the sticks, and neither of us wanted to waste the time driving back out here. One of us had to get back to HQ, so we did a divide and conquer."

"I can't picture her on the Metro."

Freddie laughed. "Me either. I had to remind her that there'd be other people there and she needed to be nice."

"She'll hate that."

"Yep. I'm sure there'll be some good stories about her ride on the Red Line."

"No doubt. Any luck figuring out who killed the woman who stole from her friends?"

"Not yet, but she gets more reprehensible with every new person we talk to."

"I just can't figure out what her plan was once everyone figured out they'd been scammed."

"Who knows? Maybe she intended to be long gone by then, but it didn't work out."

"Maybe so. How would she be able to show her face in her life after conning everyone she knew?"

"She wouldn't. Sam is talking to the husband again when she gets back to HQ. Maybe he can shed some light."

"I'd be interested to know that. I mean, anyone who steals from the people closest to them can't be planning to stick around afterward. I wouldn't. I'd be heading somewhere warm and tropical."

"That's good to know. I'd want to be able to find you."

"Duh, I'd take you with me."

Freddie laughed. "Well, that's a relief, but please don't swindle our family and friends. I kinda like my life just the way it is."

"Me too. People at the gym are talking about Nick deciding not to run."

"What're they saying?"

"Most of them are super disappointed. They had their hearts set on a Cappuano administration."

"I had my heart set on it too."

"I know. Oh well. I give him credit for having his priorities straight. So many people would put their own ambition ahead of everything, even their own family."

"Not Nick. He's waited forever to have what he has now with Sam and the kids."

"I admire him for many reasons. This is just another one."

"Do I need to be concerned about you admiring the VP?"

"Who's the husband of your partner? I don't think so."

Her dry, sarcastic tone always amused him. "Good to know."

"You aren't still worried about silly things, are you, Detective Cruz?"

"Of course not."

"Because it would indeed be silly for you to worry about me wanting anyone but you."

"Duly noted."

"In fact, I'd be happy to give you a reminder of who I really want when you get home."

"Gulp."

She lost it laughing. "I thought you might like that."

"I always like that."

"You don't know any better." She loved reminding him that she'd been his first and only, not that he ever needed to be reminded. She'd been well worth the wait.

"There's nothing better than you, baby."

"You going to be late tonight?"

"Not if I can help it. I may cut out a little early because my wife is feeling generous."

"Ha-ha, your wife is always feeling generous."

"Thank goodness for that. I'll text you when I'm on the way."

"I'll be here. I'm cooking something new tonight. It's going to take half the day."

"I can't wait for any of it."

"Be careful, Freddie. I love you."

"Love you too. See you soon."

He ended the call and pushed down on the accelerator, eager to get the interview with Townsend's wife taken care of so he could go home early. Sam wouldn't care. They worked hideously long hours and rarely took time for themselves.

Rolling into Potomac a short time later, he drove past stately homes that had him wondering what secrets they hid. Growing up with only his mom's income, they'd been short on money most of the time. He'd always assumed people who had it were immune from the problems less fortunate people faced. And while they might not have to worry about a roof over their heads or where their next meal was coming from, he'd learned that no one was immune to gut-wrenching challenges, even those who seemed to have it all.

Townsend lived in a big Tudor-style home on yet another tree-lined street with kids riding bikes on sidewalks and luxury vehicles everywhere he looked. He pulled into the driveway and parked behind a navy-blue Lexus SUV. His phone chimed with a text from Sam.

Send me the address so I know where you are.

Are you checking up on me?

No, I'm learning from my mistakes.

He knew she meant the time she'd gone to a home without telling anyone where she was and walked into a nightmare at the hands of their former lieutenant. Freddie sent her the address. *Another gilded mansion.*

With flawed people living inside with real problems.

How's the Metro?

It's great! I love it. Made a few new friends.

Freddie laughed out loud. *You're such a liar.*

Go get me a thread and hurry up about it.

I'm trying, but my boss is bugging me.

Get on it! NOW!

PITA.

Mosquito. Buzzzzzzzz. Become a yellow jacket. Get me something.

I'm going. Buzz off.

Freddie never got the last word with her, so he jammed his phone into his back pocket so he could live off that high for the short time it would last. He went up the stairs and rang the doorbell, which chimed like an air raid siren through the house. That's how Sam would describe it, anyway, and whether he wanted to admit it or not, her voice was always in his head.

She'd love to know that, which was why he could never tell her.

He rang the bell again and added some raps of the massive door knocker.

The door flew open, and a woman grabbed his arm, dragged him inside and shut the door so fast, he never saw it coming. A loud click had him staring at her in shock as she pointed a gun at him. He held up his hands.

"What the fuck do you want?" she asked as she twisted and turned a convoluted set of locks.

"I'm a cop. Let me show you my badge."

"Move slowly."

He did as she told him, moving very deliberately to get the badge out of his pocket.

"Give me your gun."

"That's not happening."

She aimed her weapon at his heart. "Yes, it is, or I'll end you right here."

As Freddie contemplated the shit storm he'd been pulled into, he tried to figure out what Sam would do. She'd draw her weapon and take her chances with getting shot herself, so that's what he ought to do too. Except he'd been shot once before, and it had totally sucked. He had no desire to go there again, especially with his beautiful wife waiting for him at home.

So he withdrew his weapon from the hip holster and handed it to her, butt first, hoping he wouldn't live to regret not shooting her when he'd had the chance.

SAM HAD FORGOTTEN HOW MUCH SHE HATED PUBLIC transportation, especially since everyone stared at her the whole time they were on the train. New people came on. More staring. She was probably trending on Twitter.

Her phone dinged with a text from Nick.

What're you doing on the Metro?

Sam laughed. Yep, she was trending all right, or her detail had ratted her out. She'd forgotten about them. *I like to keep things interesting.*

Seriously, Samantha. What are you doing there?

She loved when he called her Samantha. He was the only one in the world who did. *I gave Freddie my car so he could finish up in Montgomery County while I go back to HQ to interview two people who've been in lockup since last night and are screaming about their rights.*

Why didn't you let the detail take you!??

What detail?

Not funny, Samantha. I don't like you on public transport without backup.

I'm fine. Don't worry.

Right. Don't worry. Should I not breathe too?

Please keep breathing. I need you alive and well.

Same, which is why I'd rather you not be in crowded places by yourself.

Still totally fine. I assume my agents are around here somewhere.

You don't know for sure!?!

I forgot about them.

Honestly, Samantha. And you wonder why I don't sleep at night.

She glanced up from her phone to check which stop they were at. Out of the corner of her eye, she noticed a young man approaching a woman who was standing, her hand wrapped around a metal bar for balance on the moving train.

The guy said something to her, which had her recoiling. "Get away from me."

"Make me."

For fuck's sake. Sam sighed as she stashed her phone in her pocket and stood to get involved. Approaching the twosome, she pulled out her badge and held it up for the young man to see. "A word to the wise: You never know who's watching you be a douche. Move along," she said to the shocked man, who clearly knew he knew her from somewhere even if he wasn't sure where. "*Now.*"

He glared at her before moving to the other end of the car and taking a seat, but Sam felt his gaze fixed on her as she checked to see if the woman was all right.

"I'm fine, but thank you for intervening."

"He didn't actually touch you, did he?"

"No, but he grossed me out by telling me what he'd like me to do with him."

"Where're you headed?"

"Gallery Place."

"Me too. I'll get you a ride to wherever you need to go when we get there."

"Thanks. That's really nice of you."

"No problem." There were few perks to her job, but being able to summon a ride for someone in need was certainly one of them.

"I've admired your career," the woman said shyly. She had silky dark hair and pretty brown eyes. "I'm a senior at American, studying criminal justice. I want a career like yours someday."

"That's nice to hear, but sometimes a career like mine means having to deal with dickwads like him. It's not as glamorous as it seems."

"Oh, I know, but I still can't think of anything I'd rather do."

"You sound like me way back when. Do you have LEOs in your family?"

"My dad and grandfather."

"Ah, so it's in the blood, then. Was for me too."

"I was sorry to hear about your dad."

"Thank you. It was a tough loss. He was my buddy."

"I could tell that from the way you talked about him." She smiled. "I'm a little obsessed, and now you've come to my rescue, completely justifying my massive girl crush."

Sam laughed. She liked this kid. "What's your name?"

"Valerie Southern."

"Nice to meet you, Valerie."

"Very nice to meet you too, Lieutenant."

"You can call me Sam."

Valerie fanned her face. "You're going to have to give me a minute."

Sam laughed as an idea hit her. "You want to come with me to HQ to hang out for a bit? Check out the front lines?"

The young woman stared at her, eyes agog. "Are you for real right now?"

"Sure," Sam said, feeling unusually generous. She also wanted to make sure the younger woman wasn't bothered again by the guy who'd hassled her. "If you want to. No pressure."

"Of course I want to."

"Do you have somewhere to be?"

"Yep, but I'll get out of it." She got busy texting on her phone and let out a laugh. "My friends are freaking out. They know about my girl crush."

"You should know I'm very happily married."

"My crush extends to him too. Coolest couple on the planet."

"I don't know about that..."

"I do. Take my word for it."

"If I must," Sam said, amused by the woman's moxie.

"You must. Who's the dude over there glaring at you?"

Sam glanced over her shoulder to find Vernon right behind her. Whoops. "Um, well, he's a Secret Service agent they put on me after the whole damned world freaked out about my husband's decision not to run, and truth of the matter is, I forgot about him. I think he's pissed."

"I was crushed when I heard your husband isn't going to run. You have no idea how many people I've talked to who are devastated. Everyone I know was hoping he'd be president."

Sam winced. "Sorry to disappoint."

"The thing is, I get it," Valerie said, sighing. "I've read about his upbringing and saw his effed-up mother spouting off again last night. I think it's cool he wants to be with you and your kids."

"I do too, but don't tell anyone I said that."

"I never would. Meeting you is the sickest thing to ever happen to me, and even though you don't know me at all, you can trust me. I'll never repeat anything you say to me."

"That's a good quality to have. Usually takes people a lot longer than their senior year in college to realize they get further in this world if they just keep their damned mouth shut most of the time."

"I agree. I'm forever telling my friends to stay the eff off Twitter and just live their lives, for crying out loud."

"Never spent one full minute on Twitter, and I'm doing just fine."

"You're doing better than fine. Do you have any idea how many young women look up to you?"

"Um, no?"

"Thousands. You're our spirit animal."

"Ah, what's a spirit animal?"

Valerie looked at Sam like she was crazy or from another planet. She was probably both. "A spirit animal is like a teacher or a guide for others to emulate. Usually in the form of an actual animal, but since you're a mammal, you count."

"Ah, good to know. I'm often animal-like first thing in the morning when not yet caffeinated."

Valerie cracked up. "Me too."

The train pulled into Gallery Place. Freddie had told her to switch lines there, but she'd had enough of the Metro.

"This is our stop," Sam said. "We've a bit of a walk from here." Which she wasn't looking forward to in the brisk wind.

"Are you in a rush?"

"Always."

Valerie tapped around on her phone. "I ordered us an Uber. It'll meet us on the street."

"You're good to have around."

"So are you. Thanks for what you did with that weird dude."

"No problem."

"What about your Secret Service agent?"

"What about him?"

"Don't you have to stay where he tells you to?"

"Nope. I don't want him following me, so it's up to him—and his partner—to figure out how to do it. I'm not about to make it easy for them."

"Even though they're fellow LEOs?"

"Don't make me feel like a jerk."

Valerie put up her hands as they rode the escalator to street level. "I didn't mean to do that. I'm just wondering."

"Now I feel like a jerk." Exasperated by delays on top of delays, Sam held up at the top of the stairs and waited for the agent to catch up. "We're taking an Uber to HQ." Then she turned and continued walking toward the curb. "Happy now?" she asked Valerie.

"It was very nice of you to tell him."

"I do what I can for the people."

CHAPTER TWENTY-ONE

As they walked, Sam withdrew her phone to call Freddie and was annoyed when his voice mail picked up. "Damn it, Freddie." He ought to have something by now. She called him again, and again it went straight to voice mail. "What the hell?"

"What's wrong?" Valerie asked.

"My partner isn't answering his phone." Sam wasn't sure if she needed to do something about that, or if he was maybe on a call or in a dead zone. She'd try him again in a few minutes. He'd better pick up or else. In the meantime, she shot him a text. *Answer your fucking phone or you'll be a grasshopper forever.*

"That's our car," Valerie said, pointing to a black sedan.

"Mrs. Cappuano," Vernon called out to her.

Sam turned to him.

He gestured to a black SUV. "We're happy to provide transport wherever you need to go."

"Thank you, but I'm all set."

"We'd prefer that you ride with us."

"I understand that, but I'm good."

The agent stood with his hands on his hips, annoyance coming off him in tangible waves.

Sam took Valerie by the arm and headed toward the car. "Hurry, before he does something stupid like try to force me to go with him."

"You have to deal with this every day?"

"Nope. Just today and yesterday. Hopefully, they'll be gone by tomorrow when the fuss dies down about Nick not running."

Valerie followed Sam into the car. "Um, I don't think it's going to die down that fast. You really have no idea how upset people are, do you?"

"I tend to operate on a need-to-know basis, and that falls into the category of don't want to know. I understand people are disappointed, and I certainly get why, but it's what's best for him and us right now."

Sam's phone rang with a call from Malone. "Excuse me. This is my captain. What's up, Cap?"

"Gonzales has been released from rehab. He's on his way home with Christina now and expected here at zero nine hundred tomorrow to meet with me, the chief and Faith Miller."

"Am I invited?"

"That's why I'm calling. Thought you might want to be there."

"You thought right."

"I also pulled the Worthington file. It's on your desk."

"Thank you."

"Finally, I have two very unhappy individuals who've been on ice since yesterday, their lawyers here and charging by the hour, just waiting on you."

"I'm ten minutes out, and they're first on my to-do list. Do me a favor?"

"Anything for you," he said, his tone dripping with sarcasm.

"Ask Patrol or Montgomery County Police to check on Cruz? Whatever is quicker."

"Why?"

"He's not answering his phone, and he should be."

"Calling him now, hang on."

In the background, Sam could hear the call go straight to voicemail. A chill of fear chased down her spine. "Let's get Patrol out to check on him. He's got my car in Potomac." She gave him the address. "He was going to see the wife of Mark Townsend, who was one of Ginny McLeod's victims. We decided to split up so I could get back to HQ to interview the husband and Realtor."

"I'm notifying Patrol. Hang on."

Acting on pure fear, Sam leaned forward to ask the Uber driver if they could divert to Potomac.

"He can't really do that," Valerie said.

"Can you pull over, then?"

The driver pulled to the curb.

"Come on," she said to Valerie.

On the sidewalk, Sam waited for the Secret Service vehicle to come to a stop and then got into the back seat, moving over to make room for Valerie.

"I need to get to Potomac as fast as you can," she said. "It's urgent."

As Vernon made a U-turn in traffic and activated flashing lights, Sam prayed that Freddie hadn't done something stupid like leave his phone in the car while he interviewed Mrs. Townsend. She'd promised Valerie some time on the front lines and could only hope she wasn't taking the young woman into a nightmare.

THE WOMAN EYED FREDDIE WITH SUSPICION. "TELL ME WHY YOU'RE here."

He sat on a sofa in the living room while she paced and waved the gun around.

"Did Mark send you?" She had stringy brown hair that hadn't been washed in a while and was so thin, her collarbones stood out under a loose-fitting T-shirt. Her hazel eyes were big and wounded, her cheeks sunken in, her complexion sallow. Once upon a time, she'd probably been stunning. Now she appeared unwell.

"What? No. I'm investigating Ginny McLeod's murder and—"

She shocked the shit out of him once again when she slapped him across the face. "Don't you *dare* speak that evil woman's name in my house!"

Freddie rubbed at his face. "Ma'am, assaulting a police officer and holding him at gunpoint are both crimes punishable by years in prison."

"Do you honestly think I care about that? My life is already ruined. What the hell difference will it make if I ruin your life too?"

Freddie knew he should've been afraid before then, but he'd figured he'd find a way out of this the way he always did. The possibility that she might kill him just because actually scared him. "It'll make a difference to me, my wife, my parents and friends."

"You shouldn't have come here." She stared at him with unseeing eyes that indicated a serious departure from reality.

"I realize that now."

"Mark is fucking her." She tightened her grip on the handgun and glared at a spot on the wall behind him. "That bitch Tina. He's fucking her." She turned her glare on Freddie. "Did you know that?"

Freddie wasn't sure whether to admit he knew or pretend he didn't. He made a snap decision. "Who's Tina?"

"The woman my husband is fucking! Her husband killed himself, and now she's stolen my husband. And Ginny... It's all her fault! None of this would've happened if she hadn't taken the money. She did this. She needs to pay."

"Do you know who hurt Ginny?"

"Ginny is hurt?" Now her eyes glittered with what could only be called glee.

"Ginny is dead."

"Good. She didn't deserve to live among decent people."

"Did you hurt Ginny?"

"What? No. I wanted to, but I haven't left the house in months. I can't... She... She took that from me too. She took *everything*."

Freddie kept his gaze fixed on the gun, waiting for an opportunity. His cell phone had been ringing repeatedly, which meant Sam or hopefully someone else from work was trying to reach him. He hoped it was Sam. She would do something about the fact that she couldn't get an answer. For a fleeting second, he thought of Elin, but when despair threatened to overtake him and cloud his judgment, he forced himself to focus on Mrs. Townsend.

"What's your name?"

"My name? It's Hattie."

"I'm Freddie. Freddie Cruz. I'm a detective with the MPD, and I'm married to Elin. We just got married a little over a month ago."

"Marriage is for fools."

"Maybe so, but I like it so far. I love my wife very much. I waited my whole life to meet her, and when I did, I knew almost immediately she was meant for me. I love her, and she loves me, and if you kill me, you'll ruin her life along with mine. I promised her I'd never let that happen, and I don't want to break my promise to her."

"You can't trust her. The minute something goes wrong—and it will—she'll forget all about why she ever loved you in the first place."

Well, that was a rather depressing thought... "It doesn't always work that way."

"Yes, it does. We were fine until Ginny stole our money, and Mark decided if he was going to be poor, he was going to be poor with someone else. That never would've happened without her taking everything from us."

"Why did you decide to invest?"

"*Because!* She made us an offer no one could refuse. One hundred percent return on investment? Who *wouldn't* do that?" As she spoke, she waved the gun around in a way that added to Freddie's anxiety. "I know what you're thinking. We were stupid to be taken in by her, but you would've done it too. *Double your money* in two years? Anyone would've done it!" She came closer to Freddie, the gun aimed at his face.

He couldn't believe this was happening. He'd come to ask her some questions and had gotten pulled into a nightmare.

"Tell me the truth. You would've done it too, wouldn't you?"

Staring at the gun, he said, "Absolutely. Anyone would have. You'd be crazy not to."

His answer seemed to please her. Thank goodness. She dropped the gun to her side as his phone rang again.

"If I don't answer that, they're going to come looking for me."

She seemed to think about that for a second. "Get rid of whoever it is."

Freddie released the deep breath he'd been holding while waiting for her to give him permission. He grabbed the phone from his back pocket and took the call from Sam, giving thanks to the Lord above that it was her. "Hey."

"*What the fuck?* Why weren't you answering?"

"I told you before." He made an effort to keep his voice calm and flat. "I don't care about you. I never have. Stop bothering me with your lies."

"Freddie... I'm coming. We're coming."

"That's good. That's what needs to happen. Now don't call me again." He returned the phone to his pocket. "All set."

"It's already happening to you too. People from outside your marriage will want to ruin it. They're jealous because you have something they want. That's what happened to us. Other women wanted my husband, but we were fine until that bitch stole everything from us. Mark never looked at anyone else until Ginny ruined us. And now..." She paused, blinked, her eyes full of tears as she looked at Freddie with utter desolation. "What am I supposed to do now?"

"You turn to your family and your friends to get you through it, and you rebuild your life. It's what people do when things don't work out like they hoped. They start over."

"I don't want to start over."

"You have to. It's the only way forward. Things didn't work out with Mark. So find someone else who will love and appreciate you."

"How can I do that when I can't even leave the house? That never used to be a problem, but now..."

"What did you do before?"

"I owned a bookstore, but after Ginny took the money, I couldn't afford to stay open. I had enough for a year, but when we realized the money was gone and the investment was a scam... That store was my whole world, and then it was just gone. Fifteen years of work, just gone." Her helpless shrug tugged at him. "I don't know what to do."

"Yes, you do. You get a therapist to help with the agoraphobia. You get a lawyer to help with the divorce. You sell this beautiful house and get yourself a nice cozy little apartment you can easily afford on the proceeds from the sale. Then you set up an online profile, and you meet other people who've been disappointed in past relationships and find your happy second chance. You can do it, Hattie. I know you can."

"That sounds really nice," she said with a small smile that softened her demeanor. "You make it sound so easy."

"It won't be easy. It'll take a lot of hard work and emotional upheaval, but at the end of it, you'll come through stronger and more able to face whatever happens next. And you'll be rid of a husband who dishonored you by turning to another woman. Think about how amazing that new life will be and how vindicated you'll feel when you pull it off without him. He doesn't deserve you, but there's someone out there who does. You just need to find him."

"You really think I can find someone else?"

"I really do, but first you have to give me that gun and let me go. Otherwise, you're going to end up in really big trouble. We can chalk this up to a misunderstanding, but only if you give me the gun." He held out his hand while giving her a pleading look. "Please, Hattie. Give yourself a chance to be happy again by doing the right thing. Give me the gun."

In the seconds it took her to make up her mind, Freddie's entire life flashed through his mind, the good, the not so good, the beautiful, the ugly. The highlight reel ended with Elin's exquisite face smiling at him the way she did all the time, as if he was the center of her world. He was, just like she was for him.

"Please, Hattie. Don't do something that can't be fixed. We can still fix this, but if you hurt me or continue to hold me against my will, I can't help you."

"You'll help me?" she asked softly.

"I swear to God."

Another moment passed during which Freddie never blinked as he held her gaze.

She handed him the gun.

He quickly removed the bullets. "Now give me mine too."

Reaching behind her, she withdrew his weapon from the back of her jeans and handed it to him, leading with the business end.

He quickly turned it toward a far wall and then put it back in his holster, relieved to know he'd live to see another day. "I want you to have a seat while I go talk to my team. We're going to get you some help, okay?"

"You won't leave, will you?"

"Not until you have what you need. I promise, Hattie. I'm going to help you."

"Th-thank you," she said, sobbing. "I'm sorry about the gun and that I hit you."

"It's going to be okay. Give me one minute. I'll be right back." Taking both weapons with him, Freddie backed out of the room, since he had no way to know if there were other weapons, and frisking her might damage their fragile accord. He pulled his phone out and called Sam. "All clear," he said when she answered.

"What the hell happened?"

"I'll tell you when I see you. In the meantime, I need Dr. Trulo, and it has to be here. Can you ask him to come? This isn't a criminal thing. It's a mental-health situation."

"Did she pull a gun on you?"

"We'll talk when I see you."

"Yes, we will, and I'm almost there."

"How'd you get here so fast?"

"Two words: Secret Service."

CHAPTER TWENTY-TWO

S am was so relieved, she felt sick. He was okay. Whatever had happened with Townsend's wife had been handled, and he was okay.

"Are you all right?" Valerie asked.

Sam had almost forgotten she was there. "I am now. My partner has neutralized the situation." She called Captain Malone. "Tell the cavalry to stand down."

"Is he okay?"

"He is now."

"Jesus, Sam. What the hell?"

"I don't have all the details yet, but he's fine."

"Thank goodness. I'll call off the alert."

"Thanks." Next, Sam called Dr. Trulo.

"Hey, I was just thinking about you. We're all set for seven tonight."

"That's good, but I need you on something else," she said, filling him in on Freddie's request.

"Potomac, huh?"

"'Fraid so."

"Tell Detective Cruz I'm on my way."

"Get Patrol to bring you with lights and noise."

"That's a fine idea. Be right there."

Sam ended that call and put through another to Freddie. "The doc is on his way with Patrol."

"Good."

"Now tell me what happened." The Secret Service SUV came to a stop at the curb of the Townsends' address in Potomac. Sam got out of the car, drawing the ire of Jimmy, who had gotten out to open the door for her. Slapping her phone closed, she approached her partner, who was outside the large home. She took a quick and careful look at him, and other than a red mark on his face, she didn't see anything amiss.

"She came to the door with a gun, jerked me inside, made me hand over my weapon. It happened so fast, Sam. I had no time to react."

Sam's heart nearly stopped at the thought of what *could've* happened.

"Ginny's scheme wrecked her life. She's become agoraphobic. She knows about Mark and Tina. She's distraught. I promised I'd get help for her if she let me go and turned over the weapons."

"What happened to your face?"

"She smacked me when I mentioned Ginny's name."

"So let me get this straight. She held you at gunpoint, took your weapon, assaulted you and held you hostage for at least an hour, and you're looking for a psych hold rather than an arrest."

He held her gaze, never blinking. "Her life was destroyed by Ginny. She's become paranoid, can't leave her house. She owned a bookstore before the scam that she had to close because she couldn't afford to keep it open. She's not a criminal. She's heartbroken."

"She *pulled a gun on you*, Freddie. She could've killed you."

"I'm aware of that. I'm asking you to trust my judgment, Sam. This isn't someone who needs to be arrested. She needs a doctor, possibly in-patient treatment and a chance at a new life. Locking her up won't accomplish anything. Hattie is entitled to the same compassion we all want for Gonzo."

A black luxury SUV came to a skidding stop at the end of the driveway, and Mark Townsend got out, looking wild-eyed and frazzled. "My neighbor called to say something was happening here. Is it Hattie?"

"She's fine," Freddie said in a cold tone Sam hadn't thought her kindhearted partner was capable of.

Mark gestured toward the house. "I'll just go in and check on her."

Freddie stood in his path. "Stay out of there. You're not welcome here."

"What the fuck does that mean? This is my house."

"You're going to need to find somewhere else to stay."

"Why?"

"Hattie will tell you herself when she's ready. For now, leave. And don't come back."

Mark stared at Freddie, seemingly trying to decide if he was going to take him on. Luckily, he made the correct choice, stormed off and drove away with his tires squealing.

"I need to go in with her, because you know he's going to call her. Send Trulo in when he arrives?"

"I will."

"As soon as she's set, I'm going home to see my wife. I'll make up the time later."

"Don't worry about it. Thanks for not getting killed."

He shot a grin over his shoulder. "I do what I can for the people."

IT WAS NEARLY THREE THIRTY BY THE TIME SAM GOT BACK TO HQ, with Valerie still along for the ride. After she stashed Valerie in one of the observation rooms, she went straight to the interrogation rooms to take care of Realtor Barbie and Ken McLeod. She started with Ken, bursting into the room and taking him and his young, pale-faced attorney by surprise.

"It's about freaking time," Ken said. "I have rights, you know. I didn't kill my wife, and I didn't know about her scheme."

"You want to know what everyone I've talked to, even your own children, has said about you?"

The mention of his children seemed to take some of the starch out of him. "What?"

"How could he *not* know?"

"I didn't know! I had nothing to do with it!"

"Where did you think the money was coming from?"

"Ginny was a very successful businesswoman long before this. There was always money. I didn't notice any difference."

"You didn't notice when millions started rolling in?"

"Ginny handled our finances. She always did."

"You didn't think anything of her asking everyone you knew, everyone your children knew, to invest in her latest venture?"

"I didn't know about that either."

"Mr. McLeod, you'll have to pardon me for pointing out that no one is as clueless as you're trying to make me believe you are."

"Ginny and I did our own thing. She had her work. I had mine. We didn't talk a lot about what we were doing. She was always into big things, working her deals, bringing people together to invest in projects, and she'd had huge successes."

"So then why did she suddenly decide to start ripping off her family and friends?"

"I honestly don't know."

"Even after the shit hit the fan with multiple federal investigations, you never said, 'Hey, honey, what's up with you taking money from people we know and then ghosting them when they ask about their investments?'"

"I never called her honey."

"You know what I'm asking. Answer the question."

"I asked her what caused the Feds to get involved, and she said it was a misunderstanding that she was working on rectifying."

"And that was it? You just took her word for it and went back to your clueless little world while she stashed millions of dollars that belonged to your family and friends in offshore accounts?"

"She said it was a misunderstanding, and she was working it out. What was I supposed to do? Force her to tell me every detail?"

Sam leaned in closer to him across the table. "Let me tell you what I would've done if I found out my husband took money from family and close personal friends and then seemingly took off with it. I'd have *found the fucking money and given it back*. Did you even try to find it, or try to get her to tell you where it is?"

"No."

"Why not?"

"Because I stayed out of her business, and she stayed out of mine."

"Even after the FBI and IRS came calling? Even *then* you were hands-off?"

"She told me she was handling it. What was I supposed to do?"

"Something. You were supposed to do *something*."

"Is there a point to this interrogation?" the lawyer asked.

Sam wanted to throat-punch him. "The point is, Mr. McLeod, no one believes you when you said you didn't know anything."

"Well, too bad. That's the truth, and I passed a polygraph. The polygraph believed me."

"Polygraphs can be faulty. That's why they aren't admissible in court. You'd have to be almost willfully ignorant to what she was doing to miss what was happening in your own home. Were you purposely avoiding what she was up to so you could play dumb later?"

"I'm not playing dumb."

"So you're just dumb, then? Because you'd have to be to not realize she was scamming the people closest to you." Sam picked up a printout listing the victims and their relationships to the McLeods. "Your own brother, sister-in-law, closest friends, neighbors, coworkers... What was the end game? How did Ginny plan to explain to these people what became of their investments?"

"I don't know."

"Where were the two of you planning to go? Because you must've had a plan for where you were going to be when the shit hit the fan with every person in your life coming for you. What was the plan, Ken?"

"I didn't have a plan. If she did, I was unaware of it."

"Did you actually *speak* to your wife on any kind of regular basis?"

"About what was for dinner and who was taking the trash cans out to the street for pickup. That kind of thing."

"Wow, I really wish I had that kind of marriage, said no one ever."

"I have to object to your tone, Lieutenant," the lawyer said.

"Fuck you. I object to this man and his wife stealing millions from hundreds of people and then hiding the money somewhere only the two of them know and refusing to give back what they took. You ruined people's lives, Ken. Don't you care about that at all?"

"*Ginny* ruined people's lives, and of course I care about it."

"If that's the case, what're you doing to try to figure out where she hid the money?"

"I've turned over everything relevant to the federal investigators, and I've been retained here for more than twenty-four hours to answer your questions. What more would you have me do?"

"Where did she hide the money?"

"If I knew that, I would've told the Feds months ago. I don't know. She wouldn't tell me."

"So you actually asked her?"

"She said it was being taken care of, and I wasn't to worry about it."

"And that was good enough for you?"

"I couldn't exactly beat it out of her."

"I'm trying to decide whether you're pathological or just stupid."

"I don't have to sit here and be insulted by you."

"Yes, you actually do. In fact, maybe I should charge you with impeding a homicide investigation so I can keep you here a little longer to do some deep thinking about where the money might be."

"You can't charge him with that if he's cooperating," the lawyer said.

"Wanna make a bet? Your version of cooperating and mine are very different."

"He's told you what he knows."

"Which is dick," Sam said.

The lawyer flinched at her terminology. Poor baby. Had she offended him?

"He's told you what he knows," the lawyer said again, more pointedly this time.

"I'm going to be really honest with you, Ken," Sam said. "If I find out that you knew anything that could've helped us figure out who killed Ginny or make restitution to her victims, I'll throw the book at you so hard, it'll give you a skull fracture. I'll charge you with multiple felonies and do everything in my power to make your life a living hell. Do you understand me?"

"My life is already a living hell. My wife was murdered. My children, family and friends don't speak to me. There's nothing you can do that's worse than the hell I'm already living in."

"Don't be so sure about that."

"Is he free to go?" the lawyer asked.

"For now." Disgusted with him and his client, Sam got up to leave the room and nearly ran smack into Avery Hill in the hallway.

"Oh damn. I knew I was forgetting something I was supposed to do today."

"I'm hurt."

Sam laughed. "No, you're not. I've got one more thing to do, and then I'll find you in my conference room."

"Sounds good."

"To you, maybe."

He walked away, laughing.

Sam collected herself, took a deep breath and went into the room where Realtor Barbie and her middle-aged male attorney were waiting. Cheri looked quite a bit worse for wear after a night in jail. Her mascara was smudged under her eyes, her hair had gotten greasy, and the glow of the orange jumpsuit made her skin look washed out.

"It's about time," the attorney said.

"Oh, I'm sorry. Did I inconvenience you during my homicide investigation?"

"You have no good reason to retain my client."

"Sure I do."

"Are you going to tell us what that reason is?"

Sam took a seat across from them, noting Cheri looked terrified. Good. "I believe Cheri knew exactly what Ginny was up to and aided and abetted her crimes."

Cheri gasped. "I didn't!"

"Right at this moment, one of my very best detectives is tearing your life apart. He's looking at everything, lifting every rock and peeking behind every door. If there's anything there, he'll find it. Like, for instance, if you got a kickback for your fake-ass 'showings,' Detective Green will find that. If your influx of cash doesn't match up with your commissions, he'll notice that. If you've got money hidden somewhere, he'll find it. He's one of the best I've ever worked with, and *nothing* gets by him."

Sam never blinked as she stared down Cheri and watched her wilt before her eyes. "Do you have children, Cheri?"

She sat up straighter. "Three. Why?"

"How old are they?"

"Seventeen, nineteen and twenty-one."

"So two in college. Is that right?"

She glanced at the lawyer before offering a tentative nod.

"Where do they go?"

"Um, one goes to George Mason, and the other goes to Virginia Tech."

"Good schools. Tuition is expensive, isn't it? Especially with two in college at the same time, which you'll have for a while with your younger one coming up, am I right?"

"Y-yes."

"What are you getting at, Lieutenant?" the lawyer asked.

"Detective Green will be ripping their lives apart too. If they paid for college without loans, he'll want to know where that money came from. If they're driving nice cars, he'll find out how they paid for them. If they've got anything to hide, Green will find it. He's like a bloodhound. He makes the IRS agents that investigated you during the federal investigation look like Cub Scouts. I bet they never thought to investigate your kids, did they? Is there anything for him to find?"

Cheri shifted in her seat, her shoulders slumping. If body language was any indication, Sam had scored a direct hit by mentioning her kids.

"You don't have to answer that, Cheri," the lawyer said.

"You're right. She doesn't have to answer anything. But I'll take great pleasure in charging her with impeding a homicide investigation. It's one of my favorite things to charge people with. It leads to lots of ugly press about people who get in the way of me catching murdering scumbags. Real estate is a reputational business, isn't it, Cheri? I imagine yours has taken a bit of a hit since the Feds came swooping in on Ginny and uncovered your role in her scheme."

"My client wasn't charged with anything."

"*Yet*," Sam said. "She hasn't been charged *yet*." She slapped her hand on the table, startling Cheri. "The jig is up, Cheri. Tell me what you did with the kickbacks from Ginny!"

Cheri broke down into sobs that echoed through the tiny room. "I wanted to help my kids," she said haltingly.

"Shut up, Cheri," the lawyer growled.

"No, I can't do this anymore, Al. I can't do it." She smeared mascara across her face when she wiped away tears. "Ginny swore to me that there was nothing illegal about what she was doing. I told her I couldn't endanger my license under any circumstances, because that's how I supported my family after my divorce. My kids were heading to college, so when Ginny came to me with an 'opportunity,' I took it."

"How did you know her?"

"We played tennis together at a racquet club in Gaithersburg. We had friends in common. They introduced me to her, and she seemed thrilled to hear I was a Realtor. That first day, she told me she'd been looking for a good Realtor in our area to work on some deals she had going. We exchanged cards, she called me the next day, and we began working together shortly after."

"What did working with her entail?"

"She'd identify a property and ask me to show it to groups of people."

"How did you get paid?"

"By the showing. She paid me five hundred per."

Sam let out a low whistle. "Five hundred bucks to do a showing? And you never thought there was anything odd about her showing properties that never sold?"

"Ginny said she was putting together a group to purchase the buildings, and that was going to take some time. She asked me to show the properties. I showed them."

"How many showings did you do for her?"

"A couple thousand over three years."

"How many thousand? Two, three, four?"

"Maybe two."

"Two times five. I'm no math whiz, but that's, like, a million dollars. Am I right?"

Cheri squirmed in her seat. "Something like that."

"That's a lot of money to do showings. Did you follow a script that Ginny wrote?"

"I told people about the properties, their potential, the comps in the area. That kind of thing. Basically, I made it seem like an attractive investment."

"When you knew it was all part of a scam."

"No! I didn't know that! Not until the Feds arrested Ginny. I had no idea."

"How'd you find out that you'd been part of a scam?"

"When the Feds came to my office and told me. I honestly didn't know. I'd take a polygraph if you wanted me to."

"Stop talking, Cheri," the lawyer said.

"I would! I didn't know what she was doing!"

"Fair enough," Sam said, "but you had to suspect there was something hinky about it."

"I didn't. She asked me to do showings. I did showings. I'm a Realtor. That's what I do."

"Not once, ever, did you ask yourself what Ginny might be up to?"

"No."

"Well, I suppose if I was making that kind of easy money, I might not ask questions about it either. Or wait, maybe I would because I'd want to know *why* I was making the easy money and how it might come back to bite me in the ass, but that's just me. I'm skeptical that way."

"Is there anything else you need to ask my client, or is she free to go?"

Sam eyed the woman for a full minute before she said, "Where were you on Sunday afternoon?"

"What? Why?"

"Because I'm wondering where you were when someone took a garden tool to Ginny's neck. So... Where were you?"

"I didn't kill her," she said, sending a frantic look toward the attorney, who patted her arm reassuringly.

"She knows you didn't kill her, Cheri," the lawyer said in a condescending tone that infuriated Sam.

"Is that right?" Sam asked him. "And why do you say that?"

"Because you would've led with that if you suspected her," he said smugly, as if he was some sort of expert in interrogation techniques.

"Actually, that's not true. I tend to save the big questions for last, when the person thinks I'm done with them. Like now. Cheri thought we were done, but, oh wait, not so fast."

The lawyer scowled at her. "She didn't kill Ginny."

Ignoring him, Sam focused on Cheri, who shriveled slightly as Sam glared at her. "Where were you on Sunday afternoon?"

"I had two open houses, one from twelve to two and another from three to five."

"And where were you from two to three?"

"In the car, driving from one to the other."

Sam slid her notebook across the table. "I need addresses for each open house."

"Why?"

"Because I'm going to check. So make sure you tell me the truth, unless you want to end up right back here again. And I've got to say, orange really isn't your color."

Cheri's hand shook as she wrote down the addresses and pushed the pad back to Sam, who scanned what she'd written.

"How long did it take you to get from Bethesda to Germantown?"

"About... half... half an hour."

Why was she stammering? "You had an hour, and the drive only accounted for half of it, so what did you do with the other half?"

"There was a lot of traffic, so it took longer."

"But you just said it took half an hour."

"I meant that's how long it should have taken."

"Are you trying to get arrested for murder, Cheri?"

"No! I didn't kill her!"

"By my reckoning, you have thirty unaccounted minutes right around the time someone was bashing Ginny with a garden tool."

"I was *driving*!" Cheri directed a wild-eyed look at her attorney. "Tell her to listen to me."

"Lieutenant, my client didn't kill Ginny, and this interview is over." He stood, gathered his belongings and lifted his chin to tell Cheri to get up and follow his lead.

Sam sat back and waited to see if he'd actually try to walk out of the room. Wisely, he stopped short of that.

"Is my client free to go?"

"For now."

"What does that mean?" Cheri asked in the shrill tone that was beginning to grate on Sam's nerves. "For now?"

"Just what I said. I reserve the right to speak to you again if I need to, and if I find out you used those thirty minutes to kill Ginny, I'll be coming for you."

"I didn't kill her!"

"Did you spend all the money she gave you?" Sam asked.

"Most of it. I paid off my house, paid my kids' tuition."

"And you understand there're people out there who're in danger of *losing* their homes because of the money they lost, right?"

"That's not my fault! I didn't take their money. Ginny did."

"So you said, but if I find out you lied to me in here, I'll make you very sorry."

"I didn't lie," she said, her voice wavering and her eyes filling. "I wish I'd never met Ginny."

"But I bet you're awfully glad that mortgage is paid off, am I right?"

"We're through here," the lawyer said.

Sam looked at Cheri with utter disgust, got up and left the room. These people were so fucked up. How could Cheri *not* question the reason she was showing those buildings, or why Ginny would pay her five hundred bucks to do showings? How could she never ask *why*?

The more she found out about Ginny and her scheme, the more she felt for the people who'd been taken in by her. Maybe they'd been stupid or greedy or whatever you wanted to call it, but they hadn't deserved to lose everything.

CHAPTER TWENTY-THREE

P er the instructions she'd received by email the day before, Christina waited for Tommy in the rehab facility's reception area. She'd left Alex with Clara, an older woman who lived in their building who'd become like a grandmother to him, because Christina needed some time alone with her fiancé. It'd been a very long few months without Tommy at home to help with the parenting and everything else. But it'd been an even longer ten months since his partner had been killed, sending their lives into a downward spiral.

The loss of Detective Arnold had been devastating. The collateral damage to Tommy had been almost as devastating. He'd gone from a healthy, productive, fully engaged partner, father and detective to a shell of his former self, a man so shattered, he could barely function. He'd turned to pain meds for relief, and for a time, Christina had feared she'd lose him forever to either death or addiction.

Now he seemed more like his old self than he had since that terrible January night when Arnold had been gunned down feet from Tommy. Christina was full of foolish hope that they might actually get their happily ever after, despite the many roadblocks they'd encountered over the last two years.

At some point in the last few weeks as she counted down to the day he'd be released from rehab, she'd begun to think of herself for the first time in months. She'd taken the time to figure out what she wanted most from this second chance and had a few things to talk to him about if the time was right.

That was the thing with him lately. It was all about timing, and it never used to be that way. Before Arnold had been killed, she'd never had to tiptoe around Tommy or choose the right moment to discuss something with him. They'd had their ups and downs, but their relationship had been solid until that fateful night upended their existence.

Sometimes, she felt selfish for focusing on how Arnold's death had impacted her family, but she never forgot the wonderful young man they'd lost that night. And neither did Tommy.

She checked the time on her phone. Four o'clock. He should be out anytime now, and they could restart their lives. Drawing in a deep breath, she tried to calm her out-of-control nerves. That was another thing that was new—being nervous around him. The last time they'd been together, when he came home for Skip Holland's funeral, she'd experienced a bit of the old magic that had been so present between them from the start. She'd clung to the memories of that night ever since and was desperate to find out if they could recapture that magic once he was finally home to stay.

The door from the inner sanctum of the rehab center swung open, and there he was.

Christina stood to go to him, but found herself frozen to the spot as uncertainty assailed her.

Then he smiled, his handsome face lighting up with pleasure at the sight of her, and everything in her relaxed somewhat as he came toward her, dropping his bag on the floor and putting his arms around her. He held her as only he could, and as she breathed in the familiar scent of him, she exhaled the deep breath she'd been holding for months now as she waited to see if he would survive the loss of his partner, if they would survive as a couple and a family.

"Hey, baby," he whispered. "So happy to see you."

Christina clung to him. "Same."

"Where's my buddy?"

"With Clara. I thought we could use a minute to ourselves."

"Good thinking. I can't wait to see him, though."

"He can't wait to see you either." She pulled back to look up at the handsome face that had become the center of her world since they met at Sam and Nick's New Year's Eve party almost two years ago. "Are you all checked out?"

"Yep."

"Good."

He took her hand, bent to retrieve his bag and nodded for her to lead the way. They emerged into cold air and encroaching darkness.

Christina hated November most years. So cold and dark, with the long winter stretching out before them. But this year, November felt like spring to her as she and Tommy hopefully got their long-awaited restart.

"Do you mind if I drive?" he asked. "I can't believe I actually miss driving."

"I don't mind at all. I'm sick of driving."

He held the passenger door for her. "Thanks for coming up to see me so often and for bringing Alex. You guys saved my sanity."

"Of course we came to see you. We missed you so much."

"I missed you too." He leaned in to kiss her before he went around to get into the driver's seat. For a long time, he didn't move, and then he turned to her. "I know I've said this to you before, but it bears repeating. I'm so sorry for what I've put you through."

"You don't have to apologize to me, Tommy."

"Yes, I really do. I let my grief take over every aspect of my life, including my relationships with you and Alex. I shouldn't have let that happen."

Christina reached for his hand and cradled it between both of hers. "You didn't *let* anything happen. An awful thing was done to your beloved partner. Every ounce of the blame belongs on the shoulders of the man who killed him. I don't hold you responsible for any of it. No one does."

"Some people do, I'm sure."

"No one who matters blames you, Tommy, and that's what I want to talk to you about. You're not taking that plea deal."

"Yes, I am."

"*No*, you're not.

"How do you even know about that?"

"I hear things. Things I should be hearing from you, I might add."

"I was going to tell you."

"When? After you signed something that would effectively end your once-promising career?"

"I need to take responsibility for what I did so I have credibility with my colleagues."

"Okay, so take responsibility without pleading guilty to a crime that'll ruin your career."

"What do you mean?"

"There're other ways you can take responsibility without pleading to a crime. Tell me you realize that."

"Um, well, you may have to fill in the blanks for me. How am I supposed to do that?"

"You give an interview to a reporter you trust. You come clean on what the last year has been like for you since that awful night in January and confess to the mistakes you made in the name of grief. You own it without letting it ruin you."

"And what do I do about the people within the department who think I need to pay for breaking the law?"

Christina leaned in toward him, looking him dead in the eyes. "Fuck. Them."

He laughed. "Well, all righty, then."

"I'm dead serious, Tommy. Anyone in the department who'd criticize how you handled the murder of your partner can go fuck themselves. They don't know what you've been through unless it's happened to them, and thank God it hasn't happened to them. Skip understood what you went through because he lived it too. He's the only one I know who could possibly get it—and he did understand. Better than anyone. The rest of them don't matter to you or to us. If they never respect you again, so what? You can't control what other people do. You can only control how you react to them, and if you take that plea, you're giving them power over you that they don't deserve. They haven't *earned it* by having their partner killed right in front of them."

"You've given this a lot of thought."

"It's all I've thought about since I heard you were considering the plea. *Please* don't do it. You may think it'll fix things, but it'll only make everything worse in the long run. When you get a few years out from the horror of this last year, you'll regret having signed away your career."

"You make good points. There's a meeting about it tomorrow with the chief, Malone, Sam and the AUSA overseeing the case."

"I want to be there."

"We can make that happen."

"Good. And just so you know, I'm going to say the same thing to them that I said to you."

"I figured as much."

"Someone needs to fight for you, Tommy, and that's going to be me—and Sam. She's as upset about this as I am."

"With you two on my side, I can't lose." He leaned across the center console and reached for her, kissing her the way he used to before disaster struck, with hunger and tenderness and sweetness. "I love you so much. You'll never know how many times thoughts of you and Alex saved me."

"We love you too."

"Thank you for not giving up on me, Christina. I wouldn't have blamed you if you had."

"I love you too much to give up on you, but I'm ready for things to be different, Tommy. Even before Arnold was killed, we'd gotten a little off track, and I've made a few decisions for myself that I hope you'll agree with."

"Like what?"

"I'm going back to work part-time, mostly from home, doing some stuff for Nick. He's wanting to ramp up his school visits, and I agreed to coordinate that for him and to accompany him on some of the local ones. But he wants to expand his visits into other parts of the country, so I'll be working on that."

"That's a great opportunity for you."

"I love being Alex's mom and taking care of him and you, but I'm ready to get back to work. I need something that's all mine."

"I understand that completely. I wondered when you decided to stay home if you'd be happy doing that in the long term."

"I'm happy, but I could be happier with a little outside stimulation."

"What else is on your agenda?"

"I want to have a baby."

"That we can do. In fact, I'd take great pleasure in making that happen."

Christina laughed at the suggestive way he said that. "I'm sure you would."

"What else?"

"We're going to need to find a bigger place to live."

"Let's make sure I still have a job before we do that."

"You'll still have a job. If they fire you for things you did after you lost your partner on the job, you'll file the biggest lawsuit in the history of workplace injustice lawsuits, and they know that. There's no way they'll fire you. And let's not forget you're a damned good detective who they'd be crazy to let go. And they know that too."

He tipped up her chin and kissed her again. "I gotta say, this fierce side of you is a huge turn-on."

She snorted out a laugh. "You haven't had sex in weeks. It probably doesn't take much."

"Nah, baby, it's all you. I can't wait to sleep with you in my arms tonight. I've missed you so much, and not just since I've been here. For months now."

"Everything is going to be okay now, Tommy. I know it is."

"Let's get out of here. I've had more than enough of this place."

"I'll be forever grateful to them for giving you back to us."

"I'm back, and everything will be better. I promise." After he'd driven out of the parking lot and headed them toward home, he looked over at her. "When are you going to marry me?"

"As soon as possible."

"Maybe we can do it on Thanksgiving and surprise the hell out of everyone."

"That'd be fun."

"Really?"

"Really."

"You don't want something bigger and better?"

She shook her head. Once upon a time, she might've wanted bigger and better, but life had taught her to be thankful for smaller things. "All I want is you and Alex and our life together. I couldn't care less about anything other than that. We have so much to be thankful for. Thanksgiving seems like the perfect time to take that next step. Both our families have been on hold until we figure out our plans, so how about I tell them dinner's at our house this year?"

"Sounds perfect to me."

After Dr. Trulo arrived at the Townsend home, Freddie briefed him on what'd taken place with Hattie and the promises he'd made to her. "I'm convinced that with the proper care, Hattie could make a full recovery from the agoraphobia and paranoia that've set in since she and her husband were victimized by Ginny McLeod."

"The murdered woman who defrauded her friends and family?" Trulo asked.

"Right. The Townsends were among her victims, and when you talk to Hattie, you'll understand the impact that's had on her, which led to today's events."

"What about you, Detective? I understand she pulled a gun on you and assaulted you."

"I'm fine. Let's worry about her. She's the one who needs your help, not me."

"I'll take care of her, but I want to see you in my office tomorrow to discuss this further."

"I told you, I'm fine."

"Nonnegotiable, Detective."

Freddie stared at the doctor for a long moment, hoping he

would blink. He didn't. "Fine. I'll see you tomorrow. Can I take you in to see Hattie now?"

"Lead the way."

An hour later, Freddie drove away in Sam's car, heading for home in Woodley Park. He needed to see Elin right now. She was the only thing he could think of as he drove faster than he should've, tempted to use the lights and siren to get there faster. He resisted, but just barely. It took ten precious minutes to find a parking space near their building and another ten to jog the short distance home. He took the stairs two at a time and nearly dropped his keys twice as he tried to get in the door.

Elin saved him when she pulled it open, her white-blonde brows furrowing with confusion. "I'm glad it's you. I thought someone was trying to break in."

"It's me."

"What's wrong?"

"Nothing. I just need this." He put his arms around her and held her so tightly she let out a squeak.

"Freddie! Let me breathe."

"Sorry." He dropped his head to her shoulder, filled with relief to be back with her when he'd had reason to wonder if he'd ever see her again.

"You're freaking me out." She ran her fingers through his hair and gave a gentle tug, compelling him to look at her. "What happened?"

"Nothing." If he told her, she'd worry about him even more than she already did. "Just a weird day, and I couldn't wait to see you."

"You're supposed to be working for a few more hours. You said you'd be home late."

"I cut out early."

"Why?"

"Because I wanted to see you."

"You don't do things like that when you're working a new case. What gives? And don't tell me it's nothing."

"Something happened, but I don't want you to worry. I was

completely fine. Well, most of the time, I was completely fine, but it was kinda weird and..."

"What happened, Freddie?"

"I went to interview one of the people our vic scammed."

"By yourself?"

"Yeah, Sam had to go back to HQ to interview two people we had in lockup for almost twenty-four hours. We decided to split up because we were way out in Maryland."

"What happened?"

"When I got to the woman's house, she pulled a gun on me, and, well, she basically took me hostage for a very short time."

"*Jesus,*" Elin said on a long exhale.

"I talked to her and made her see I could get her help to deal with the issues she's developed since Ginny McLeod stole their money. Dr. Trulo came, he's helping her, and it's all fine. But I wanted to see you."

She looked up at him with the stunning blue eyes that had never failed to slay him from the first time he ever saw them. "Why did you want to see me so badly?"

"I always want to see you."

"Why, Freddie?"

"Because," he said, sighing, "for a minute—and it was only a minute or two—I was afraid I might not see you again, and that made me sadder than I've ever been in my life."

She wrapped her arms around him and brought his head to rest again on her shoulder. "How will I bear to let you go back to it tomorrow?"

"That's why I didn't want to tell you."

"You arrested her, right?"

"No, she'll be on a seventy-two-hour psych hold, during which we hope she'll be convinced to seek in-patient help."

"She held you hostage."

"She's mentally ill. Arresting her won't do anything but make a bad situation worse."

"She could've killed you."

"She didn't. We should have a baby."

"*What?* Where's that coming from all of a sudden?"

"It's not all of a sudden. I've been thinking about it for a while now."

"What happened to not wanting to bring children into this messed-up world we live in?"

"Sam made me see that we can't judge our own lives and how we live them by the screwed-up stuff we see on the job, because it's out of proportion to regular life."

"And after you have this scary experience, suddenly you're ready for a baby?"

"Not just because of that. Don't you want one too?"

"I do, but not right away. Can we have a year to enjoy being married before we have a baby?"

"I suppose we can do that, but we're going to need to do a lot of practicing so we're ready when the time comes."

She laughed, as he'd fully expected her to. "If we practiced any more than we already do, we wouldn't get anything else done."

"I'm fine with that since there's nothing else I'd rather do than practice with you."

"Starting now?" she asked as he walked her backward toward their bedroom.

"Starting right now."

"Hey, Freddie?"

"Yeah, babe?"

"Thanks so much for not getting killed today. I wouldn't know how to live without you."

"All I could think of the whole time was you and getting home to you. That'll always be my top priority."

CHAPTER TWENTY-FOUR

S am had almost forgotten about Avery waiting for her in the conference room, until she returned to the pit with Valerie in tow and heard him in there talking on the phone. Days like this tested her fortitude, and this one wasn't over yet by a long shot. Then she remembered the grief group meeting, and she groaned out loud.

"What's wrong, Lieutenant?" Cameron Green asked.

"Everything is wrong. I hate this case, my partner got taken hostage, I've got the proctology meeting with Hill and the grief group tonight, and this day has officially reached endless status. Other than that, I'm just dandy."

Green's lips quivered as his eyes danced with amusement.

"If you laugh, you're fired."

"I wouldn't dare laugh, but I do have something that might interest you."

"What's that?"

Cameron glanced at Valerie, brow raised in inquiry.

"This is Valerie, a criminal justice senior at American," Sam said. "Valerie, this is Detective Cameron Green. She's interning with me today. You can speak freely in front of her."

"Two things, actually. One, Jeannie got signed statements from all of Ken Sr.'s golfing buddies that he was on the course all afternoon."

"Well, that's something, I guess."

"This is even better," Cam said. "Multiple trips to the Cayman Islands by our friend Mandi McLeod over the last two years."

"Okay..."

"You know the Cayman Islands are a tax haven, right?" Cameron asked.

"They're a popular place to store money you don't want subjected to taxes," Valerie added.

"That's right," Cam said, seeming impressed by the young woman.

"I think I knew that," Sam said, intrigued by the info. "The Feds didn't pick up on the trips?"

"I don't think they did, because they investigated Ginny and Ken—hard—but didn't dig much deeper. I found this connection through the daughter's social media, a private Instagram account called Finsta that I managed to access through means we're better off not discussing. She posted five different sunset shots that were tagged at Seven Mile Beach, Georgetown, Grand Cayman, over the last two years."

"Multiple trips or pics from the same trip?"

"Judging by the dates, four different trips."

"And there's no sign of the parents being there at the same time?"

"Nothing public and no sign of the expenditures on their financials from around those dates. I figure Mandi must've paid under some sort of alias or had a fake passport or some way to travel undetected."

"This is great work, as usual, Detective. Go pick up Mandi McLeod at Catholic University." Sam wrote down the name of the dorm and her room number. "Take O'Brien with you and ask Patrol to back you up." After Freddie's mishap earlier, she was taking no chances.

"Will do."

"We'll let Ms. McLeod spend the night at the three-hots-and-a-cot hotel downstairs and deal with her in the morning."

"Are we charging her?"

"Not yet. Let me talk to her first and get a feel for what she knew and when she knew it. To hear her tell it earlier, she was nothing but outraged at what her mother did. I'm not sure if she was a willing coconspirator or she took four innocent vacations to the Cayman Islands over two years. And until I know which, I don't want to charge her."

"Got it."

"Give me an update when you're back with her."

"Will do."

"After that, you can take a half day."

Cameron laughed. "Gee, thanks, Lieutenant. You're a generous boss."

"I do what I can for the people." Referring to the legendary Skip Holland Half Day made her feel closer to her dad.

"So," Sam said to Valerie, "that's about what it's like around here on any given day."

"This has been the coolest day of my entire life. Watching you interrogate suspects was breathtaking. You're so good."

"Thank you." Sam handed her a business card. "Call me when you're ready to start your career. I might be able to help."

"I'll never forget how getting hassled on the Metro turned into the best thing to ever happen to me."

"Please don't repeat anything you saw or heard here."

"I never would. Can I hug you and take a selfie?"

"If you promise to make it quick and not post the selfie on social media."

"Swear to God."

Sam gave her ten seconds for the hug and the photo. "Keep in touch."

"I absolutely will. Thank you again for an unforgettable day."

"Sure thing." Sam watched her head toward the lobby exit, hoping she'd hear from Valerie again. She had a feeling the young woman would make an outstanding law enforcement officer.

"Lieutenant," Avery called from the conference room. "Ready when you are."

"Ugh, the proctologist beckons."

"You do have a way with words, LT," Green said as he signaled for O'Brien to join him as they went to find Mandi McLeod.

"I'm coming, Hill. Let me grab my water." She went into her office, took her hair down from the clip that held it out of her way while she worked and found the now-warm bottle of water she'd bought earlier from a vending machine in the break room. Chugging half of it, she grabbed a pad and pen and went into the conference room to get the meeting with Hill over with.

"I'm here. What do you want?"

He grinned as he stood to close the conference room door. "Charming, as always."

"Charm is my middle name." Sam always hated to admit, even to herself, that Avery Hill was a fine-looking man with light brown hair he wore swept back off his forehead, prominent cheekbones, golden eyes and a South Carolinian accent that could make even the most stalwart of panties go damp. Her friend Shelby Faircloth, Avery's new wife, was one lucky woman. Not that Sam ever gave him a thought when he wasn't right in front of her face, but she never failed to notice how handsome he was.

"What can I do for you, Agent Hill?" she asked, using her sweetest, most solicitous tone.

"I want to talk to you about some of your favorite people— Stahl, Conklin and Hernandez."

"Oh joy. My favorite old boys' club."

"Before we do that, though, I wanted to tell you my team is doing some digging into your mother-in-law. Nothing to report yet, but we're finding some interesting things."

"That doesn't surprise me in the least. She's scum."

"It might take a while, since we're doing this between other things."

"That's no problem. Whatever it takes."

"So about the reason we're here... I'm sorry to do this to you, Sam. I truly am."

She shrugged. "I'm starting to get past the initial shock of Conklin and Hernandez, and I'm well past the realization that Stahl was always a dick."

"We're reviewing their past cases and digging deep into whether Conklin and Hernandez's involvement in your dad's case was a one-off or if there was a pattern."

Sam's stomach dropped. "Jesus. It never occurred to me that Dad's case could be the tip of an iceberg. The thought of there being more makes me feel sick."

"You and a lot of other people around here. I want you to know—we're not looking to discredit this department as a whole. Only the people who deserve to be discredited. We're well aware of the great work you and many others are doing here every day."

"Thank you for that, but I certainly know that not everyone approaches the job the same way you and I do."

"When you think back to working with Stahl and Conklin, what stands out?"

"Stahl was always a pain in the ass because he could as the LT. And when he moved to Internal Affairs, it was even worse. He was drunk on his own power. He tried to make an issue out of overhearing Detective Arnold make a joke about how he hadn't been invited to my wedding."

"What kind of issue?"

"An IAB hearing kind of issue. He never missed a chance to bust my balls any way he could think of. It was nonstop. When he was my actual boss, it was a full-on nightmare for me."

"Did you know why?"

"Nope. I assumed it had something to do with my dad. They came up through the ranks together, never really got along, butted heads, etc. So when Stahl had Skip's daughter under his command, he made sure to fully maximize the opportunity."

"That must've been fun."

"All kinds of fun that occurred at the same time I was married to passive-aggressive Peter, and my father had been recently paralyzed in a shooting on the job. Neither my boss nor my husband gave me an ounce of slack during that time. Let me tell you, those were the good old days."

"Sounds like it. Did you suspect Stahl of cutting corners when he was your LT?"

"All the time. He was constantly telling us to hurry up, get him something, didn't matter what it was. Mostly, we ignored him, but he was relentless in his efforts to close cases at any cost."

"Do you think he manufactured evidence or anything like that?"

"Not that I could ever prove, but his methodology was always questionable."

"How so?"

"He would skip over people the rest of us wanted to interview and tell us to focus on the most likely suspect, but I've found the most likely suspect isn't immediately obvious."

"Can you think of any cases that might've been glossed over or handled badly by Stahl, Conklin, Hernandez or anyone else, for that matter?"

"As a matter of fact... Hang on a second." Sam left the conference room to go into her office to retrieve the Worthington file. When she returned, she closed the door and laid the file folder on the table. "Calvin Worthington, age fifteen, was fatally shot in Southeast on his own property fifteen years ago." She placed a photo of the smiling young man on the table and pushed it across to Avery, followed by the medical examiner's photo of the chest wound that'd ended his life.

"I was in my first year in Patrol, and I took the call. I've never forgotten his mother's agonizing grief or the way the case seemed to go cold almost immediately. Stahl was the detective assigned to the case, and that was the first time I tangled with him. I kept asking him what was being done to find Calvin's killer, and he told me to mind my own business and stay in my lane. He was so annoyed that a lowly Patrol officer questioned him. Later, I realized that the fact my last name was Holland made it doubly galling for him."

"The file is rather thin for a homicide."

"Exactly."

He opened the file and flipped through the pages, scanning the reports. "You offered a more detailed description of events just now than the detectives who investigated it did."

"They barely investigated it. I remember being enraged that they didn't give it much attention, but it happened during an outbreak of shootings and domestics, and the case just got overlooked. But I never forgot Lenore or her terrible grief. When I saw her the other day for the first time in years, I knew exactly who she was and why she'd come. She said she heard I'd closed my dad's case after four years, and even though fifteen is a lot longer, maybe I could take another look at Calvin's. She reminded me he would've been thirty this year."

"Such a tragedy. You just wonder how people survive this stuff. I look at Noah and think I'd die if anything happened to him."

"I know that feeling, but the human spirit is resilient. Somehow, we survive things we think will break us. I know it's nowhere near the same thing as losing a child, but a few weeks ago, I couldn't imagine life without my dad. And here I am, breathing and functioning and living without him. Life goes on even when you're sure it won't."

"I guess so. Your grief group starts tonight, right?"

"It does."

"That's a really incredible thing you're doing. It'll help a lot of people."

"I hope so."

"Do you mind if I keep the Worthington files to take a closer look?"

"Not at all. I'm knee-deep in the McLeod case, but I was planning to revisit Worthington after I close this one. I got the okay from the brass to devote some time to it."

"I'll get the files back to you tomorrow. Talk to me about Ramsey. His name has come up a few times during our investigation."

"Is that right?" Sam asked, smirking. "He's another of my BFFs within the department."

"What's his beef with you?"

"Good question. If I had to guess, it would be something like I'm female, younger than him, I have fewer years on the job and outrank him. And that would be solely because of who my father was and the fact that the chief was my uncle Joe growing up. There could be no other reason for me lapping him."

Avery rolled his eyes. "The fact that you excel at your job has no bearing on it."

"None at all."

"He's jealous."

"Maybe, but he's also dangerous. I think he's trying to railroad Gonzo out of spite toward me." She filled him in on the details of what Gonzo had done and her suspicions of how it had come to light.

"Wow."

"There's a meeting tomorrow at which everyone who matters in this department will beg Gonzales not to take that deal. If he does, his career will be all but over. He needs to remind people *why* he ended up with an addiction to pain meds."

"Absolutely. What happened to Arnold—and to him by extension—was one of the worst things I've ever experienced as an LEO. I can't imagine what it was like for him."

"It was a nightmare. Arnold drove him crazy with his earnestness, eagerness and overall puppylike demeanor. He was the sweetest kid, and Gonzo was good with him, but half the time he wanted to gag him. He was aggravated with him that night and told him he'd let him take the lead if he'd just shut up. That's the part that stays with Tommy now. He believes he put him in front of that gun."

"He gave Arnold exactly what he wanted."

"You and I know that, but you can't tell him that. To him, he set his partner up to be murdered."

"It's an awful thing to live with."

"It is, and who can blame him for doing whatever it took to survive it? Most people around here empathize with him, but not Ramsey. He's out to ruin Gonzo's career in some sort of misguided attempt to exact revenge on me. It's all so screwed up."

"I heard the reason he threatened you most recently is because someone uncovered signs of a possible extramarital affair."

"Is that right?"

"Uh-huh." He gave her a probing look. "You know anything about that?"

Sam made an effort to keep her expression neutral. "Not a thing."

"He must have other enemies within the department."

"That wouldn't surprise me. When you act like a jackass ninety percent of the time, that comes back around on you."

"True. What about Conklin? Was there ever anything to indicate he wasn't a good cop?"

"Only the thing when retired Captain Wallack went missing, and his wife told Conklin, who kept it to himself for two weeks, during which Wallack's stepson forced him to shoot innocent people."

"Did he say why he didn't tell anyone?"

"Because he thought Wallack, who's a recovering alcoholic, might've relapsed. He said he was trying to protect Wallack's reputation. Conklin is in recovery too. My dad was actually the one who dried him out and saved his career when things got out of control for him back in the day. Ironic, huh?"

"It's obscene," Avery said with a forcefulness that Sam appreciated. Good cops were appalled that Conklin had held on to secrets related to her dad's shooting for four years. And Avery was a good cop, even if he was a Fed. "So when he didn't report Wallack's disappearance, was that the first time you knew him to do anything that wasn't by the book?"

She nodded. "You'd have to ask the chief and Malone and people who go further back with him than I do, but I think it was the first time anyone ever questioned whether he was legit. I remember being shocked when I found out what he'd done and feeling sick that I had to report it. Finding out another officer has done something questionable is the worst feeling, especially when he's the deputy chief and a longtime friend of your father's. At least I thought he was. I've since found out otherwise."

"Have you had to report colleagues other times?"

"Here and there. Most recently when one of the department's sharpshooters, Sergeant Dylan Offenbach, was off the grid during the sniper shootings, and our investigation uncovered that he wasn't where he was supposed to be. Rather than attending the conference he'd checked out for, he was off cheating on his wife, with whom he has five children and a sixth on the way. He accused me of ruining his life, but if you ask me, he did that all on his own. I heard he got busted down to Patrol, and he blames me for everything."

"You're just Miss Congeniality around here, aren't you?"

Sam laughed at the title. "So it seems. The thing is, when I first started on the job, my dad gave me the most important advice I've ever gotten about how to do it right. He said if you find out something your superior officers need to know, you report it to them immediately. You don't delay even to take a leak. You report it. I've always lived by that rule, even when it caused me heartburn with my colleagues. I'm not the one doing something I shouldn't be doing."

"And they know that. They just need someone to blame."

"Whatever," Sam said with a shrug. "The fact I'm a woman calling them out, not to mention the daughter of a martyred hero and the 'niece' of the chief, doesn't help."

"Not an easy spot to be in."

"Nope, but when you try to do the right thing most of the time, you sleep pretty well at night. That's not to say I haven't screwed up, because I have. Show me someone who hasn't, but I *try* to do the right thing, and that irritates people around here sometimes."

"I see the same thing in our agency. People do stupid things and then can't believe when they get caught and disciplined. That never sits well, but I just want to say to them if you hadn't done what you did in the first place, we wouldn't be having this conversation."

"Exactly. Trust me when I tell you I take zero pleasure in catching a fellow officer doing something shady. Even Ramsey or Stahl or someone I can't stand, because it makes us all look bad when one of us is bad."

"That's a fact. This has been really helpful. Thank you for taking the time."

"Can I ask you what the expected outcome of this investigation might look like?"

"I'm honestly not sure yet. I'm seeing some patterns here and there, but right now, we're mostly just talking to people."

"Does that include people like Stahl, Ramsey, Hernandez, Offenbach and Conklin?"

"It may. I'd like to get their perspectives just for my own edification. I'd like to hear their justifications, if nothing else."

"Conklin would tell you he was protecting his wife. City Councilman Gallagher and the others involved in the gambling ring had threatened her if he didn't stay in line."

"I can see that as a valid concern, but if you don't have anything to hide in the first place, then no one can threaten you with it."

"Right. That was another of my father's pearls of wisdom—don't give them anything to use against you."

"Have you ever thought about writing a book about being a high-profile female legacy Homicide detective?"

"Uh, well, no, not exactly. Reading and writing with dyslexia isn't something I do for a hobby."

"You ought to think about it. You could dictate it to someone else, the poor bastard, and have them type it up."

"Haha, I could make Freddie do that."

"I think it would be very interesting reading, and with your platform as the second lady, it'd probably be a huge bestseller."

"Just what I want—more public attention than I already get."

Avery smiled. "I'd read it. And I'm totally serious. I think your story would make for an amazing book."

"I'm flattered you think so." Sam took a surreptitious glance at the clock. She had ninety minutes until she had to pick up Roni. "Are we done for now?"

"We are. Thanks again."

"I'm going to run home and see my kids before the meeting tonight. See you later."

"Have a nice visit with the kids, and good luck with the meeting tonight."

"Thanks." Sam was almost relieved to find the pit empty when she emerged from the conference room. She ought to care where everyone was or if anyone was still working, but right now, she just wanted to see her kids before she had to be back. In her office, she went to grab her keys and remembered that Freddie had her car. "Damn it."

As much as she hated to admit it, the Secret Service was about to come in handy.

CHAPTER TWENTY-FIVE

At home, Sam jumped out of the SUV before Jimmy could get the door, earning her an annoyed glare from the agent.

"Is my little girl making friends again?" Nick asked from where he stood in the doorway with Nate.

"Always." She loved the weight of Nick's arm around her shoulders as he escorted her into the house. "

"I can't believe you actually let them drive you home."

"Freddie had my car. They were handy."

"Ah, I see. What're you doing home so early? I thought you had your grief group tonight."

"I do, but I saw a chance to escape for a minute and took it."

Shelby came into the kitchen, her son, Noah, on her hip, stopping short when she saw Sam there. "Mom's home early."

"It's temporary," Sam said. "Gotta go back in a bit. Where is everyone?"

"The twins are upstairs getting changed to go to the park, and Scotty's at basketball practice. I texted to see if he wants to go with us to the park when he gets home."

"Can we go?" Sam asked Nick.

"Sure. Let me just tell Brant."

While he went to do that, Sam said to Shelby, "Why don't you and Noah cut out early too? We can do the park run."

"Are you sure? I don't mind doing it."

"I'd really like to, if that's okay. I feel like they don't get enough of me."

"Yes, they do, Sam. They love you so much, and they know you're working."

"Still, I wish it could be more."

"It's enough. They're doing great. All three of them."

"I'm glad you think so. Go take some time with your own family. I just saw your husband. He's probably home by now."

"In that case, this old preggo lady will take you up on that."

"I want to be you when I'm 'old.'" Sam gave Shelby a hug and kissed Noah's cheek. "Thanks for all you do around here to make it all happen. We'd be lost without you, but I don't want you doing too much while you're pregnant. You have to let us know if you need relief or time off or anything."

"I'm fine. Don't worry about me. I love every minute with the kids. I'll see you in the morning."

"Have a nice evening."

Shelby's pregnancy struck Sam with a pang for the first time in a long time. Her sister Angela was expecting her third, Tracy had three, Shelby was having her second... And Sam couldn't have any. Sometimes, life was unfair, but in the grand scheme of things, she refused to look at her glass as anything other than half full. Her life had been extraordinarily blessed, especially since Scotty and the twins had joined their family.

Speaking of one of her greatest blessings... Nick returned to the kitchen, seeming surprised to see her there alone. "Where's Shelby?"

"I gave her the rest of the day off, which I just realized might not have been the best idea I ever had if you're going to need her later."

"Nope. I'm free for the evening, so no worries."

"Oh good. I wanted to take the kids to the park ourselves. Well, with numerous Secret Service agents, that is."

"I get what you mean."

The kitchen door burst open, and two adorable soon-to-be six-year-olds came rushing in, excited to go to the park.

Aubrey let out a happy squeal when she saw Sam, who scooped her up into a tight hug.

"How's my baby girl?" she asked, using the nickname Sam's dad had given her when she was littler than Aubrey was now.

"Good. Do we have to wear coats to the park?"

"Yep, and hats."

"I hate hats," Alden said.

Nick plopped a hat on Alden's head and held his coat for him. "They keep your head warm."

"Are they gonna let us walk?" Sam asked.

"I think so. I requested that."

She fired off a quick text to Celia to invite her stepmother to come along on the outing. "How far out is Scotty?"

"Two minutes," Nick said. "I told him we'd wait."

While two excited Littles bounced off the walls, waiting for Scotty to get home, Sam ushered them outside and down the ramp toward Celia's home. Her heart still ached every time she looked at the ramp that led to the front door of her father's house. She was coming to accept that the ache would never go away.

Celia came out, wrapping a scarf around her neck and pulling on gloves.

"Celia, you forgot your hat," Aubrey said.

"So I did. Be right back." Celia went back inside to get her hat and then joined them on the sidewalk in time to see Scotty's Secret Service detail arrive.

The twins were so excited to see Scotty that Sam could barely hold them still until he emerged from the back of one of the big SUVs. Only when he was ready for them did Sam release their hands.

He caught them up with an arm around each of them, carrying them like sacks of potatoes. "Anyone looking for some little kids?" he asked Sam and Celia.

"They're all yours, champ," Nick said when he joined them. "Let's go burn off some energy."

The agents kept a respectful distance in front and behind them as they walked the three blocks to the playground that the little ones loved. When they were within sight of the park, the three kids took off running toward the swing set and other equipment. Everything came to a halt when the other parents realized who was joining them.

Sam kept her eyes on the kids while hoping no one would talk to them.

"Ugh," Celia said. "Look away, people. Nothing to see here."

"Right?" Sam said. "The staring is so annoying."

The agents fanned out around the perimeter, making a bubble of sorts around their family. Sam ignored them and everyone else and focused on the kids, pushing Aubrey and Alden on the swings and riding the seesaw with Scotty until the Littles wanted to join them.

Sam wrapped an arm around Aubrey, Scotty took Alden, and Nick took pictures with his phone while Celia called out encouragement. Just another family out for some late afternoon fun, or so she told herself. With Secret Service agents all around, she could never slip completely into the fantasy that they were just like everyone else.

"How can you not run?" a middle-aged man called to Nick. "You owe it to the country to run."

"Sorry, but I'm with my family right now."

"I pay your salary. You can talk to me for one minute."

"Not now I can't."

When the man took a step closer, Brant was there to discourage him. "Back off. Now."

"Or what?" the guy asked. "You fucking politicians are so full of yourselves."

"Dear God," Celia muttered.

"You don't need to talk like that with kids present," Nick said.

"Don't act like you care about kids if you're running away from your obligations to everyone's kids."

Leaving the belligerent man to the Secret Service to deal with, Nick turned his back on him and returned his focus to his own family. "Sorry about that," he said to Sam.

"Don't apologize. You didn't do anything."

"Apparently, I've disappointed a lot of people."

And he hated that. She could see that as clearly as she saw his handsome face and sinfully sexy lips. "You don't owe them anything, Nick. Tell me you know that."

"I do, but it's hard to realize I've let people down. I had no idea they were so... invested."

"You didn't?" she said with a laugh. "Really?"

"Not like that." He gestured to the man who was receiving a talking-to from Brant and Nate.

She hated seeing him dejected.

"Did I do the wrong thing, Samantha?"

"No. You made the best decision for yourself and our family, and you can't start second-guessing because people are disappointed. Someone else will run, and it'll all be fine."

"I hope you're right."

"When have you ever known me not to be?"

He laughed, kissed the top of her head and went to supervise the twins, who were climbing the rock wall.

"Don't let them go any higher," Sam said.

"They go to the top all the time, Mom," Scotty said.

"They do not!"

"They do too." He cracked up at the horrified face she made at him. "What was that guy saying to Dad?"

"Nothing worth repeating."

"Why are people mad at him for being honest about what he wants and what he doesn't want?"

"That's a very good question. Personally, I'd rather not have a president who doesn't particularly want the job, you know?"

"Yeah, even though it would've been sick to live in the White House."

"You say that now, but it'd be so confining."

"More confining than now?"

"Confining on a different level. People watching everything you say and do. Nonstop scrutiny and security issues and life-and-death decisions." Sam shuddered. "I can't imagine it for the life of me."

"Dad could do it."

Sam put her arm around Scotty and gave him a quick squeeze.

"No doubt he could do it, but he has to want to. And therein lies the problem."

"I hate that people are mad with him for doing what's best for himself and his family."

"That's annoying for sure."

Scotty looked up at her, eyebrows furrowed with concern. "You don't think anyone is mad enough to try to hurt him, do you?"

Sam couldn't bear to consider that possibility. "I really hope not, but try not to worry. Brant and the other agents are watching him all the time. They won't let anything happen to him."

"Sometimes, having the Secret Service around is a drag. Other times, not so much."

"I hear you, pal." Sam glanced at her watch and groaned. "I hate to say it, but I've got to go back to work. I have a meeting tonight."

"The grief group, right?"

"That's right."

"Do you think maybe I could come? Is it something kids are allowed to do?"

"Of course you can. I'd love that. I'm sorry that I didn't think to invite you."

"It's okay. You've got a lot going on."

"I do, but I'm always here for you. You know that, right?"

"Duh, yes, I know that. Do I have time to grab something to eat before we go?"

"If we head home right now."

"Let's roll."

Sam told Nick and Celia that she and Scotty were heading home as he ran off to tell the twins he and Sam were leaving. "He's coming with me tonight," she said to Nick.

"Is that right?"

"His request."

"What a fine idea. I'm sorry I didn't think of it."

"I said the same thing."

"Good thing our son is smarter than both of us put together." Nick kissed her forehead. "You gonna be okay at that meeting?"

"Should be. You gonna be okay at home with the Littles?"

"Sure thing. We got this. I'll wait up for you."

"Don't do that if you feel tired."

"I'll wait."

She left with a smile for him and a wave for Celia, who was pushing Alden on a swing. "Will I see you at the meeting?"

"Not tonight," Celia said with a small, sad smile. "Maybe at some point, but I'm just not there yet."

"I understand."

"I hope it's a wonderful success, though."

"Thanks." As Sam walked past Brant, she said, "The crazies are crazier than usual lately."

"Yes, ma'am."

"Don't look away."

"I never do."

She felt confident that Nick would be safe with the earnest young agent in charge of his protection, but she worried anyway.

Sam's detail and Scotty's escorted them home. Sam made turkey sandwiches for her and Scotty that they took with them to eat while the Secret Service transported them to HQ, with plans for a stop to pick up Roni on the way. Sam agreed to ride in one of their SUVs so she could be with Scotty, not because she needed them to protect her.

Two days with a detail had reminded her why she hadn't wanted one in the first place.

"What'll happen at this meeting?" Scotty asked between bites of his sandwich.

"Dr. Trulo is in charge and facilitating it."

"What does that mean? Facilitating?"

"He's going to lead the discussion."

"What kind of doctor is he?"

"A psychiatrist."

"Otherwise known as a shrink."

"Yes," Sam said, amused by him as always.

"And we like this guy?"

"We like him very much. He's been good to me over the years, and when I brought the idea for a grief group to him, he's the one who really made it happen."

"In other words, he did all the work while you got all the credit."

"Something like that." She nudged him with her elbow. "You're too smart for my own good."

His laughter filled her with an unreasonable joy. "Watch out for when I lap you and take over the management of the family."

"I'm keeping my eye on you, buster."

"Did you find the person who killed that lady who stole from her friends?"

"Not yet."

"I've been thinking about her. What do you suppose her plan was? It wasn't like they weren't going to find out she'd ripped them off."

"I think she was probably planning to leave the country."

"By herself? Didn't she have kids?"

"Yeah, but they were pissed with her because she scammed their friends' parents."

He thought about that for a second. "So she was going to leave the country and not take her husband and kids?"

"Her kids are adults, so it's not like she would have left behind little ones."

"Still. They're her kids."

"That's true," Sam said, mulling that over. "You think they were in on it?"

"I don't know, but I'd wonder how much they really knew."

"We think the daughter might have been running money to the Cayman Islands, which is a tax shelter, meaning that people who deposit money there don't have to pay taxes on it in the U.S."

"Do you think the daughter knew what she was doing?"

"We're talking to her tomorrow, but she'd have to be pretty stupid not to know why she was being sent there."

"Did they send her with suitcases of cash?"

"That's what I want to know too. And P.S., if you're interested in a career in law enforcement, we might have a spot for you on the MPD."

"Not if we get to him first," Deborah, Scotty's lead agent, said over her shoulder from the front seat.

"There's a bidding war for me," Scotty said with a big grin.

"How do you know about bidding wars?"

"Video games. That's how I learn most of the coolest stuff, which is why school is so not necessary."

The agents in the front seat laughed while Sam tried not to join them. "Your father would have a heart attack if he heard you say that."

"Which is why we aren't going to tell him. Got me?"

"I got you." The motorcade pulled onto Roni's street.

"Why are we stopping here?"

"We're picking up my new friend, Roni. Her husband was killed recently by a stray bullet. They'd just gotten married."

"God, that's so sad."

"It's awful. I had to talk her into coming tonight. I hope she hasn't changed her mind."

"I hope not either."

"Be right back."

CHAPTER TWENTY-SIX

S am waited for the agents to open the door and then got out of the vehicle to go up the stairs to the vestibule to buzz for Roni. "Hey, it's Sam," she said when Roni answered. "You ready to go?"

"I'll be down in a minute."

As she waited on the stoop, Sam was relieved that Roni hadn't bailed. The door opened, and Roni stepped out, stopping short at the sight of the motorcade parked outside her home. "Um, what's all this?"

"My son asked if he could come to the meeting. Since he's under the protection of the Secret Service, we are too. Is that okay?"

"Oh sure. I guess."

"Sorry for the big production. If you're friends with me, you have to deal with an occasional motorcade."

"That wasn't part of our original agreement."

Sam laughed at her witty comeback. The more time she spent with this woman, the more she liked her. She gestured for her to lead the way into the SUV. "After you." When she got in after Roni, she said, "Roni, meet Scotty. Scotty, this is my new friend, Roni."

Scotty shook Roni's outstretched hand. "Wow, you must be really cool, because my mom usually hates people."

"And now I'm mortified," Sam said, glaring playfully at Scotty. "You're not supposed to tell *people* that."

Roni laughed helplessly, and even though Sam wasn't happy about Scotty spilling her secrets, she was thrilled to see Roni so delighted.

"I don't hate *all* people, just the *extra* ones."

"I gotcha." Roni wiped laughter tears from her eyes. "And it's so nice to meet you, Scotty."

"You too. I'm very sorry about your husband."

"Thank you. I'm very sorry about your grandfather."

"Thanks. It totally sucks."

"It really does."

And right there, Sam thought, grief group was already spinning its magic for people who needed to know they weren't alone with their losses. Roni asked Scotty about school, and they quickly bonded over their shared disdain for math. "My husband was a math genius. I used to tell him he was lucky I ever went out with him after I found that out."

"I don't know if I could do it," Scotty said gravely. "I'd fear that our differences would be too great if my wife was a math geek."

"He had other qualities that helped me forget about that one major failing."

"My dad is a total school geek. He gets so mad when my mom and I diss on school, but he got straight A's his whole life. He has no idea what the rest of us go through."

"The struggle is real," Roni said.

"So real. When he helps me with math, he makes it seem so easy. But I suck at it on my own."

"Here's a pro tip for you—sucking at math doesn't mean you're going to suck at life. Trust me on that."

"My mom says the same thing."

"And your mom ought to know. She most definitely does *not* suck at life."

"But she did suck at math," Scotty said, making them all laugh.

As they walked into HQ through the main doors, Sam marveled at the difference between daytime, when the press staked out that door, and nighttime, when the area was deserted.

"In case you don't already know this, your kid is pretty awesome," Roni said when Scotty preceded them into the building.

"Oh, I know. I can't take any credit, though. We found him that way."

"He's adorable, sweet, articulate and funny as hell."

"We love him madly."

"I can see why." Roni looked around at the MPD lobby. "So this is where it all goes down, huh?"

"Nah, this is the fancy part. Come see my pit."

"You work in a pit?"

"That's what we call the Homicide squad's neck of the woods. Follow me, and I'll show you." Sam led her through the corridors to her home away from home. "Here it is in all its glory." Her third-shift detectives, Carlucci and Dominguez, were just coming on duty and stood up from their desks to greet Sam.

"This is Detective Dani Carlucci and Detective Gigi Dominguez. My friend Roni Connolly."

"Nice to meet you both," Roni said, shaking their hands.

Sam thought her eyes were playing tricks on her when Gonzo walked into the pit for the first time in months. She went to hug her close friend and sergeant and introduced him to Roni.

Gonzo shook her hand. "Nice to meet you. I heard about your husband. I'm so sorry. I lost my partner to murder earlier this year."

"I read about that. I'm sorry for your loss too."

"It's so good to see you here," Sam said to Gonzo.

"It's nice to be seen." Gonzo hugged Scotty, Carlucci and Dominguez. "I figured I might catch the meeting tonight, if that's okay."

"That's more than okay. We'd love to have you."

"LT," Carlucci said, "just so you know, when they tried to pick up Mandi McLeod, she was gone. Her roommate said she left shortly after you were there earlier and hasn't been around since."

"Damn it."

"Detective McBride took the liberty of checking to see if she was with her brother, but there's no sign of him either."

Sam thought about that for a second. "Put out a BOLO for them. Alert local airport and train station security to be on the lookout for them. And let's call Jesse Best," she said, referring to the commander of the U.S. Marshals. When you needed to find someone, the marshals got it done. The "Be On the Look Out" alert was more specific than the "All Points Bulletin" request, and usually led to apprehension when the suspects were located.

"We're on it," Dominguez said.

"Let me know if anything breaks overnight. I'll be here for the next hour or two and at home after that."

"Will do."

Though she wanted to stick around and work the case, she had other obligations tonight. "Let's head upstairs to the lieutenants' lounge."

"I'll be right up," Gonzo said, ducking into his cubicle.

"Lieutenants have their own lounge?" Scotty asked as they walked toward the stairs. "That's sick."

"So sick I've only been in there, like, twice."

"How come?"

"Who has time to lounge around in lounges? Not me." Sam wanted to groan when she saw the one person she'd hoped would be long gone for the day by then.

Sergeant Ramsey was coming out of the SVU offices as they went by.

It was too much to hope that he'd let them pass without comment. "Hey, Holland, I know you had something to do with the bullshit that came through interoffice mail, but don't think I'm going to take that lying down. I'm coming for you."

With her hand on Scotty's back, Sam compelled him to keep moving, but her son glanced at her in alarm.

"Do you hear me, Holland? You'd better watch your back."

Roni spun around. "Shut up, you moron. That's *her kid* with her. Why don't you just move along?"

Ramsey shot a filthy look at Roni but took her advice, to Sam's great relief.

Sam glanced at her. "Just so you know... Never again in our entire friendship will I ever love you more than I do right now."

"I usually hate to peak early, but in this case, it was worth it."

Sam laughed. "You have no idea how much I enjoyed hearing you call him a moron."

"I think I probably get it. I'll confess to having read about your past run-ins with him. I recognize him from the coverage."

"Yeah, he's a problem."

"Do I need to worry about him making good on those threats?" Scotty asked.

"Nah, he's a windbag."

"Is he the one you 'accidentally' pushed down the stairs that time?"

"Maybe?"

"Good," Scotty said. "Looks like he deserved it."

Sam hated that she had to set him straight, but she had to be the parent once in a while. "So, buddy, the thing is, I never should've let that happen. He said a crappy thing to me, but he didn't deserve to be injured over it." She was such a liar, but thankfully, Scotty couldn't see that. Or at least she hoped he couldn't. "And for the record, I only punched him. He fell down the stairs all by himself. But I absolutely should not have punched him." She had no regrets, but her son didn't need to know that.

"I get you. Dad always says that we can't solve problems by creating more problems."

"Dad is very wise."

"Someone's got to be." Scotty snorted under his breath and held the door to the lieutenants' lounge for her and Roni to go in ahead of him.

"I *love* your kid," Roni said to Sam.

"I do too."

Sam was pleased to find a large turnout for the grief group. She recognized several faces from past cases, including Lenore Worthington, and a few surprises, such as her old friend Roberto and his girlfriend, Angel. Roberto rolled his wheelchair toward Sam.

"If it's not the most fly detective in all the land," Roberto said, smiling up at her. He had short dark hair and friendly brown eyes.

Sam bent to hug him and then stood upright to hug Angel, who also had dark hair and eyes. "Good to see you guys."

"You too," Angel said. "We saw something on Facebook about the group and decided to check it out."

They'd both been victims of violent crime in the past and were perfect for the group. "I'm so happy to have you here. This is my son, Scotty, and my friend Roni." After she introduced them all, she looked around but didn't see Dr. Trulo. *Uh-oh.* "Excuse me for one second. I need to make a quick call." Sam walked away, flipped open her phone and put through a call to Dr. Trulo, who answered on the second ring. "Please tell me you're in the building."

"I'm about fifteen minutes out. I just got Hattie Townsend checked into a residential facility in Bethesda, and traffic is a bitch, as usual."

"Uh, what am I supposed to do with the group?"

"Get them organized in a circle and start by telling them a little about why we formed the group, what we hope to accomplish and then let everyone introduce themselves."

"I guess I can do that."

"You got this, Lieutenant. I'll be there soon."

Not soon enough, Sam thought. "All right. See you very soon, I hope."

Trulo hung up, laughing.

Sam gulped and took a deep breath before turning to the gathered group of about fifty people. "Hey, everyone." When she had their attention, she said, "Thanks for being here. Our facilitator, Dr. Trulo, got called out to assist with a case this afternoon and is on his way back now. He wants us to organize ourselves in a circle, so let's see if we can do that much without his help."

Scotty rolled his eyes at her and started arranging the chairs with an efficiency that impressed his mother and the other adults.

"Looks like your kid is as fly as you are, mama," Roberto said.

"He's way more fly than I am. He's gonna take over the world someday."

"Speaking of world domination, I was sad to hear your old man isn't going to run. He'd have been a dope president."

"I think so too, but between us, the kids and I are looking forward to having him all to ourselves."

"Heard you took in those twins after their parents were murdered."

"They're the sweetest kids. We love them so much."

"That was a dope thing you did, lady cop."

"It felt dope. I like being a mom."

"Looks good on you."

Scotty gestured to her, pointing to the circle of chairs.

"Let's get this show on the road." Sam led Roberto and Angel to the chairs. She moved one to make room for his wheelchair and then sat next to him. "I think I probably know most of you," she said, "but for those who don't know me, I'm Lieutenant Sam Holland." She'd planned to say more, but the words got stuck on her lips when Nick walked in and took a seat in the circle, drawing every set of eyes in the room to him.

"And that," Sam said, "is my husband."

He gave a little wave as everyone else laughed. Nick Cappuano needed no introduction.

Later, Sam would ask him why he hadn't told her he was coming and who was with the kids, but for now, she was thankful to have him there. "Dr. Trulo is on the way to save you all from me, but until he arrives, he suggested we begin with introductions and a little bit about why we're here and what we hope to accomplish. Dr. Trulo and I had the idea for the group as a way to bring together some of the people we encounter in our daily work, for support and help through the difficulty of losing a loved one to violence.

"Everyone in this room understands the pain of tragic loss, but our losses bear the additional burden of the way in which they happened—suddenly and violently, thrusting us into the web of law enforcement and criminal justice. I lived in that world long before my father was shot on the job and left a quadriplegic in a case that went unsolved for four long years. The shock of his shooting, the pain of his new reality, the fear over his precarious health were the most stressful things I've ever been through. It took my dad almost four years to succumb to his injuries, but our lives changed forever on the day he was shot.

"I feel blessed to have gotten that extra time with him, but I was always aware of the hell in which he lived after the shooting. He died suddenly last month, so my grief, and that of my son Scotty and our entire family, is still fresh, especially since learning a man we considered a close friend was involved in covering up the details of the shooting.

"The death of a loved one by violence is complicated, no matter how or when it happens. We hope this group will become a source of comfort and fellowship to those of you who've walked this journey and that you'll find new friends who understand better than anyone else ever could what it's like to travel that path."

She nodded to Roberto, encouraging him to go next. "Hey, y'all, I'm Roberto, and I met my friend the lady cop here when she was undercover in a crew I was running with at the time. I was working for some bad dudes, and when shit got real, I ended up in this chair. The lady cop came to see me in the hospital, offered me a way out and kept her promise to help me find a good job. My girl, Angel, she got snatched off the street and roughed up, and when they sent her back to me, she was broken. We've both been through hell, but at least we have each other. I'm pretty sure I would've died without her to give me a reason to go on living."

"Same for me, baby," she said softly. "Hi, everyone, I'm Angel, and like Roberto said, when I was kidnapped and raped, I thought my life was over. I've found out since that I can still feel joy and excitement and pleasure. It's just taken me a while. I'm glad to be here. Thank you, Sam, for organizing this."

"I'm Lenore, and my son, Calvin, was shot and killed fifteen years ago when he was fifteen. I've now lived without him longer than I had him with me. The case remains unsolved, which is part of what keeps my grief so present. That we've never been able to get justice for him is something I live with every day." She glanced at Sam. "I'm hoping a renewed interest in the case will lead to some answers."

Sam gave her a quick nod, hoping she could keep that silent promise.

"I'm Trey. My daughter, Vanessa, was killed in one of the recent drive-by shootings."

He was one of the people who'd inspired Sam to want to start the group. She'd never forget responding to the scene of Vanessa's murder or his unbearable heartache.

"She was six and so sweet and..." Trey looked down, took a breath and released it slowly. "I was a single dad, and she was my whole life. I don't know what to do without her. People keep telling me it'll get better in time, but I don't think it will. When Lieutenant Holland invited me to come to this meeting, I hoped maybe it would help to be around other people who've been through the same thing I have."

"We're glad to have you here, Trey," Sam said.

He nodded, his lips tight and his handsome face twisted with torment.

"My name is Joe, and my beautiful wife, Melanie, was also killed in the drive-by shootings. She was expecting our first child, so I lost them both. Mel never did anything to deserve what happened to her, and I've been dealing with a lot of anger since she was killed. Some days, I fear it's going to boil over and take me under, but I keep pushing through because that's what she'd want me to do. But it's the hardest thing I've ever had to do."

The woman next to him took hold of his hand. "I understand that feeling, Joe. I'm Danita, and my son, Jamal, was also killed in the drive-by shootings. He'd been to see a movie about space at the Air and Space Museum with two of his friends and was shot for no good reason on the walk home. I know all about unreasonable anger and the kind of grief that makes you wonder how you can go on living. I've been lucky to have my daughters to help me through it, but every day since we lost Jamal has been a struggle." She glanced toward Lenore. "My son was also fifteen. Like you, I thought I was almost home free. He was a good boy who almost always did the right thing. I was pretty sure he was going to grow up to be a good man."

"He would have," Sam said. "Everyone we talked to raved about what a fine young man he was."

"Thank you," Danita said, wiping away tears. "That means a lot."

"I'm Tommy, an officer with the MPD. My partner was killed three feet from me in January, after I let him take the lead for the first time because he was bugging me. We were on a stakeout in the cold. We were tired and hungry and annoyed. I told him if he'd stop being a pain in the ass, he could take the lead with questioning our suspect when he finally showed up. Arnold was like a happy little kid, running through it with me, how he'd approach the guy, what he'd say. I've relived that last hour with him so many times. We got out of the car, and he was dead less than a minute later. I've had a really hard time accepting that he took a bullet that should've been mine, but through lots of therapy, I've come to understand it was his time, not mine, even if I'll always be so sorry he had to go when he did. He was a good guy, a great cop in the making. I miss him, even if he was annoying sometimes."

Gonzo took the tissue one of the other women handed him and pressed it to his eyes. When he looked up, Sam sent him a reassuring chin lift and a nod, hoping he knew how proud of him she was.

"I'm Scotty, and the lieutenant is my mom. I wasn't part of her family when my grandpa Skip was shot. I met my future parents after Gramps had been in the wheelchair for two years already. So I never knew him before, but I heard lots of stories about how he was a terrible dancer and gave the best parties and was a great cop. I would've liked to have known that version of him, but I'm really thankful I got to know him at all. He taught me a lot in the short time I knew him, things like how important it is to keep your word and that the measure of a person is whether they do the right thing when no one is looking. Stuff like that. I know I'll always remember him and the things he taught me."

Roni handed Sam a tissue that she accepted with a grateful smile.

Nick gave Scotty's shoulder a squeeze. "I'm Nick, and you've met my wife, Sam, over there, and my son, Scotty. I lost my best friend and former boss to murder almost two years ago. I was chief of staff to Senator John O'Connor at the time of his murder, and when I lost him, I also lost my job and my identity and a friend who'd been by my side since I was eighteen. I was tapped to take his Senate seat, which later led to being asked by President Nelson to replace Vice President Gooding when he fell ill, and here I am, vice president because my best friend was murdered. Sometimes, it's hard to wrap my head around the way it all happened. But I like to think John would be pleased and maybe shocked to see me now. He'd definitely have something to say about it." He ended with a small grin that belied the pain he carried with him from the loss of John and the events that followed.

"I'd also like to add that, like Scotty, I didn't know Skip before he was injured, but I grew to love him for many of the same reasons Scotty did, plus one more really important one—he made my wife into the best cop and person I've ever known, and I'll always be thankful to him for her."

Sam dabbed at her eyes again. "No fair."

Everyone else laughed, which relieved some of the tension that had come from hearing everyone's stories.

"I'm Roni. My husband, Patrick, was killed a month ago when a stray bullet found him on a sidewalk when he was out grabbing a sandwich for lunch. We were newlyweds, madly in love and just happy, you know? I thought I was set for life once we got married. I never imagined having to live most of my life without him. I think a lot about the day before he died, when I was supposed to go to the grocery store but forgot and went straight home instead. I was moaning about forgetting and said I'd go back out. But Patrick told me not to sweat it. He said he'd go out for lunch the next day. I wonder if maybe if I'd made it to the store, he wouldn't have left the office to get lunch, and he'd still be here with me. I know there's no sense second-guessing something that's already happened, but I'll always be sorry I didn't make it to the store that day."

Sam reached for Roni's hand and gave it a squeeze, her heart breaking all over again for the other woman. What a thing to have to live with, the feeling that something you did or didn't do might've indirectly cost someone else their life—and that someone being the person you love most in the world.

"I'm Joseph, and my son, Daniel, was killed when he was in the wrong place at the wrong time. Someone looking for revenge against an ex-boss locked the boss and my son in a freezer, where they froze to death. I try not to think about what that must've been like for them, if it hurt or how long it took for them to die. Daniel was my pride and joy, the focus of my entire life, and losing him... I've been really struggling. When Lieutenant Holland called me about this group, it felt like a badly needed lifeline, so thank you for organizing this."

"Thank you for coming, Joseph," Sam said. "I've thought of you so often since that night, and I'm very glad to see you here."

"Thanks for having me. Hearing what happened to others makes me feel less alone with my loss."

That, Sam thought, was the entire purpose of the group.

By the time Dr. Trulo joined them half an hour later, the group was immersed in a conversation about how other people in their lives didn't understand their grief and expected them to get over it on others' timetables and how some of the people they'd been closest to before the tragedy hadn't stuck around afterward.

Sam scooted her chair closer to Roni's to make room for the doctor.

"How's it going?" Trulo asked in a whisper.

"Better than I ever imagined."

"Congratulations, Lieutenant," he said with almost fatherly pride that touched her broken heart. "You've done a very good thing here."

"Couldn't have done it without you."

"Yes, you could have. This was all you. I was just your glorified admin behind the scenes."

Sam laughed. "Bullshit, but okay. If you say so."

"I say so."

CHAPTER TWENTY-SEVEN

"Who's with our Littles?" she asked Nick when the meeting had concluded.

"Celia offered to stay with them when I said I'd like to come."

"That was nice of her. I thought Tracy and Angela were coming."

"Angela wasn't feeling well, and Mike ended up having to work late."

"I was hoping Derek would come too," Sam said of their friend Derek Kavanaugh, who'd lost his wife, Victoria, to murder.

"He said he hopes to get here eventually, but I guess tonight wasn't possible."

"I need to speak to someone," Sam said. "I'll be ready to go in just a minute."

"Take your time, babe."

She went over to talk to Lenore, who was standing with Danita, probably comparing notes about losing their teenage sons.

"Sorry to interrupt," Sam said, "but I wondered if I could speak to Lenore for a second."

"Of course," Danita said. "I'll definitely call you for coffee, Lenore."

"I'll look forward to that."

After Danita walked away, Lenore smiled at Sam. "Your group is already doing so much good."

"I'm glad to hear that. I wanted to tell you I've received permission to take a look at Calvin's case. It'll be after Thanksgiving before I can get to it, but I'll keep you informed."

"I appreciate anything you can do."

"I'll give it everything I've got," Sam said.

"That's more than anyone has given it thus far."

"I'll be in touch."

"I hope you have a blessed Thanksgiving."

"Same to you."

"It's a little overwhelming to realize how many people need your group," Roni said when they were on the way home with Nick and Scotty in one of the Secret Service SUVs.

"At times, it can be," Sam said, "which is one of the reasons I wanted to do it. We do what we can to get justice for murder victims and their families, and then we move on to the next case. I found myself wondering what became of people like Trey Marchand, who lost his little girl in the sniper case. I wanted to know he was okay."

"It's nice of you to care so much."

"Don't tell people I'm nice, or we can't be friends."

To Scotty, Roni said, "Is there, like, a handbook or something that comes with her?"

"Dude, if there was, I sure could've used it a coupla years ago."

Sam play-punched his arm as Nick laughed.

"But I can definitely give you some pointers, such as don't enter any room that she might be in with my dad without either knocking or covering your eyes."

"Don't tell all our secrets, buddy," Nick said.

Sam noted a hint of yearning in Roni's expression that made her ache for the other woman's loss.

When they pulled up to Roni's house, she turned to hug Scotty.

"It was so great to meet you, Scotty, and you too, Mr. Vice President."

"Please call me Nick."

"Er, um, Nick."

"I hope we see you again soon, Roni," Nick said.

"I hope so too."

Sam got out to hug her on the sidewalk.

"This was good for me," Roni said. "Thank you for making me go."

"Thank you for letting me make you. You have plans for Thanksgiving?"

She nodded. "I'm going to my parents' house. There'll be a big crowd there, which I hope will help."

"I hope you're able to enjoy that a little. I'm here for you. Anytime you need a friend. Call me, text me, come by my house on Ninth Street, stop by the office. I'm here."

"That means so much. I've stopped hearing from a few people who probably don't know how to deal with me right now, so it helps to have some new friends to lean on."

"I'm not just saying it either. I honestly don't like a lot of people, but for some strange reason, I really like you."

Roni laughed—hard. "I am so *honored*."

"You should be."

"I haven't laughed in weeks. You're already batting a thousand, and you will be hearing from me."

"I'm counting on that. Take care of yourself."

"You too."

Sam got back in the car. To the agent holding the door for her, she said, "Wait a sec until Roni gets inside."

"Yes, ma'am."

Per Sam's request, the car didn't move until Roni closed the door behind her. "I really like her."

"Does she have any idea how lucky she is?" Nick asked, amusement dancing in his lovely eyes.

"She does, because Mom told her," Scotty said.

Nick laughed. "I'm sure she did."

"As I recall, *Scotty* was the one who told her I hate people and that she was lucky I liked her."

"She needed to know," Scotty said. "I stand by my statement."

"Spoken like a future politician," Nick said.

"Or police officer," Scotty said.

"Wait, what?" Nick asked. "Since when?"

"I'm just keeping all my options open."

"I couldn't handle worrying about both of you."

"Mom will be too old to run the streets by the time I get there."

Sam shot him her best perp glare. "Who you calling *old*?"

"You're not old now. You will be *then*."

"And I'll still be able to kick your ass."

"She will, pal," Nick said. "I wouldn't mess with her."

The silly conversation was what they needed after airing out their pain at the meeting. "Thanks for coming tonight, you guys. Meant a lot to me to have you there."

"It was really cool," Scotty said, "to hear what those people have been through. It makes you realize you're not alone with whatever your thing is."

"That was our goal in starting the group. I'm so glad you came and that you got so much out of it." She paused before she added, "I hope you know you can always talk to us about how you're feeling about losing Gramps."

"I do, but I know it's so hard for you too. I don't want to make it worse for you."

"You couldn't make it worse. Knowing he was loved by so many has made it easier for me to cope with losing him. Everyone I talk to who knew him has something funny to share about him, or something meaningful about how he touched their lives. I loved hearing the advice he gave you and how you'll always live by his wise words."

"I will for sure. I want to make him proud of me."

"He was so proud of you. He used to tell me all the time what a remarkable kid you are and how much he loved you."

"I really miss him," Scotty said. "Every day after school, I want to go see him and tell him everything that happened. He always wanted to hear the latest news."

"He looked forward to seeing you. You made his last years so much happier than they would've been otherwise."

"I'm glad I could do that for him, but he did a lot for me too."

They arrived home a short time later and went up the ramp to the front door, where a Black female agent Sam didn't recognize greeted them.

"Mrs. Cappuano, I'm Kourtney with a K, one of the agents on your detail. It's a pleasure to meet you."

"She says that now," Sam said to Nick as she shook hands with the new agent. "Great to meet you Kourtney with a K. If you've talked to Vernon and Jimmy, you already know it's not a pleasure to protect me. I apologize in advance."

"Vernon did mention that Fuzz could be challenging."

"Ugh, again with that nickname. I hate that name."

"I've heard that as well," Kourtney said, smiling.

"And yet no one cares that I hate it."

"That's above my pay grade, ma'am."

"Don't call me ma'am, and we'll get along fine."

"Yes, ma'am—I mean, Lieutenant."

"Better."

Nick moved her forward with a hand to her back, and she felt a thrill of excitement run through her, knowing he was ready for their end-of-the-day time alone together. She was more than ready.

"I need to call Freddie really quick and also check in with Carlucci."

"Make it snappy," Nick said with a playful smile.

Motivated to get the tasks done as quickly as possible, Sam put through the call to Freddie.

He answered on the third ring. "What?"

"Did you mean, 'What, Lieutenant'?"

"Yeah, that. What?"

"I was checking to make sure you're okay."

"I'm fine. You? How was the grief group?"

"It went really well. People seemed relieved to have a place to talk it out."

"That's great. I love that."

"You're sure you're okay?"

"Yep."

"I don't like when shit like that happens."

He huffed out a laugh. "Neither do I, but I handled it."

"Thank you for not getting shot or killed or any other dreadful thing."

"I do what I can for the people."

"Trademarked."

"Oh right, sorry. Anything new with the case?"

"Green might have something implicating the daughter in the scheme."

"No shit?"

"No shit." She told him about the trips to the Cayman Island.

"How did the Feds not find that?"

"I don't think they investigated Ginny's kids. Just her and Ken. Green dug into a private Instagram account, something called Finsta?"

"Yeah, I've heard of that. Wow, that's a bombshell."

"Yeah, and now we can't find her or her brother. We've got people looking for them, including the U.S. Marshals."

"You think the kids had something to do with her murder?"

"I really don't know yet, but I'd say at least the daughter had a hand in the scam."

"Why don't we use Ken Sr. to lure them in?"

"What're you thinking?"

"He contacts them, tells them he needs to see them, that it's urgent, etc."

"That might work. I'll tell Carlucci to get with him and set it up. Good thinking. I'll see you in the morning."

"Call me if anything pops overnight."

"Will do." Sam ended that call and put through another to Carlucci.

"Hey, LT. I was just going to call you. I heard from Jesse Best that the marshals apprehended Mandi and Ken McLeod Jr. at BWI, about to hop a flight to the Bahamas."

"Were they now? Well, that's excellent news."

"Best's team is bringing them in, and I was going to put them on ice until you're here in the morning, unless you'd like us to handle it some other way. I was also planning to run their financials to get the lowdown on when they bought tonight's plane tickets."

"Sounds like a plan. They'll probably lawyer up anyway."

"No doubt."

"Good call on the financials. I'll see you in the morning. Call me if anything new pops."

"Will do, see you then."

Sam called Freddie back.

"What now?"

"What now, *Lieutenant*."

"Yeah, yeah, what's going on?"

"Best's team got them at BWI, preparing to board a plane to the Bahamas."

"Is that right?"

"They'll be waiting for us in our cooler in the a.m."

"That gives us something to look forward to."

"Right. See you at six thirty?"

"Ugh, do we hafta?"

"Let's get this wrapped up before the holiday, when everything comes to a screeching halt and makes our lives twenty times more complicated."

"Fine. See you then."

"You bring the coffee." Sam ended the call before he could object to her order, which made for a rather satisfying end to a seemingly endless day. She went upstairs, checked on the sleeping twins, kissed them both good night and covered them up. Then she crossed the hall to knock on Scotty's door.

"Enter."

"Are you all set?" she asked, noting he had papers spread out on his bed and the Caps game on TV.

"Define 'all set.' I still have a tiny bit of math homework to do."

"Define 'tiny bit.'"

"Thirty, maybe forty minutes of pure hell."

"Do I need to send Dad in?"

"Nah, I think I got it, but I'll send out an emergency text if needed."

Sam went to him and leaned in to hug him. "In case I forget to tell you every day, you're my favorite thirteen-year-old boy named Scotty."

"Gee, thanks."

She kissed the top of his head. "Love you."

"Love you too. Thanks for letting me go with you tonight."

"If there's ever something I'm doing and you want to go, just say the word. If there's no chance of anyone shooting at me, you're more than welcome wherever I am."

"Thanks."

"Don't stay up too late."

"Night."

Sam went into her room and shut the door, leaning back against it to release a deep breath. "This was one *long-ass*, mo-fo day."

Nick was already in bed, scanning briefing books, his sexy-as-fuck chest on full display.

Inspired by that chest, she started pulling off clothes right where she stood and dropping them on the floor.

He glanced up, saw what she was doing and did a double take. "What is happening?"

"Only good things."

"I love good things." He tossed the briefing book on the floor and held out his arms to her when she sashayed across the room, naked as the day she was born, to join him in bed. "And you, my love, are the goodest of good things."

"Don't let people hear you say that. You'll be criticized for poor grammar."

"No one but you will ever hear that."

"I love when I get to have you all to myself at the end of the day."

"I love when you have me all to yourself too.

She straddled him and came down on top of him as his hands cupped her breasts.

"I have the sexiest wife in the whole world."

"Yes, you do."

His laughter did such amazing things to his already sinfully handsome face. Sitting up, he pulled her in closer and drew her nipple into his mouth. Sam let her head fall back as she let go of the stressful day and lost herself in the magic they created together. How she'd ever lived for so many years without him amazed her.

Sinking her hand into his thick hair, she squirmed on top of him, pressing against his hard cock and trying to move things along.

"Patience, love."

"No patience."

He grasped her ass and held her in place, taking his time with one breast and then the other, moving back and forth until he had her on the verge of begging. And then he moved them both and brought her down on his cock, joining their bodies in a moment of utter perfection that kept her addicted to him and this and them. If they lived forever, she would never get enough of him.

"How do you do this to me every time?" she asked, winding her arms around his neck and holding on tight.

"The same way you do it to me. Every single time."

"Hold on tight," he said in the second before he turned them and settled on top of her without losing their intimate connection.

"Smooth move, Mr. VP."

"You liked that?"

"I like all your moves." She drew him into a hot, tongue-twisting kiss and then drew back with a groan when her phone rang. "I have to get that."

"Seriously, Samantha?"

"Seriously, Nicholas. Hold that thought."

"I'm holding." He pressed into her to make his point, not that his point needed to be made.

Sam twisted under him to grab her phone off the bedside table. "Holland."

"Sorry to bother you, Lieutenant," Carlucci said.

"No bother. I wasn't doing anything." She smiled up at Nick, who glared at her and thrust into her again. Sam had to bite her lip to keep from giving away what she'd been doing—and was still doing—when the phone rang. "What's up?

"When we ran Mandi McLeod's financials, we found that she

made forty-two dollars' worth of purchases at a hardware store a half mile from her parents' home on Sunday around two thirty."

"Hot damn! Good work, Carlucci."

Nick raised her leg, filled her completely and captured her nipple between his teeth, giving a gentle bite that had her gripping his hair in a tight handful.

"I thought you'd want to know that," Carlucci said.

"Absolutely. Thanks for the call. I'll see you first thing."

"See you then."

Sam slapped the phone closed and tossed it aside.

Nick smoothed his tongue over her nipple. "Are you back?"

"In case you didn't notice, I never left."

"Oh, I noticed. I notice everything about you." He wrapped his arms around her and picked up the pace, leaving her breathless as he drove them to the finish line in a frenzy of heat and desire so intense, she wondered how she survived it. And it was like that every single time.

Lying in his arms afterward, she breathed in the fresh, clean scent of his skin and loved the tickle of his chest hair against her face. "Thanks for coming tonight. I know it took some doing, but I appreciated it."

He ran his hand over her back in soothing circles. "I wanted to be there for you, not just to support your new endeavor, but I knew you'd be talking about your dad. I didn't expect it to be so cathartic to talk about John for the first time in a while."

"I know he's never far from your mind."

"I think of him every day and imagine him mocking me in my mostly useless role of VP. He'd get such a kick out of that."

"I wouldn't let him mock you."

"You wouldn't be able to stop it. That was our groove. We were always busting each other's balls about something."

"Sometimes, I wonder if I would've liked him."

"Only because you investigated his murder, so you know how he really lived his life. If you'd met him before that, you would've liked him. Everyone did."

"Hmm, I'll have to take your word for it. Gonzo looks good, doesn't he?"

"He does."

"We're meeting in the morning about the plea deal," she said, yawning.

The next thing she knew, her alarm was going off, and Sam woke up in the same place she'd been the night before—wrapped up in Nick's arms, her head on his chest. Before him, she hadn't been able to bear being touched while sleeping. Now, she was most comfortable surrounded by him. She shut off the alarm and took one second to enjoy him before they had to go their separate ways for another long day.

CHAPTER TWENTY-EIGHT

"Get up, Samantha," Nick said, his voice gruff with sleep.

"I'm up."

"No, you're not. You're on your way back to sleep."

"Don't act like you know me so well."

He pinched her butt, making her startle. "Up."

"Did you sleep?"

"Like a dead man. I need that same cocktail before bed tonight too."

"That cocktail is available to you anytime you need it."

"Cocktail hour is my favorite time of day."

"Every second with you is the best part of my day, especially if there're some kids tossed in the mix. And I'm not going to see them this morning either."

"You'll have a whole week with them next week."

"I can't wait. I want to do everything—movies and crafts and baking and games and all the stuff I never have time to do."

"We'll do it all. I promise."

"On that note, I gotta go tell Freddie he can stay in bed a little longer."

"How come?"

Sam sat up, pushed her hair back from her face and reached for her phone. "Because I've got something I need him to do on the way in." She put through the call to her partner.

"I'm up," he said, sounding as grouchy as Sam felt.

"Good, but I'm calling to give you another forty-five minutes in bed."

"Okay, bye."

"Freddie! Listen. I want you to go to a hardware store near the McLeods' and find out exactly what Mandi bought at two thirty on Sunday. Get me a receipt and security video of her in the store if they have it. I'll have Carlucci text you the address."

"Got it, will do."

"Call it into the pit the minute you know and get it in writing from the store."

"Okay."

"Thanks. Set your alarm again."

"Yes, Mom."

Sam slapped her phone closed, called Carlucci and then headed for the shower.

"Damn, that's a nice view," Nick said from the bed.

She put some wiggle in her walk just for his benefit.

Thirty minutes later, she headed out to work and was met on the ramp outside her front door by Vernon and a new woman.

"This is Belinda. She's on your detail today. Belinda, this is Mrs. Cappuano."

Sam shook hands with the tall, red-headed agent. "Nice to meet you, and actually, I'm Lieutenant Holland for the next eight to ten hours." She prayed it would be the lesser end of that range.

"Such an honor to meet you, Lieutenant. I've admired your career."

"Thank you. I need a ride to work this one time."

Vernon smiled. "As you know, we'd prefer to drive you."

"You get your wish today." While he held the door, Sam got in the back of the SUV, adrenaline zipping through her veins at the thought of maybe closing the McLeod case and perhaps returning some of the missing money to Ginny's victims. Wouldn't that be something? To do something the Feds hadn't been able to accomplish would be a huge victory for the MPD at a time when the department could really use a win.

"When we get to HQ, go straight to the morgue entrance in the back please." She cringed at the thought of her colleagues seeing her arriving in a Secret Service vehicle. Fortunately, she didn't warrant and entire motorcade.

"Yes, ma'am," Belinda said.

The media was still staked outside the building. Didn't they ever get tired of the futility of waiting for something that would never happen? Not once in all the months that Nick had been vice president had Sam ever given them anything useful. And yet they still showed up every day with hope in their hearts. Better them than her. She'd rather chase murderers than a story that wasn't going to happen. But hey, to each his or her own.

When they arrived at HQ, she ducked inside, hoping to avoid anything that got in the way of her plans for the morning. With just over two and a half hours until the meeting about Gonzo, she was hoping to use most of that time to sew up the McLeod case.

They were close. She just needed the last few details to lock it up.

Carlucci and Dominguez were in the pit when she strolled in. "Ladies! It's a fine day to solve a murder. What've you got for me?"

Dominguez, who was petite, with gorgeous brown skin, hair and eyes, turned to Sam, her eyes rimmed with red.

Sam stopped short. "What's wrong?"

"Ugh, I'm so sorry to be crying at work. Boyfriend trouble."

"Are you okay?"

"I will be once I show him the door."

"That's the way. Let me know if you need anything."

"Thank you, Lieutenant."

"No worries. We've all been there. It's the worst."

"Yes, it is." Gigi made a visible effort to shake it off. "In other news, we've got Mandi and Ken McLeod Jr. in the cooler, and their father has been calling every six minutes to demand we release them."

"Is that right?"

"He's been quite insistent," Carlucci said. "He says we have no grounds to hold his children, and we need to let them go immediately, or he's going to the media."

"And you told him where they were found and where they were going?"

"We did," Carlucci said. "He said they were going to the Bahamas for a long-planned trip for Thanksgiving." The tall, blonde detective put two pieces of paper on the desk in front of Sam. "Except we can prove they purchased the tickets yesterday afternoon, which takes the steam out of that explanation."

"Very well done, as usual, ladies." Sam loved the buzz of knowing they were closing in on murdering scumbags. "Cruz is going to call in as soon as he has anything from the hardware store."

"The thing is," Gigi said, "I'm still having trouble picturing one of them actually killing their own mother."

"I think it was heat of the moment," Sam said. "Maybe Mandi went to the house to have words with her mother about what she'd done to her life by scamming her friends' parents, and when things escalated, she reached for the closest available thing and swung."

"So you think she didn't mean to kill her?" Gigi asked.

"I think maybe she wanted to," Dani said, "but didn't go there planning to do it."

"That's what I think too," Sam said. "Let's see what she has to say. Put her in interview one and him in interview two."

"Will do," Gigi said.

After Dominguez left the pit to see to Sam's orders, Sam glanced at Dani. "Is she okay?"

"She will be once she gets rid of him. I think he's getting rough with her, but she denies it."

"Do we need to have a talk with him?"

"I asked her that, and she pleaded with me to let her handle it, so I'm trying to do that. She promised me last night that this is it. She's going to end it with him."

"What do we know about him?"

"He's got a sealed juvie record, but nothing as an adult. I did a deep dive on social media and picked up a vibe that he's not a good guy when it comes to women. I tried to tell her that without letting her know I was looking into him. Fine line, you know?"

"I hear you. Thanks for watching out for her."

"She's like my baby sister. I want to stab that dude through the heart."

"I got a rusty steak knife you can borrow anytime you need it."

Dani laughed. "I may take you up on that."

"Do I need to worry about her?" Sam asked.

"I'm keeping an eye on it. I'll let you know if we need to get more involved."

"Do that."

"Thanks, LT."

"I'm going to bring her in with me when I talk to Mandi," Sam said. "Give her something else to think about."

"Good call."

"I'll take you in with Ken."

"Let her do them both. She needs it more than I do right now."

"Sounds good. And keep being generous to your fellow officers, Carlucci. You'll never regret it."

"I'm lucky to work with awesome people. Gonzo looked great when he was here last night."

"By all accounts, he's doing very well."

"I'm relieved to hear that."

"Me too. The poor guy has been through hell."

"I heard they're going to charge him..."

"Not if I can help it."

Dani cracked up. "Why did I know you were going to say that?"

"Because you know bullshit when you see it, and so do I."

"I'm so glad you're all over that. Here's the rest of what you need to know about our friends Mandi and Ken."

Sam spent the next few minutes scanning the reports from the marshals who'd apprehended the siblings and reviewing financials for both of them.

Gigi returned a few minutes later. "They're in the rooms."

"Any talk of lawyers?"

"Not to me, and I didn't see anything about that in the reports from the marshals. They both seem scared shitless."

"Good. Come in with me, Dominguez."

Her entire demeanor brightened. "Really?"

"Really. Let's do it."

Sam went into her office to grab her notebook and pen, put her hair up in her favorite clip and headed for interview one with Detective Dominguez. When they burst into the room, Mandi startled and then seemed to shrink into the orange jumpsuit. Her hands were shackled.

"Detective Dominguez, you can remove the cuffs from Ms. McLeod."

"Yes, ma'am."

While Dominguez took care of that, Sam stared at Mandi, taking pleasure in the way she wilted. Fluorescent lighting tended to make even the prettiest people look wan and sickly. "So, Mandi. We meet again."

"I told you everything I know the first time."

"Did you, though?"

"What does that mean?"

Sam took her time withdrawing the report on Mandi's financials from one of the file folders and placed it on the table in front of Mandi. "See the item we highlighted? That's your card being used at a hardware store half a mile from your parents' home on Sunday, when you told us you were..." Even though she knew the list by heart, Sam opened her notebook, scrolled back a few pages and glanced at Mandi. "At study group, napping and writing a paper all day. You said you never left campus. So which is it? Did you never leave campus, or did you make a trip to the hardware store near your parents' home around the time your mother was killed?"

"I... Um, I'd like to speak to a lawyer, please."

Sam pushed the notebook and pen across the table to her. "Write down your lawyer's name and number."

"I, uh, I don't know who to call. Our family's lawyer was one of the people my mother scammed."

"We'll call the public defender's office for you."

Sam and Gigi got up and turned to leave the room.

"Wait. Where're you going?"

"Once you make that request, we can't talk to you until your lawyer arrives."

"You need to let me out of here."

"Sorry, but that's not happening anytime soon."

Mandi broke down into gut-wrenching sobs. "I didn't do anything!"

"Then you shouldn't have anything to worry about."

"Don't go. I don't want to be here."

"I'm not allowed to talk to you until your lawyer gets here, and I've got other stuff to do until then."

"Please. I've never been in any trouble. I didn't do this."

"We'll talk about it when your lawyer gets here. It's apt to be tomorrow, though. The public defenders are always backed up."

She shook her head. "I don't want a lawyer."

"Are you officially rescinding your request for an attorney?"

Mandi nodded and used the sleeve of her jumpsuit to wipe her eyes and nose.

"Are you sure? Because that might not be the smartest idea."

"I'm sure. I want to get out of here."

Sam and Gigi returned to their seats.

"Detective Dominguez, please record this interview and add that Ms. McLeod has declined her right to an attorney."

Dominguez did as requested.

When she was done, Sam said to Mandi, "We're listening."

"I... I wasn't entirely truthful about Sunday."

"We already know that. Why did you go to your parents' house?"

"Because my brother asked me to meet him there. He wanted to talk to my mom about where the money was and what could be done to make restitution to the people she stole from."

"But you knew where the money was, because you made the deposits in the Cayman Islands, right?"

Mandi hadn't been expecting that. Her mouth fell open and then snapped shut. "I... I don't know anything about that."

"Save it, Mandi. We can put you in Georgetown, Grand Cayman, four times in the last two years." Sam put the printouts from her social media in which she'd posted about being there.

"How did you... That account is private."

"Funny thing about social media. Nothing is really private if you know how to dig deep." Which Sam had no idea how to do, but thankfully, she had detectives who did.

"That doesn't prove anything other than I took some vacations."

"In one of the most notorious tax havens in the world? Try selling that to someone who's buying that BS. You know exactly where the money is. Does your brother know that you know? And you might want to start being truthful, because we're talking to him next."

"He knows I went on vacation. That's all it was."

"And your mom never asked you to deposit cash or a bank check in a Cayman account while you were there?"

"I don't know anything about that."

"I'm sending a detective to Georgetown tonight. I'm going to have him match up the security footage from the dates you were there with every bank on that island."

"I used the ATM at one bank to get out cash."

"And that was it? He's not going to find that you made any deposits while you were there?"

"What if I said I did but had no idea why I was doing it? Would that matter?"

"Potentially. If you were to provide account numbers and other salient information that would allow for restitution to your mother's victims, I'm quite certain there'd be room to negotiate on any other potential charges you might be facing."

"What other charges?"

"Murder, for one."

"I didn't kill her!"

"But I think you know who did, and you helped clean up after that person. If you know who killed her and don't tell us what you know, you can also be charged with hindering our investigation."

She started crying again, sobs jolting her petite frame. "I was just a college kid minding my own business. My mom offered to pay for my vacations if I did a favor for her while I was there. I'm not sure how that's a crime."

"It's a crime because you've known all along where the money is stashed and you denied it."

"She told me she'd kill me if I breathed a word of it to anyone. 'They'll never think to investigate you,' she said. And the Feds didn't. No one asked me anything until you came to my dorm."

And until Cameron Green dug into the financials and social media for the entire McLeod family. Why in the world hadn't the Feds done that too?

"Who killed your mother?"

"Why does it matter? Didn't she deserve it?"

"That's not for me to decide. My job is to find out who killed her. Whether or not she deserved what she got is for a higher power to determine." Sam leaned in. "*Who* killed her?"

Mandi shook her head as tears streamed down her face and sobs echoed through the room.

"Who did it, Mandi?"

"My brother! He did it. He went to the house to beg her to do the right thing and give back the money, but she told him there was no way that was happening. They got into a fight in the garage, and when she told him to stop being a whiny baby, he grabbed the closest thing and just swung it at her. He didn't mean to kill her."

"How did you hear about it?"

"He called me, hysterical. Told me to come quickly. He needed my help."

"What did he need you to do?"

"He couldn't find anything with bleach in the house, so he asked me to get some and disposable rags and garbage bags."

Sam took notes as Mandi ran through the list. "What did you need the garbage bags for?"

"I think he was going to try to get her out of there, but there was just so much blood."

"Did he tell you what he did before he sent you to the store?"

"No, but I could tell it was something horrible, because I'd never heard him sound so freaked out."

"When he asked for bleach and garbage bags, you still didn't suspect murder?"

"No, I figured he'd dropped a bottle of merlot on one of my mother's Turkish carpets or something like that."

"What did you think when you got to the house and saw what'd happened to your mother?"

"I freaked out. Completely lost it. I hated her for what she did to our lives, but I didn't want her to die. Not like that. And my brother... He was just out of his mind. He's not a murderer, Lieutenant. He's a really good guy. You have to understand what she did to us, what she did to everyone."

"I'm having a hard time feeling sorry for you, Mandi, when you knew all along who killed her and where the money was and didn't tell anyone."

"She said she'd kill me!"

"And you actually believed your own mother would kill you if you did the right thing and told the authorities where she hid all that money? Or, I should say, where *you* hid it for her."

"I didn't know that's what I was doing."

"So you say."

"It's the truth!"

"Even when the shit hit the fan with the Feds, it never occurred to you to say, 'Oh, by the way, I know where the money is stashed'?"

"Not if I valued my life. My mother was very clear about what would happen to me if I told anyone what I knew. She said if I ever breathed a word of any of this, even if she was gone, I'd pay."

"Whose idea was it to go to the Bahamas?"

"Mine. I wanted to get my brother out of the country."

"Why there and not the Caymans, where the money is?"

"Just because I helped her make the deposits doesn't mean I have access to the money. Only she had that."

Sam pushed a yellow legal pad across the table to her. "Write it all down. I want every detail of the runs you did for your mother to the Caymans, what happened Sunday, how you and your brother decided to cover up his involvement, your plans to flee to the Bahamas. All of it. Detective Dominguez will stay with you while you do."

"Are you going to tell my brother what I told you?"

Sam looked at her, wondering if she was for real. "Yes, I'm going to tell him."

"You can't! He'll hate me."

"What did you think I'd do with that info?"

"Get him to tell you what happened without implicating me. Please? Isn't it enough that our lives were ruined by our mother? Don't take him from me too. *Please.*"

Sam didn't want to be moved by her, but she was nonetheless. "I'll see what I can do, but if he's not willing to admit his involvement, I'll tell him I already know what happened. Either way, he's going to be charged, and you will be too."

"For what?"

"Lying to us, obstructing our investigation, possible money laundering, embezzlement. That kind of thing."

Mandi put her head down on her crossed arms and wailed.

Sam walked out of the room, pissed off and annoyed.

Captain Malone was waiting for her.

CHAPTER TWENTY-NINE

"Did you catch that?" Sam asked the captain.

"The highlights."

"I've hated this case from the outset, and I hate it even more now."

"I can't believe we might've found the money and the Feds didn't," Malone said. "I kinda like that."

"I figured you might. This department could use a big win like that, and it's all thanks to Green. He's a star."

"Yes, he is. Cruz reported back from the hardware store—the same things Mandi said she bought."

"I'm glad it matches up. That's another box checked."

"You believe her when she says it was the brother."

"It fits our theory that the murder was heat of the moment, that the murderer grabbed the first thing they could reach, and it went down from there."

"So the charge will be manslaughter?"

"That's what I'm thinking. I don't believe he went there that day intending to kill her." Sam checked her watch. "I have just enough time to talk to him before Gonzo's meeting."

"I'll let you get to it."

"You want to come in with me?"

He blinked, seeming surprised. "Oh, um, sure."

"Are you? You still remember how, right?"

"Don't be a smartass."

"That's like telling me not to breathe, Cap."

"Don't I know it."

Sam led the way into interview two, where Ken McLeod Jr. was pacing like a nervous cat. If his sister were to be believed, he had good reason to be nervous. "Have you been advised of your rights regarding counsel?"

"I have. I waived my right to counsel."

Sam turned on the recorder. "Interview with Kenneth McLeod Jr., Lieutenant Holland and Captain Malone present. Subject has waived his right to an attorney. Have a seat, Mr. McLeod."

"I'd prefer to stand."

"Have a seat, Mr. McLeod."

He sat, hands on the table, posture wary and distrustful. "I don't know why I'm here."

"You don't?"

"No."

"Let me tell you something they taught us in Law Enforcement 101. Innocent people don't run."

"We weren't running. We were going on vacation for Thanksgiving."

"And when did you decide to take this vacation?"

"Yesterday."

"Right after your mother was murdered. Odd timing."

"She wasn't in our lives. Her murder had no impact on us."

"None at all? Your mother was whacked in the neck with a yard tool and bled out on the floor of her garage. That didn't affect you at all?"

"Not the way you think it would. She hurt a lot of people with what she did, including my sister and me. It's no wonder someone killed her."

"Do you have any idea who might've killed her, Ken? And before you answer, I want you to really think about your options here. If you know something and don't share it, you can be charged with a felony count of impeding a homicide investigation."

"I told you. I don't know anything."

Sam had to give him credit, he never blinked, fidgeted or

anything that murderers usually did when confronted by cops after committing the ultimate crime. "Were you at your parents' home on Sunday?"

"No."

Again, he gave no indication he was lying.

"What if I had a witness who can put you there?"

"Your witness is lying. I haven't been anywhere near my parents' house in months. I'd be willing to take a polygraph, if necessary."

Interesting, Sam thought. *If he's lying, he's one hell of an accomplished liar.* "Why did you and your sister decide to go to the Bahamas days after your mother's murder?"

"I told you—because Mandi is on Thanksgiving break from school, and we both wanted out of here for the holiday, seeing as we no longer have a family to spend it with."

Sam hated that the explanation actually made sense, but she couldn't reconcile what Mandi had told her with the cool customer sitting before her.

"So you're close with your sister, then?"

"We've had our differences over the years, but we've stuck together during this nightmare our mother brought down on us."

"What kind of differences?"

"The usual sibling shit. Who got to use the car our parents made us share as teens, who took whose earbuds and didn't return them. That kind of stuff. Things were a lot better between us after I left for college, and we weren't living together anymore."

Recalling her own sisters saying the same thing once upon a time, Sam stood. "We'll be back."

"I haven't done anything. You can't hold me here indefinitely."

Sam let him have the last word and left the room with Captain Malone following her out.

"What're you thinking?" Malone asked when they were in the hallway.

"That the sister is minimizing her own involvement and pointing the finger at her brother to save her own ass."

"What do you want to do?"

"I want to talk to Mandi again."

"I'll watch from observation."

Sam led the way back to interview one, where Dominguez was overseeing Mandi's efforts to record her version of what'd happened.

Mandi popped up out of a slouch, her eyes wide with fright. She looked like someone who had something to hide. "Did you talk to Ken?"

"I did."

"And?"

"He says he didn't do it."

"He's lying!"

"See, the thing is, I don't think he is."

"He is! He did it!"

"Convince me."

"I told you! He called me at one thirty on Sunday in a complete panic. I left my dorm to get the things he said he needed, and I was at my parents' house by three and found him standing over my dead mother."

"He says he hasn't been to their house in months. Did he tell you why he went there that day?"

"To beg her to do the right thing and give back the money."

"Does he know you made the Cayman deposits for your mom?"

She blinked and squirmed, and Sam could almost see smoke coming out of her ears as she tried to figure out how to reply to that. "No."

"How did you explain your frequent trips there to him?"

"I told him I was taking a break from school. Like I said, this was long before we knew what my mother was really doing. I had no clue she'd stolen the money I was depositing for her until the Feds charged her."

"And then you knew exactly why she'd sent you to the islands and basically implicated you in her crime. The way I see it, Mandi, you had much more of a motive to end her than your brother did."

"I didn't do it."

"So you say."

A knock sounded on the door, and Sam got up to see who was

interrupting her interrogation. The only time that happened was if someone had found something that would help.

Cameron Green gestured for her to come out of the room.

Sam closed the door behind her. "What's up?"

"After we found Mandi's ties to the Cayman Islands, I did some digging in some of the other more notorious tax shelters and found something interesting in Delaware. The VMcL Corporation was formed just over two years ago, and I thought you might be interested in who's on the four-person board of directors. The company's assets are listed at fifteen million."

Sam took the paper he handed to her and scanned it quickly. It listed Amanda McLeod as chair, Kenneth McLeod Jr. as vice chair, Kenneth McLeod Sr. as treasurer and Virginia McLeod as director-at-large. "Great work as usual, Green. This helps."

"Are you liking the daughter for this?"

"I want to, but she insists it was the brother, who's the coolest-under-pressure dude I've ever encountered if he murdered his mother. I don't know what to believe. We need a warrant to dump their phones and the father's," she said, adding Ken Sr. on a hunch. "She insists the brother called her at one thirty in a freak-out, asking her to get stuff for him from the hardware store and then meet him at the parents' house. I need to know if that call happened and if you can put him in the area on Sunday. I'll ask Malone to get the warrant."

"Once we have it, I'll get with Archie to track them," Green said. "We can track the pings to isolate his location."

"Do hers and the father's too. Let's figure out who's telling the truth here."

"On it."

Sam ducked her head into the observation room. "Cap? Can you come here, please?"

"What's going on?" she heard Mandi ask Dominguez. "I didn't do anything! You need to let me go!"

Captain Malone stepped out of the room and closed the door behind him.

"We're going to track the cell phones to see who's telling the truth. Can you take care of the warrants?"

"I will. Good call, no pun intended."

She handed him the paper Green had provided. "In the meantime, Green has found a corporation in Delaware worth fifteen million, and guess who's on the board of directors?"

Malone scanned the sheet. "Well, I'll be damned."

"Let's go ask Ken Jr. if he knew he was vice chair of the board."

They went back to interview two.

"Got another question for you, Ken. Have you ever heard of a corporation called VMcL?"

"No. Why?"

Sam placed the paper on the table in front of him. "I assumed you would've heard of it since you're the vice chair of the board of directors."

"What? No, I'm not."

Sam pointed to the place where he was listed. "Yes, you are."

He looked up at her, shock etched into every corner of his face. "I know nothing about this, Lieutenant. I swear to God."

Sam believed him.

"I can't believe she'd use me this way." He shook his head. "Who implicates their own kid in a crime of this magnitude? Who *does that*, Lieutenant?" He seemed on the verge of tears. "She was my *mother*. Wasn't she supposed to protect me?"

Sam had heard Nick ask the same heartbreaking questions about his own mother. "Yes, she was."

"I don't know what to do. I had no idea she'd done this, and now I suppose I can be held criminally liable for things I had nothing to do with."

"This may be an opportunity to fix some of the wrong your mother did."

"How so?"

"As a director of the company, I'd imagine you'd have the ability to determine where the money goes."

He brightened visibly. "I would, wouldn't I?"

"I think so."

"I'll do anything I can to make this right for the people she stole from."

"Hold that thought." Sam retrieved the paper about the company's board of directors. "We'll be back."

Sam left interview two, and while Malone went to see to the warrants for the phones, Sam returned to interview one. "What's the deal with the VMcL Corporation?"

Mandi's brows furrowed. "I don't know any company by that name."

Sam put the printout on the table. "That's strange, because you're the chair of the company's board of directors." She pointed to the place where Mandi could see her name.

"I am? How's that possible if I've never heard of the company?"

"I don't know. You tell me."

"I don't know either! She never told me anything about this."

"The company has fifteen million in assets."

"Oh. Well... I didn't know."

"Now you do."

"I'm not sure what you want me to say about it. I didn't know she made me the chair of a company I'd never heard of. I didn't know she was sending me to the Caymans to deposit stolen money. I didn't kill her."

"You were pretty oblivious all the way around, huh?"

"I was in *college*, Lieutenant. Did you go to college? Do you know what's involved?"

"I went to college and grad school—with dyslexia—so yeah, I know what's involved."

"I didn't have time to pay attention to what she was doing with her business."

"But you had plenty of time to take trips to the Cayman Islands whenever she needed you to."

"Those were *vacations*. Since when are vacations illegal?"

"They're not, unless you're actually on the payroll to stash money in tax-free havens."

"I wasn't. She didn't give me a dime except for my tuition. My brother and I were always expected to work, and we did. They even made us share a car in high school so we wouldn't be spoiled. None of our friends had to share a car with their siblings. We were the only ones."

Poor baby, Sam wanted to say. *How did you ever survive such hardship?*

After hearing how Ginny had raised her kids, Sam needed more insight into who she had been as a person, how she'd ended up defrauding friends and family and what her relationships with her kids had been like.

She left Mandi and went to talk to Ken Jr. again. "Who was closest to your mother?"

"Her sister, Janet."

"Did your mother steal from her?" Sam didn't recall seeing anyone named Janet on the list of fraud victims.

"No, but probably because Janet is an artist and never really had money to steal. She knows my mother better than anyone."

"Write down her address and phone number."

CHAPTER THIRTY

To save time, Sam decided to call Janet rather than visiting her in person. Since she was looking only for background, she could do that over the phone. She used her cell so the MPD number wouldn't show up on Janet's caller ID.

Janet answered on the fourth ring, sounding winded. "Hello?"

"Janet Milton?"

"That's me. Who's this?"

"Lieutenant Sam Holland with the Metro PD in Washington."

"The vice president's wife."

"Yes."

"Is this about Ginny?"

"It is."

Janet sighed. "What can I do for you, Lieutenant?"

"I'm looking for some insight into your sister."

Janet's harsh laugh echoed through the phone. "You and everyone else."

"Talk to me about her relationship with each of her kids."

"What about them?"

"Was she close to them?"

"She was before she decided to become a criminal. After that, things were a bit strained, to say the least."

"Before that, was she closer to one of her children over the other?"

"She always had a special bond with Mandi. Ken Jr. was independent from a young age. He didn't 'need' Ginny the way Mandi did."

"How so?"

"Ginny referred to Mandi as her Mini-Me. They did everything together. At times, she would say she worried that being so close to Mandi was making it difficult to be her parent. She hated saying no to her but knew she needed to so she didn't create a monster. Have you spoken to the kids?"

"I have. I'm going to be honest with you, Ms. Milton. I have them both in custody and suspect one of them might've killed your sister."

A long silence met her statement.

Sam was about to ask her if she had any thoughts on whether one or both of Ginny's kids would be capable of murder when Janet started talking.

"I can't see Ken doing that, because as far as I know, he hadn't seen either of his parents since before the federal charges were filed. But Mandi... I don't know. She says she hasn't seen them, but I have a hard time picturing her not seeing Ginny on a regular basis."

"Even after Ginny stole from the parents of Mandi's friends?"

"Even then. I was with Ginny two months ago at her house, and we were talking about what'd happened and what she'd been trying to do with the investment opportunity and how she hadn't intended for it to go the way it did."

"What did she intend?"

"She genuinely planned to go through with the purchase of a property that would be the next high-end planned community, but endless red tape and unexpected zoning challenges had messed up everything. She said no one understood how difficult it was to put together something as complex as what she was trying to do, and with people getting anxious about their money and what'd become of it, she'd run out of time. While I was there that day, Mandi came into the kitchen and stopped short when she saw me."

"She told us she hadn't seen either of her parents since before the federal charges were filed."

"That's not true. This wasn't that long ago, and she was definitely there. Don't get me wrong, Lieutenant. I love my niece—and my nephew. I loved my sister despite her many flaws. I'm not trying to get either of them in trouble."

"I understand. We're just trying to get at the truth. What are your feelings about Ken Sr. not knowing about the scam?"

"I think he's full of shit, but then, I've always thought that. He's a blowhard. Has a big opinion of himself and isn't afraid to share it with anyone who'll listen."

"So you think he knew about the scam."

"No question. I've always believed that, but the Feds couldn't prove it, which is why he wasn't charged along with Ginny."

"What did she tell you about his involvement?"

"That he didn't know. She never deviated from that throughout the investigation."

"Do you think he threatened her in some way?"

"I wondered that, but she was adamant that everything was fine between them and that he had nothing to do with the scam."

"Would she have told you if things weren't good between them?"

"I don't think so. She never had a bad word to say about him in all the years they were together, even to me, and we talked about everything. Sometimes, I'd wonder how she could stand him because he was so pompous, but that didn't seem to bother her."

"Is he close to the kids?"

"To Ken more than Mandi. He used to joke about how he didn't 'get her' and how it was a good thing he had a son, or he might think he was the problem."

Sam had already gotten an asshole vibe from Ken Sr., and Janet's insight only added to it. "Wasn't he angry to find out she took money from their family members, colleagues, friends?"

"If he was, I never saw that, which is another reason why I believe he knew exactly what she was doing. How else do you explain why he stayed with her after she took money from his brother, his former coworkers, their mutual friends? Would you stay with your spouse if he did something like that?"

Since Nick would never do such a thing, that wasn't something she needed to worry about, but she wasn't about to say so. "It does seem odd to me that he didn't raise more of a stink."

"He didn't raise a stink because he *knew*, Lieutenant. He knew what she was doing and maybe even endorsed it."

"What I don't get was their end game. So they steal from everyone, stash the money somewhere and then stick around long enough for the investors to get squirrely and report them to the authorities. Why weren't they long gone? They had more than enough to live comfortably forever."

"It was probably because of our mother. Her health has been declining over the last year, and Ginny always took care of her. She wouldn't leave her."

"Even if it meant getting caught in a web of her own making?"

"Even if. She was very devoted to our mother and vice versa, especially since Mother has been in an acute care facility for dementia."

"Are you devoted as well?"

"My mother and I have never once seen eye to eye on anything. We aren't close. I visit my parents once or twice a month, but Ginny was there every day. She was the one who followed my mother's plan for her life. I had my own ideas and wasn't afraid to express them."

"Does she know your sister is dead?"

"She does. I was there yesterday to share the news with both my parents. After basically accusing me of lying about what happened to Ginny, she finally understood I was telling her the truth when I showed her an online story about Ginny's murder. Mother was devastated and asked me to leave. That about sums up our relationship. But then again, she refused to believe her precious Ginny did anything wrong with the investment either. She kept saying it had to be a misunderstanding, because Ginny would never do something like that."

"Do you believe she could do something like that?"

"I loved my sister, Lieutenant. We were always close despite being two very different people. But I do believe she was capable of scamming people. She had a taste for the high life, and after Ken lost his job—"

"Wait. When did that happen?"

"Just over two years ago. He got 'reorganized' out of a job after thirty years with his firm."

"Huh, isn't that around the time that the Feds allege Ginny's scheme began?"

"Right around then."

Sam consulted her notes. "He was an estate attorney."

"Right."

"How does a guy his age in that profession get reorganized out of a job? Wouldn't he be a partner in his firm by then?"

"In most cases. He never achieved partner status. It was something that made him—and Ginny—bitter. They sued his firm when they let him go, but it didn't go anywhere."

"He told me she had a gambling addiction."

"No, she didn't."

"You're sure of that?"

"One hundred percent sure. She never gambled in her life. Ginny liked money—gathering it, having it, spending it. No way she'd ever gamble it. That wasn't her nature at all."

Now Sam knew Ken Sr. and Mandi had both lied to her. That was enough to charge them with impeding her investigation, which would buy her time to figure out the rest of what they'd lied about. She had a feeling there'd be additional charges coming their way.

"Thank you for your time, Ms. Milton. This has been very helpful."

"Do you know who killed my sister, Lieutenant?"

"I'm not completely sure yet, but we're getting closer."

"Will you let me know when you do?"

"I'll do that. If you think of anything else that might be relevant, please call me back on this number."

"I will."

"Thanks again." Sam ended the call with the usual satisfying slap of her flip phone and sat back to ponder what she'd learned from Janet. Then she picked up the phone on her desk and put through a call to Patrol, trying to remember who had taken Hernandez's place after his arrest. She had no idea.

"Patrol. Officer Baker."

"This is Lieutenant Holland. Could you please ask someone to pick up Kenneth McLeod at his brother's home in Chevy Chase?" Sam recited the address. "He's apt to be confrontational, but I don't expect him to be armed or dangerous. Read him his rights and tell him he's being charged with interfering in a homicide investigation."

"Yes, ma'am. We'll get right on it."

"Thank you."

Sam hung up and thought it through from every angle. The call to Janet had been illuminating in more ways than one. Not only did she know for sure that Mandi and Ken Sr. had lied to her, she also knew Ken Jr. was most likely innocent of any involvement in his mother's death. She just needed Archie to confirm that for her.

An hour later, the man himself appeared at her door. "I've got the cell phone data you requested."

"Gimme," Sam said.

He handed over several pages that had names on the top. "I did the daughter, the son, the husband and Ginny's phone too."

"Perfect, Archie. Thanks." As Sam tried to read what was written on the page, the words swam before her eyes into a mixed-up jumble of letters and numbers. Goddamned dyslexia reared its ugly head at the worst possible times. She glanced up at Lieutenant Archelotta. "Give me the gist?"

"Sure, no problem. I could find no record of a call from Ken Jr.'s phone to his sister's on Sunday afternoon. His phone only shows pings from his home and a nearby park on Sunday."

Wow, Sam thought. So much for Mandi's efforts to pin the murder on her brother.

"There was a two-minute call from Ken Sr. to Mandi that was made at one twenty. She was at school when she received the call."

"And where was he when he made it?"

"At his house."

"And not on the golf course like he told us. Hot damn. That means not only did he lie, but the three friends who told us he was playing golf with them all afternoon lied too. We've got a lot of people to arrest."

"Sounds that way."

Captain Malone came to the door. "We're getting ready to start the meeting with the AUSA and Gonzales. You coming?"

Sam glanced at the clock on the wall and saw that it was one minute before nine. "I'm coming." She gathered the cell phone info to take with her. "Thanks for this, Archie. You just made my case for me."

"Happy to help."

"You always do," she said with a warm smile.

"Good luck with the meeting," Archie said. "I think it's madness they're going to charge him with a crime after what happened to Arnold. A lot of people think that."

"Appreciate that. I know he would too."

Archie nodded and took off toward the stairs to go back to his kingdom on the second floor.

Sam walked with Malone to the chief's conference room. "I think the husband killed Ginny, and the daughter helped him after the fact. I also believe the two of them know where the money is."

"I heard the Feds expended a big effort trying to find it."

"They focused their efforts on Ginny and Ken Sr. They never investigated their kids, which Green did, and that's what led to Mandi's trips to the Caymans."

"That'll make for a rather nice headline, especially with the FBI investigating us at the moment."

"That thought never occurred to me, Captain."

His bark of laughter echoed through the hallway. He gestured for her to go ahead of him into the conference room, where Chief Farnsworth, Assistant U.S. Attorney Faith Miller, Gonzo and Christina waited for them with Nick's lawyer friend Andy Simone.

Sam was surprised to see Christina there too. "Morning, everyone."

"Morning," Gonzo said.

He looks good, Sam thought. *Really good. Like the Tommy he was before disaster struck.*

Captain Malone shut the conference room door and sat next to Sam across from Tommy and Christina. The chief and Faith sat at either end.

"Faith," the chief said, "this is your meeting."

"Thank you for coming in, Sergeant," Faith said. "As you know, we're here to discuss the possibility of a plea deal pertaining to the charges of possession of narcotics as well as illegal acquisition of narcotics, both of which are felonies. We've agreed to plead the charges down to misdemeanor counts."

"He's not taking that deal," Christina said.

Gonzo smiled at her. "I've got this, honey." He glanced at Faith. "No deal."

Faith cast a confused glance at Andy. "I thought we had an agreement."

"My client has had time to consider all his options and has decided not to accept the deal," Andy said.

Faith looked to the chief for direction.

"Sergeant Gonzales," Farnsworth said, "the floor is yours."

"Thank you, Chief, and to all of you for your support over the last ten months, the worst time of my life. Losing Arnold the way we did nearly ruined me, and I allowed that to happen because the grief was so immense, it swallowed me whole. I don't say that lightly. It drowned out everything else in my life, even the two people I love the most." He took Christina's hand and held on tight. "I did things during that time I'm not proud of, many things, including scoring pain meds on the streets out of desperation. Whatever it took to drown out the pain. I'm not proud of how I behaved or the things I did to survive. In rehab, I learned I have to forgive myself for those things, or I won't be able to stay sober. I've learned I have to put my sobriety and health above everything else in my life, even my fiancée and son. If I want to stay healthy for them, I have to do it for myself first."

He looked right at Faith. "In my right mind, Ms. Miller, I never would've done what I did. I was sick—with guilt, grief and regrets I'll carry with me forever. I walked that amazing young man straight into a slaughter. I'll relive the horror of that night every day for the rest of my life. But I'm not a criminal. I'm a victim of the same man who killed my partner, and that's why I'm not accepting the deal.

"I understand that you have a job to do, and I respect that. I understand that by not accepting the deal, I'm forcing you to consider taking my case to trial. If that's what you and USA Forrester believe needs to happen, so be it. But I won't willingly sign anything that effectively ends the career I've worked so hard to have. I'm a good cop, Ms. Miller. I'm good at what I do, and I want to continue doing that job for as long as I possibly can. If I plead guilty to these charges, that won't be possible."

Sam wanted to stand up and cheer. Her Gonzo was *back*, with the same fire in his eyes he'd had for the job before that tragic night last January. "If I might add something," Sam said. "I believe the only reason you're aware of the lengths Sergeant Gonzales went to in the effort to survive the loss of his partner is because of the vendetta Sergeant Ramsey has undertaken to try to discredit me and my squad. After the grand jury failed to indict me for assaulting Ramsey, he's been hell-bent on causing trouble for my officers and me any way he can. The information about Sergeant Gonzales purchasing drugs on the street, which sparked the investigation, came from one of Ramsey's informants. That doesn't make what Sergeant Gonzales did less of a crime. However, it does indicate the lengths that some people within this department will go to in order to harm others."

"I've suggested that Tommy give a media interview," Christina said, "during which he'll take ownership of his struggles in the aftermath of Arnold's murder as well as the things he did to feed his addiction. If he comes clean and does so within the context of the larger story surrounding Arnold's death, I believe he'll be tried in the court of public opinion and forgiven for his so-called crimes."

"I agree with that one hundred percent and was going to suggest the same strategy," Sam said to the woman who'd been an adversary during her investigation of John O'Connor's murder. They had since become friends.

"I'm glad you think so, Lieutenant," Gonzo said. "Even though I hate the idea of going public with this nightmare, Christina is right. If I tell my story in my own words and take ownership of the mistakes I made, I can only hope most people will understand that the crimes I committed were due to my illness, not my character."

"Your character has always been unimpeachable, Sergeant," Chief Farnsworth said. "I'm sorry if we didn't do enough to support you after Arnold's tragic death."

"You did what you could, sir. I believe now that everything that happened since the night Arnold died occurred because of a greater purpose. It was meant to teach me things I can use to be a more empathetic police officer and human being. There had to be some meaning in this. I refuse to believe Arnold died for no reason."

"You've given me a lot to consider, Sergeant," Faith said. "I need to speak to USA Forrester and determine whether he intends to pursue the charges."

"I understand, but I'm giving the interview either way."

"That is, of course, your prerogative. I'll take your input back to Forrester and let you know how we plan to proceed."

"Thank you for your consideration," Gonzo said.

"Of course. For what it's worth, I was never comfortable with these charges, but it wasn't my decision to make. I can't promise you anything, but I'll remind USA Forrester that I've had concerns about this case from the get-go."

"I appreciate your support."

"I'll be in touch."

After Faith had left the room, Gonzo said, "I want to thank all of you for sticking with me through this nightmare. Knowing you all have my back has made a huge difference."

"We do have your back," Sam said. "We always will. What happened was such a tragedy. I came in here ready to fight to keep you from compounding that tragedy with another one. But you took care of that for me. I'm proud of you, Tommy."

"Thanks. I'm trying."

"We can all see that," Malone said. "Whenever you're ready to come back to work, let us know."

"I'm aiming for around the first of December, if that's okay."

"Works for me," Sam said. "You should give the interview to Darren Tabor. He'll do it right."

"That was my thought too."

Sam nodded, feeling confident that Gonzo and his story would be in good hands with Darren. "I've got to get back to it. We're closing in on Ginny McLeod's murderer. We think it was the husband, which means the three golfing buddies who vouched for him are going to need to be arrested too. Lots of paperwork in my future."

"Don't you mean in Cruz's future?" Gonzo asked with a smile.

"Of course that's what I mean."

"Glad to see some things around here haven't changed."

"Nothing has changed, except we miss you—and Arnold."

"Thanks. It's nice to be missed. Christina and I would like to invite you and your families to our place for dessert on Thanksgiving." He glanced at the chief. "You too, of course, sir."

"I do love me some apple pie," the chief said.

"I'll make sure there's plenty with your name on it."

"My wife and I would be delighted to join you, Gonzo."

"Holy crap. The chief is coming, honey."

Christina smiled at him. "So I hear."

"We'll be there," Sam said.

"Us too," Malone added.

"This is going to be the best Thanksgiving ever," Gonzo said to Christina.

"It sure is."

CHAPTER THIRTY-ONE

As Sam left the chief's conference room, a disturbance in the lobby had her running to find out what was going on. Two young Patrol officers had Ken McLeod Sr. in custody and were attempting to get him to Central Booking. He was fighting them every step of the way.

"You stupid bitch!" he screamed when he saw Sam. "What're you thinking arresting me? I'll have your badge and your ass! I have an alibi!"

"That's full of holes," Sam replied.

"What the hell does that mean?"

"You'll find out soon enough." To the officers, she said, "Get him booked and take him to interview two."

Ignoring the man's continued diatribe, Sam walked to the pit.

"McBride," she said, "spring Ken Jr. from interview two. Tell him he's free to go and thank him for his cooperation."

"Yes, ma'am."

While Jeannie took care of that, Sam went into her office, downed half a bottle of water and took another look at the cell phone reports Archie had compiled. This time, the words behaved themselves so she could actually read them. She focused first on Ken Sr. The pings put him on the golf course from noon to one ten. At one forty, the phone registered a ping at his home, and by two ten, he was back on the golf course.

"Hey, Cruz!"

Freddie popped up from his cubicle and looked into her office. "You bellowed?"

Sam signaled for him to come in. "The three men who said Ken Sr. was playing golf with them all afternoon—can you please make arrangements to have them arrested?"

"All of them?"

"All of them."

"Who's gonna do those reports?"

Sam sent him a salty look. "Who do you think?"

"Why did I know you were going to say that?"

"Why do you ask questions you already know the answers to?"

"What am I charging them with?"

"Obstructing a homicide investigation by lying for their friend."

"I'll take care of it. Does this mean we've found Ginny's killer?"

"I believe we have—along with most of the money she stole from her victims."

"I thought the Feds couldn't find it."

"They couldn't, but Green did."

"Wow, that's awesome."

"It is, and it's just what we need right now."

"No kidding. All right, let me go start arresting people."

"It's going to be that kind of day. We're charging Ken Sr. and possibly Mandi too. Stand by for paperwork."

"I'm standing by," he said. "I live to serve you."

"That's why you're the best partner I ever had."

"Yeah, yeah, save the charm, Lieutenant. I'll still do your paperwork whether you charm me or not."

"I am rather charming when I'm about to arrest a bunch of scumbags."

"Arresting scumbags does bring out the best in you."

A red-faced young Patrol officer appeared in the doorway to her office. "Mr. McLeod is in interview two, Lieutenant. My partner is watching him."

"Thank you, Officer..."

"Daniels, ma'am."

"Officer Daniels. Appreciate the assist."

"I'd say it was no problem, but Mr. McLeod put up one hell of a fight."

"Guilty people tend to put up the biggest fights." Sam couldn't wait to square off with Mr. McLeod. After Officer Daniels took off, Sam said to Freddie, "I'm taking Green in with me. He did some great work on this case."

"He does great work on all of them."

"I like to spread things around when I can."

"No worries. I'll be buried in paperwork."

"You're a good sport, Freddie Cruz."

"I have to be to put up with the likes of you," he tossed over his shoulder as he left the office.

Sam picked up her folders and notes and prepared for battle. "Green!"

"Yes, ma'am?"

"You're with me. Let's go."

Cameron seemed surprised, but he responded quickly, walking with her to interview one.

"Follow my lead," Sam said.

"Yes, ma'am."

Sam burst into the room, once again startling Mandi. That never got old.

"Can I leave now?" Mandi asked.

"Not so fast."

"Why not? I told you I didn't do anything."

"Well, you lied to us."

"No, I didn't!"

"Yes, Mandi, you did." Sam put the cell phone report in front of Mandi. "See this? The proof is in the pings."

"What does that even mean?"

"Your cell phone disproves your story."

"What? How?"

"Look here." Sam pointed to the ping at Mandi's dorm. "That's you at one o'clock on Sunday afternoon." She pointed to a different ping. "That's you at two thirty at the hardware store near your parents' home. That's you at your parents' home, and then that's you back at campus at three thirty. You had a busy afternoon."

"I told you I went to the store and my parents' house after my brother called me in a panic."

Sam put yet another report in front of Mandi. "That's a printout of your incoming calls for Sunday between noon and five p.m. There's no call from your brother, but interestingly, there're two from your father." Sam took the cap off a highlighter and colored the two numbers.

Mandi looked down at the pages and swallowed hard.

"What I'd like to know is why you pointed the finger at your brother for a crime you know your father committed?"

"I... He... My father... He threatened me."

"Threatened you how?"

"He said he'd tell everyone that I knew where the money was all along unless I did everything I could to protect him."

"Including implicating your brother?"

"His instructions were very clear. By any means necessary. He would've ruined my life if he told people that I knew where the money was and never said anything."

"Even though it was true, right? You knew where it was and never said anything."

Mandi broke down. "I didn't know that until after the charges were filed. I pleaded with her to do the right thing, to return the money, but she just kept saying that wasn't the plan. We had to stick with the plan. Except it wasn't my plan. It was hers, and when I deposited those cashier checks in the Cayman Islands, I didn't know where the money came from. If I'd known..."

"What would you have done?" Green asked.

She swiped at the tears that slid down her cheeks. "I... I don't know, but I wouldn't have done that to our family and friends. She... She was my mother. She asked me to do this for her, and it was a bunch of free vacations. It never occurred to me why she was really sending me there. I didn't know the Caymans were a tax shelter until you told me that."

Sam wondered if she'd ever been as stupid or naïve as this

young woman. No, she'd been born smarter than Mandi McLeod would ever be. "Do you know the account numbers?"

She hesitated before she nodded. "She made me memorize them so there wouldn't be a paper trail."

Too bad Ginny hadn't also told her to stay off social media while she was "on vacation" in the Caymans. Her Finsta posts had been her undoing—whatever Finsta was. Sam was clueless about such things. Thankfully, Cameron was hip to it all. "Write them down."

Sam waited, feeling breathless with victory, as Mandi wrote down the account info. Between that and the money associated with the Delaware corporation, they'd found most of what'd gone missing. After Mandi pushed the notebook back across the table, Sam said, "Stay put. We'll be back."

"But..."

Sam sent her a quelling look that had her thinking better of what she'd been about to say. With Green in tow, she left interview one and went into interview two, startling Mr. McLeod. That too was satisfying. "You've been apprised of your right to an attorney, Mr. McLeod?"

"I have. I don't need one. I haven't done anything."

"Detective Green, please record this interview."

He shifted on the recorder and noted who was present in the room.

"Mr. McLeod," Sam said, "have you waived your right to an attorney?"

"I have because I haven't done anything that would require the services of an attorney."

Stupidity apparently comes naturally to Mandi McLeod, Sam thought. "Mr. McLeod, you're being charged with the murder of your wife, Virginia, as well as numerous other obstruction charges resulting from the lies you told me and other officers during our investigation."

For a second, his arrogant demeanor slipped, but then he recovered himself. "I didn't kill her."

"We can put you at the house at her time of death."

"No, you can't. I was playing golf with three of my friends—the only friends I had left, because they didn't have anything for my wife to steal."

"They're being arrested as we speak for lying to us and obstructing a homicide investigation."

Another chink appeared in his armor. "They didn't lie."

"Yes, they did. They lied when they failed to tell us about the nearly forty minutes you were gone from the course during your round of golf."

"I went to use the bathroom."

"At home?"

"No, at the clubhouse."

Sam put the cell phone report down in front of him. "Funny, but the location of your phone tells a different story."

"What?"

She pointed. "See that right there? That's you and your cell phone at your house at the time of your wife's death."

"I didn't take my phone to the club with me that day. I always leave it at home when I'm playing golf so I won't be disturbed."

"That too is a lie." Sam pointed to three lines on the report. "That's you at the golf course, that's you at home, and that's you back on the course after you killed your wife. The pings don't lie, Mr. McLeod. You're under arrest for the murder of Virginia McLeod. You have the right to remain silent. Anything you say can and will be used against you in a court of law. You have the right to an attorney—"

"I'd like to call my attorney," he said, looking scared now, which was thrilling to Sam. The most pompous people were always the most fun to take down.

"Write down the name and number, and I'll reach out."

"I, um, I no longer have a personal attorney."

"Shall I call the public defender's office?"

He blanched at that. "Absolutely not."

"You should know Detective Green here has also managed to track Mandi to the Cayman Islands, where she helped your wife stash money, and he also uncovered the VMcL Corporation in Delaware. We'll be turning that info over to the Feds, along with the account numbers in the Caymans that Mandi gave us."

Cameron smiled and waved at Mr. McLeod.

She loved to see him enjoying this victory.

McLeod's mouth fell open in disbelief. "Mandi wouldn't *dare*."

"See, that's where you're wrong, Mr. McLeod. When faced with a long prison sentence or doing the right thing, your daughter chose the right thing. It's a lesson she somehow managed to learn while growing up with you and your wife as her role models. Congratulations on raising a daughter with a conscience. Too bad you don't have one of your own."

"Ginny ruined my life! She got what was coming to her!"

"I'll remind you this interview is still being recorded, Mr. McLeod."

"I don't care. You tell me what you would've done if your wife stole from most of your friends and family members and then refused to tell you where the money was hidden or to leave town because her shrew of a mother had fallen ill. When forced to live among the very people she stole from, what would you have done, Lieutenant?"

"I think we're finished here, Detective Green." Sam made a big production out of shaking Green's hand. "Congratulations on the great work you did on this case. You were the one to tie Mandi to the deposits in the Cayman Islands. Without that, we might never have gotten her to flip on her father. We might've let her blame her brother, who's completely innocent of any crimes. That would've been truly tragic."

Though that wouldn't have happened, because they could prove he never called his sister that fateful afternoon. But Ken McLeod Sr. didn't need to know that. Not to mention, restitution would be made to Ginny's victims, which made for a satisfying end to a revolting case. "Our work here is finished."

EPILOGUE

It took until ten p.m. to book, charge and write up the reports on the McLeod case, but when Sam left HQ that night, she was on vacation for a week. They were hosting Thanksgiving at their house, and the only way she could pull that off without foisting everything onto pregnant Shelby's shoulders was to take time off. And she planned to fully wallow in this staycation by not taking any work calls during her break.

However, murder never took a break, and with Freddie and Jeannie also taking time off for the holiday, she'd left Cameron Green in charge for the week. He'd more than earned the right to step up a bit with his superior work. The young, earnest detective had a bright future ahead of him, and Sam could easily picture him in a command role at some point.

Vernon and Jimmy were waiting for her outside the morgue door when she emerged into inky darkness.

"Oh damn," she said. "I forgot all about you guys."

"It's a good thing we aren't allowed to get our feelings hurt," Vernon said.

Sam flashed him a grin. "I've got to be the worst person you've ever been assigned to."

"Not the absolute worst, but damned close."

Sam laughed as he walked her to her car. "Touché. Sorry to be a pain in the ass. I'll be sticking close to home for the next few days, so you can stand down."

"Heard you closed the McLeod case," Jimmy said. "Is it always the husband, or does it just seem that way?"

"Not always. But this is one I'm glad to be done with. The whole lot of them made me sick."

"Greedy bastards," Vernon said.

"You said it. I'm going home. I'll try not to lose you on the back streets."

"Gee, thanks."

At the car, Sam stopped and turned to Vernon. "Has the recent uptick in threats against my husband died down at all?"

"Not really, but we're monitoring them. Nothing to worry about."

"Easy for you to say."

"We find in most cases, people are all talk and no action."

While Sam took some comfort in that information, she was well aware it took only one nutjob to change everything. The thought made her shudder and left her feeling queasy.

Vernon held the car door for her until she was settled.

"Thanks for what you do, Vernon. Even when it doesn't seem like it, I do appreciate you all."

"Thank you, ma'am. It's an honor to protect you and your family."

As Sam drove home, she tried to decompress from the action-packed day and deal with the extra adrenaline that always kicked in when they wrapped up a case and arrested a murderer. While stopped at a light, Sam put through a call to Ken McLeod Jr.

"This is Lieutenant Holland," she said when he answered, sounding wary. Who could blame the poor guy? "I wanted to let you know your father has been arrested for the murder of your mother."

"I heard he was taken in. My uncle called." His dull, flat tone conveyed a world of hurt and bewilderment. "Did he say why he did it?"

"Apparently, she wouldn't tell him where the money was and wouldn't leave town because of your grandmother, and he was frustrated at having to live among the people she stole from while being shunned by most of them."

"I certainly know how that feels. It's the worst."

"I have some good news for you on that front. One of my people was able to determine that your mother used your sister to make deposits to accounts in the Cayman Islands. She made your sister memorize the account numbers so there wouldn't be any paper trail. Mandi gave us those numbers, and we've turned them over to the Feds. With that and the cash in the Delaware company, your mother's victims should get most of their money back."

"Really? That's amazing! Oh my God." Now he sounded tearful. "That's the best news I've had in months."

"Did you have any suspicion that your mother was using your sister to run money out of the country?"

"I had no idea. Honestly, I haven't stayed close to my family since I left for college. When my sister asked me to go away for Thanksgiving, that was the first time I'd heard from her in a while. Their goals in life were very different from mine. I just want to work and live my life. I don't need the flash and the cash they were all so obsessed with."

"I'm sorry for what you've been through."

"Thank you. Can I ask... Is my sister being charged too?"

"She's being charged with two felony counts of being an accessory after the fact pertaining to your mother's murder. We believe she was unaware of the true nature of her 'errands' on your mother's behalf, and she was instrumental in helping us to recover the money, so she's getting a pass on that."

"Will she go to jail?"

"I believe she'll do some time, but it shouldn't be a long stretch. Cleaning up after a murder and then lying about it, not to mention trying to frame an innocent man, are serious crimes."

"Did she say why she tried to pin it on me?"

"Your dad threatened to cut her out of everything if she didn't protect him."

"So they both put money ahead of me. That's good to know, especially after I was nearly an accessory myself by going along with her plan to leave the country."

"I'm sorry, Ken. I know this is a bitter pill to swallow."

"It is what it is. I'm glad to know the truth about them. It helps me to move forward on my own."

"I wanted to let you know we've started a grief group for people who've lost family members to violent crime. I know that your grief is a little different from most of our participants' experiences, but grief is grief. If you think you might benefit from the interaction with others, we'd be happy to have you."

"I'll think about that."

"It's an open invite. Now, a year from now, whatever works. I'll text you the info, and you can decide."

"Thank you for everything. I can't tell you what it means to me that my mother's victims will receive restitution. When will they get that news?"

"We'll be issuing a press release in the morning that'll make it public."

"I can't wait for that. It's time for this nightmare to end. I'll always be thankful to you and your team for that."

"I'm glad we were able to find the money. I'll ask the prosecutors keep you informed of your father's and sister's legal proceedings if you'd like to know."

After a long pause, he said, "That's okay. I'm not really interested in what becomes of them. They made their beds, so to speak. I'm moving on."

"Fair enough. I'll send you the grief group info. I'm here if I can do anything for you going forward."

"You've given me the best possible gift by finding that money. That's all I need. Take care, Lieutenant."

"You do the same."

Sam ended the call with a feeling of satisfaction and optimism that Ken Jr. would land on his feet after the hell his family had put him through. He seemed like a decent young man with a bright future ahead of him. She pulled onto Ninth Street a short time later and was waved through the security checkpoint. As she went up the ramp, feeling exhausted, exhilarated and excited to be on vacation, the front door opened, and there he was. Her love, her life, her reason for being.

Her heart gave a happy leap at the sight of him in a long-sleeved T-shirt and sweats, his hair rumpled and his jaw covered in late-day whiskers. He was, without a doubt, the sexiest man she'd ever laid eyes on, and he was all hers.

Forever.

She sped up her pace and jumped into his outstretched arms, letting out a whoop of excitement.

"Mom's on vacation," Nick said to Nate, who laughed as she dropped her purse and coat inside the door while Nick continued to hold her.

"We nailed a murderer *and* found the missing money. Best day ever."

"Better than March twenty-sixth?" he asked of their wedding date.

"Second only to that." In his ear, she whispered, "Straight to bed."

"I *love* vacation Sam."

"She's not that different from workweek Sam."

"True, but I love all my Sams, no matter what." Nick carried her up the stairs, past the Secret Service agent positioned in the hallway outside the kids' rooms and straight up another flight of stairs to their loft.

"And now the whole Secret Service knows it's booty-call time for the second couple."

"Eh, whatever. Let them think whatever they want." He put her down and went to light the beach-scented candles that reminded them of their trips to Bora Bora.

Sam pulled off her clothes and crawled onto the double lounge, holding out her arms to him.

He stretched out next to her and pulled her in tight against him.

"You're overdressed for this party," she said, tugging on his T-shirt.

His hand on her face anchored her for a deep, passionate kiss. "I want you to know something," he said, kissing her neck and down to her breasts.

"What?" Sam asked, breathless.

"I'm always so bloody thankful when you walk through that door at the end of a workday. So very, very thankful."

"I hate that you worry about me the way you do."

"Can't help it."

"I'm worried about you too."

He raised his head to meet her gaze, his gorgeous hazel eyes conveying confusion. "Why?"

"I hear the threats against you haven't dropped off."

"That's nothing to worry about. People love to hear themselves talk. You know that."

"Still... I worry."

He smoothed the hair back from her face. "Don't worry. I'm very well protected. And guess what else?"

"What?"

"I cleared my schedule so I can be off with you."

"Best day ever!"

"I can't let you handle cooking the turkey all on your own."

"That's what it's really about, right? Protecting Thanksgiving dinner."

"Scotty did suggest it might be a good idea for you to have some 'qualified help,' was the term I believe he used."

"I'll be having a talk with him tomorrow."

"Is he wrong?"

"Shut up and kiss me before I forget why I'm in such a good mood."

Smiling, he did as directed like the good husband he was, and as he made love to her, Sam held on tight to him and his love and the euphoric feeling she'd brought home with her. Seven full days to spend with him and their kids. Nothing could top that.

SOMEHOW, SAM MANAGED TO COOK A PRETTY DECENT THANKSGIVING dinner, with the "qualified help" of her sisters, their mother Brenda, Celia and Shelby, who'd decided to stay in the city rather than go home to her family, as morning sickness had been making her miserable.

"Has to be a girl this time," Shelby had joked at one point. "Only women cause this much trouble."

In addition to Shelby, Avery and baby Noah, Sam's sisters and their families were there, as well as Freddie, Elin and his parents, along with Nick's father, Leo, his wife, Stacy, and their twin sons. Elijah was also home for the long weekend, much to the delight of Alden and Aubrey, who'd barely left his side since his arrival.

Scotty was enthralled by Elijah, who included Scotty in everything he did with his brother and sister. Sam and Nick had let Scotty stay up late playing video games with Elijah the night before, which had thrilled Scotty.

After dinner, they went around the table, and everyone said one thing they were thankful for. "We did this when we were kids. Remember, girls?" Sam asked her sisters.

"I remember," Tracy said. "It was your thing, Mom. You should go first."

Brenda looked around the table, smiling at her daughters and grandchildren. "I'm thankful to be here with my girls, their families and friends today. Thank you for including me, Sam."

"It's good to have you here." The twenty years in which Sam hadn't spoken to her mother after her parents' marriage fell apart seemed like a distant memory now that they'd made peace with the past. "I'm thankful to be here with all of you and to have added Elijah, Aubrey and Alden to our family this year. We love you all very much."

"Thank you so much for all you've done for us," Elijah said. "I'm not sure what would've become of us without you guys, and it's such an incredible relief to me to know my babies are well cared for when I can't be here. They're probably too shy to say so, but Alden and Aubrey are thankful for you guys too."

"I'm thankful for them and you," Scotty said to Elijah. "It's so cool to have siblings."

"We feel the same way," Elijah said, smiling at Scotty, who beamed back at him.

Sam's heart wanted to explode at the way Elijah included him and seemed to fully understand that he'd inherited another younger brother.

"I'm thankful for this family," Nick said, "the family I've always wished for and hoped for and often thought I'd never have. You all are the best thing to ever happen to me, and after this last week, I'm especially thankful to know I'm off the hook for the next election and able to be right here—the only place in the world I really want to be."

"Thank goodness for that," Sam said.

"We all feel that way," Tracy said dryly. "No one wanted to deal with *her* while you were off campaigning."

"Preach it, sister," Angela said.

"Preach it, Auntie," Scotty said.

Sam stuck her tongue out at each of them. "Just because it's true doesn't mean you gotta be mean."

Smiling at their banter, Celia said, "I'm thankful to you guys for getting me through this difficult first month without my love. I know you miss him as much as I do, and we're all trying to figure out life without Skip at the center of it. But I'm thankful to be part of this family and to know I get to keep you, even though he's gone."

"You're not getting rid of us," Tracy said.

"Although you may wish you had," Sam said.

"Never," Celia said emphatically.

"I'm thankful for my kids, the three that live in this house, as well as my baby Noah," Shelby said. "The one on the way is giving me some grief, but I can't wait to meet him or her. I'm also thankful for my wonderful husband, Avery, who has made me so happy."

"Same goes, darlin'," Avery said. "You and Noah have given me so much. And I'm thankful for the friends who've become like family to us."

Freddie, Elin and his parents gave thanks for each other as well as their friends.

"Wait," Sam said to Freddie. "You forgot to be thankful for me as your most awesome partner."

"I didn't forget anything," he said, making everyone laugh hysterically.

"That's hurtful," Sam said with a teasing glint in her eye, "because I'm very thankful for you, partner."

"Fine. If you're going to be that way, I'm thankful for you too, even when you're a gigantic pain in my ass."

Sam dabbed at her eyes. "I'm so moved."

The food, the family, the love and the laughter kept Sam from focusing overly much on the person who was missing from the holiday gathering. She'd cooked the giblets for him, even though no one else was interested in eating them. Her sisters noticed, though.

"It's sweet that you cooked them for Dad," Tracy said when they were cleaning up the kitchen.

"I thought about taking them to the cemetery, but they'd probably attract buzzards."

"Can we stop talking about giblets?" Angela covered her mouth. "I'm already sick from eating too much."

Sam held up the boiled neck of the turkey, another part her dad had loved to gnaw on. "You want this?"

"Ugh, get rid of that nasty shit," Angela said, turning a worrisome shade of light green.

The sisters had a good laugh and then a good cry as they remembered Skip and his love of all things Thanksgiving.

Their day was capped off by dessert at Gonzo and Christina's. As the Secret Service conveyed them to the gathering, Sam rested her head on Nick's shoulder. She'd much rather be napping than going out, but there was no way she'd disappoint her friend by missing his get-together.

She yawned loudly.

"She's gonna fall asleep in the apple pie," Scotty said.

"I am not!" Sam said.

"Are you taking bets, son?" Nick asked. "Because I'm betting on a full face-plant."

"I'll remember you bet against me," Sam said.

"Don't start being gross," Scotty said. Glancing at Elijah, he added, "They're so *weird*."

Elijah laughed. "I feel you. My parents were like that too. Always kissing and crap."

"It's the worst."

"Actually, it's not so bad," Elijah said. "You'll find out soon enough."

"Ew," Scotty said. "I thought I liked you."

Sam had to bite her lip to keep from laughing out loud, knowing Scotty wouldn't appreciate it. Thankfully, they arrived at their destination before she could lose her composure.

"He's in for such a wake-up call," Nick said, low enough that only she could hear him as they followed the four kids out of the SUV.

"Anytime now."

Gonzo and Christina's apartment was full of friends, family and colleagues, enjoying an amazing dessert buffet full of pies, cakes, cookies, brownies and all things sweet. The atmosphere was even more joyful after the news had come the day before that USA Forrester had decided not to pursue charges against Gonzo. That had been a huge relief for all of them, no one more so than Gonzo, who credited Christina with giving him the fortitude to fight the charges.

None of them were under any illusions that the story was dead, however. Once Ramsey found out about it, there was apt to be more trouble ahead. Gonzo planned to meet with Darren Tabor over the weekend to give him the exclusive story of what he'd been through since his partner's murder. Hopefully, that story, coupled with the dirt they'd dug up on Ramsey, would take some of the wind out of the hateful sergeant's sails.

News that Metro PD Detective Cameron Green had done what the Feds had failed to do and found the missing money had been met with jubilation among Ginny's victims and some badly needed good press for the department. Sam made sure Cameron got full credit for the find, and he'd been enjoying his moment in the limelight.

"Have you seen our hosts?" Sam asked Nick as she looked around for them.

"Not yet."

Avery Hill made his way over to Sam, holding his son, Noah.

"Hey, I was hoping I'd get the chance to talk to you before you left on vacation."

"I busted out of there the second I closed the McLeod case."

"So I heard. I wanted to tell you I went through the Worthington case files, and I agree it's worth another look. Our old friends Conklin and Stahl made some very questionable decisions during that investigation, such as it was. We're finding that was somewhat of a trend with them."

"Ugh, seriously?"

"I'm afraid so."

"Have you told the chief?" Sam asked, glancing at Farnsworth, Malone and their wives, standing together in a corner with drinks and relaxed expressions on their faces. Sam didn't want anything to ruin this day for her beloved chief, who'd gone through the wringer while grieving the loss of his best friend.

"I've briefed him that there're some irregularities that'll need to be addressed."

"Is this going to get ugly for us?"

"Don't you mean uglier? It could, but it's also an opportunity to right some old wrongs."

"I'd be down with that. Lenore has waited long enough for justice. I'll jump on that the second I'm back to work."

"Let me know if you could use some help."

"You do the same, Agent Hill. We managed to find that missing money, after all."

"You're never going to let me hear the end of that, are you?"

"Not ever."

Avery laughed, which made Noah laugh too. Lowering his voice, he said, "I'm still working on the other thing, with the MIL. More to come on that."

"I look forward to anything that can help get her out of my husband's life forever."

Sam looked around for Gonzo and Christina, but still didn't see them. The apartment wasn't that large, but there was no sign of them until they finally emerged from a bedroom ten minutes later. Christina wore a white silk dress and a radiant smile. Tommy was dressed in a suit, holding baby Alex, who was also wearing a suit.

"Um, what's happening?" Sam asked.

"If I had to guess, I think we're here for a wedding," Nick said.

"Shut up. No way!"

Freddie and Elin worked their way over to Sam and Nick. "Are you thinking what I'm thinking?" Freddie asked Sam.

"I sure hope so."

Gonzo whistled to get everyone's attention. "Hey, so Christina and I want to thank you all for coming to celebrate Thanksgiving, my homecoming from a long, difficult journey and... our wedding!"

Their guests cheered and applauded.

"Before we make it official, I just want to say to all of you— thank you. Thank you for sticking with me through the darkest days of my life, for supporting me, Christina and Alex while I was away, and for being here today to help us celebrate this new beginning. And now, without further ado..." Gonzo glanced at Nick. "Are you ready, Mr. Vice President?"

"You bet."

"Wait," Sam said. "*What?*"

Gonzo grinned at Sam. "I asked Nick to officiate and to keep the secret."

"Another thing he'll pay for later," Sam muttered.

"It's not every day that you get the vice president to officiate at your wedding," Gonzo said.

"I'm honored." Nick joined them in the corner of the living room that'd been set up with flowers Sam hadn't noticed before. "On behalf of all the loved ones who've gathered for this special occasion, let me say how thrilled we are to see two people who belong together getting their long-awaited happy ending. Since this is my first time officiating at a wedding, Tommy and Christina promised to make it easy on me by writing their own vows. Christina, whenever you're ready."

Tommy handed Alex to his mother and took hold of Christina's hands. He looked healthy, happy, relaxed, and Sam decided she was most grateful on this Thanksgiving for his recovery.

"Tommy Gonzales," Christina said, already battling tears,

"almost two years ago, I met you on New Year's Eve, and you changed my whole life in the course of that first night. I'd never experienced anything like the sheer thrill that came from being in the same room with you. I quickly found out that, contrary to what I'd thought, I'd never actually been in love before, because everything was different after I met you. In the last two years, we've been through a lot, including becoming parents overnight to Alex. You and Alex are the greatest blessings in my life, and I love you both so much. I promise to love, honor and cherish you as my husband for as long as I live. Thank you for choosing me, Tommy. You've made me the luckiest woman in the world."

Gonzo was openly weeping by the time she finished.

Sam wiped tears from her eyes as she watched her beloved friend marry his true love. For a time, Sam had balked at them dating. Her world and Nick's colliding had freaked her out, but it'd happened several times since then, and she'd learned to live with it as long as everyone was happy.

"I can't believe you think you're the lucky one, baby. That's all me. From the first second you looked my way, I've felt like the luckiest SOB who ever lived. That a cool, classy, competent, successful woman like you would love me has always been one of the greatest miracles of my life. That you stayed with me after what I've put you through is yet another miracle. I know how incredibly fortunate I am to be standing here with you, having you vow to love me forever, and I promise to never take you or your love for me and Alex for granted. I can't wait for everything with you and our little family. I love you always."

Nick walked them through the exchange of rings, which brought about more tears when Gonzo kissed the back of Christina's hand and then reached for Alex to make him part of their big moment.

"By the power vested in me," Nick said, "it's my great pleasure to declare Tommy and Christina husband and wife. Tommy, you may kiss your bride."

"Yes, please," Gonzo said, putting his arms around her and staring into her eyes before kissing her softly and sweetly.

They hugged for a full minute, and only when Alex began to

protest did they break apart, laughing and crying and looking genuinely thrilled.

God bless them both, Sam thought as she clapped, wiped away tears and celebrated their beautiful friends' joyful union.

MUCH LATER, SAM LAY NEXT TO NICK IN BED, STILL STUFFED TO THE point of imminent explosion. "Why do I do this to myself every year?"

"Because it's *so* good. Your stuffing was amazing, by the way."

"It's my grandmother's recipe. It's so easy—white stuffing bread, sautéed onions, ground-up sausage, Old Bay and water. You mash it all together, let it sit overnight and then bake it in the oven. I crisp up the top in the broiler. And just talking about it makes me want to sneak downstairs and eat it cold, even though I'm about to vomit from being so full."

"That's the sign of a successful Thanksgiving."

"Feeling like you're going to vomit?"

"Being too full to have sex."

"Don't make me laugh. It hurts to laugh. You know it's bad when we don't want to have sex."

"It's the best kind of bad. Today was awesome."

"And you! Keeping secrets!"

Smiling, he looked over at her. "I didn't think you'd mind since it was for such a good cause."

"It was awesome. I'm thrilled for them and so hopeful he's going to be okay."

"I think he will be. It's not like he's suddenly going to be over what happened to Arnold, but he's learning to live with his grief in a more productive and healthy way."

"I sure hope so. And in other news, it seems like the nonsense over you deciding not to run is finally tapering off."

"Thank God for that. I've got to be honest. I really didn't think people would care as much as they did."

"How'd that work out for you?"

His snort of laughter made her smile.

"It's not easy being married to the most popular man in the world."

"What*ever.*"

"Have you given any more thought to your plans for after you leave office? I don't want you sitting around here drinking beer and going to pot. I expect to be kept in the manner to which I've become accustomed." Being silly and ridiculous with him was one of her favorite things to do.

"There goes my plan to retire early."

"That's *not* happening."

"I'm giving more thought to the idea of teaching—and maybe writing a book."

Sam looked over at him. "What kind of book?"

"A memoir about growing up the way I did and how I ended up vice president. I think it's a pretty cool story."

"It's a great story, and I love the idea of you writing a book."

"I'm glad you do, because I've actually had some interest from a couple of publishers who've reached out to see if I might want to do it after I leave office."

"That's so cool! Why didn't you tell me?"

"I am telling you."

"When did this happen?"

"Earlier in the week. And they're offering the kind of money that'll keep you in fancy shoes for another year or two."

"And you're just telling me now?"

"You were busy with stuffing and turkey."

Sam turned on her side, groaning from the agony of moving. "I'm never too busy to hear that kind of news. I think you should totally do that. You could show so many struggling kids that there's always hope."

"That's what I was thinking too."

Sam rested her head on his chest. "It's a really good idea."

"Glad you think so."

She was well on her way to dozing off when the phone on his bedside table rang. She felt guilty because her first thought was, *Thank God it's his phone and not mine.* The only way she'd be called in to work was if something huge happened, and she was praying for huge things to stay far, far away while she was on vacation through the weekend.

Nick reached for the phone they called the "bat line" to the White House and stayed reclined when he took the call. "This is Nick." He was always so humble and normal, never affected by his lofty position or title.

"Mr. Vice President, this is Tom Hanigan."

Sam could hear the president's chief of staff because she was still lying in Nick's arms.

"Hey, Tom. What's up?"

"Sir, I regret to inform you that President Nelson was found dead in the residence thirty minutes ago. EMS was called, but they were unable to revive him. We need you to come to the White House immediately. The Secret Service is standing by to transport you and your wife."

Sam felt as if she'd been electrocuted, and Nick was barely breathing.

"I understand," Nick said. "I'm on my way."

How could he sound so calm when a nuclear bomb had just gone off in their lives?

He put down the phone and looked over at her, his eyes gone flat with shock. "You heard that?"

Sam swallowed hard. "I did."

They stared at each other for a full minute.

Nick was the first to blink. "I'm the president."

Fade to black on the Fatal Series, and introducing... The First Family Series!

HOLY CRAP, I'VE BEEN SITTING ON THIS BOMBSHELL FOR MONTHS, having to bite my tongue not to accidentally give away the surprise! I know some of you are sitting there asking WTF is happening. Let me explain...

Earlier this year, I left the publisher of the first fifteen Fatal books. As I was writing *Fatal Fraud*, it became clear to me that the way forward for me with Fatal was unsustainable with no ability to market or promote the earlier books. I can't make another company do something, and as such, it was obvious I needed to end that chapter in Sam and Nick's story and start a new one.

The idea for the First Family Series came to me as I was writing *Fatal Fraud*, after Nick announced he wasn't going to run in the next election. I thought, what if he made that decision public, and then Nelson dropped dead? He'd be inheriting a job he just told the world he didn't want. Not to mention the implications for Sam and their children, and holy moly, I can't WAIT to write the First Family Series! *State of Affairs*, Book 1 in the new series, will pick up *one second* after Nick gets the phone call from the White House chief of staff letting him know the boss is dead and will follow the Cappuanos through this enormous transition from second family to first family.

I promise you this: All the things you love best about the Fatal Series will be coming with us into the new First Family Series, only there'll be some added focus on Nick's job (not too much—I promise) in addition to Sam's job, which she'll continue, despite an enormous uproar. There'll be glamour and international intrigue and all sorts of amazing things to come, beginning with *State of Affairs* in April 2021. We've included a sneak peek at *State of Affairs* and preorder information below.

All the characters you love in the Fatal Series will remain on the landscape, albeit some of them in new and different roles, but everyone will remain present. I understand that change is often scary, even fictional change, but I'm so excited for this new chapter in Sam and Nick's life, and I hope you are too.

Because this development is a rather major bombshell for Fatal readers, I ask that you discuss this ONLY in the Fatal Fraud Reader Group at *www.facebook.com/groups/fatalfraud/* so it can be a surprise to everyone when they get the chance to read *Fatal Fraud*. I'm also going to ask that you PLEASE not include mention of this development in reviews of *Fatal Fraud*. I want every reader to have the "holy shit" moment at the end of this book that you got to have, so please help me keep a lid on this until most of the hard-core series fans get a chance to read this book. Thank you so much for that!

I want to thank the loyal Fatal readers who've come on this journey with me, Sam and Nick thus far and invite you to join us at 1600 Pennsylvania Avenue for the next part of their story. I can't wait!

So many people to thank as I wrap up the Fatal Series and move into this new and exciting adventure with these characters I love so much. First and foremost, to the amazing team that supports me every day: Dan, Emily and Jake Force, as well as Julie Cupp, Lisa Cafferty and Tia Kelly. You ladies are the BEST, and I'm so fortunate to work with you as well as our awesome cover designer, Kristina Brinton. HUGE thanks to Capt. Russ Hayes, retired, Newport, RI Police Department, for his invaluable input to every one of the Fatal books.

Many thanks to Kim Killion at The Killion Group for figuring out a way to do a photoshoot for the new series during a pandemic, using real-life couple Joshua Verax and Maria Fekaris as our models. I'm so excited about the amazing images we have to use on an endless number of new First Family books.

Thank you to my front-line beta readers Anne Woodall and Kara Conrad, who've been with me from the start, as well as my editors, Joyce Lamb and Linda Ingmanson. And thanks to my "last line of defense" Fatal betas: Elizabeth, Irene, Sarah, Jennifer, Maria, Jenny, Juliane, Viki, Sheri, Betty, Marti, Kelley, Gina, Tiffany, Ellen, Maricar and Mona. A huge thanks to my pal Tracey Suppo for reading, too!

To all the readers who've embraced Sam and Nick's story since *Fatal Affair* debuted ten years ago, thank you for your endless support and enthusiasm for these characters and this series. You make my "job" so much fun. Much more fun to come from the White House!

xoxo

Marie

STATE OF AFFAIRS

CHAPTER ONE

A full minute after ending the bombshell call with the White House chief of staff, Nick Cappuano stared into the eyes of his wife, Samantha, looking to her for calm in the midst of calamity. He wasn't seeing calm in her lovely eyes, however. He was seeing the same panic he was feeling.

President David Nelson had been found dead in the residence.

Nick was going to be president of the United States of America.

The Secret Service was waiting to transport them to the White House so he could take the oath of office.

Five minutes ago, they'd been in bed, commiserating after eating too much at Thanksgiving dinner. And now... Now, he needed to breathe, to remain calm, to do what needed to be done for his family and his country. "Say something."

Sam licked her lips and looked up at him with eyes gone wild. "I... I don't know what to say."

"It's going to be okay. You and me... We've got this. There's nothing we can't handle."

She laughed, but it had a maniacal edge to it. "If you say so, Mr. President."

Mr. President.

She was the first to ever call him that, which was as it should be. She was the most important person in his life.

He held her precious face in his hands and gazed into her eyes.

"Before we leave this room and step onto the biggest stage in the world, I want you to hear me when I tell you this won't change anything that matters. This—you and me and our family—will not change. I swear to you, Samantha."

She nodded and reached for him.

He took her into his arms and held on tight to the love of his life, determined to do whatever it took to reassure her even as he tried not to freak out himself. No one needed a president who was freaking out.

President.

This could not be happening. But it was. David Nelson was dead. Nick couldn't wrap his head around the last five minutes.

Still holding Sam, he said, "We need to get up, get dressed and make ourselves presentable for pictures that'll be in history books for the rest of time. But no pressure or anything."

Again, Sam's laughter had a hysterical edge to it. "I... We should tell people. Like Graham, Terry, my sisters... Your dad."

He shook his head. "They'll find out in the morning. For right now, we need to focus only on getting ourselves to the White House."

"Scotty. He'd never forgive us if we didn't take him."

"Agreed. I'll go get him up and tell Elijah what's going on so he knows he's in charge of the Littles." Aubrey and Alden, the twins Sam and Nick had recently taken in after their parents were murdered, would be six on Saturday. Leaving them with their older brother, who was home from Princeton for the Thanksgiving holiday, was the right thing to do.

"Will we be allowed to come back for them?"

"Of course, or we'll have the Secret Service bring them to us. Try not to worry. We'll figure it out one step at a time."

Sam looked around at the bedroom that was their private sanctuary, their calm in the storm of their crazy lives. "We're going to have to move. This won't be our home anymore."

"This will *always* be our home. We can come back here any time we want to." He pulled back to kiss her forehead and then her lips. "We have to go, Sam. Are you going to be able to do this?"

He watched as she took a deep breath and summoned the

fortitude to take this formidable next step on their journey. "I'm about to prove to you that I meant it all the times I said there was nothing I wouldn't do for you."

Smiling, he said, "I love you more than anything. Don't ever forget that."

"Same."

They got out of bed, and he pulled on a T-shirt and pajama pants, took the child monitor they kept in their bedroom to alert them if the twins woke up, and went to wake Scotty. Sam was right. Their thirteen-year-old son would never forgive them if they didn't bring him with them. Opening the bedroom door, he found his lead agent, John Brantley Jr., waiting to speak to him.

"Mr. President, sir. We're ready to transport you and Mrs. Cappuano to the White House."

"We need about ten minutes to pull ourselves together. I'm going to wake Scotty. He'd want to be there, and I need to tell Elijah what's happening." The twins' older brother and legal guardian was home from Princeton for the holiday weekend.

"Yes, sir."

"We'll be quick." Nick went into Scotty's room and sat on the edge of the bed. "Scotty." He gave his son's shoulder a gentle shake. In the glow of the Capitals' nightlight, he watched his son's eyes open.

"What's wrong?"

"President Nelson has died."

His son's eyes went wide as the implications hit him immediately. "*Holy crap.*"

"That's putting it mildly. The Secret Service is waiting to take Mom and me to the White House. Mom said you'd never forgive us if we didn't bring you with us."

"Hell, yes, I want to be there."

"You have to hurry."

"Work clothes, I presume?"

Nick smiled and nodded at their code word for the clothes he wore when he accompanied Nick to official events—khaki pants, navy blazer, dress shirt and tie. He got up and headed for the door.

"Dad?"

He turned back to his son.

"Are you freaking out?"

"Trying not to."

"How about Mom?"

"Same."

"Are we bringing the Littles too?"

"We're going to have them stay here with Elijah for now. I think it would be confusing and upsetting for them until we have time to explain what's happening."

"That's a good call."

"Glad you agree. I'm going to tell Elijah. Hurry up and get ready, okay?"

"I'm hurrying, and in case I forget to tell you later, I'm super proud of you, even if it's gonna be a bit of a shit show at first."

Nick grinned. "Thanks, bud. That means the world to me. We'll get through it. Like I told Mom, nothing that really matters will change. As long as we're all together, we can handle whatever comes our way."

"I guess we're gonna find out if that's true. Thanks for getting me up. Mom was right—I never would've forgiven you if you hadn't."

"We had a feeling. You probably know this, but you can't say anything to anyone about this until the official statement is released by the White House."

"I never would."

"Thanks. Be back in a few."

Nick went up to the third floor, where they'd made a bedroom for Elijah across the hall from the loft he'd put together as a sanctuary for him and Sam to get away from it all. He knocked on Elijah's closed door.

"Come in."

Nick opened the door to find Elijah stretched out on the bed watching a movie on his laptop.

"What's up?" Elijah asked.

"I have to tell you something that you can't tell anyone. I need your word."

"You have it."

"President Nelson was found dead in the residence a short time ago. Sam, Scotty and I are headed to the White House so I can be sworn in."

"Holy. *Shit.*" Elijah sat up on the bed. "I, um... *Wow.*"

He handed the child monitor to Elijah. "We're going to leave the twins here with you for now. I think it would scare them if we woke them in the middle of the night to take them with us."

"Agreed. That's better. I'll talk to them when they get up, and then we can figure out what's next. But Jesus, Nick... I mean..."

"Believe me, I know. As I said to Sam and Scotty, nothing that matters will change. We're still a family. You and the twins are still our family, and we're going to stick together and get through this. I promise."

The young man nodded, but Nick saw the wariness, the fear, the uncertainty they were all feeling.

"Try to get some sleep. It's going to be a crazy few days."

"Ah, yeah, sure," Elijah said, laughing. "Not seeing a lot of sleep in my future tonight."

"I don't want you to worry about anything."

"I'll try not to."

"We'll be in touch as soon as we can about getting you and the kids to us."

"Okay."

Nick wasn't sure what else he could say to reassure him, so he left it at that and returned to his room, where Sam was emerging from the shower, wrapped in a towel.

"I'm hurrying."

"Thanks, love." Nick got in the shower and ran a razor over his face, being careful not to cut himself in his haste to get ready. His mind ran a mile a minute, but he concentrated only on the task at hand. Shower, shave, get dressed, get in the car, go to the White House, take the oath. If he took this one minute and one step at a time, he could hold it together to do what needed to be done.

At least he hoped so.

Holy shit, holy shit, holy shit. That was the only thought in Sam's head for the first ten minutes after "The Call" that changed their lives forever. Thankfully, she'd spent some time on her hair earlier in the day and only needed to give it a good brushing to make it presentable. Her hands trembled ever so slightly as she applied makeup and mascara. *Dear God...* Nick was going to be the *president.*

He'd only just told the world of his decision not to run in the next election. Her relief had been overwhelming. She hadn't wanted him to be president, to be subjected to the scrutiny and stress that would come with the most important job in the world. She'd been thrilled to know he would become a private citizen again in three years, when his term as vice president ended and they got back to "normal," whatever that was anymore.

This couldn't be happening.

Except it was, and their lives were going to be turned upside down once again. She'd believed him when he said nothing that mattered would change. Their marriage was solid, and they were a formidable team.

But this...

She glanced in the mirror at him in the shower, seeing the tension in his shoulders that no one else would notice. But she saw it. She saw *him*, and as the dizzying array of implications settled on her, the weight of it threatened to crush her.

Yes, they'd known this was possible when Nick became vice president, but David Nelson had been a healthy man in his late sixties with decades left to live, or so they'd thought. She flattened her hands on the marble vanity and hung her head, trying to relieve the tension in her neck.

Nick had said nothing that mattered would change, but they both knew everything would.

The scrutiny, the security, the criticism, the *insanity...* Panic bubbled up inside her. What would she do? They'd make her leave her job a police officer, the job that had defined her adult life. That realization filled her with a pervasive sadness that only compounded the sadness she'd been living with since she lost her beloved dad just over a month ago. What she wouldn't give to be able to talk this through with Skip Holland.

He'd tell her to toughen up and do for Nick what he'd always done for her—support her one thousand percent. He deserved nothing less from her, and would get everything she had to give him, no matter what she had to sacrifice.

And then he was there, with his hands on her shoulders, kneading the tension from her muscles. He kissed her neck and made her shiver. "Whatever you're thinking, just stop. It's you and me all the way, babe."

Sam turned into his embrace and breathed in the fresh, clean scent of home, taking comfort in the familiar when everything had become uncertain in the span of a one-minute phone call.

"We really have to go," he said.

"I know." Sam gave herself another second to cling to life as she knew it before she reluctantly let him go, donned a robe and went across the hall to get dressed in the closet he'd built for her. Thinking of photos that would last forever and in deference to the death of President Nelson, she chose a demure black dress, slid on her diamond engagement ring and the diamond key necklace Nick had bought her as a wedding gift.

Taking a quick look in the full-length mirror on the back of the door, she decided she was presentable enough to be in photos that would be studied for generations to come. She stepped into the black Louboutins with the distinctive red soles that Nick had bought her for Christmas last year, ran damp hands over her skirt to smooth the lines and tried not to think too far ahead of the next couple of hours.

She took a deep breath and released it slowly, determined to be there for him the way he always was for her. So much of their life together had been about her—her job, her family, her needs. This was about him, and she was determined to support him in every possible way as he took on the role that would define his life—and hers, whether she wanted that or not.

"You can do this," she told her reflection. "You can do it for him. You *will* do it for him."

A soft knock on the door sounded.

Sam opened the door to him dressed in a navy-blue suit with faint pinstripes, a white dress shirt, a navy-blue-and-red-striped tie and an American flag pinned to his lapel. He looked handsome, sexy, competent and slightly petrified. The rest of the world would see the calm, cool, competent man he was under pressure. Only she would know how he really felt.

"You look beautiful," he said softly, aware of ears all around as the Secret Service hovered nearby.

"Funny, I was just thinking the same about you." Flattening her hands on his lapels, she looked up at him. "Is Scotty ready?"

He nodded.

"Are you?"

"As ready as I'll ever be."

She slid her hands down his arms and took hold of his hands, giving a gentle squeeze. "Then let's get going."

"Before we go, I just want say... You certainly didn't sign on for this."

She went up on tiptoes to kiss him. "I signed on for *you*, come what may."

"But this..."

"This will turn out to be our greatest adventure yet." She wasn't sure she believed that herself, but she needed *him* to believe it. "I love you, and I'm right here with you. Always."

"That's all I need to know."

"Let's do this thing."

Preorder right now at *marieforce.com/stateofaffairs* to read the rest of *State of Affairs* in April 2021, and find out what happens when the Cappuanos arrive at the White House as the new first family!

ALSO BY MARIE FORCE

Romantic Suspense Novels Available from Marie Force

The Fatal Series

One Night With You, *A Fatal Series Prequel Novella*

Book 1: Fatal Affair

Book 2: Fatal Justice

Book 3: Fatal Consequences

Book 3.5: Fatal Destiny, *the Wedding Novella*

Book 4: Fatal Flaw

Book 5: Fatal Deception

Book 6: Fatal Mistake

Book 7: Fatal Jeopardy

Book 8: Fatal Scandal

Book 9: Fatal Frenzy

Book 10: Fatal Identity

Book 11: Fatal Threat

Book 12: Fatal Chaos

Book 13: Fatal Invasion

Book 14: Fatal Reckoning

Book 15: Fatal Accusation

Book 16: Fatal Fraud

Contemporary Romances Available from Marie Force

The Gansett Island Series

Book 1: Maid for Love *(Mac & Maddie)*

Book 2: Fool for Love *(Joe & Janey)*

Book 3: Ready for Love *(Luke & Sydney)*

Book 4: Falling for Love *(Grant & Stephanie)*

Book 5: Hoping for Love *(Evan & Grace)*

Book 6: Season for Love *(Owen & Laura)*

Book 7: Longing for Love *(Blaine & Tiffany)*

Book 8: Waiting for Love *(Adam & Abby)*

Book 9: Time for Love *(David & Daisy)*

Book 10: Meant for Love *(Jenny & Alex)*

Book 10.5: Chance for Love, *A Gansett Island Novella (Jared & Lizzie)*

Book 11: Gansett After Dark *(Owen & Laura)*

Book 12: Kisses After Dark *(Shane & Katie)*

Book 13: Love After Dark *(Paul & Hope)*

Book 14: Celebration After Dark *(Big Mac & Linda)*

Book 15: Desire After Dark *(Slim & Erin)*

Book 16: Light After Dark *(Mallory & Quinn)*

Book 17: Victoria & Shannon (Episode 1)

Book 18: Kevin & Chelsea (Episode 2)

A Gansett Island Christmas Novella

Book 19: Mine After Dark *(Riley & Nikki)*

Book 20: Yours After Dark *(Finn & Chloe)*

Book 21: Trouble After Dark *(Deacon & Julia)*

Book 22: Rescue After Dark *(Mason & Jordan)*

Book 23: Blackout After Dark

The Green Mountain Series

Book 1: All You Need Is Love *(Will & Cameron)*

Book 2: I Want to Hold Your Hand *(Nolan & Hannah)*

Book 3: I Saw Her Standing There *(Colton & Lucy)*

Book 4: And I Love Her *(Hunter & Megan)*

Novella: You'll Be Mine *(Will & Cam's Wedding)*

Book 5: It's Only Love *(Gavin & Ella)*

Book 6: Ain't She Sweet *(Tyler & Charlotte)*

The Butler, Vermont Series
(Continuation of Green Mountain)
Book 1: Every Little Thing *(Grayson & Emma)*
Book 2: Can't Buy Me Love *(Mary & Patrick)*
Book 3: Here Comes the Sun *(Wade & Mia)*
Book 4: Till There Was You *(Lucas & Dani)*
Book 5: All My Loving *(Landon & Amanda)*
Book 6: Let It Be *(Lincoln & Molly)*

The Treading Water Series
Book 1: Treading Water
Book 2: Marking Time
Book 3: Starting Over
Book 4: Coming Home
Book 5: Finding Forever

The Miami Nights Series
Book 1: How Much I Feel *(Carmen & Jason)*
Book 2: How Much I Care *(Maria & Austin)*
Book 3: How Much I Love *(Dee's story)*

The Quantum Series
Book 1: Virtuous *(Flynn & Natalie)*
Book 2: Valorous *(Flynn & Natalie)*
Book 3: Victorious *(Flynn & Natalie)*
Book 4: Rapturous *(Addie & Hayden)*
Book 5: Ravenous *(Jasper & Ellie)*
Book 6: Delirious *(Kristian & Aileen)*
Book 7: Outrageous *(Emmett & Leah)*
Book 8: Famous *(Marlowe & Sebastian)*

Single Titles

Five Years Gone

One Year Home

Sex Machine

Sex God

Georgia on My Mind

True North

The Fall

The Wreck

Love at First Flight

Everyone Loves a Hero

Line of Scrimmage

Historical Romance Available from Marie Force

The Gilded Series

Book 1: Duchess by Deception

Book 2: Deceived by Desire

ABOUT THE AUTHOR

Marie Force is the *New York Times* bestselling author of contemporary romance, romantic suspense and erotic romance. Her series include Gansett Island, Fatal, Treading Water, Butler Vermont, Quantum and Miami Nights.

Her books have sold more than 10 million copies worldwide, have been translated into more than a dozen languages and have appeared on the *New York Times* bestseller more than 30 times. She is also a *USA Today* and *Wall Street Journal* bestseller, as well as a Speigel bestseller in Germany.

Her goals in life are simple—to finish raising two happy, healthy, productive young adults, to keep writing books for as long as she possibly can and to never be on a flight that makes the news.

Join Marie's mailing list on her website at *marieforce.com* for news about new books and upcoming appearances in your area. Follow her on Facebook at *www.Facebook.com/MarieForceAuthor* and on Instagram at *www.instagram.com/marieforceauthor/*. Contact Marie at *marie@marieforce.com*.

Manufactured by Amazon.ca
Bolton, ON